WHEN SHE TOUCHES

WHEN SHE TOUCHES

A NOVEL

A DISCOVERY OF DESTINY AND A GIFT LIKE NO OTHER

Sheryl M. Frazer

ISBN-9781688985490

Registered Copyright with the Library of Congress

Dedication

To all the blessed Souls that now blissfully soar amongst the stars.
To all the incredible heroes that selflessly show up to do
battle against Covid-19 every day.
And to you, my dear reader, for staying strong in these trying times.

ACKNOWLEDGEMENTS

THIS STORY TAKES the reader from the mid 1900's to present day. I had wonderful memories as I came upon certain time periods, remembering the shows that were popular as well as the songs playing on the radio.

Thanks to some of the people who made us laugh during those times and brought realism to the story, like Jerry Seinfeld, Lucille Ball, and the Tonight Show with Jay Leno. I also want to thank a couple vocal artists that brought a richness to the plot and could really pull at the heartstrings, Paul Anka, Bob Marley, and Luther Vandross.

TABLE OF CONTENTS

CHAPTER 1

THE DREAM

AN UNRELENTING CHILL had coiled around her body like an invisible serpent caressing its prey just before devouring it. Dressed only in a light summer dress and sandals, Genevieve tore at the clip holding her long, dark hair in a vain attempt to warm her bare shoulders and stop the uncontrollable chattering of her teeth.

Fog hung weighty in all directions, insufferably damp and opaque. As her anxious green eyes strained to see through it, nothing was perceivable, save for some faint rumblings heard in the far distance. With arms outstretched, Genevieve groped in the unyielding haze as she moved toward the sound. She was keenly aware of being alone, but it was the visceral feeling of *loneliness* that painfully rippled through her body. As her lip quivered, she moved forward.

Minutes passed, and the veil of fog began showing signs of retreat. Strangely, as it did, the dreary emotions *within* Genevieve, also began to recoil.

She had just begun to quicken her pace when she came to a sudden stop. With her ears perked, Genevieve's pulse started to gain speed. Somewhere, not too far away, there was warbling, otherworldly chant calling her name with a tonality foreign to anything she'd ever heard.

An odd energy was now pulling her closer as the anomalous tones slowly continued to reverberate, "G e n e v i e v e." With each step, the ensemble of ethereal voices was becoming clearer. Genevieve could feel an indescribable vibration emanating from the sounds, and the closer she got, the more intense her emotions became. As her mind tried interpreting the sensation, Genevieve only knew it resembled love, yet nothing she would be able to describe or had ever experienced before.

Then, the last trace of fog disappeared.

Blinking, in a state of confusion, Genevieve knew her eyes must be deceiving her, as a vast sea of people were spread out before her. Curiously, they were all lying on beds. Some were on hospital beds, others on regular beds, some, even on simple cots or mats. People of every age and walk of life were there. As Genevieve slowly moved her head from side to side, the multitude had her complete attention, yet Genevieve had no understanding as to why the vast bedridden choir had summoned her.

The sky slowly became dark and cloudy. Lightning flashed above, but the thunderous sound afterward never materialized. Rain came and went but fell silently with no sensation to Genevieve's skin. Nothing mattered but the state of reverie in which Genevieve had become a willing captive.

Not knowing if years or just moments had passed, Genevieve noticed that, in the far distance, those she barely could see had started to drift upward, still lying on their beds. As she watched, one by one, they made their exit into the dark, ominous clouds above. When those closer to her started to lift off the ground, Genevieve could see they were smiling; their eyes fixated on her as they continued their ascent, singing her name until they disappeared.

Then, the last bed, and the one closest to Genevieve began to rise. On it, was a young woman in her late teens, approximately the same age as Genevieve. Frowning, Genevieve sensed a familiarity, yet knew she had never seen the girl before. When the teenager had risen to eye level, the young woman began to speak. "We know the great strength that dwells within you, Genevieve. Your spirit is extraordinarily fearless. Trust the path that will unfold before you. It will become more important than you can imagine."

As the girl rose slightly above Genevieve, she reached out her hand. Genevieve ran quickly forward and grabbed hold of it. There were no words, but Genevieve clearly understood the young woman as if she was communicating telepathically. "You will begin to understand once your daughter is born."

Frantically, Genevieve tried to hold on tight, but the young woman's fingers slipped away. As the bedridden teenager watched Genevieve while rising higher and higher, Genevieve implored her, "Don't go! I don't understand what's happening here. *PLEASE*, what are you trying to tell me?"

With her one arm still stretched upward, Genevieve could only watch as the mysterious teenager silently disappeared into the clouds above.

All of a sudden, a crack of thunder snapped behind her, making Genevieve jump. Moments later she felt the rain pelting, icy cold, against her face. Looking around, she realized that once again she was abandoned and alone.

With a moan, she dropped to her knees. Not caring how badly her hot tears stung against her frozen skin, Genevieve angrily screamed toward the dark grey sky, "You *have* the wrong person! I'm no one special—I'M NOT EVEN PREGNANT!"

With a sudden jerk, Genevieve opened her wet eyes and felt her body trembling. Brushing the tears away, she took a deep breath and blew it out in an attempt to calm down. *It was only a dream,* she thought. With a quivering chin, she closed her eyes again, trying to pull everything back into her consciousness and analyze it. *Why did a dream upset me so much?*

Squeezing her eyes tight, Genevieve shivered when loneliness began to insinuate itself. Shaking her head vigorously, she quickly buried the thought. She took another deep breath. After a few moments, Genevieve felt her body relax as she recalled the intoxicating feeling that came later in the dream.

Lying flat and very still, Genevieve tried to see if the euphoric phenomenon was something she could conjure up again, at will. *Nothing.* Whatever it was, it was gone now. *What in the world could people in beds possibly mean? What did the girl mean about a path to follow? 'You will begin to understand once your daughter is born.' What daughter? We just got married and haven't even discussed children yet. And, why did they make me feel so incredibly important? I'm certainly no superhero.*

Trying to figure out the abstract dream was beginning to give Genevieve a headache. Still, she couldn't help but whisper the young woman's final words, which weren't relayed as words at all, "…once your daughter is born." With a flashing grin, Genevieve thought, *at least that didn't seem so unbelievable… someday.*

Letting the dream fall away, Genevieve noticed the first signs of light peeking through the drapes. Rolling to her side, Teddy was still in a deep sleep. Genevieve relaxed and closed her eyes. *Mrs. Walker*, she thought with a sigh. The past year continued to feel surreal; the intense and unexpected romance, the fairytale wedding, as well as the honeymoon in Hawaii they had just returned home from.

Having had so much of her happiness and stability ripped away from her in the past, Genevieve had a hard time believing anything good would last. But she knew, deep down, this would last, it *had* to. For, at seventeen, she had never known love and wasn't looking for it, but he found her anyway—Theodore Ian Walker. *He* was the good that would last a lifetime.

CHAPTER 2

❧

LOVE AND DESIRE

SMILING, GENEVIEVE OPENED her eyes and quietly observed her new husband as he lay sleeping. Moving closer, she gently placed her arm on his chest, resting her hand over his heart. Without realizing it, Genevieve started to tap her finger to the invisible sound in her head, *ta-dum, ta-dum ta-dum.*

It was just over a year ago, at Wainsworth Estate in Bamburgh England, where it all started. Seventeen-year-old Genevieve had just arrived at the upscale resort for an extended vacation with her family. Teddy, age twenty, was a porter, leading Genevieve and her family to their cabin. The moment the two set eyes on each other an unfamiliar obsession began for each of them. Within days Teddy and Genevieve became inseparable, and, along the way Genevieve lost her virginity to him. On her last day at the exclusive resort, when Genevieve thought she would never see him again, Teddy proposed.

Life felt perfect now. Taking a deep breath, Genevieve inhaled traces of Teddy's musk perfume and moved even closer.

Even though her husband seemed to be blissfully asleep, desire had taken over. Genevieve began kissing his neck, her breath warm on his skin. Teddy didn't stir. Lifting her hand from his chest, Genevieve gently ran her fingers through his thick, wavy black hair. Although his eyes remained closed, a smile appeared. Genevieve slid her finger down, along Teddy's dimpled cheek as she pressed her anxious lips to his. As he kissed her back, Genevieve could feel his heart begin to speed up, and knew he was ready to play.

The fervent craving was palpable. Like a drug, Genevieve had become addicted to the painfully intense pleasure she received while having sex. It seemed odd though, and Genevieve wondered why every time Teddy made "umm" sounds as she caressed *his* body, she, herself, felt erotic stimulation.

At a quarter past seven, the snooze on the alarm went off for the third time, signaling Teddy to get up and get ready for work. The newlyweds were temporarily living with Genevieve's Aunt Melinda and Uncle Steven, who were Genevieve's guardians, and, for all intents and purposes her mother and father.

Teddy sat up and turned the alarm clock off. With his back to her, Genevieve ran her finger slowly down his spine and beyond, then uttered, "Come on, lay back down."

Genevieve knew she was pushing it but couldn't resist the temptation to lead her husband astray for just a little longer. With a look of triumph on her face, Genevieve watched as Teddy laid back down next to her. *He took the bait!*

A moment later, he rolled his body over and laid on top of her.

She was ready…

His crystal blue eyes were seductively intense…

She closed her own and began quietly moaning with renewed anticipation.

Then, leaning close to her ear, Teddy whispered in his Scottish type brogue, "Ye sly one…thought ye'd get me in trouble, didn't ye?"

Genevieve opened one eye to see if there was still a chance.

Displaying a crooked smile, Teddy slowly shook his head. Then, quickly rolling out of bed, he winked at his temptress before heading to the attached bathroom to take a shower—as cold as possible.

"Hmmph!" Genevieve uttered as she laid flat on the bed, pulling the sheet over her.

A couple of minutes later, she heard Teddy humming in the shower. It brought her back to the dream, and the mystical sounds while her name was being sung, and the words, "Trust the path that will unfold before you." She pondered, *Maybe my path is to be wife and mother to Teddy's children.* With a slight frown, Genevieve somehow suspected there was more in store for her.

Whatever the future held it was a mystery to be solved later. Only the moment at hand and the wet, soapy man in the next room mattered right now. Flinging the sheets away, Genevieve hurried to the bathroom, turned up the heat, and joined her new husband in the shower.

Genevieve was feeling optimistic about life now, but that was not how it began.

When very young, Genevieve lived with the sole purpose of pleasing her mother, the wife of a career military man. It was a constant struggle as Liv, Genevieve's mother, spent much of her time depressed and distant while Genevieve's father was away fighting the war.

In the spring of 1968, Genevieve's already fragile world shatter to pieces. Her father, Zeffran Clarke, a Marine, had just died in Vietnam. Her mother, and the woman she adored, abandoned Genevieve and her three-year-old sister, Tess, after their father's funeral. Liv told Genevieve she was going to spend time in a hospital. She explained that without Genevieve's father, she had lost the desire to live and believed people at the hospital could help her. Genevieve wanted to keep her mother close, but something deep inside her felt it was selfish to do so. Therefore, with her mother's promise to come back soon, Genevieve didn't protest.

Days later Genevieve received the crushing news, that her mother would never come back. Her mother's sister, Aunt Melinda, got word that Liv was dead. She had left the mental hospital of her own volition, even though the doctor treating her had strongly advised against it. Although Liv's body was never recovered, there had been an eyewitness who said he saw a woman fitting her description entering the surf. That, along with sufficient evidence left on the beach, a strong rip current, and the staff's assessment of Liv's mental state, all led to the official conclusion: Missing, presumed dead due to suicide.

Upon hearing that, eleven-year-old Genevieve crumbled deeper into a dark void with bitter feelings of worthlessness and abandonment. For days afterward, she laid in bed, catatonic, not understanding why her mother didn't love her enough—why she wasn't important enough.

Then, Genevieve was blindsided. Her *very* wealthy aunt and uncle, who had no children of their own, took Genevieve and Tess into their home, choosing to raise the girls as their own. It felt foreign and circumspect at first. Genevieve assumed they would change their mind, but they never did. Their love never faltered.

As Genevieve got into her later teens and her friends were going steady and falling in love, Genevieve felt disconnected, again. She lacked any excitement or anticipation with those she dated, finally deciding her mother's warped sense of passion and desire must have damaged her own understanding of it as well.

Yet, on a family vacation, after traveling thousands of miles, across a vast ocean, a young porter with a disarming accent and a killer smile appeared as if by divine fate. It was then that Genevieve began to suspect things didn't happen randomly.

The synchronicities *did* happen. The love and abundance surrounding her now would never have happened if it weren't for Genevieve's tragic beginning.

Unfortunately, it is not the blessings we tend to dwell on, but those darker moments.

The past we cannot let go.

Ghosts we allow to haunt us.

CHAPTER 3

FAMILY

WHEN TEDDY FIRST arrived in Scottsdale, Arizona where Genevieve lived, he quickly became Uncle Steven's protégé, quickly excelling in his apprenticeship as a commercial real estate developer.

Now, after five months of shadowing Steven, an icon in his field, Teddy was enrolled in night classes for finance and urban development. Genevieve however, still not clear on a career path, was set to finish up the last few units she needed in general education.

August 1975 was almost over. The Walkers had been married just under two months with classes starting in a few days, but Genevieve sensed something was off. The feeling had been that way for about a week now.

It was simmering hot Friday morning at the estate. Genevieve had spent the morning with Haddie, her Friesian mare in an attempt to feel better again. Yet, today as they finished their ride together, Haddie's magic wasn't working. The odd, uneasy feeling persisted.

After an afternoon of busy work, Genevieve eventually found herself sitting in the living room, staring at the family portrait of Uncle Steven, Aunt Melinda, Tess, who was five years old at the time and herself, at age thirteen.

Focusing her attention on Aunt Melinda's beautiful face, and the proud smile she displayed, Genevieve thought about how much her aunt meant to her.

When she was very young, Genevieve remembered Aunt Melinda's striking presence whenever she and Uncle Steven came for a visit. Slightly older than her sister Liv, Melinda had a shapely model's body and stride with clothes to match and was never seen without her striking red lipstick.

Genevieve had always been in awe of her aunt but never pictured her as the motherly type.

Still, it was Aunt Melinda who cradled Genevieve in her arms for hours while Genevieve sobbed after learning her mother had died. It was she who gave Genevieve a healthier view of the world through her patient guidance. Aunt Melinda was the one that made sure the family traveled every year and were exposed to different cultures, or, as Tess would always say, "exotic places." And it was this intuitive woman that knew, before anyone else, how much Genevieve loved Teddy. As she continued to stare at her aunt, Genevieve brushed a tear away. *I wish you'd been my mother from the start.*

As Genevieve closed her eyes, a sudden rush of understanding enveloped her. *Mother.*

Opening her eyes, Genevieve looked down. Now the feeling she had been experiencing made sense. *A mother...me?* A grin started to form but quickly disappeared as creeping thoughts of doubt filtered in. *The two of us parents? We aren't even living on our own yet. Maybe I should have been more careful. How will Teddy take the news? Aunt Melinda? Uncle Steven?*

Peering into the large foyer, Aunt Melinda was sitting on the elegant open stairway. She was petting their dog, Egan, while watching Tess, now eleven, and her best friend Samantha practice a dance routine for an upcoming recital.

Then, Genevieve heard Teddy and her uncle entering through the back door. Uncle Steven, a robust man, that was even an inch taller than Teddy at 6' 2", must have been telling one of his jokes, as Genevieve rarely heard Teddy laugh *that* hard. Getting up, Genevieve went to greet them. As she entered the back room, she saw Teddy wipe a tear from the side of his eye, while trying to control his laughter. "My goodness, Uncle, that must have been quite a joke!"

Uncle Steven put his hands up and blurted, "It wasn't me. Really!"

With a smile and narrowed eyes, Genevieve replied, "Okay...then what could possibly be so funny?"

Meandering closer to her husband, Genevieve was just about to kiss him when he burst out laughing again, spraying her in the face.

With eyes wide, he apologized, "Ah naw, *so* sorry my love."

Genevieve reached to wipe her face just as Aunt Melinda walked in. "What's going on in here?"

Genevieve shook her head, but the infectious laughing was beginning to amuse her. "I don't know, but it must be good because it caused Teddy to spit all over me!"

Then both the men snorted with laughter again. Smiling, Genevieve and Aunt Melinda just gave each other a puzzled look.

"Whew…" Teddy said and took a deep breath. "Okay, well, somehow we started talkin aboot the weddin reception on the way home." Genevieve stopped smiling, as there was only one thing from the reception that could make them laugh *that* hard, and it was something she was quite ready to forget.

Glancing at Genevieve, Teddy saw the look on her face. "Aww, don't look tha way. It turned oot to be a great, romantic moment, Gen!"

Aunt Melinda nodded, giving Genevieve an empathic smile. "Well, I have to admit, it was something we'll never forget. However boys, for once, let's hear it from *Genevieve's* point of view."

Although shaking her head and rolling her eyes, Genevieve decided to engage while the other three gave her that, *We-love-you-no-matter-what* look.

Clearing her throat, and looking downward, she began, "Well, it had been several hours, and the reception on the lawn was just starting to die down. My feet were killing me, so I slipped away from some friends I had been talking with to find an empty table so I could take my heels off and rest a bit. As I sat there, with my bare feet up on a chair, I watched the two of you (looking at her aunt and uncle). It was mesmerizing to watch the way you danced and laughed together. You were just so…" Genevieve searched for the right word as she stared at them, "I guess I'd best describe it as enchanting!"

Uncle Steven, quiet now, winked at his wife, and she smiled back.

Looking downward again, Genevieve continued. "All the twinkling lights made the aura of the evening even more romantic. I sat there observing how different groups of people had migrated to different areas, while Egan was in his glory as Tess and some of the kids were chasing him around." Genevieve smiled. "It was such a great day."

The four of them became quiet, replaying the evening in their own minds.

"Then, at the far end of the reception area, even past the last awning, I spotted him." Genevieve looked up at Teddy. "He was with a group of his friends, but I could see that his eyes were fixated on me."

Genevieve noticed how caught up Teddy had become, listening to her version of the night. Tilting her head, "We just stared at each other for a long time. Then I saw him excuse himself and start to walk toward me. When I saw him getting a bit closer, I began to stand up, and when I did, I felt an odd pull on the back of my dress.

"I can still picture it in slow motion. We started moving toward each other, only I didn't realize a thread on my back zipper had got caught on the chair and was unraveling with every step. As I began to move faster, the chair fell over and lodged on the awning poll. "Just ten feet apart and my strapless gown dropped to my waist, tripping me and causing me to fall forward at Teddy's feet."

Teddy took Genevieve's hand while the other two just smiled but said nothing.

"There I laid, stunned! But Teddy just smiled, took his jacket off and covered me before anyone actually realized what had happened. Then, instead of helping me up so I could get out of the rather revealing predicament, he laid down next to me and began kissing me all over my face."

With a playful grin, Teddy reminded, "As I mentioned in our weddin vows, it was your mishaps tha first caused me to fall in love with ye, anyway."

Genevieve countered, "Well, maybe it was my unconscious way of getting you excited for our honeymoon that night!"

Even though Aunt Melinda was enjoying the romantic banter, Uncle Steven made a gagging sound as he started to walk away, "Geez kids, get a room for heaven's sake!"

As the foursome began to disperse, Genevieve felt a wave of queasiness overtake her playful mood and remembered her suspicion. Holding Teddy's hand, Genevieve could only hope he'd understand. *What if he doesn't want children? Why have we never brought the subject up before?*

CHAPTER 4

I HAVE SOMETHING
TO TELL YOU.

GENEVIEVE SAT IN her car, looking straight out at nothing in particular. Still parked in the urgent care parking lot, there was a whirling sound going on in her mind, as if trapped in a tornado. She was envisioning the next few hours as she told her family about her motherly status: Teddy's shocked, blindsided look, Uncle Steven's eyes raised upward as his mind grappled at the inconvenient timing, while Aunt Melinda displayed surprised confusion, masked in an unconvincing smile. Tess, well she'd be happy. She loved babies, and there would be nothing else to contemplate in her eyes.

The doctor said the baby would be due around the end of May; seven weeks pregnant. Genevieve closed her eyes, *I'm really pregnant.* After a moment, a shiver ran through her as she thought of her mother. *No matter what, I'll never be like her.* As the words formed in Genevieve's mind, a feeling of resolve calmed the tremulous mood within.

It was Saturday, and as Genevieve drove into the circular driveway of the massive estate, Teddy was washing Egan, or possibly it was the other way around as Teddy's hair glistened, wet in the sun, his T-shirt hung drenched and clinging to his body. Just as he looked up to see Genevieve pulling in, Egan shook his soapy lathered fur, covering Teddy with suds.

With an amused grin, Genevieve watched her unassuming husband struggle to hold the golden retriever in place. She often wondered why Teddy

14

had not found someone before her with his striking features and athletic body.

As Genevieve parked the car near the wet duo, Teddy ordered Egan to stay put and ran around to the driver's side of the car and opened the door. Genevieve knew precisely what he had planned, but it was a scorching hot August day in Arizona so, as she stepped out, she gladly let Teddy wrap his wet frisky body around hers.

Pleased with himself, he teasingly asked, "Hey there bonny lass, want a bath? I'll give ye one, cheap. I'm sure Egan won't mind sharin with ye."

As they looked over, Egan had hightailed it out of the tub and was running across the yard.

"Well," As Teddy bent down closer to Genevieve's face with raised eyebrows, "I guess ye've got the bath all to yourself then."

Noticing an odd look on Genevieve's face. Teddy tilted his head with a perplexed frown, "Wha's goin on Gen? Where did ye go just now?"

Summoning courage, Genevieve kissed him, hard. Teddy's frown quickly faded as he pressed his wet body against hers. After a couple of minutes, he took Genevieve's hand and headed for the house. Genevieve knew she had to stop stalling, and, noticing the bench by the front door, steered him over to sit down.

The bewildered look reappeared on Teddy's face once again. Not knowing how to lead into the subject, Genevieve decided to give him a hint, "Remember what happened on our honeymoon…that day at the waterfall?"

The memory of the sensual interlude behind the cascading water flashed into his head. As Teddy smiled and nodded, Genevieve knew she had to be more direct. Nodding back, Genevieve added, "Well, we probably should have used some protection."

After a few agonizing moments, Teddy's eyes got wide. He didn't say a word for several more seconds, but somehow, as Genevieve held his hand, she sensed he was genuinely happy.

"I didn't plan this Teddy. I know how hard you're working and now with classes about to begin…"

Teddy squeezed Genevieve's hand. "One thin my mum would always say, 'Nivvor leik fer the perfect time laddie, but bless each moment *fer* its perfection.' Teddy kissed Genevieve, "Don't ye worry, love. The time is perfect, and this baby of ours…perfection."

As Teddy put his hand on Genevieve's abdomen, she began to laugh and cry at the same time. It was a mixture of relief, but even more so, the stunning way Teddy always made her feel.

At dinner, they broke the news to the rest of the family. Uncle Steven ran over and lifted Genevieve out of her seat and gave her such a squeeze she thought she heard a rib crack. Aunt Melinda literally screamed in delight and said, "I can't *wait* to be a grandma!" Then, stopping abruptly, and looking at Genevieve and Teddy she inquired, "Will it be okay if the little one calls me that?"

Genevieve had grown to love Melinda as her mother but was never able to call her by that name. Maybe it was because she had been older when she came to live with her aunt and uncle, but never because they didn't deserve the title. Tess, on the other hand, only being three at the time, could have easily called Melinda and Steven, Mommy and Daddy. Yet, the toddler followed her big sister's lead, and no one ever pressed to change it. Genevieve later felt regretful as she believed Aunt Melinda would have loved being called Mom.

Walking over to her aunt's chair, Genevieve bent down and wrapped her arms around the elegant woman's shoulders, softly saying, "You already *are* this little one's grandma." Aunt Melinda's perfect red lips began to tremble. Then she whispered, "I'm so glad."

Genevieve looked over at her sister who was being very quiet. "So, nothing to say?"

Tess looked at her aunt and pondered. "I was thinking about the talk we had last year. You know, *that* talk." Aunt Melinda smiled with an encouraging nod to keep going. Then the eleven-year-old grimaced as if she'd just got whiff of a rotten potato and said, "I like babies, but it's a

16

gross way to get one. I hope there's another way to have one by the time I get married!"

While everyone laughed, Genevieve remembered the way her baby had been conceived. As she looked at her husband, she thought, *Never fear sister, there are definitely more ways than you can imagine!*

CHAPTER 5

TEARS FALL

APRIL 1976

Was that an arm or a leg? As Genevieve reclined in a warm bath, she watched a small bump rise in her belly and felt the rolling motion of her baby trying to get comfortable in its cramped home. *We're almost there little one, just a few more days.* "Teddy, can you come in here and help me get up?"

Teddy came in from the bedroom where he had been studying for his accounting class and knelt next to the tub. In examining his wife's compelling emerald green eyes, he could see the bath had not done its job to soothe her. Without saying a word, he helped Genevieve maneuver to a sitting position.

As she surveyed her swollen middle, Genevieve murmured, "This little person seems very anxious to leave me. Look at me, Teddy, I'm huge. I just don't see how I'm supposed to get all this, (pointing to the bulge in front of her), out!" The two watched as another bump rolled up and then slowly disappeared. Teddy smiled, but Genevieve continued to have a bewildered look on her face. "I know it's been done forever, but what if *I* can't do it?"

Teddy sat down on the floor and ran his fingers down Genevieve's arm. "Every day tha's gone by, I've watched your body change and pictured our baby, wonderin if it chose us to be its parents. I think it did, Gen, and I think it's anxious to meet ye and be held in your arms. I know wha tha love feels like, and there's just nothin betta. You'll do just fine."

Genevieve wiped her eyes with her forearm. "I don't know, Teddy. Do you think our little one could give me a pass and call a stork to do all the heavy stuff?"

Teddy got back on his knees and kissed his wife on the head. "Where's the adventure in tha? You don't need any stinkin bird, love. Trust me. You've got this! Besides, I'll be with ye every step of the way, and I promise I'll smell betta than wet feathers!"

Genevieve finally smiled.

Helping her up, Teddy grabbed a towel and wrapped it around her as she stepped out of the bathtub. Still with a slight grin on her face, Genevieve took the clasp from her thick dark hair, letting her long, loose curls fall around her. Moving some hair from around her shoulder, Teddy began lightly kissing her neck, arousing feelings that had waned in recent weeks. As she let the towel drop to the floor, Teddy continued to caress her. The tenderness in his eyes, as he gently loved her, allowed the angst Genevieve had been feeling to subside, realizing how foolish it had been to worry. Later, as the two began drifting off to sleep, Genevieve closed her eyes and thought, *What could possibly go wrong with a love like this?*

Something feels wet. It was April 25th, and Genevieve was now a few days overdue. As she laid in bed, trying to shake the fuzzy feeling in her head, she realized her water must have broke. Throwing the sheet back, Genevieve could see that the mattress was dark. Confused, she reached over and turned on the light. Confusion changed to panic as she gasped, *Oh God!* "TEDDY!"

Teddy lunged upward, hearing the alarm in her voice. As he looked over, he saw what she saw; blood, and not just a little. Jumping out of bed, he began dialing 911 then realized it would take too long. It was barely five in the morning, and as Teddy scooped Genevieve up and rushed out of the room, Uncle Steven, who had just come downstairs to get breakfast, heard the commotion and came running over. Genevieve's gown, wet and red, hung ominously from below the blanket in which she was wrapped. "I've got to get her to the hospital, now!" Teddy panted.

Uncle Steven called Geoffrey his chauffeur, who lived on the estate, to pull the car over right away.

Genevieve whispered loudly in Teddy's ears as they headed toward the door, "Teddy, I can't lose this baby, we have to hurry!" Genevieve was feeling light-headed and didn't know how much blood she had lost. Placing her in the back of the town car, they all knew they were racing against time.

Geoffrey flew through the back streets, ignoring residential stop signs as few people were moving about anyway. Genevieve started feeling mild contractions, and with each one, more blood oozed from her body.

By the time they got to the emergency room, her panic had abated. Genevieve felt a fuzzy, surreal fascination watching the flurry of nurses and doctors tending to her. Before long, she was being wheeled down the corridor to surgery. She knew something had gone wrong, yet, never felt more peaceful. Even while hearing the doctor tell Teddy and her uncle, "We'll do the best we can to save both of them," Genevieve sensed a disconnect from the reality at hand—beyond fearfulness.

Then, she felt a sudden jolt as Teddy's hand was being forced from hers when the double doors began closing. Trying to put on a reassuring smile for her terrified husband, Genevieve murmured, "It will be okay, honey, I feel fine." However, he didn't seem to believe her. With space quickly separating the two of them, Genevieve imagined jumping off the gurney and running back to him. But she barely had enough strength to keep her eyes open, thinking, *I just wish I could have kissed him good-bye.*

She watched as the three most important men in her life stared back at her through the double door windows. Before they disappeared from view, Genevieve heard Teddy yell, "Be strong, Gen! Ye can't leave me now!"

Arriving in the operating room, Genevieve laid complacent under glaring lights. She felt pricks from needles, but they didn't hurt, nothing hurt. With a tranquil smile, she closed her eyes. *Sleep, that's all I need...*

Within moments she felt a violating cold moving through her limbs, shocking her awake. As she looked around her, she could see IV's of blood pumping into each arm and leg. *I'm sooo cold*, she thought. Her body began to shiver, and her jaw soon rattled uncontrollably. *Oh my God, I can't stand this!* Genevieve mustered enough energy to shout, "Stop! I'm freezing!"

Just then, a nurse came in with a heavy silver covering. They hurried to wrap her upper body and arms with the insulated blanket. Then Genevieve felt a sharp contraction and couldn't help but scream in pain.

The doctor moved close to Genevieve's face and spoke softly. "Genevieve, we've just given you a spinal block because we have to do a cesarean section. Your baby is in distress and can't come out the normal way."

Genevieve closed her eyes, frowning, and tried to focus on what was being said. Barely mumbling, "What do you mean…I don't understand."

"You have what is called placenta previa. It's where the placenta covers the cervix and not only blocks the baby's passage but as the cervix begins to open, the placenta hemorrhages, causing excessive bleeding. You've lost a lot of blood, and we're pumping as much as we can, as fast as we can, but unfortunately, we didn't have the luxury of warming it as much as we normally do. That's why you are so cold. Be strong for me, Genevieve! You're about to meet someone very special."

As the doctor prepared for surgery, Genevieve closed her eyes and remembered she had felt that uncontrollable cold before. It was in the dream she had months ago. Then, recalling her doctor's words, "Be strong for me, Genevieve," the cryptic dream began to coalesce. Fighting against the pain and disorientation, Genevieve tried her best to recall what she had all but forgotten. Summoning the message from deep within her, the same voice whispered, *'We know the great strength that dwells within you.'* Genevieve's eyes opened wide as she thought, *Yes, and the girl talked about my daughter.*

When she glanced at the doctor, he gave Genevieve a reassuring nod as he asked the nurse for the scalpel. *Am I having a baby GIRL?* Genevieve asked herself. *Is that dream becoming my reality?*

Pure willpower was keeping Genevieve from falling into the quiet abyss that beckoned. Feeling the pressure of the incision, Genevieve took a deep shuttered breath, *Be strong Genevieve. Be strong for her!*

CHAPTER 6

ARIELLA

MOMENTS PASSED. THE surgical staff moved swiftly and resolutely, but Genevieve's angst had come back with a vengeance. She couldn't tell if her racing heart was because of the caustic cold that was engulfing her body or the fear that her little one would never take a breath. Whatever it was, it was excruciating.

With a pulling sensation, the doctor announced, "She's out."

"She…" Genevieve murmured. Then, immediately afterward, her eyes got wide, "I can't breathe!"

Not hearing Genevieve, the doctor turned to her with a smile and uttered, "You have a little girl." Genevieve's eyes went up, and pain, like she'd never experience ripped at her chest.

The last thing Genevieve remembered was thinking, *Be strong for me, Ariella!*

It had been almost two hours since Genevieve was taken away. Aunt Melinda and Tess had arrived forty minutes earlier, and a nurse came out shortly after, to explain why Genevieve had been hemorrhaging. Now, all were sitting stoically in the waiting room, numbed by the unexpected turn of events.

Just as Teddy got up to pace the floor, again, the surgeon walked in. The family rushed to meet him halfway. Looking at Teddy, the doctor said, "You have a beautiful baby girl, eight pounds, five ounces."

Teddy blinked and whispered, "Ariella." Then focused on the doctor's face that looked far from jovial, "Wha aboot my wife? Is she okay?"

With all imploring eyes fixated on the doctor, he drew a deep breath. "First, let me say, your wife is alive, but there were complications. As you know, she had lost a lot of blood, and the only way to save her was to replenish the loss as fast as possible. We would normally have enough time to warm the refrigerated blood but, if we had waited, she surely would have died. We attempted to warm her body as best we could, but she also had to endure the trauma of a cesarean." As soon as the baby was born, Mrs. Walker went into cardiac arrest."

Aunt Melinda let out a shocking cry. Tess wiped her eyes while clinging tightly to her aunt. Uncle Steven shook his head and muttered, "Oh my God." Geoffrey, who loved Genevieve like a granddaughter, struggled to stay composed.

Teddy frowned at the doctor as he tried to make sense of it all. "Ye said she's alive, but wha is her condition?"

The doctor replied, "After we felt she was stable, she was moved to the intensive care unit. If her condition continues to improve, she should be able to move to the maternity wing later today. Her heart is holding in a good sinus rhythm now, and there are no signs of tachycardia. Her body temperature has normalized as well. I'm administering one more unit of blood and have given her an injection of iron, as her level was very low."

Then, with a grin, the doctor added, "She's still very weak Mr. Walker, but she's been asking for you."

Teddy turned to the family. Tears were still visible in Aunt Melinda's eyes, but she had the biggest smile he'd ever seen. Teddy knew everyone wanted to see Genevieve and seemed hesitant to leave them behind, so Aunt Melinda nudged his arm, "Go! We'll be right here waiting!"

For the first time in hours, Teddy drew a deep cleansing breath and smiled. "I'm a fatha!" Uncle Steven gave him a firm pat. Tess grabbed his arm, pulling Teddy down so she could give him a kiss. When he glanced up, Geoffrey had turned slightly and was wiping a tear from his eye. As Teddy stood upright, Geoffrey quickly turned back around, reached into his coat pocket and handed Teddy a cigar.

Steven laughed, "Good man, Geoffrey. You're always prepared, no matter the circumstance. Tonight, you, me and Ted will celebrate with Cuba's finest and a bottle of whiskey!"

Melinda shook her head at her husband. "I suppose this *is* the best excuse you'll find to light up one of those smelly sticks."

"Aye," Teddy said as he tucked the cigar in his shirt pocket, "It will be a good way to end this day." As he and the doctor headed toward the door, Teddy assured, "I'll be back to get ye in just a little while."

Following the doctor, Teddy hurried up and down corridors until the surgeon pointed to her room. Genevieve was lying quietly, eyes closed. Slipping silently into the room, Teddy noticed the color had come back to her face again. Bending down, barely brushing his lips to hers, Genevieve's eyes slowly opened, and a satisfied, sleepy look appeared on her face. "I needed that you know."

Pulling a chair next to the bed and sitting down, with his hands hidden behind him, Teddy whispered, "Aye, so did I. Ye shouldn't scare a new fatha like tha! I have somethin for ye." Then Teddy laid a soft stuffed animal next to her and mumbled, "Maybe the stork *would* have been a betta option this time."

Genevieve picked up the bird and stared at its crossed eyes and long beak. "Now, where would have been the adventure in that?" Slowly she moved her blissful gaze to Teddy, "Have you seen her yet?"

"Naw, naw yet. The doctor said they wanted to run some tests on her and monitor our baby for a few hours."

Genevieve grabbed Teddy's arm, "She's alright, isn't she?"

"I think she's fine. To be honest, a lot of the stuff he was sayin didn't make much sense to me. But affta he was finished, I just asked him tha same thing, and he said he didn't foresee any complications."

Genevieve nodded and released her firm grip on Teddy, letting her arm fall back on the bed. Teddy took her hand that felt cold, and warmed it in his own, while he watched her drift slowly back to sleep.

CHAPTER 7

LIGHTNING BOLT

"She should be out for a while."

As Teddy watched Genevieve sleep, a nurse came in to adjust the I.V. "She's coming off some strong meds right now. I hear you're a new father?"

Teddy smiled. "Aye, I am."

"Well, I think it would be a good time to meet your new—daughter, correct? Your wife is in good hands, Mr. Walker. She'll never even know you were gone."

Teddy laid Genevieve's hand at her side without her stirring. "Are ye sure she won't wake up for a while?"

The nurse nodded. "Go, take a peek. You have some time."

Teddy beamed, "I won't be long."

With a good sense of direction, Teddy wound his way back to the surgical waiting room where the family was still waiting. Walking up to them he said with a smile, "Gen looks good. She's still on some strong drugs and sleepin right now. How aboot we visit Ariella?"

There was no hesitation. In the nursery, Ariella was the only female surrounded by four infant males. Aunt Melinda shook her head as she turned toward Teddy, "Look at that, she's already attracting the boys." Teddy's nose was touching the glass, and Aunt Melinda could see he was utterly dumbstruck in love. With a slow blink and gentle smile, Aunt Melinda put her arm around Teddy's waist as she returned her gaze to Ariella.

Uncle Steven glanced at the nurse tending to the infants. "Hey, Ted, if you want to hold Ariella, I could call the nurse to let you in."

Teddy shook his head. "I can wait." Just watching his precious newborn as she slept was enough for the time being. He wanted to share the first intimate moments, holding his daughter, with Genevieve.

Once the family knew Genevieve would be okay, Uncle Steven and Geoffrey left for a few hours so Steven could finalize some business, while the others took turns visiting Genevieve in the I.C.U. By late afternoon, Genevieve was finally moved to a room in the maternity wing. Once settled, the nurse said she'd bring the baby to her. Aunt Melinda wanted the new parents to have some time alone, so she and Tess left to grab some dinner, saying they'd be back in an hour or so.

No sooner had they left, Genevieve heard something rolling down the corridor, getting louder by the moment. The yearning to hold her daughter was overwhelming. As the nurse appeared at the door, she quietly announced, "She's here." and in rolled the newest chapter to their lives.

Bringing the bassinet next to the bed, Genevieve could see that Ariella was awake, wrapped tightly in a receiving blanket. Speaking softly, the nurse said, "She's doing really well, but I think she'll be hungry soon. I understand that you want to breastfeed her, is that right?

Genevieve smiled while looking at her daughter and nodded.

"That's great. However, dear, you'll need to postpone that for a little while. We need to make sure the medications and high dosage of iron you were given won't be passed on to the baby. I hope you understand."

Genevieve eyes never veered from the baby as she whispered, "I understand."

Adjusting the blanket around Ariella, the nurse added, "Okay then. There is a bottle next to her and diapers and supplies below. If you need any help, press the call button attached to the bed. Otherwise, I'll be checking back with you later." She gave Genevieve a quick grin and left the room.

"Teddy, can you pick her up?" Genevieve pleaded.

Teddy gently put his hand around the base of Ariella's head and wrapped the other around her body. Bringing her up high on his chest, he introduced himself to his newborn. She seemed mesmerized as she listened to the hushed lilt of her father's voice. Genevieve saw Teddy's eyes filling with tears.

Watching the two of them, made her heart melt, and Genevieve knew, by far, they were the only medicine she needed.

After a minute or so, Teddy laid the infant in Genevieve's open arms and sat next to the bed. It was surreal to feel the warmth of Ariella's tiny body, that weight now independent of her own. While Genevieve gently touched Ariella's silky-smooth cheek, an unfamiliar feeling began to build. Finding her daughter's tiny fingers, tight in a fist, Genevieve uncurled them and watched them quickly wrap around her index finger. The feeling was getting stronger. Genevieve took a deep breath. The emotion was becoming so intense it almost hurt, but only because Genevieve didn't think she could contain the euphoric feeling about to burst from within her.

Teddy could see his wife struggling and became alarmed. "Gen, wha's wrong. Is your heart okay? Should I call the nurse?"

"No! No, but take the baby for a minute please, Teddy."

Teddy lifted Ariella and gently put her back in the bassinet. Then looking at Genevieve, "Wha's goin on?"

Genevieve felt the strong feelings dissolving. "I don't know. I knew how much I would love her, but as I held Ariella, I..." Genevieve, slowly shook her head, "I can't describe what I felt—there are no words that come close to this feeling. It was love I guess but, the feeling was almost unbearable and intoxicating. I felt like I was going to explode!" Genevieve looked at Teddy and started to laugh. Then she looked at her daughter. "Let me hold her again, Teddy."

Teddy was pretty sure the drugs were causing Genevieve to hallucinate. With raised eyebrows and a nonchalant grin, Teddy suggested, "How aboot *I* hold Ariella, and we all lie on the bed togetha?"

Genevieve blinked slowly in agreement, "That's even better." Slowly moving over to make room, Genevieve felt the raw sting of her stitched incision and winced. Teddy picked up Ariella and laid next to his wife.

"Are ye sure ye feel alright?"

"Never better," Genevieve stressed.

As they snuggled, Genevieve began stroking the fuzzy dark hair on Ariella's head. After a few minutes, Teddy gave the baby to Genevieve as he could tell she yearned to hold her. The baby was perfectly content as she focused on her mother. The longer Genevieve touched her infant's skin, the faster the feelings returned, until she had an epiphany, "It's coming from her!"

"Wha in the world are ye talkin aboot? Wha's comin from her?"

"Oh, my God! I thought the feeling was something I was feeling for her. Teddy, these aren't my feelings, they're hers!"

Teddy was speechless, staring back at Genevieve, blankly.

Genevieve tipped her head down and closed her eyes as she held Ariella. No one spoke for a short while. Teddy had a frown that wasn't going away as he watched the serene faces of his wife and child. Thinking it was time to talk to a nurse, Teddy started to move off the bed, but Genevieve opened her eyes and pulled him back. "Teddy, I'm fine, really I am." Tears were evident in her eyes. She held his hand, and they both watched their baby as Ariella drifted off to sleep.

Knowing what Teddy had to be thinking, Genevieve scrambled for a way to convince him she wasn't crazy or delusional. "I never told you about a dream I had just before I knew I was pregnant. I remember it vividly now, yet it was abstract in nature. I still don't understand what some of it was about, but just before I woke up from it, I remember a young woman held my hand, and though her mouth wasn't moving, I could understand what she was saying; like her emotions were conveying a message to me. I remember her message, 'It will start to become clear when your daughter is born.' Now, after holding my *daughter*, I understand what the woman meant."

After several moments, tears began to trickle out as Genevieve's eyes darted back and forth, recollecting times in her past. "My mother! Oh God, it makes sense now. No matter how happy she pretended to be, when she'd hold my hand, or I'd sit on her lap, I got so sad. She was *always* so sad. And I can remember feeling *so* happy when holding Tess when she was first born. I'd even get upset when Mom would take her away from me. I was too young to understand what was happening, since I was barely eight years old, but I'm sure it was because it felt a lot like this!" As her mind raced, Genevieve had a look on her face as if she'd just learned the secrets to the universe. "I always seemed to sync to the feelings of others when we were close. But I always thought they were *my* feelings of happiness when the person near me was happy. And

I confused empathy for what was actually sadness, when they weren't. I never had any other reasonable explanation as to why my feelings could change so drastically. There have been times though, I felt I was going crazy."

Teddy interjected, "Why didn't ye ever tell me aboot this?"

Genevieve looked at him and shook her head. "I didn't think there was anything *to* tell. I didn't know that I was different. I just thought it was normal, at least for me." Genevieve wiped her face and smiled. But it wasn't normal, or even me! I don't understand this feeling of Ariella's, but it feels like what I would imagine is heaven. *That* definitely couldn't have come from me. I've never had a feeling like that, ever! I hate to say it, honey, but it even beats sex!"

Teddy didn't know how to take Genevieve's comment. If their sex was the best high she'd ever known, and it undeniably was for him, then how could he ever compete with heaven? Realizing it was apples and oranges he acknowledged, "I can only say, since one feelin is primal and the other celestial, I'm glad at least tha I was the best earthly high ye'd ever experienced."

Genevieve put Ariella in Teddy's arms as the baby began to cry. "Don't say it in the past tense, mister. I plan to experience that earthly high many times over with you, and hopefully very soon. "Now, feed your baby!"

CHAPTER 8

PULLING AT THE HEARTSTRINGS

THEIR HOUSE WAS finally move-in ready. It had been ten months since Ariella, whom everyone now called Ella, was born. Uncle Steven had assigned Teddy a prominent account to manage four months prior, and the quick learning intern had secured two new ones entirely on his own. Uncle Steven's company, Teel Development Corporation, was in high demand, and Steven let Teddy know that once he had a few more years of experience, he planned to make him a partner.

Genevieve had been honing her newfound skill as an empath. She had just finished a night class in psychology and signed up for another, becoming engrossed in the whole phenomenon. The intense feelings she had with Ella slowly began disappearing when the baby was about six months old. Not only did Genevieve miss the euphoria her child emitted, but she also wondered why it vanished so mysteriously. Then, a few weeks ago, while visiting a potential client of Teddy's whose wife just had a baby boy, Genevieve asked if she could hold him. In just a few moments, she reaffirmed the incredible feeling infants embody. As if heaven holds them close until they've had time to acclimate to physical life on their own.

Now, *believing* there had to be a reason behind her ability, Genevieve started delving into how she could put it to good use. Just understanding an emotion coming from someone doesn't help *them* with it at all, since they are the one having the feeling anyway. And, pretending to know more than that, would be no better than those who prey on lost individuals looking desperately for answers—answers Genevieve had no way of knowing. So, the quest to understand the *why*, continued.

Genevieve had just come back from the realtor's office. The papers would be ready to sign tomorrow. It was exciting, yet Genevieve had always been comforted by the protected wings of her aunt and uncle, not to mention how devoted and doting they were with Ella. Genevieve knew it would be hard, especially on her aunt, who was enjoying every aspect of Ella's development.

It was quiet when Genevieve entered through the front door. Walking silently through the foyer, Genevieve peeked into the living room, and there on the couch sat Aunt Melinda, with Ella sound asleep in her arms. Startled to see Genevieve, Aunt Melinda quickly wiped a tear that had fallen. With concern, Genevieve sat next to her aunt. Putting her arm around her and resting her head on Melinda's shoulder, Genevieve *expected* to feel sadness coming from her aunt, but instead, it felt more like longing or possibly regret. The two emotions were still a bit confusing for Genevieve to read.

Kissing her aunt on the cheek, Genevieve whispered, "You know how much I love you, right? And this little one would be lost without her grandma. We'll be here so much you'll hardly know we ever left."

Aunt Melinda ran her fingers through Ella's dark ringlets without stirring her. "I wish I'd been around more when you were a baby." Melinda lamented. "Now that you know what your mother was going through, or feeling, it must have been even more difficult for you than I imagined. It's essential to know you're important and loved." Aunt Melinda looked at Genevieve, whose eyes had become misty. "I love you, my girl. From the day you were born, you've *always* been especially close to my heart. And, despite all that happened, you turned into an incredible human being, *so strong!* This little darling doesn't know how very blessed she is to have you as her mother."

Genevieve choked back tears, "And you as her grandmother."

Ella's eyes slowly opened and seeing her mother, reached for her. As Genevieve was about to take her daughter, an acute feeling of longing *and* regret pierced Genevieve like a knife, it was coming from her aunt. For the first time, Genevieve sensed two distinct emotions at once.

As Ella wrapped her arms around Genevieve, nuzzling her face against her mother's, Genevieve took her aunt's hand, and stressed, "You came into my life exactly when I needed you the most. I don't regret how things were when I was small, because, as you said, it made me stronger. And I *don't* want you to ever be remorseful about things that were out of your control back then. You have the most unselfish love I've ever known. I don't think you can fathom just how much I trust and look up to you. If I am what you say I am, then I owe every bit of it to you."

Aunt Melinda burst out crying. Little Ella popped her head up, and, seeing her grandmother in tears, crawled back into her lap and hugged her as Melinda wrapped her arms desperately around the baby. Genevieve frowned as she thought, *I didn't realize our leaving would affect her so strongly. Or, am I misunderstanding the focus of her emotions? Is Aunt Melinda thinking about us or something else? What other reason could there be?*

After a minute, Aunt Melinda's beautiful smile was back as usual, and she started playing finger games with Ella. Genevieve, now worried about her aunt's state of mind, put her hand on her aunt's arm but soon relaxed. The negative feelings had been replaced with feelings Genevieve understood well these days…belonging.

CHAPTER 9

MAKING NO SENSE

April 1980

"I'm so sorry Genevieve, I know how much you wanted this baby."

Nodding to her friend Jennifer, as the two sat on Genevieve's couch on an otherwise typical Wednesday morning, Genevieve wondered if she'd ever bear another child. Yesterday was the second miscarriage in two years. The first pregnancy, just over a year ago, was lost at the beginning of the third trimester, when Genevieve was thoroughly enjoying the movements of her baby, boy. It was a devastating loss that shook Genevieve and Teddy to their core.

This time, Genevieve barely found out she was pregnant, and now it was over. Her obstetrician, Dr. Sagon, said there was no underlying reason she couldn't carry a fetus to term, so why was this happening then? Was it the complications of having Ella? The doctor had said it wasn't, but now that it happened again, was he having second thoughts? When Genevieve and Teddy left the doctor's office yesterday, after confirming what she already knew, Dr. Sagon said he could do some testing, but honestly believed she would be a mother again. *From your lips to God's ears,* Genevieve thought.

Steering away from a love she'd never know, Genevieve focused on four-year-old Ella who was sitting not far away in the living room. She had sunk deep in a beanbag chair, along with Jennifer's two-year-old daughter, Chrissy. Ella was handing Chrissy one fish cracker at a time as they watched Sesame Street together.

Jennifer and Stuart Kohl had become good friends of the Walkers. Ever since Genevieve's old high school friend, Stuart, came to their wedding with his fiancé, it seemed as if the two couples serendipitously began running into each all-around town. Pretty soon, they were planning outings together.

Genevieve and Teddy were present at Stuart and Jennifer's wedding a year after their own and were some of the first visitors after Chrissy was born.

Only two weeks prior, while telling the Kohls she was pregnant, Genevieve also decided to tell them about her empathic ability. She was very protective of who she included these days, and for a good reason. While her aunt and uncle, as well as Teddy and Tess, were not concerned, others felt violated by it. They saw it as a personal and very private invasion that she had no right to know. Genevieve had to consider the implications at all times now. Still, it wasn't like she could turn it on and off at will. The only way to shut the ability off was to stay away from physical contact with another or wear gloves, and gloves were not the fashion these days. Nevertheless, she always kept a pair with her wherever she went.

Telling the Kohls was particularly scary. She didn't want to lose their friendship, but the closer and more comfortable everyone became, the more Genevieve and Teddy knew it was only a matter of time before they would find out anyway. It was a risk, but she couldn't bear to let them be blindsided by circumstance, there had to be trust.

When Genevieve saw their intrigue and fascination that day, she glanced at Teddy, who nodded and winked at her. Jennifer moved next to Genevieve and deliberately held her hand, letting Genevieve feel her excitement mixed with trust, to prove she did not see it as a devilish curse.

With the crackers gone and the show over, the two little girls struggled to find their way out of the soft, pillow-like chair. The mothers took wicked pleasure watching as their girls struggled to escape the massive rolling beast that was holding them in its clutches. After a minute, Ella figured out it was easier to slide down off it than trying to use her legs as leverage. Once she had maneuvered to a standing position, Ella reached down and pulled Chrissy's legs until the little one was lying flat on the floor. Jennifer winked at Genevieve, "That's one way to do it."

After a quick lunch, Jennifer and Chrissy headed home, and Ella and Genevieve headed upstairs for some rest. Genevieve had fought her emotions since the miscarriage, trying to put her trust in what was *meant to be*. Still, it was sadly mystifying. In the quiet solitude of her bedroom, she let the

34

tears flow, imagining all that could have been. Eventually, the physical and emotional fatigue overcame her, and sleep became a welcome escape, or, so Genevieve hoped.

"I love you!"

In Genevieve's dream, she heard a little girl yelling the words, over and over, as a blur of children whirled by on a Merry-Go-Round not far from where Genevieve was standing. As she tried to spot the child on the fast-moving ride, pipe-organ music started to play, becoming louder and louder, until nothing could be heard above it.

Desperation was setting in. Genevieve had the feeling time was running out to find the child. Then, with relief, Genevieve felt the softness of a little hand in hers. As she looked down to see who it was, Genevieve realized her eyes were closed, and, no matter how hard she tried, her eyelids remained unmovable. While Genevieve continued to struggle, the child's hand was suddenly torn away, followed by a blood curdling-scream.

"Mommy!" Ella hollered from her bedroom. Genevieve opened her eyes, disoriented. The clock read 4:18 p.m. Sitting up, Genevieve could still feel her heart racing, and the scream that made her skin crawl.

From the time Ella was born, Genevieve realized her dreams might be more than rambling, insignificant gibberish. Therefore, if she could remember any of it, Genevieve would write it down in a journal, kept by the bed, feeling that they may contain hidden messages she was supposed to interpret. Often lately though, Genevieve found herself blind at some point in her dreams. Sometimes, just when she needed to see something, her sight was taken away. She was beginning to realize there was a purpose behind it. To not rely so much on what was seen, but more on the feelings the dream projected. *What was the meaning this time? Who loves me? Is it the baby I lost?* she wondered. After hastily jotting down a few words and sentences, the prism of fragmented images and sounds quickly flickered and disappeared.

Shaking her head, Genevieve called to Ella, "I'm coming, honey!"

When Genevieve entered Ella's room, Ella was sitting on the edge of her bed. Noticing that her daughter was about to cry, Genevieve sat next to her. "Mommy, why were you shouting?"

Genevieve frowned, "What are you talking about, baby? I was sleeping, like you."

Ella shook her head, "No, you weren't. You were screaming, "Stop! Don't look up! S T O P!" Ella wrapped her arms around her mother. "You scared me. Who were you screaming at?"

Genevieve had no recollection of what Ella just told her. Giving her daughter a tight squeeze, she assured her, "I must have just been dreaming, Ella. Did I say anything else?" Ella shook her head.

Although the dream felt scary and intense, Genevieve hoped it didn't mean anything, for there was very little to go on. Nevertheless, she added what Ella heard her say to the journal as well. Then the two went downstairs so Ella could play with her new Strawberry Shortcake doll and Genevieve could start dinner.

CHAPTER 10

TIME FOR A CHANGE

FALL 1981

It seemed like it had been ages since Genevieve had been on a plane, even though it had only been six years. But, feeling Ella was old enough to start experiencing life outside of Scottsdale, Genevieve and Teddy accepted an invitation from Aunt Melinda and Uncle Steven to travel with them to Jamaica. Tess, her best friend Katrina, and Geoffrey were coming as well. A client of Uncle Steven had offered his five-bedroom vacation home in Negril, as a "thank you" after Uncle Steven's firm bought one hundred and forty acres near Ft. Myers, Florida, to develop a residential community.

Flying in Uncle Steven's company jet, that he had bought earlier that year, Ella sat glued to the window as it sped down the runway. As the small craft lifted off, the airy, weightless feeling made Ella's eyes and mouth open wide as she looked to her parents for a reassuring nod that all was okay.

Genevieve was *really* looking forward to some quiet, alone-time with Teddy. The last year had been daring, scary, and lonely, as Teddy branched out, away from Uncle Steven's firm.

Initially, Uncle Steven had a lot of frustration and even resentment when Teddy talked to him about his decision. Although ever grateful for all Uncle Steven had done, Teddy became conflicted when observing the vast uprooting that happened during large land development projects. So, after much study, he realized a more natural urban landscape, with nature molded around housing communities was the way he wanted to go. In the spring, Teddy felt the time was right and made the brave decision to move in that direction.

Several talks later, Uncle Steven gave Teddy his blessing and said he admired the way he listened to his 'gut'. But then, of course, Steven had to add, "When I listen to my gut, on the other hand, people steer clear of the bathroom…for *hours!* Now that's one powerful gut, don't you think, Ted?"

Still, Genevieve knew her uncle was very disappointed that his vision to have Teddy as a partner would never be realized.

At about the same time, while taking yet another marketing class, Teddy met fellow student, Solomon Santaro. Although the two were very different, not only in personality but in their ideas toward marketing, they oddly hit it off. Both coincidentally had degrees in real estate development.

Sol had come from money and had a slick, polished air about him. There was something that bothered Genevieve about his demeanor, but not knowing what, she decided not to dwell on it. She was glad for her husband's new friendship and trusted Teddy, knowing he was always a great judge of character.

With the decision to form his own business, Teddy then felt Sol was the logical person to be his partner. Sol had what Teddy could surely use; additional seed money to build the company, and a clever pitchman. Someone with an aggressively suave, "You can't live without this" oration, compared to Teddy's more disarming, "I love it, I know ye will too" approach. That way, depending on the client's disposition, they had it covered.

Between the non-stop wooing of potential clients, scouting new projects, and forming the business Walker and Santoro Inc., Genevieve felt the only time she spent with Teddy was when he collapsed, exhausted, next to her at night. But now, with the company's first project in Oregon, due to break ground in a few months, Sol assured a nervous Teddy, that he would keep the momentum going as potential clients were beginning to take notice.

"It's only a week, Ted. Go have some fun with that sexy wife of yours." Sol demanded. "I can handle anything that comes up here. It's only seven days for God's sake!"

After the plane had reached its cruising altitude, Teddy pulled out a folder Sol had given him with land potentials up for sale. As he opened it, Genevieve reached over and gently closed it. Teddy, still looking down at the folder, smiled and took Genevieve's hand and squeezed it. Leaning on his shoulder,

Genevieve whispered, "Let it all go. Just for a few days, anyway. I promise to show you what you've been missing."

Teddy kissed Genevieve's head. Then, glancing over to Ella, who was talking with her grandpa, murmured, "I can't wait."

Genevieve lifted her head and grinned.

Looking more animated, Teddy whispered, "Naw, really, I can't *wait*. Tell me, Gen, do ye think we'd be the first to initiate this plane to the Mile-High-Club?" Then, narrowing his eyes, "Or do ye think your aunt and uncle have already beaten us to it?"

Genevieve snorted in laughter so loud it drew the attention of everyone in the cabin. Trying to keep her voice hushed, "Do you think they would… or did?" Shrugging, Teddy had a cockeyed smile while watching Genevieve contemplate the possibility.

After a few moments, Genevieve closed her eyes and shook her head, trying to push away the visual, "No. No, can't do it. It would be weird now, not to mention obvious! Pick a place. A new one that's not in the clouds and I'll meet you there."

With a continued daredevil look, Teddy nodded, "I'll figure one oot by nightfall. So be ready!"

"Oh, I'm ready," she quietly confirmed. Then, barely above a whisper, Genevieve sang her favorite Bob Marley song, as her lips almost touched her husband's, "One Love, One Heart, *let's get together* and feel alright."

When the pilot announced he would be touching down in a few minutes, Uncle Steven, who had Ella fast asleep on his chest began to wake her up gently. Tess and Katrina, who had spent the last hour flirting with the male attendant reluctantly went back to their seats as he prepared the plane for landing. Teddy made a final, killer move, beating Geoffrey at a game of chess, while Genevieve and Aunt Melinda continued to look at travel brochures for tour excursions that sounded interesting.

When the plane door opened, a warm, humid blast of topical air rushed in. "Welcome to Jamaica" a large sign said as they entered the airport.

After the two-hour trip to Negril was over, everyone piled out of the large van as Tany, their housekeeper and cook, came out to greet them. With the sweetest Jamaican lilt, she welcomed "*her family*" to their home. Once settled in, Tany took them to the large balcony that overlooked the ocean, just two blocks away. It was incredibly enticing, but so was the spicy aroma of Jerk Chicken wafting from the kitchen. With surrounding clouds getting darker and the day getting later, everyone decided the beach could wait until tomorrow. However, both Teddy and Genevieve knew something else couldn't.

CHAPTER 11

JAMAICA MON

THE RAIN WAS coming down so hard they all got up from the dinner table just to watch it. Tany laughed. "You've never seen rain before?"

Staring out the large picture window in the living room like they were watching a suspenseful movie, Tess replied, "Not with raindrops this big and loud." The rain fell copiously for almost an hour. Then, like that, it was gone, save for a sprinkle from a small, transient cloud that scurried by as if trying to catch up with the stormy clouds ahead of it.

Later in the evening, after the last of the family had made their way to their bedroom, Teddy took a couple bottles of Red Stripe beer out of the refrigerator, grabbed Genevieve's hand, and walked out onto the large balcony. It was pitch black, but the chirping sound from the Jamaican tree frogs could be heard everywhere. The consistent sing-song pattern gave off an enchantingly romantic ambiance. Having noticed a shelf full of candles on the way out, Genevieve went back inside and grabbed a handful, found some matches, and after lighting them on several tables nearby, joined Teddy in a large hammock that he had dried with a towel.

The setting was perfect. As they drank the local favorite, the two relaxed quietly for a while, savoring the mating call of a hundred tiny frogs. The modest breeze of tropical air, however, wasn't enough to cool the heat building as Teddy and Genevieve laid close, their faces a faint glimmer next to the candlelight.

It had started as a slow burn after the plane trip and kept building throughout the day. Genevieve could feel Teddy's eyes on her, even when she wasn't looking, yet knowing the craving was growing stronger as each hour passed. Now with his hand in hers, she felt his feverous passion ricocheting within her.

Teddy took the empty bottle from Genevieve and put both on the deck below them. As he turned back around to face her, she found it funny how, after six years of marriage, she could still feel such anticipation yet, be vulnerable about what was coming next. Although she supported Teddy's dedication to building a career and understood why he came home so tired at night, it had caused a lonely distance for Genevieve. As the past few months went by, Genevieve would often stare at her exhausted husband as he slept, craving his touch.

While Teddy stroked Genevieve's cheek with his fingers, a flood of emotions she had been holding back, began to surface. Pressing his open lips against hers, Teddy started slowly unzipping the back of her dress. With an unfair advantage, Genevieve magnified the feelings she was having by mixing them with Teddy's. As his already strong, potent feelings reacted like a chemical to her own, every touch she felt intensified.

As he removed her underwear, Teddy whispered, "God, I love ye." Genevieve was sure he could feel her quivering as he knew precisely what she wanted, and skillfully kept her on the edge for so long it left her moaning and breathless. She had missed this...she had missed him.

The two were consumed with each other for over an hour when Genevieve felt a drop fall on her shoulder, then another on her face. Within a minute, the heavy rain was back. They began to laugh as the water quickly drenched their bodies. However, the deluge did not deter, but became yet another aphrodisiac as sight, now blinded by the opaque darkness, was replaced with the feel of their slippery bodies sliding over one another as they continued their undaunted rendezvous.

The next day came sooner than expected. Everyone else, who got a good night's sleep, was noisily moving around the house. By eight-o-clock, Ella tried to open her parent's bedroom door, but it was locked. "Mommy, let me in!" It took almost a minute and another holler from Ella, before the door finally opened and Genevieve's sleepy disheveled self, appeared. With a concerned frown, Ella questioned, "Mommy, are you okay?"

Glancing over at her niece, Aunt Melinda smiled. "I think she's just fine, honey. Maybe she didn't get enough *sleep* last night." Genevieve gave her aunt a puzzled frown. Aunt Melinda, who had gotten up during the night after hearing noises, *knew* there was no *maybe* about it, and gave Genevieve a wink.

Still frowning, Ella peered into the dark room and saw her daddy fumbling with his pajama bottoms. "Daddy, why are you putting your pajamas on now? It's time to get up." Genevieve closed her eyes and could feel the flush in her face.

Ella looked around bewildered.

Aunt Melinda, trying not to laugh like all the rest were, whispered to herself, "Out of the mouths of babes."

The next week went flying by. Genevieve relished every moment with Teddy and Ella. Teddy only received one call from Sol all week, and it was just to make sure his partner wasn't feeling *so* 'Irie' that he'd decided never to work for a living again.

Late in the afternoon, the day before they were to fly home, Genevieve and Teddy were laying in the hammock on the balcony. It had become her favorite spot, for many reasons. All week long she and Teddy made a point to be there as the sun set beautifully on the horizon. Those carefree moments, as the simmering red globe drifted downward, always put Genevieve in a state of reverie. As if the rest of the world, and the reality that went with it, didn't exist.

But as with all great trips that come to an end, as Genevieve watched the final gorgeous sunset with Teddy, time began ticking again, and she secretly began to wonder if soon she'd lose the attention *and* lover, she had finally reclaimed.

Teddy sensed a hint of melancholy in Genevieve's far-away look while she silently observed the sunset. The week had given him the time to reflect and realize what had been slowly slipping away. Taking her face and turning it to meet his, Teddy quietly confessed, "I'll nivvor take ye for granted again, Gen." Pausing to find the right words, he continued. "But I need ye to understand. I've only been workin this hard because I didn't want to let ye doon. I see the way you've always looked at your uncle, the love and admiration for who he is and wha he's accomplished. And rightly so, he's amazin. I want ye to see me tha same way too. It's knowing ye are near me, tha keeps me goin, no matta how beat doon I feel. Still, if I were to lose ye in the process, it would all be meaningless."

Genevieve took a deep, slow breath. "First of all, I don't love my uncle for his money. I love him for loving me when he could have walked away. I love him for showing me what a family is all about. When I first met you, I sensed the two you were made from the same cloth; that your love runs just as deep as his does.

"Who knows, maybe my uncle felt unsure and needed to prove himself also in the early years of his marriage. That was before I knew him. But who I love, never has, and *never* will be measured by the money they make. However, *like* my uncle, as long as what you do excites you and gives you satisfaction, then that *does* matter to me.

"I still hope someday soon I'll know that feeling as well—wondering if this ability of mine will have a purpose and I'll enjoy the kind of fulfillment you both do."

Realizing she was starting to digress, Genevieve put her focus back on her husband. Slipping her arms under Teddy's and closing what little space there had been between them, the two held a long tender kiss before Genevieve moved her lips to Teddy's ear and breathed, "I love the feeling coming from you right now. It's all I could ever want. I just wish you could feel what I feel for you every day. Then you'd never doubt yourself, ever again."

Teddy looked at Genevieve. Shaking his head, he admitted, "I don't know if I could handle the complicated feelins of a woman, especially *my* woman— seems much too scary to me. Ye know the old sayin, 'God only gives ye wha ye can handle.'

Genevieve's eyes narrowed, and a knowing grin appeared. "That's quite true, sir. But, since God gave you someone, such as *me*, there's no doubt, you're quite capable of handling more than just about any other man on the planet!"

CHAPTER 12

GENEVIEVE'S CALLING

AFTER FINDING OUT she was pregnant a month after the Jamaica trip, Dr. Sagon took every precaution in the hopes Genevieve would carry *this* baby to term. Still, there were complications, as in the third trimester Genevieve's blood pressure began to escalate. Preeclampsia was diagnosed, medication and bed rest were ordered. With little improvement however, Dr. Sagon decided it would be best to deliver the baby early, than take a chance on a ticking time bomb.

Baby Broc was delivered two weeks premature, but he was perfect. Genevieve knew her son was healthy and had plans to stick around the moment she held his sleeping body and touched heaven along with her new infant.

However, Genevieve's understanding of heaven was minuscule at best. The mysterious way she could feel emotion like no one else was a mere precursor for what was to come. Later that fall, on what was to be a fun way to spend a Saturday, four-year-old Chrissy Kohl was rushed to the hospital, due to a horrific freak accident at a carnival. She laid deep in a coma the following morning, with little hope for survival. Chrissy's parents rushed to see Genevieve and pleaded with her to do what she had never done before, feel the emotions of someone who was close to death. Their hope was that maybe Chrissy would somehow know that Genevieve was with her, to comfort her.

On that morning, the Kohls took turns describing to Genevieve and Teddy, the scene of the accident. They had just finished riding the Merry-Go-Round when Chrissy saw a man selling balloons on the other side of a large walkway. Chrissy escaped her mother's grasp and ran toward the colorful orbs, high in the sky. As she ran, full speed, eyes held upward, the little one never noticed that two carnival workers were carrying a massive beam as she rushed toward it.

As Jennifer continued to speak of the horrendous accident that followed, everyone became overwhelmed with emotion. As Genevieve's wiped a tear away, she suddenly shuttered with Déjà vu, recalling a dream she had had about a Merry-Go-Round.

Fear was telling Genevieve she'd only find dark and morbidly sad emotions by accepting the Kohl's request. Feelings that could very well scar her for the rest of her life.

Asking to be excused for a minute, Genevieve went upstairs and quickly thumbed through her journal until she found the entry. She felt the hair on her arms stand on end when she read her penned words—the cryptic notes of a whirling Merry-Go-Round; a little girl's hand in hers, and Ella, hearing her mother yelling, "Stop, don't look up!"

When Genevieve came back downstairs, Jennifer could see there was still fear in Genevieve's eyes. After Genevieve settled back down on the couch, Jennifer came over and sat next to her. Looking imploringly into Genevieve's eyes, Jennifer said, "I had a vision you should know about." Taking Genevieve's hand, Jennifer wanted her friend to understand what she was about to relive.

Quickly, Genevieve felt a foreign emotion of hysteria pressing at her chest. Jennifer slowly closed her eyes and continued. "As soon as Chrissy was in the ambulance, I followed and went to sit next to her. I was in a sheer panic. Chrissy was unresponsive. Her forehead was bright red, and I could see it swelling right before my eyes! The paramedic, sitting on the other side of her, was administering an I.V. and hollered at the person driving to hurry. When I looked down next to me, Chrissy's arm was hanging off the stretcher and a little plastic diamond ring she had won, was still on one of her little fingers. I reached down to hold her hand in mine." Then Jennifer opened her eyes and looked directly at Genevieve. "When I did, *everything* became calm and in my mind Genevieve, I clearly saw *you* holding Chrissy's hand."

Genevieve's chin began to quiver as she nodded to Jennifer. She made her decision. It was to embrace love instead of fear.

First encounter in Chrissy's hospital room:

Genevieve closed her eyes, bracing for what she was sure would come next. Instead, she felt deep gratitude calming her, followed closely by confidence and trust. The emotions coming through were much too complex and had a maturity way beyond that of a four-year-old. *That* was when Genevieve realized, she wasn't receiving feelings from Chrissy, but of the child's Soul!

Once Genevieve had made the revelation, she was flooded with the feeling of ecstasy. However, instead of relishing the emotion as she did with an infant in her arms, Genevieve felt tears escaping her closed eyes, knowing the feeling meant heaven was near. In this case, it could only mean one thing, Chrissy was headed back home.

Within moments however, a feeling of frustration became evident. Thinking it was Chrissy, Genevieve opened her eyes and looked at the bruised little face in front of her. With no visible reaction from the little girl, Genevieve closing them again, and thought a question, *Can you hear my thoughts?*

When a giddy feeling of joy responded, Genevieve laughed out loud and everyone in the room began to feel hopeful.

Genevieve's real connection to heaven had just begun, as the euphoria she felt *only* meant the Soul was in Its natural state of blissful happiness.

That event uncovered the extraordinary purpose for which Genevieve had been hoping. The conversation continued for hours, relayed by a sequence of complex emotions responding to Genevieve's questions as she thought them.

It was a stunning revelation and turning point. Chrissy eventually recovered. However, Genevieve learned during that encounter that the accident had been by design—a way the Soul might reach her. It was willing to risk the death of Its host and the one Genevieve loved dearly, just so Genevieve could finally know the piece of the puzzle she'd been missing. Genevieve was to be a messenger for the Soul.

CHAPTER 13

※

WORD SPREADS FAST

A FEW DAYS after Chrissy's accident, a woman appearing to be in her early forties approached Genevieve while she was visiting the Kohls in the hospital. She said her name was Beth and asked if Genevieve would come with her to her husband's room just around the corner from Chrissy's.

Beth explained that her husband, Nick had been found beaten and shot in the head the night before. The night nurse had told her about Genevieve and thought she might do for Beth what she had done for the Kohl's; provide peace and understanding where none was to be found.

Still very unsure of her abilities, Genevieve agreed with the encouragement from Jennifer to follow Beth. Unlike with Chrissy, where loved ones surrounded the helpless toddler and Teddy was by Genevieve's side, Nick's hospital room had a sterile loneliness that permeated the air. As Genevieve stood hesitantly by the stranger's bedside, her angst felt debilitatingly strong. *Why did I agree to this?* She thought. However, as Genevieve turned to look at Beth's pleading eyes, she realized her new path had already begun.

After asking Beth for her permission, Genevieve took the woman's hand and held it. They both stood observing the man before them who was disfigured by the beating, his head heavily bandaged, lying motionless on the bed. Since Genevieve knew nothing about either of them, she hoped that by feeling Beth's emotions, she might learn something that wasn't obvious. Anger and despair were dominant, but Genevieve also felt suppressed fear. "Beth, were you with your husband last night?"

"No, I had been in a counseling session."

Genevieve questioned, "As the counselor, or being counseled?"

Gently pulling her hand away from Genevieve, Beth frowned, "I'm a marriage counselor. Why do you ask?"

Genevieve took a deep breath and let it out. 'I don't know if the nurse told you, but this type of communication is very new to me. I just thought it would be good to know a little about you and your husband first. Can you tell me anything about last night, where he may have been?"

Beth continued her frown as she turned toward her husband. "He should have been home. Nick is a lawyer and was prepping for a trial that was going to begin today. I had talked to him just before my session began and nothing seemed out of the ordinary. Then, later in the evening, as I was finalizing my notes, I got a call from the police. Our neighbors found him down the street after hearing a gunshot. I don't understand any of it. We live in a good neighborhood. He isn't one to take walks at night. I…"

Genevieve watched Beth become lost in thought. "Are you sure you want me to proceed?"

Beth took her focus off her husband and, giving Genevieve a cursory glance, whispered, "Yes."

Genevieve took a chair and moved it next to the bed. Although wishing Teddy was there with her, she was now committed. *You can do this, Genevieve,* she thought.

Taking Nick's hand, she let the emotions begin to stir within her. Closing her eyes, she could feel the indescribable love that she only experienced while the Soul was accessible. Genevieve waited for it to begin its emotional conversation. If the experience were anything like the first one, it would start communication with a feeling.

Blame. *That's an odd emotion coming from the Soul,* Genevieve pondered. The heaviest negative feeling Genevieve had received from Chrissy's Soul was minor frustration. But then, that situation was different. The Soul's purpose in that communication was only to help Genevieve understand her ability. In doing so, almost all of the emotions were positive. This Soul had something else to project, and it was feeling blame. But for whom?

Do you blame yourself for what happened?

The feeling felt positive.

Do you know who hurt you, Nick?

Again, the emotion was positive.

Genevieve took a deep breath while she waited for the next emotion to reveal itself.

Forgiveness.

Forgiveness, for whom? Genevieve queried in her thought, *"Do you forgive yourself or the person who hurt you, Nick?"*

Frustration. The same uncomfortable frustration Genevieve felt when Chrissy's Soul couldn't convey *Its* intended message.

Puzzled, Genevieve continued to search for a connection. Then, out of nowhere, a single word rose in her mind, *Beth.*

It was happening again. As with Chrissy, there were times in that emotional conversation that Genevieve found herself asking questions that seemed odd or out of context. Questions that had not occurred to her at all, yet they had led to a clearer understanding.

A feeling of hopefulness infused Genevieve's body as she asked, *Am I understanding correctly, that the feeling of forgiveness is meant for Beth?* Genevieve could almost feel the Soul smiling, and Genevieve smiled herself.

Beth saw Genevieve smile, the first sign of any emotion since the communication began. Not knowing whether she could interrupt or not, she fought the urge to speak, and remained silent, taking solace that whatever was happening seemed to be positive.

Genevieve felt another question arising, *Do you want Beth to know this?*

The sudden eagerness startled Genevieve. Opening her eyes, she looked at Beth. "He blames himself. But wants you to know he forgives you."

Beth's eyes filled with tears. Genevieve knew the words made sense to Beth, even though she herself was nowhere near putting any of the pieces together.

Trying to control her shaky voice, Beth asked, "Does he know who did this to him?"

Genevieve nodded, "Yes, I got a positive response to that question."

Beth's fear was now showing through her eyes as she murmured, "Was it Trent Ivy?"

Genevieve had no way of knowing until the name was uttered out loud. At that moment, she felt the Soul's positive confirmation flooding her body. Genevieve only nodded in reply.

Beth walked over and sat at the end of the bed and wiped her eyes. Glancing at Genevieve then down at the floor she confessed, "Nick and I have made a lot of mistakes. Our biggest was letting everything become more important than each other. It became obvious when Nick had an affair last year. By the time I found out it was already over, but it destroyed me. Nick did everything he could after that, to make it up, and I truly wanted to move on, but I just couldn't help wondering every time I saw him glance at an attractive woman—did he want her? Cliché, right? It all became so ironic, doing what I do. I mean, who in their right mind would take advice from someone who didn't even have a handle on their own marriage? Nothing in my life was making sense anymore."

Beth slowly blinked and shook her head. "Then a potential client walked through my door, someone who didn't have a handle on his life or marriage either, Trent Ivy.

His wife had already filed for divorce, so I told him I didn't think there was anything I could do for him. He asked if he could have just one session to talk about some things that were troubling him. I felt bad, so I agreed, but shouldn't have. He had the classic signs that drive a partner away, jealousy, self-doubt, compulsive behavior. At the end of the session, he put the charm on, telling me how beautiful I was and how much he wished he had someone in his life like me. I should have known better, but I was still feeling betrayed and undesirable. When he began…" Beth stopped abruptly and looked at her husband.

With a long pause, she continued. "A few days ago, I ended it. I was afraid of the way Trent might react if I saw him, so I cowardly did it over the phone. He kept calling me after that, but I wouldn't pick up. I had to make him understand there was nothing to discuss.

"I knew how damaging an affair could be. I knew first-hand how Nick had hurt me. Still, I didn't do it out of revenge. I really *had* hoped that Trent could fulfill something I needed somehow. But the feeling I had when I was with him didn't make me feel better or wanted. It left me even emptier inside, and all I craved was to have my life with Nick back."

Beth continued to stare at her husband. "I understand exactly how Nick felt now," she said. Then, turning to Genevieve, "But I won't get a chance to try and make it up to him, will I?"

Genevieve, still holding Nicks' hand, was beginning to feel a distance from the Soul. With Chrissy, it felt like it was moving deeper within the child. Today, however, it felt like it was drifting away. Genevieve wanted to give Beth some feeling of peace but hadn't received any emotional response from Nick since Beth started talking.

Genevieve looked nervous as she thought, *Nick, what can I tell her?*

Then, like walking along an art gallery wall, Genevieve felt emotions, distinctly framed, one after another:

Understanding, passionate love, belief, and finally, appreciation.

It was Nick's final love message to his wife.

It was through Nick that Genevieve learned that the Soul never leaves with regrets or anger. Nick's Soul only used the negative feeling of blame to define a circumstance in life, not to characterize a flaw of negativity within itself.

In the end, every Soul Genevieve would ever communicate with released Itself from the human host feeling only the purest of love. Even as Nick's Soul revealed Its last detectable feeling, there was no trace of blame for itself or anyone else. The journey was complete, and It was happy to be going home.

It gave Genevieve some comfort in knowing that even though *her* mother never understood how remarkable maternal love could be, when the final moments came for her, she did. Genevieve had witnessed the way the Soul integrates with Its host, exuding unbounding love for everyone as Its time on Earth comes to an end. Genevieve knew her mother had felt *this* kind of love for her—something Genevieve had always longed for. Yet, it could only be in the knowing now. A fleeting emotion of maternal love that died when her mother did, years ago.

CHAPTER 14

IT GOES DEEPER

Late March 1983

"Is this how I do it, Mommy?" Ella took one cooked pea at a time, smashed it and put it in front of her eight-month-old brother. Turning from the sink, Genevieve watched as Broc's hands pounded on the high-chair tray, impatient with his sister's teasingly slow method of feeding him.

"You're doing fine Ella. I'll have his meal ready in a minute." Then, walking over and bending down to look at Broc's cute cherub face, she said, "Be patient there, little guy. You're lucky to have a sister who's willing to help out." Broc squinted his eyes and gave his mom a jack-o-lantern grin, as if he actually understood. "Yeah, that's more like it," Genevieve said, kissing him on the nose and walking back to finish her task.

Just then, Broc grabbed hold of the hard-plastic bowl Ella was holding, full of peas. It flipped over, spilling the vegetable all over the floor as it ricocheted off the linoleum and bounced halfway across the large kitchen.

Broc blinked several times at his sister, then, leaned over the side, innocently stared at his handiwork.

Ella, however, had a look of total exasperation. As Genevieve came over to calm her daughter down, Ella warned, "Mommy, you better wear your gloves. I'm really mad right now!"

Genevieve tried to contain a laugh. "Okay, I've been warned. But you know, it's perfectly normal to feel frustration, Ella." As Ella watched Broc's vain attempt to reach for the little green dots surrounding his high-chair, Genevieve knelt down and wrapped her arm around Ella's waist and felt her daughter's annoyance dissipating. "Do you think a cookie would make you feel better?" Genevieve hinted.

Ella turned and looked at her mother eye to eye as she placed her small hands on Genevieve's cheeks, "I think it will take at least two. I'm still *really* mad."

As Genevieve pursed her lips and acted surprised, she detected her daughter's dimpled smile and blue eyes sparkling in triumph. "So, is this how you've been negotiating with your father lately?"

Ella continued to smile and shrugged. "Maybe. I don't know what that means."

Genevieve grinned, thinking, *Well maybe not, but nevertheless, you do it quite well.* It was the first time Genevieve wondered what her daughter might grow up to be. *A charming negotiator. Yep, you're more like your father every day!*

After lunch was over and Ella got the dessert she had bargained for, the doorbell rang. "Good," Genevieve said, glancing at her watch. "The Garlands are here to watch you and your brother for a while."

The older couple who lived down the street were one of only a few that the Walkers felt entirely comfortable with, outside of family, to watch their children.

As Genevieve carried Broc, Ella skipped along, trying to keep pace with her mother as they headed for the door. "Where are you going, Mommy?" Ella chirped.

"To the police station," Genevieve replied.

Ella's carefree expression turned frantic. "Are you getting arrested for touching people?"

Genevieve cringed. Pausing for a moment before opening the door she stated calmly, "No, honey. There is a detective that wants to meet with me. He thinks I may be able to help him. And Ella, can you do me a favor? Let's keep Mommy's touching ability to ourselves for now, okay?"

Ella frowned slightly and shrugged, "Okay."

Once the Garlands had settled in, Genevieve snuck away before Broc noticed. He had been going through separation anxiety lately, and it seemed to be better for him, and Genevieve, when he didn't know she was leaving.

On her drive to the station, she replayed something that had been weighing heavily on her mind. Late last year, when Genevieve learned how deep her ability went, one thing Chrissy's Soul impressed upon her was she would also be able to help those who couldn't communicate with the outside world due to a physical circumstance or trauma. *Was my interaction with Nick and his murder what the Soul meant? Beth was really the one that solved that case. Can I do the same on my own?* As she parked her car, Genevieve hoped she'd get the chance to find out.

Brunner Chao, a young detective at the Scottsdale P.D., had heard the rumors of Genevieve's ability, but no one at the precinct believed in "that spiritual mumbo-jumbo." As his co-workers made jokes, Brunner laughed along with them. However, many years ago, he had witnessed his little sister, Hui Yin come back from the dead, almost an hour after drowning in a pond in his homeland province in Gansu, China. When Hui Yin awoke, she found her mother crying over her as she cleaned the mud from Hui Yin's body and prepared her for burial.

Later that same day, Hui Yin told Brunner about a loving being comforting her. She felt as if it was a part of her somehow. She knew she had been in a long conversation with it but could not recall the specifics. Hui Yin knew that it helped her in deciding to come back.

Brunner had never forgotten that day. So, the rather ambitious, "out-of-the-box" thinker, decided to test Genevieve in a sort of unauthorized audition, to see just how credible she was, with the hopes she might help him solve a case that was going nowhere.

Hearing Genevieve had checked-in at the sergeant's desk, Detective Chao went to greet her. Putting his hand out, he inquired, "Mrs. Walker?" Genevieve quickly nodded and shook Brunner's hand.

The detective seemed distracted as he handed a file to the clerk behind the counter and then glanced at the clock on the wall. Turning back to face Genevieve he said confidently, "Your background check turned out just fine."

Genevieve looked puzzled, "I didn't know you were doing that, but okay."

Brunner shrugged, "It's just procedure, that's all. Say, I'm on my way to a suspected robbery right now, so I got to run. Can you meet me this evening at the Mayo Clinic? It's about the person in room 4025. His name is Dillon Michaels. Does 7:00 p.m. sound okay?"

Genevieve frowned as she thought she had come for an interview. As Brunner headed towards the door, Genevieve shook her head, baffled as to why she had to come to the precinct at all. With no details of what the detective expected of her, a feeling of insecurity began to flutter in her stomach. Before he was out the door, Genevieve blurted, "Would you mind if my husband tagged along, just this one time?"

Brunner nodded and smiled, "Don't mind at all. Whatever works for you, works for me."

Detective Chao, realizing he probably came off as being a bit of an ass, called Genevieve later that afternoon to apologize for not being able to meet with her properly or brief her on the case that had him baffled.

"Just so you're aware," he said, "Dillon's condition is stable, but he suffered a stroke and doesn't seem to recognize anyone. He seems unaware of his surroundings and unable to communicate. The lab test showed a high level of cocaine in his system, probably not meant to kill him, but Dillon also has high blood pressure—a dangerous combination.

"About three weeks ago, he and his girlfriend went to their favorite grille to have a beer and burger after work. Both Dillon and his girlfriend, Dharma, consider themselves astrology nerds, star mapping, and that sort of thing. They're even into UFOs and searching for life on other planets. Dharma said neither of them touched drugs and even a beer that night was a rare choice. But, it was St. Patrick's Day and it seemed like a green beer would be a fun way to celebrate Dillon's first full month at his new job.

"Before the dinner had finished however, Dillon started hallucinating, seized and collapsed soon after. Several patrons sitting around the couple were interviewed, as well as the chef, and the couple's server, but nothing seemed out of the ordinary, and there was no motive. Dharma said Dillon barely made ends meet and he didn't come from money either. His one-month job was as a lab tech at the Mayo Clinic Hospital. Before that, he was finishing college and had been a part-time grocery checker at a local market. I heard you might be able to reach him on different level. Maybe you can get him to talk to you, so to speak."

Genevieve was glad Brunner called to fill her in, but clarified, "There's no speaking that goes on, so I hope you aren't expecting me to fall into a trance and start talking like Dillon. It would be easier I suppose if that was the way it worked. Instead, however, I translate the emotions I feel coming from his Soul. Emotions that hopefully will tell you what you need to know."

7:00 p.m.

The minute Genevieve and Teddy walked into the hospital room of Dillon Michael, Detective Chao noticed the warm, empathetic nature in Genevieve's green eyes. Walking up to the bed, Genevieve acknowledged Brunner, but her focus was on Dillon. Brunner sensed cautious optimism that she might be the one he needed.

As Teddy stood at the doorway, Genevieve took Dillon's hand as he stared blankly at the ceiling. Without theatrics or fan-fair, Genevieve just closed her eyes. She had no idea what may or may not happen in this case, as he seemed awake but unable to communicate. Would it be Dillon she would be interacting with, or his Soul?

With her eyes closed, Genevieve felt Dillon's hand lock around hers. Surprised, her eyes flew open to see if anything had changed. However, the same blank expression remained on Dillon's face, so she closed her eyes again. Trying not to impose her own assumptions on what might be revealed, Genevieve let her thoughts disperse. Within moments she began to feel something stirring, and she knew it was what she had felt before—the Soul.

That confirmed a more profound truth. *It IS the Soul that communicates if the body cannot, no matter the circumstance!* As Genevieve began imagining all the people who were just like Dillon, she began to shake, overwhelmed by the scope of all those that could use her help. But then a feeling of thankfulness warmed and calmed her like a soft, soothing blanket.

Why are you thankful, Dillon?

Thankfulness morphed into appreciation.

For me?

Dillon's hand clenched tighter around Genevieve's. Sensing Dillon's movements might be more than involuntary muscle contractions, Genevieve felt compelled to confirm a suspicion as she asked, *Does Dillon understand my thoughts also?*

Genevieve felt satisfaction in reply.

With a sharp breath, Genevieve's eyes opened as she focused on Dillon's. *Then Dillon will learn, as I do, what happened to him?*

As his flat facial affect continued to stare, a complete feeling of assurance was as good as a definite "yes."

Over the next two days, Genevieve worked painstakingly through trial and error to understand the meaning behind each emotion. By the time she was done, however, Genevieve knew that the person who had drugged Dillon was a bartender. She knew it was due to jealousy, not of Dillon but of someone at the grille that night. Finally, she was able to ascertain it was given to him by accident. That was all the Soul would offer.

Curious, but not convinced that anyone could really get to the truth through emotions, Brunner went back to the grille. Luckily both bartenders who worked on the night of the crime were present when Brunner showed up.

One, named Sid was in his early thirties, tall with a thin build, blue-green eyes and black hair slicked back. "How about a drink on the house?" Sid asked as he tempted Brunner into trying his latest libation masterpiece. But after Brunner held steadfast, reminding Sid *twice,* that he was on duty, Sid turned his attention to other patrons sitting at the bar. With continued prodding, Sid finally answered the detective's questions hastily, and with little detail. He told Detective Chao that it was a jam-packed evening. The usual regulars stopped in, but otherwise, no one came by that he knew.

The other bartender, Mattie, in her early forties, a bit stocky with an infectious laugh, wanted to know all about Brunner's work, family, hobbies, always diverting the conversation back to the detective. Brunner began to wonder if the deflection was just the habit of an engaging bartender, or something more calculating. Eventually, she too gave a similar account of her evening.

With no smoking gun, Brunner asked the owner if he could see the silent security tape of that day.

Fast-forwarding to the dinner hour, the detective observed that Sid seemed to have an obsessed focus on a couple that was sitting at the bar. Rewinding the tape, Brunner stopped and pressed forward when he saw the couple arrive and sit down. The detective could see that although Sid seemed to know them both, it was the woman Sid most engaged with. Soon after, Dillon and his girlfriend showed up and were seated at a table.

The hair on the back of Brunner's neck began to rise. *Damn Genevieve! Could it be true?* With Mattie exhibiting no unusual behavior, Brunner decided to put his full focus on Sid.

Moving close to the screen and wishing there had been sound, Brunner steadily watched as the bartender gave the man, a tall glass of green-colored beer. Then, as Sid placed the emerald brew in front of the woman, she grabbed his arm and said something that seemed to upset him. For over a half-hour the bartender kept a close eye on the two. However, they seemed oblivious to him, or anyone else, as they laughed together and occasionally kissed.

As Detective Chao continued to watch intently, the other bartender, Mattie, asked Sid a question. Nodding, he went into the back room and came out with a bag of limes. When Sid noticed the couple at the bar had departed, he began looking around his station, agitated. Then he focused on a waitress. She had just delivered two glasses of green beer she had picked up from behind the bar and served them to Dillon and his girlfriend.

Immediately afterward, Dillon and his girlfriend clicked their glasses together and took a swig. Seeing that, Sid takes off, swiftly moving to the men's bathroom where he stays for almost ten minutes before going back to work. Five minutes later, Dillon is seen convulsing.

Even though it was apparent on the silent footage that people were panicked and several of the grille's staff were seen running over to assist Dillon, Sid barely glanced over, busying himself by washing glasses.

Detective Chao told Genevieve after Sid had been arrested, that the woman at the bar was Sid's roommate, Sunny. After interviewing her, Sunny informed the detective that Sid had been pushing a relationship with her for months, even though she had made it clear she wasn't interested. Sunny had come by that night to make a point. She told Sid she was moving in with the man she was with; one they both knew very well—their "Wallstreet" looking drug supplier, Reece.

In a fit of jealous rage, and knowing Reece was already high as a kite, Sid slipped a high dose of cocaine in a beer, primed and ready when his adversary signaled for another round.

With the mystery solved, Genevieve asked Brunner if he wanted to come with her to say good-bye to Dillon. "First rule of thumb, Genevieve, don't get attached. You can't do anything more for him now."

Genevieve shook her head, "How do I stay unattached when my sole, sorry, play on words, purpose, *is* to attach myself to the victim, deeply."

With a shrug, Brunner acknowledged the dichotomy and, feeling a bit guilty for putting her in it, agreed to come along.

Dharma was sitting by Dillon's bed as they entered the room and thanked them both for solving the case. Then Genevieve took Dillon's hand, to let him know his attacker was in jail. The Soul had no emotion other than its default state of unfettered love. But Dillion's hand twitched as his eyes blinked rapidly. With barely a whisper Genevieve said, "I knew you'd want to know." Then squeezing his hand, she silently added, *I hope you will enjoy another green beer with your sweetheart, someday soon.*

As Genevieve and Brunner were leaving the room, the detective questioned, "The one thing I don't understand is how Dillon could have known who committed the crime against him."

Genevieve just smiled. "*He* didn't. Remember, my source wasn't the victim. It was with his Soul that connected us both and gave Dillon *and* me, the answers we were seeking. It's all who you know…you know?"

CHAPTER 15

TEN YEARS

1994

In the fall of 1984, Tess married Ryan Seelig, preferring to exchange their vows in an impressively ornate wedding chapel, instead of the open lawn setting Genevieve and Teddy had chosen. Several months afterwards the newlyweds moved to San Diego, California, where Ryan began a teaching career and Tess opened a daycare while expanding their family with Selene who was now eight years old, and Sara, age five.

Ella, now eighteen, who always excelled in school, had just started at Arizona State University in their undergrad program for Landscape Architecture. Her decision made for a happy dad, as Teddy had been keeping his own secret vision for her—as company employee.

However, unlike his straight-A sister, twelve-year-old Broc struggled with academics, not because he wasn't capable, but because he cared more about the social game. Just on the verge of his teen years, Broc was pushing the boundaries more and more with his father. Teddy's solution: keep his son busy, very, very busy. Now, with summer school, league baseball, *and* one-week of basketball camp over, Broc assumed he was free and clear to spend more "free" time with his friends again.

As the family sat down for dinner, a week into the new school year, Teddy, nonetheless, was ready to share his latest brainstorm with Broc. "Wouldn't ye agree, son, tha carin for somethin tha depends on ye, might help ye see life a bit differently?"

Without turning to look at his dad, Broc's eyes narrowed as he peered at his mother sitting across from him. Genevieve, however, was as much in the dark as her son, and could only offer a clueless shrug.

Teddy's newest idea was convincing his son to help out at his grandfather's busy stable. "Aye, ye know, horses are amazin animals' lad, but they need a lot of care. Your mum has great stories aboot her horse, Haddie." Then leaning toward Broc but looking at Genevieve with a feigned attempt of whispering, "Ye know, she told me once she believes they have magical powers!"

Genevieve rolled her eyes and shook her head as Teddy winked at her.

Feeling he didn't actually have a choice anyway, Broc begrudgingly agreed, however, secretly the prospect sounded like it could be fun.

Walker and Santoro Inc. was steadily growing and had won two top local awards in the past few years. Then, just last week, Sol had been notified by a phone call that their company took second place in the Professional Architect and Landscape Foundation Awards. This was quite a feather-in-the-cap for a national foundation to recognize the company's talent for incorporating nature into all their land developments.

Over the years, Genevieve had all but dismissed her uneasy feelings toward Sol. She had gotten to know his family: Leo, Sol's handsome son who was the same age as Ella, and Sol's wife, Cindy.

Cindy was one of those rare beauties who didn't wear a touch of makeup as she was blessed with natural flawless skin and long dark lashes that framed her brown eyes perfectly. And, even though she was a bit introverted, she had a great sense of humor once she opened up; typically, one glass of wine would do it. With a master's degree in accounting, Mrs. Santoro had supervised Walker and Santoro Inc.'s receivable *and* payable departments for almost eight years with aplomb.

Cindy's devotion to Sol was undeniable, yet, Genevieve had begun to notice Sol's wandering eye lately. Was Cindy aware of it as well, or, Genevieve wondered, had it been an undesirable trait of his all along?

The one thing Genevieve *was* sure of, was her relationship with Teddy. Unlike other wives, Genevieve would never be in the dark if their love was in jeopardy. The nuance of other people's emotions had become second nature to Genevieve now, and she knew her husband's very well.

Helping Detective Chao solve crimes had become Genevieve's part-time job. It was challenging and often rewarding. Still, several cases remained unsolved, and Genevieve blamed herself for not being smart enough to decipher the Soul's message and give the victims peace.

One case, early-on, involved a five-year-old little boy named Quintin who had been kidnapped. Weeks after the abduction he was found in a wheat field, alive, but barely. The police report estimated he had been left there for at least two days before he was found by the farmer while surveying his crop. The farmer's dog and close companion had veered off from his master and disappeared in the mature field that was ready for harvest. When the farmer found his dog, he was licking the face of little Quintin.

There was no evidence of abuse or sexual assault, even though the child had been found naked. At the time, Genevieve was plagued with nightmares of drowning or suffocating, waking up gasping for air. Feeling the dreams must have had something to do with the case, Genevieve jotted everything down in her journal. But, two weeks later, the little one died without warning. Struggling with enormous guilt, Genevieve felt she must have misunderstood the emotions, but there was nothing she could do, time had run out.

Another case that haunted Genevieve was now growing cold. It happened almost a year ago involving a sixty-four-year-old widow named Lucy, who was attacked while home alone the night of her husband's funeral. She had been beaten and left for dead. Her head trauma was so severe it had caused a stroke and irreversible damage was done before a neighbor came by the following day to check on her.

Unlike those, such as Dillon and Chrissy, who wanted to return to their lives, Lucy Granger, the frail widow, who had barely begun grieving the loss of her husband, now existed in a state of twilight.

Genevieve had become familiar with the feeling she called "Twilight." Unlike "Twilight Zone" in which someone is stuck in a sort of surreal no-mans-land, but wants to come back to the reality they had left, like Dillon, Genevieve understood that those in the twilight state felt the sun had already set on their life. Now they waited in quiet darkness, hidden, where they knew no one could harm them, waiting for a release—waiting for peace.

In the case of Lucy, the Soul mysteriously chose to stay. Genevieve didn't question why, as she learned long ago, from Chrissy's Soul, that every situation and circumstance is at the behest of the Soul. If the Soul stayed, there was a reason, there was *always* a reason.

Genevieve just prayed that Lucy's Soul wasn't lingering due to Genevieve's failure to bring the petite widow the justice she deserved. Every time Genevieve went to visit Lucy at her care facility, the woman's emotions were always the same: anticipation and confidence. As if Lucy's Soul was aware of something Genevieve was not. But what? All leads had dried up.

Smack!

While sitting on the couch lamenting two of the people she had failed, a bluebird crashed into the large picture window directly behind her and fell to the ledge, dazed. With her heart pounding, Genevieve stood up and spun around—her first impulse was to go to the bird's aid. But then, not really knowing what she could do for it, she settled back down on the couch, anxiously watching to see if the little creature would be able to fly away.

After a few minutes, it stood with its back to her and began fluttering its wings. Genevieve sat on the couch, fixated on the bird's movements when suddenly it made a surprise turn and stared straight at her. For almost ten seconds, the two did not move. Slowly, Genevieve began moving her hand to touch the glass near the bird. In response, the Bluebird slowly hopped closer, until only the glass pane separated them.

Just then the phone rang, startling Genevieve and making her jump. With a nervous laugh, she stood up, and, as she did, the bird turned and flew away.

Then Genevieve noticed it, *Angel wings*. The mark on the window, where the bird hit, left a perfect imprint of an angel in flight. *Angel in disguise?* she wondered. With squinted eyes, Genevieve peered over at the empty window ledge and felt a little shiver tickle the back of her neck. As she quickly walked past the impressive smudge to answer the phone, Genevieve concluded with a murmur, "Angel or not, you certainly *did* make an impression!"

CHAPTER 16

MIND-READING

"IS THIS GENEVIEVE Walker?" A soft-spoken woman asked over the phone.

"Yes, this is she."

Genevieve could hear the woman cover the phone and argue with someone on the other end. In a few moments, she came back on. "Excuse me, I don't know exactly how to say this, are you a mind reader of sorts?"

Genevieve rolled her eyes as she got several calls a month from people wanting their fortunes told. *Time to get my number changed, again,* she thought. "No, ma'am, I'm not, and I don't have Tarot cards either. Goodbye."

Just as Genevieve was about to hang up, she heard the woman say, "Wait, don't hang up!"

Lifting the receiver back to her ear, Genevieve cautiously replied, "Okay?"

"As I mentioned, I don't exactly know what to say, but a nurse at the facility where our son now resides, told us that you have a way to talk with people that are like him."

Genevieve relaxed and took a deep breath. "I apologize for being so curt. A lot of people call me to read their palms or want me to tell them why their dead mother didn't leave them anything in her will. I can't help those people. However, I *do* have an empathic ability. If you heard of me from a nurse, then *maybe* I can help you with your son. Can I ask to whom I'm talking to?"

Her name was Jorgia Soblin. Her eighteen-year-old son, Mario, had been a victim of a car accident in which he had sustained a traumatic brain injury and was now in a vegetative state. She and her husband, Victor, had been caring for their son at home, along with private nurses, taking shifts around the clock. But in the last few days, Mario's brain waves had become erratic and his involuntary movements harder to control. It was decided by all, that moving him to St. Ann's Nursing Center, would be best to handle his changing condition, at least for now.

When Jorgia mentioned St. Ann's Nursing Center, Genevieve knew from where the referral came. She had worked there several times, and it was also where Lucy Granger was being cared for as well.

During the conversation, Jorgia kept covering the phone and Genevieve could tell there was arguing going on. "Is there a problem I should know about, Jorgia?"

"My husband thinks I'm crazy for calling and keeps telling me to hang up."

Not surprised, Genevieve questioned, "So, Jorgia, what answers are *you* looking for?"

Jorgia's voice became shaky, and Genevieve could hear the despair as Jorgia grappled with her son's decline. "He was always so bright, selfless—happy to help anyone. Mario was supposed to graduate from high school this year, and even in his condition, the class voted him "Most Likable.""

There was a long pause, and all the arguing on the other end of the phone had ceased. Genevieve heard Jorgia crying, trying to compose herself so she could continue. "I'm not sure he has much time left Mrs. Walker. I want him to know how proud I am of him, how proud we both are of him. I want to hear my son again, even if it's through his feelings."

Genevieve always tried not to associate her life with those she helped. But when hearing Jorgia's story, Broc flashed through her mind, and all Genevieve wanted to do was squeeze him tight, and make sure he knew how much she loved him.

Without hesitation, Genevieve said she'd come by the care facility later that day after she had picked Broc up from school and taken him to the stable to work.

The nursing facility was the largest of its kind in the Scottsdale area with three large wings, two floors high. Before going to see Mario, Genevieve stopped by Lucy's room, which was just down the hall from Mario's and brought some flowers. Her room seemed so lonely. As far as Genevieve knew, no one ever came by to see her. Lucy and her husband had never had children of their own, but she *had* worked part-time at a daycare center near her home. As Genevieve held Lucy's hand, she asked, *Did you ever want children, Lucy?*

A feeling of quiet contentment told Genevieve Lucy had been happy with the way things were, at least before her husband died. But then everything changed. Lucy didn't even have time to adjust to her new role as a widow before she was viciously attacked. It broke Genevieve's heart every time she looked at Lucy's scarred and disfigured face.

But like a good friend, Lucy's Soul didn't want Genevieve to dwell on futility. Soon, the familiar feelings of anticipation and confidence buzzed like an electrical current, zapping Genevieve out of her melancholy.

With a slight smile, Genevieve reiterated, *I wish I understood these feelings of yours, Lucy.*

Trust, was the feeling that replied.

Trust. Genevieve just stared at the woman she wished she had known before everything happened to her. Shaking her head, Genevieve got up and whispered, "I'll come back to see you soon."

It was almost 4:30 p.m., and as Genevieve entered Mario's room, Jorgia quickly got up from her chair and gave Genevieve a firm handshake. "Thank you for coming, Mrs. Walker."

Genevieve stressed, "Please, call me Genevieve."

Jorgia looked different than Genevieve had pictured her. She was tall and slim, maybe in her early forties. Her hair was dark red, long, permed, and tied loosely behind her. She had striking hazel eyes and was wearing a stylish spandex exercise outfit. "I love what you're wearing," Genevieve complimented, trying to put Jorgia at ease.

With an exasperated sigh, Jorgia confessed, "I plan to go to the gym after I leave here. It's the only way to relieve my frustration and anxiety."

With a reassuring nod, Genevieve walked over to Mario. His eyes were closed. "Is your husband here?"

Jorgia shook her head, "No, he said if I want to waste my time on this, I'm on my own." Realizing how it must have sounded, Jorgia hastily added, "No offense! He's just that way."

Genevieve shook her head, "No offense, truly. There was a time I would have thought just as he does now. I didn't really understand what my empathic ability was for until the Soul of a small child finally helped me to understand."

Jorgia took Genevieve's hand. "I'm just glad I found you, and I believe there's a reason for it too. Because, when the nurse told me about you, I typically would have pictured the same opportunistic scam you mentioned on the phone. But instead, I felt strongly compelled to ask for your number. Of course, when I did, Victor yelled, 'Are you kidding!' He's been furious since Mario's accident—even longer than that actually."

Smiling at Jorgia but feeling she should clarify a statement she had made earlier on the phone Genevieve emphasized, "Jorgia, it's not that I don't believe there may be something to those that read palms or see things others don't. After realizing what *I* could do, I became more open-minded to other abilities as well. But, yes, there are definitely those who have no skill as an empath, and prey on other people's desperation for monetary gain. I want you to know I don't. The only money I ever accept payment for is when I work as a consultant for the police. It was something that Detective Chao, who I work with, insisted upon."

"If I can help you, by reaching out to Mario, then that's what I believe I'm meant to do. Maybe Mario can help you in some way; give peace to you *and* your husband as well." Jorgia became misty-eyed and nodded.

Letting go of Jorgia's hand, Genevieve spotted a chair in the corner and moved it next to the bed. "Sometimes it takes a while. If you're hungry, you could grab a bite to eat and come back."

Jorgia shook her head. "I'm not going anywhere."

CHAPTER 17

ALL BY DESIGN

ON GENEVIEVE'S VERY first Soul encounter with Chrissy, she learned the extent of what the Soul could do to convey Its intent to her. Besides responding with emotional responses, It had the power to guide her by creating questions in her mind. Not being questions she would have asked, to Genevieve's surprise, they always had a significant purpose in the asking.

Then, as she began using her abilities more and more for crime-solving, Genevieve noticed a shift. She often worked harder to understand the simplest intent of the Soul.

It was during a case in 1988 that Genevieve found out why.

Genevieve had become mentally exhausted and utterly frustrated while consulting on a high-profile case that had made national news. Even with guided questions, little progress was being made to solve a double homicide shooting and attempted murder. Resolution felt elusive after almost three days of communing with the Soul of the young shooting victim; a man named Elijah, whose condition was quickly deteriorating.

Agitated with the twenty-questions game, that, in reality, had been more like sixty, Genevieve finally asked the man's Soul a question that had been confusing her. *If you have the power to guide my thoughts so I ask relevant questions, then why not simply let the answers appear in my mind the same way?*

The feeling that responded could best be described as unbiased or detachment.

Still puzzled, Genevieve digressed from the case, so that she could understand the Soul's response. With little effort, the Soul seemed almost eager to explain. The impartiality was due to the fact that the Soul was not, and never would be, interested in crime and punishment. Retribution held no purpose,

69

as the Soul carried no anger or need for justice; it would *never* be the Soul's concern.

It begged the question, posed in Genevieve's mind, *Why, then, in that case, are you interacting with me at all when my goal is to solve this crime?* The Spirit acknowledged the only reason It assists, is because the violation *does* matter to its human host and Earth's society as a whole. And, it is because of that symbiotic relationship It cherishes, that it communicates in such matters.

Still, there was a conflict. For the Soul does not condemn the fault of another. It sees and understands the circumstance in ways humans cannot. And, It knows the power fear has when Love feels absent, even though it never is. The Soul recognizes that at any moment, every human on the planet is capable of being a villain.

Yet, to help in the commitment to Its host, who *wants* justice, the Soul goes only so far as to reveal truth objectively. It will assist solely to open an eye; to show hidden realities—nothing more. What results after that, matters not to the Soul, only to the humans that seek after it.

Therefore, Genevieve concluded, it wasn't what the Soul *could* convey, which always came easy when It was relaying love, but what it *would* convey in solving a crime. Because unconditional love; the essence of God, had no part in the equation.

By the end of the case, Elijah had succumbed to his injuries. But, before he did, Genevieve understood the sad circumstances that led to the tragedy.

On the day of the shooting, Elijah's mother, Alona, a fifty-six-year-old divorcee, had just discovered she had ALS, more commonly known as Lou Gerig's Disease. After downing a bottle of wine that evening, Alona, a recovering alcoholic, twenty years sober, left a cryptic, incoherent voice message on her adult daughter, Eza's answering machine. Worried, Eza called her twin brother Elijah to meet her at their mother's home. Once there, Eza's boyfriend, Gabe, who drove her there, waited out in the car while the twins entered the house.

Alarmed to see her children, Alona, with a gun in hand, began sobbing, as she told them about her condition, a disease she could not accept. Eza and Elijah pleaded with her to put the gun down. Just as the two believed they had talked some sense into their mother, Alona began lifting the gun to her head. Terrified, Elijah ran to grab it, but, Alona, in an alcohol-induced panic, quickly turned the gun outward and pulled the trigger. It passed, not only through her son but then through Eza, who was standing directly behind her brother.

Hearing the shot, Gabe ran into the house. Alona dropped the gun and staggered, disoriented to a nearby chair. Horrified, Gabe could see Elijah struggling on the floor, but breathing. When he knelt next to Eza and realized she had died, Gabe picked up the gun, and in his moment of agony, shot Alona in the head.

Scared and crying, Gabe kissed Eza. Then, before leaving, he quickly wiped his prints from the gun and dialed 911, placing the phone in Elijah's bloody hand, as Elijah struggled to stay conscious.

No single shooter, no sinister plot in play. The Soul always understood— Love was *eternally* present. Even in the moment, when no one saw it coming and the true villain appeared, fear.

Back in Mario's room, Genevieve got comfortable and took the young man's hand. It felt cold. She noticed his eyes were open now, the same hazel color of his mothers, blankly staring at the ceiling.

As Genevieve closed her eyes, a feeling of excitement greeted her. It was always so reassuring that no matter the circumstance, she was always appreciated and loved by the Souls she interacted with. Sending the feeling of thankfulness and anticipation back, Genevieve waited to see if Mario's Soul wanted to start the conversation.

A sudden powerful emotion came through, RAGE! Genevieve almost let go of Mario's hand. It was blinding anger.

Are you angry, Mario?

There was a rejection feeling to the question.

Someone else is outraged then?

Genevieve waited. Trust.

Trust? There was a pause. Then a question appeared in Genevieve's mind, *Is there someone you trust that is very angry?*

Contentment settled within her.

Responding to the only information that corresponded, Genevieve's thought questioned, *Are you talking about your father?*

The same feeling of contentment continued.

I understand he has been very distressed. Your mother said he is angry about what happened to you.

Genevieve had to squeeze Mario's hand tight, instead of releasing it as she wanted to, for she felt a sudden repulsive sense of betrayal and deception. It was so penetrating it turned her stomach.

Jorgia saw the distress on Genevieve's face, and blurted, "Are you alright?"

Genevieve quickly nodded but kept her eyes closed, not wanting to lose the momentum, no matter how the feeling resonated within her.

What are you trying to tell me, Mario? Genevieve pleaded in her thought. New, negative emotions transfused through Genevieve's body: hatred, and jealousy.

This is all so confusing. I thought the dialog with you would be to reassure your parents of your love for them and give them some peace or possible hope of recovery. Instead, Mario, this feels much more like the interactions I have with a victim's Soul as I try to solve a crime.

A feeling of assurance began to trickle in.

Crime? Genevieve was struggling with a dialog that she had not prepared for. Opening her eyes, she looked at the young man and silently asked, *Was a crime committed, Mario?*

Genevieve felt excitement brewing.

Did your father do something to you?

The response was ambiguous. At first, it felt positive, then frustration immediately followed.

Frowning, Genevieve closed her eyes again and got more basic with the question. *Did your father commit a crime?*

An overwhelming feeling of positive expectation assured her she was on the right track.

Then a question entered Genevieve's mind that seemed utterly absurd, yet she felt compelled to ask it, *Was the crime against someone I know?*

The implication almost made Genevieve laugh, positive she misunderstood the ridiculous query. After all, how could she have anything in common with people she met only hours ago? Genevieve expected the reply would be disaffirming. Besides, everyone she knew was just fine. Yet, within moments, an eager enthusiasm swirling inside her.

I know this person? I don't understand, Mario. The only person we have in common is your mother. Is it your mother?

A definite prickling feeling of negativity shot through her.

Genevieve shook her head. *What picture are you trying to paint, Mario? Rage, hatred, anger, betrayal, jealousy. These are all from someone out of control.* Genevieve realized this might take a long time. *How can I figure out who we have in common? What kind of crime did your father commit?*

While waiting and hoping Mario's Soul would reveal a new clue, the abhorrent feelings reminded Genevieve of Lucy's attack. Soon, her melancholy feelings for the dainty woman began to creep back into Genevieve's psyche.

Suddenly, a shock of concurrence blasted Genevieve's senses.

What? No! You don't know the Lucy I'm thinking of, you can't.

But Genevieve couldn't shake the overwhelming confidence that Mario's Soul was emitting. She suddenly felt disoriented—her equilibrium was revolting, making her want to vomit. Opening her eyes, Genevieve looked at Mario as her thought questioned, *This is about Lucy...Lucy Granger?*

Mario slowly closed his eyes with a feeling of sleepy satisfaction.

Genevieve jumped out of the chair, startling Jorgia, and ran to the bathroom down the hall where nausea had finally taken its toll. After a minute, as Genevieve continued to kneel over the toilet, she labored to think clearly. *Why would Mario's father do such a thing? How did he know Lucy, or did he?* With her head whirling, Genevieve knew she had to go back and talk to Jorgia, and there was still much more to learn from Mario's Soul.

Trying to calm down and stop the questions flooding her mind was like trying to stop a tsunami by standing in front of it and just putting up a hand.

How is Mario involved? Was his accident part of the crime? What about Jorgia? Was she aware of any of this? Did she know Lucy too?

As Genevieve's head started to clear, she realized no one was aware of what she had just learned, yet. And, not knowing who all was involved, Genevieve had to be very careful moving forward. Every word to Jorgia had to be well thought out as Jorgia would undoubtedly talk to her husband about the meeting.

Before Genevieve went back to Mario's room, she gave Detective Chao a call. "I may have a lead on Lucy's attacker. But you may have to help me find the pieces I'm missing. I'll call you tonight."

CHAPTER 18

SYNCHRONICITY

As GENEVIEVE ENTERED Mario's room, Jorgia jumped from her chair. "God, are you okay? I wasn't sure if I should follow, you seemed very upset." Jorgia then paused, and Genevieve noticed tears in Jorgia's eyes. Continuing with a hesitant whisper Jorgia uttered. "I'm afraid to hear what you found out. My son is dying, isn't he?"

Genevieve reached for Jorgia's arm. "No, I didn't get that from him at all, and I'm sorry for leaving as I did. Your son had a lot of strong emotions, and sometimes, when I'm not prepared, they tend to overwhelm me."

Jorgia shook her head, "I'm sorry to put you through this. I had no idea how all this worked, or what you must go through."

As Genevieve continued to hold Jorgia's arm, she felt no deception, only a mother's anguish for her son and empathy for someone she barely knew. It was evident to Genevieve that Jorgia knew very little about the severity of her husband's anger.

Forcing a smile, Genevieve mused, "I came to the realization years ago that the emotional and physical effects would go hand in hand with what I do. They are intrinsically tied to each other, so don't worry about me. As for Mario, there was a torrent of emotions he was trying to convey, but they felt very scattered. Can you tell me anything more about his accident?"

Jorgia shook her head. "Nothing noteworthy really. Mario had told me at breakfast, that day, that he would be going to his friend's house after school but would be home by dinnertime. When Victor got home from work, a little early that day, he pleaded with me to fix ribs for dinner—meaning a run to the store, which I did. Just as I was putting the groceries in my car, I heard my pager go off. It was Victor telling me to call him immediately. When I finally found a phone booth and called, he was frantic, telling me Mario was in the hospital. He said when Mario came home, they talked for a while, and after that, Mario told Victor he was going for a drive. That's all I know."

A slight frown appeared on Jorgia's face. "It was strange though because Victor and I couldn't understand why Mario was in the part of town where the accident occurred. None of his friends live around there. I've spent many a sleepless night, trying to figure out why he was on the other side of town and why he lost control of the car. The police said he was driving far too fast to make the sharp turn in that quiet residential neighborhood."

Genevieve knew she had to connect to Mario's Soul again if she was to get further along and hopefully have more to tell Brunner when she talked with him later. "Jorgia, I'd like to sit with Mario a little longer. Is that okay with you?"

"Of course," Jorgia replied. "As much time as you need. I think I'll go outside for a little walk though if you don't mind?"

Genevieve genuinely welcomed the privacy. She didn't want to alarm Jorgia any further if she was blindsided again. "Take your time. I know how stressful this can be for loved ones."

Instead of sitting in a chair, this time Genevieve sat on the edge of the bed and took Mario's hand. Questions were clear in Genevieve's mind this time.

Mario, did your father know Lucy?

She felt a positive response.

Did you know Lucy?

Again, the same positive acknowledgment.

Did your mother know Lucy?

The emotion quickly became abrasively negative.

Did your father know Lucy before you did?

Positive confirmation came back.

She was much older than your father. Were they having an affair?

A bitter hatred stung at Genevieve's senses.

So, he hated Lucy then?

If an emotion could shout YES, then Genevieve felt it loud and clear.

Is there anything else you want me to know, Mario?

She suddenly felt confined, even claustrophobic, although Genevieve had never felt that way in her life. As she dwelled within the emotion, she began to feel like she was in a box.

A Coffin?

A curt rejection was felt immediately.

Good. I didn't like where that was going. Bending her neck to the right, then the left, Genevieve knew she was feeling overly tense for some reason. Taking a few deep breaths, she waited. *I still feel closed-up or concealed, yet it's not a coffin? I can't help feeling boxed in though.*

As the thought appeared in her mind, she felt a positive expectation taking hold.

Boxed in?

Excitement was brewing. It slowly changed to a feeling Genevieve often had when people asked her what she did for a living, secrecy. Just as Genevieve resonated with *that* feeling, resentment mixed with jealousy added more complexity to the story Mario's Soul was trying to convey.

Then the transmission of feelings ended, rather abruptly. But, in doing so, it allowed Genevieve time to organize the emotional data.

Okay, boxed in, secrets, rage, resentment, and jealousy. Is that all you want me to know? I think I'll need more to go on, Mario.

Confidence poured through Genevieve like refreshing rain, rinsing off the oppressive feelings that had been building up inside her.

The confidence, it's for me?

Genevieve felt amusement mixing with assured expectations, as if the Soul was laughing.

A grin appeared on Genevieve's face.

Lucy had the same confident feelings. Could she have known I'd meet you?

Genevieve felt a nebulous response which always happened when the answer coming back was simply too complicated to understand.

Deciding to leave that question a mystery, Genevieve had only one more thing to ask.

Is there anything you want your mother to know?

Genevieve began to feel the emotions any mother would relish. Unrestrained love, admiration, and trust saturated her chest to the point it was becoming overwhelming, when Jorgia walked back in.

Slipping off the edge of the bed, Genevieve pulled Jorgia into a long embrace. Then, stepping back to face Jorgia, "I only wish you could *feel* the emotions Mario has for you. It's the one thing words will always fall short on conveying. He wants you to know how deep his love is for you, and how much he admires and respects you. Trust me though, Jorgia, these words merely shadow the depth of which I felt them for you. No matter what happens in the future, I know he wants to show them to you himself. That's an excellent sign."

Jorgia broke down and started to cry. With a nod she mouthed, "Thank you" and walked over to her son, kissing him on his forehead.

As Genevieve stood at the doorway, watching Jorgia stroke Mario's hair with her fingers and whisper in his ear, it felt bittersweet. For Genevieve knew she would also have a hand in *hopefully* uncovering Victor's crime, and, in doing so, rip Jorgia's world apart even further.

On the way out of the nursing facility, Genevieve stopped again by Lucy's room. Sitting by the bed, she held Lucy's hand. *Anticipation and confidence. You always knew this day would come, didn't you, Lucy?* Genevieve felt nothing but a soothing calm resonating.

I've got hope again, Lucy! It never ceases to amaze me how the dots connect in this vast, and unpredictable universe. Even when I felt nothing was happening for you, plenty was going on behind the scenes. The synchronicity is uncanny!

Genevieve felt unfettered love coming from Lucy for the first time since they began their journey together. *I'll see you later, my friend.*

At home, Teddy was making his favorite dish for dinner. It was the one that he had cooked up for Genevieve soon after they first met in Northumberland, England. As Genevieve opened the door, the smell of onions and bacon took her instantly back to a simpler time, when all she cared about was a casual bike ride and falling in love.

Sneaking up behind him, Genevieve wrapped her arms around the cook who was at the sink, busy washing a frying pan. Closing her eyes, Genevieve felt Teddy's warm body next to hers and murmured, "God, you feel good!"

Turning, Teddy studied Genevieve's face with narrowed eyes. "Somethin happened today, aye? Ye were goin to meet with tha young lad. But things didn't go as planned, did they?"

Genevieve tipped her head and frowned slightly. "How could you know that? Are you keeping *your* empathic abilities a secret from me?"

With a hint of a grin, Teddy plopped his wet soapy hand on Genevieve's forehead and closed his eyes. Genevieve smiled as several drops of water dribbled down her face. She decided to play along with his mischief, since she, of all people, should have known better than to ask him such a question.

As suds began covering her eyes, Genevieve tried to watch Teddy's feigned concentration before he proclaimed loudly, "I *feel* hunger arising from deep within your Soul. Hmm, but is it for food or for tha damn handsome man you're married to?"

Teddy peeked out one eye. Genevieve smirked and reached to take his hand away. With a shocked expression, Teddy opened both eyes wide, took his hand away and blurted, "Ah, the feelins are clearer now, it's not hunger, it's lust…ooh, and the naughty kind at tha!"

Genevieve couldn't help but laugh. "You're such a bad imitation of me, mister. But you may be on to something with that lusting thing." As Genevieve batted her sudsy eyelashes flirtatiously at Teddy, she admitted, "Making Panhaggerty has always been an aphrodisiac for me!"

Teddy pulled her close. "Ye think I don't know tha, woman? It's always been my secret weapon, ye know!"

Grabbing a dish towel, and drying his wife's face, Teddy continued, "But, I guess since ye have no faith in my *other* perceptive abilities, I might as well confess…I got a call from Brunner a while ago, he was tryin to reach ye. He filled me in a bit. Then he asked me to tell ye, he thinks he knows the connection between Lucy and tha family ye saw today."

Genevieve's eyes widened. "Excellent!"

Nodding, Teddy turned and finished rinsing the pan, "So, ye have to work tonight, then?"

Genevieve could hear the disappointment in his voice. "I think just a phone call should do for tonight. An aphrodisiac as strong as this one should never be wasted."

CHAPTER 19

BEST OF BOTH WORLDS

AFTER DINNER, GENEVIEVE noticed how quiet the house seemed. Ella was now living with a friend near the university, and Broc was spending Friday evening at his friend's house. Jergen was the *one* friend of Broc's that Teddy trusted. A straight-A student, Jergen was helping to tutor Broc in math, was on the tennis team at school, and held down a part-time job as a dishwasher in his father's popular Swedish restaurant. With Jergen's positive influence and Broc's greatly improved work ethic at the stable, all signs were looking positive.

Peering into the study, Genevieve saw Teddy at his drafting desk, biding time, she was sure, until her call was over. Teddy had recently purchased a Nokia Telekom cell phone. A pricey little item, but just being able to walk around the house now without a cord seemed worth every penny.

Better make the call, Genevieve thought.

Taking the phone, Genevieve walked out to the patio. *Not too bad for mid-October, there's even a decent breeze tonight.* Genevieve sat with eyes closed for a few minutes and listened to her favorite wind chime as it was pinging in the invisible air current. Knowing Brunner was still in the office Genevieve dialed the number she had memorized long ago.

"Hello, Detective Chao here."

"Hey Brunner, it's Genevieve. Hope it's okay if we just talk on the phone. I have to be somewhere within the hour."

Brunner affirmed, "Sure, that's fine. We can't do anything tonight anyway, but I found out something very interesting. I started to do a background check on Victor after you called—made a few inquiries too. He has a successful drywall business, married just once, to Jorgia, and has one son, Mario. Nothing stood out there. But then, nothing's ever that easy anyway, right?

"So, I started to look further into his past. When he was thirteen, he was sent home from school, and the juvenile authorities called when he slapped a friend's mother as she picked her son up from school. Victor apparently was upset because the woman had told her son to stay away from Victor. I got the info from the school's archived student files. I guess the friend's mother never filed any charges.

"What I could gather, it looked like he was in and out of trouble until he got to college, where he took up competitive boxing. There were several articles in the paper of his winning bouts. I have to say, after reading that, it gave me a chill, knowing the damage inflicted on Lucy!

"But then things seem to calm down. Victor got married, worked in construction as a drywaller until he branched out on his own. By all accounts, he has been a good husband and father to Mario.

"Although Victor's parents had been married, it looked like his father was out of the picture by the time Victor was about eight years old. I didn't see any child support payments or any other involvement by the father. Victor's mother died five years ago from cancer.

"Still not seeing any connection, I decided to find out why his father fell off the face of the planet, or so it seemed. His father's name was Vincent Soblin. A Vietnam vet who had been in a few skirmishes with the law, drunk and disorderly and an incident of hallucinating and punching an Asian man at a horse race. My guess, he needed professional help in readjusting to civilian life and wasn't getting any. You'd think Vincent's wife would have been the one to file for divorce, but it wasn't, it was Vincent. It looked like a bitter battle, but because of his problems, Victor's mother received full custody."

Genevieve was becoming impatient, "So, the connection?"

"*So*, two years later, after their divorce, I find a marriage license. It's for Vincent Soblin and Lucille Granger."

Genevieve stopped breathing. "Lucy was Victor's step-mother?"

"Bulls-eye! Brunner declared. "She never took her husband's name, that's why it didn't connect."

"But Mario conveyed that Jorgia doesn't know who Lucy is. Doesn't that seem odd? Genevieve inquired."

"No, not if Victor never spoke about her. Maybe Victor only knew of her but never had met her. As far as I can tell, Victor had no relationship with his father after the divorce. *But,* I found out what might have set him off and triggered the attack. Remember back when it happened? Lucy's husband, *Vincent,* had died just the week before. The attack happened on the same day as his funeral. You think that's a coincidence?"

Genevieve had a flashback to the original briefing of Lucy's attack. "Lucy's husband's name *was* Vincent! I remember that now, and *no,*" Genevieve said emphatically, "There are no coincidences, Brunner."

"I guess not." Brunner agreed. "I still don't understand how Mario knew her though?"

"That's puzzling me also," Genevieve murmured. "I can't help shake the feeling that there is more to Mario's accident than what we've been told."

Brunner sighed, "Well, I'm calling Victor in tomorrow."

Genevieve shook her head, "But you don't have anything on him."

"Well, we now know his connection to Lucy. Maybe he'll expose a secret."

A lightbulb went off in Genevieve's head...*secret!.* Genevieve understood the feelings Mario had projected in a clearer light now. *It was literal, boxed-in secrets.* "Brunner, I think Mario might have found a box maybe, or some type of enclosure that his father kept hidden, with secrets. I think that may have been how he found out about Lucy."

"Well, unless Victor tips his hand, I won't have any way to get a search warrant."

"You may not have to, hopefully. Hold off on talking to Victor. Let me speak with Jorgia tomorrow. Her son means everything to her. If my gut is right, she may be all we'll need. Standby for my call."

Hanging up the phone, Genevieve sat back and watched as the last sliver of the sun disappeared from the sky. The wind chime was still making its gentle sounds, while a hummingbird flittered at the birdfeeder which hung nearby.

Pleased with all that had been accomplished in just one short day, Genevieve closed her eyes and took a deep breath, letting it out slowly. *Two people have been hanging in limbo silently for so long. Finally, there's hope in the truth. I can't wait to make sense of it all.*

Yet, there was another thing that couldn't wait, inside. After a few minutes to rehearse what she would say to Jorgia the following day, Genevieve put work aside and opened the sliding glass door. As she stepped inside, she took a deep breath to capture the last lingering remnants of dinner before heading to the study.

Teddy was frowning at a detailed diagram laid out in front of him. Moving next to him, Genevieve breathed in his ear, "I'm ready to turn that frown upside down if you are?"

Turning, Teddy peered at her stoically, "So, ye think ye can snap your fingers and I'll come runnin, just like tha?"

Genevieve took his hand and pulled him off the stool, "Uh-huh, I do."

Teddy glanced at the overstuffed couch in the room and gently pushed Genevieve on to it. Biting her lower lip as he stood over her, she removed her silky blue blouse. Like a seductively slow salsa, Genevieve took her time, letting the desire swell. Teddy waited and watched until there was nothing left for Genevieve to remove. Then, remembering Teddy's comment, Genevieve smiled up at him and snapped her fingers.

Raising his eyebrows, Teddy tried to play along. As it was now Genevieve's turn to watch, he slowly removed his shirt. But within a minute Teddy bellowed, "Ah, forget this!" and quickly abandoned the distressingly slow striptease. He'd already waited too long to devour the tantalizing dessert now laying right in front of him. As Teddy raced to undress, Genevieve snorted with laughter knowing, at least for the moment, she genuinely had the best of both worlds.

When Teddy came to lie next to her, Genevieve took in a sharp breath, underestimating the torrid desire that had been building within her lover.

Aye, Genevieve thought as Teddy moved even closer, *these are quite the naughty feelins!*

When the two eventually headed upstairs to go to bed, Genevieve inquired, "So what was the frown about anyway? Is there a problem with the plans?"

Teddy was silent for a moment. "Naw, it's not tha. Everythin is comin along. I was makin good headway with Jason, the interested party, when Sol felt it was takin too long and started pushin harder for a commitment. It rubbed Jason the wrong way, and now I'm tryin to smooth things over. I don't know why Sol did tha. I'm goin to talk to him tomorrow when the four of us go to dinner. Ye know it's tomorrow, aye?"

Genevieve had it on the calendar, but honestly, it had slipped her mind. "Right. What time was it again?"

"Sol said Cindy made the reservation for 7:30."

"No problem. I think we're near a breakthrough in Lucy's case finally, so, although tomorrow is a workday for me, I'm sure I'll be home in plenty of time."

Teddy nodded, "The call to Brunner was a good one, then?"

"Better than I expected anyway," Genevieve confirmed. "Brunner found out that Lucy is, in fact, related by marriage to Victor, Mario's father. Through Mario's Soul, I found out both Mario and his father know Lucy, or of her, but Mario's mother, Jorgia does not. The fact that there is a physical connection between Victor and Lucy, along with the timing of the attack, makes Victor a strong suspect. But we haven't figured out a motive, yet. Mario conveyed there are secrets in a box or something like a box, which he must have discovered at some point.

"So, tomorrow, I have to explain everything to Jorgia, and hope she won't see it as a betrayal that I had no choice but to consult the police. Either way, it will undoubtedly turn Jorgia's world upside down. Hopefully, she will want the truth, no matter what. Then possibly I can ask her to look for that box. I wish I didn't have to, but I think it must be important or Mario's Soul wouldn't have let me know about it."

CHAPTER 20

BETRAYAL

It took over two hours for Genevieve to finally fall asleep, but when the alarm went off at 7:00 a.m., Saturday morning, she rushed out of bed and showered. *I wonder what time Jorgia will be up and about? God, what will she think when I tell her what I know?*

Before going downstairs, Genevieve kissed Teddy as he continued to sleep, then let out a little smirk as she peered into Broc's room. He was sound asleep, sprawled sideways on his bed. He had somehow managed to put his pajama bottoms on over his bulky tennis shoes that were still firmly attached to his feet. Shaking her head, Genevieve quietly closed the door and headed for the kitchen.

By eight-fifteen, Genevieve had finished her second cup of coffee. Taking a chance that Jorgia might be up, Genevieve called the house, Victor answered. "Hello?"

"Hello, my name is Genevieve Walker. I met with your wife yesterday."

There was a short pause, "Yes, I know who you are. Did you want to talk to Jorgia?"

"Yes, is she available?"

"Actually, she left the house an hour ago, went running."

Stress relieving already? Oh boy, Genevieve thought. "Would you please let her know I called, and that I'd like to talk to her?"

Genevieve could hear Victor clearing his throat and could almost picture him frowning. "Jorgia made it sound like you had finished with your shenanigans, my words not hers. No, you've made a believer of that woman. I think you know, however, that I don't believe, *even slightly*, in what you claim to do.

At least you didn't charge her for it, or, is that what you want to discuss with her now?"

Feeling her pulse start to rise, Genevieve tried to stay calm, "No, sir, I have no intention of charging her a penny. I just forgot to tell her something yesterday, that's all."

Genevieve heard a muffling noise, then Victor returned, "Ah, your wish is granted, she just walked through the door."

Relieved the conversation with Victor was over, Genevieve heard the two mumbling, then Jorgia came on the line. "Genevieve, hi! Victor said you forgot to tell me something?"

"Yes, sorry. A few things, actually. Were you planning to see Mario this morning?"

Sounding curious Jorgia offered, "Well, no, a little later than that, but I *can* make it over in an hour if you like, I just need to shower first."

Genevieve nodded, "I'd really appreciate it. Thanks."

After the two said good-bye, Genevieve headed for the hospital. It would have been too suspicious to ask Jorgia to come alone, so Genevieve was banking on Victor's distaste for her, hoping he'd choose to stay behind.

Genevieve had barely made it to Mario's room when Jorgia walked in, alone. Giving Genevieve a quick hug, she said, "I got so excited after you called, I hurried as fast as I could. So, what do you want to tell me?"

Looking into Jorgia's optimistic eyes, Genevieve took a deep breath and began. "Jorgia, I found out much more yesterday than I lead you to believe, and it's going to be unsettling."

Jorgia's expression began to change, "So Mario isn't going to get better after all?"

Quickly pulling the two chairs in the room together, Genevieve sat in one and motioned Jorgia to sit in the other. Then taking Jorgia's hand, she began, "Mario is strong, and everything I said to you yesterday was utterly true. But Mario's Soul had more than that to convey to me."

With a cautious, "Okay" from Jorgia, Genevieve continued by telling her about Lucy and how the case had run cold, assuring Jorgia there was a reason for telling the story. Then came the hard part. Telling her that Lucy was more than just a sad statistic, that she was Victor's stepmother.

Confusion covered Jorgia's face. "Victor never mentioned a stepmother, and only mentioned his father maybe once or twice during all the time we've been together. I don't understand Genevieve, you got all this from Mario?"

With a slow blink and nod, Genevieve confirmed, "It's amazing what the Soul reveals. At first, I received strong negative emotions of anger, rage, jealousy, and a feeling of deceit. Over time I understood Mario was conveying Victor's feelings, not his own. The purpose was to make me aware of the intensity of his father's emotions toward Lucy.

"At one point, I began thinking everything felt more like my interactions with the Soul after a crime had been committed. It was then that I was hit with a very dominant positive response from Mario. After that, I started to treat our emotional conversation the way I do when I'm trying to help solve a crime. Jorgia, because Mario's Soul assured me an offence had happened, I *had* to talk to the detective I work with. I know you weren't expecting this type of response from Mario. Believe me, I wasn't expecting it either."

Jorgia kept the same bewildered expression, asking, "I'm not sure what you're getting at Genevieve. Who are you implying did the crime?"

Genevieve braced. "From what Mario has given me, and Detective Chao found out yesterday, we believe your husband was the one that assaulted Lucy, his stepmother." Genevieve paused for a reaction. As Jorgia's frowning face stared silently back, Genevieve continued. "You said he's been angry, even before Mario's accident. Can you remember when it started?"

Finally, the meaning behind Genevieve's words seemed to have caught up with Jorgia, and her expression mutated into total incredulity. Closing her eyes slowly, Jorgia began shaking her head from side to side.

Genevieve's heart sank as she thought, *She doesn't believe me. Oh God, I made a big mistake in telling her about this.*

As Genevieve frantically thought of what to say next, Jorgia opened her eyes and began speaking. "We were all sitting at breakfast, maybe a week or so prior to Mario's accident. I had just brought Victor a cup of coffee as he read the morning newspaper. Then, out of the blue, he began cursing. A minute later he crumbled the newspaper into a ball and threw it, almost hitting Mario in the head. I asked what was wrong, but he wouldn't tell me."

Genevieve responded with a nod. "Victor probably read his father's obituary in the paper on the day you mentioned. Mario's accident happened a week after that announcement came out, and Lucy was assaulted the following day, which was also the day of Vincent's funeral.

Jorgia looked toward the ceiling as a tear began to fall. By her expression, Genevieve knew Jorgia was seeing part of the picture now, assembled from the bits and pieces that Genevieve had given to her.

Brushing the tear away, Jorgia asked, "Why would Victor do such a thing? It doesn't make sense." Then, turning to look at Mario, Jorgia's eyes opened wide with terror. "Do you think Mario, knew something? Do you think his accident has something to do with all of this?"

With a determined look, Genevieve replied, "I don't have all those answers yet. But when I was about to break off the connection, last night, I was conveying a feeling of thankfulness to Mario's Soul. Then, new emotions erupted from him, overpowering my own and letting me know we weren't quite through yet. Eventually, I understood two things even though they didn't make sense at the time: secrets and an enclosure or confinement. Then last night, when I mentally laid out all I knew before me, I understood what the Soul had been trying to tell me. It took longer to decipher, as physical objects are harder to convey through emotions. But Jorgia, it's *boxed-in secrets!* I'm pretty sure that Mario must have found some sort of box that his father kept hidden."

Genevieve paused and breathed deeply. "I don't know why Mario had his accident Jorgia, or why Victor would harm such a gentle woman. At this point, there isn't even strong circumstantial evidence on Victor. But Mario believes it, and my gut does as well. If only I knew where Victor was the night Lucy was attacked, it would help a lot."

The room became silent, save for Mario's heart monitor that continued its steady beeping. Then Jorgia blinked hard. "Oh, God, I think I do! We had been glued to Mario's side the moment he was brought to the hospital; nothing would have torn us away. But the following day, Victor left two times. The day you said was Vincent's funeral, right?" Genevieve nodded.

Jorgia paused to recollect. "Yes, I couldn't understand why he would leave his son, who was barely holding on. The first time was early afternoon. Victor said he had an emergency at work, and he'd be back within the hour, and he was. But when he got back, Victor was oddly distant. At one point, when I came back from a short break, I caught him crying as he stood over Mario. I thought Victor was being emotional over his son's circumstance—and maybe he was, but now I wonder, was it something else?

"Later that evening, he said he couldn't stand seeing Mario that way and needed a break. I didn't see him again until the following morning and noticed his right hand was bandaged. When I asked what happened, he said he punched the brick wall on the side of our house in frustration."

Looking at Genevieve, "It wasn't the wall at all, was it? It was Lucy." Jorgia's lip began to tremble.

Genevieve struggled to be strong. Speaking softly, she continued, "So, now we have compelling circumstantial evidence. But, if the box was discovered, it might give us the why—a motive for his hatred."

"And you want me to find that box." Jorgia surmised.

Genevieve impressed, "I only want the truth, for everyone to be safe, and ultimately, closure. People are hurting. Mario, Lucy, even Victor is in such a state of misery he's barely holding it together. What might Victor do if he discovered that my ability indeed had merit?

"When you called me Jorgia, you said you felt compelled to do so. But you have to ask yourself, why? Just minutes before the phone rang yesterday, a bird crashed into my window. After it flew away, I noticed it had left an imprint that looked remarkably like an angel, distinct wings spread out wide. Was it a reminder to trust in the guidance that is sent to help us? I choose to look at it that way.

"One thing I've learned over the years doing what I do, is that there is an incredible unseen power. It's always one step ahead of my every move and gives me whatever I need when I need it. But it's also subtle. What I'm trying to say Jorgia, is I believe the urge to call me was given to you for a reason. It's what you needed. It's what I needed. It's what Lucy and Mario needed as well.

"So, it's up to you Jorgia. What do you think?"

Genevieve jumped in her seat when Jorgia bellowed, "I *think* I'll kill Victor myself if he had ANYTHING to do with harming my son!"

Then returning to a little softer tone, Jorgia added, "I even *think* I know where that box may be hidden."

Genevieve was relieved to hear the determination in Jorgia's voice, but she knew Victor was a ticking time bomb, and the last thing she wanted was yet another casualty. "Jorgia, I don't care if it takes a week or longer; you have to be careful. Make sure Victor isn't going to be home when you're looking around."

Jorgia shook her head, "I can't let this purgatory continue anymore. If it's true and Victor did that despicable thing, then I've been living with a stranger and never even realized it. Don't worry about me, Genevieve. If there is a box of secrets, I'm sure the unseen power you talk about, will be there to show me the way."

CHAPTER 21

WHEN THINGS
GO SIDEWAYS

"Ye look so sexy in tha dress all I want is to take it off." Teddy teased as he walked up behind Genevieve and kissed the back of her neck.

Standing in front of the floor-length mirror, Genevieve reached back and stroked Teddy's face as they stared at each other's reflection. "You're welcome to if we skip the dinner tonight."

Teddy continued to stare at her as Genevieve began to feel his desire rising.

"Oh, no, Sir. I was kidding! Sol and Cindy have been planning a dinner out with us for weeks. Besides, I need a night out anyway, something to distract me from thinking about what Jorgia may be getting into."

Teddy whisked Genevieve around to face him. "Aye, okay. But if ye still need an additional distraction *affta* dinner..."

Genevieve winked. "We better go, we're already running late."

As they pulled into the restaurant parking lot, twenty minutes later, Teddy commented, "Can't ever miss Sol's ride."

Parking their car next to Sol's cherry-red jeep, Genevieve noticed that the plain black wheel cover on the back had been replaced by one with a menacing black panther. "Well, that's a little disturbing."

Teddy shrugged. "I think he likes causing a disturbance. In fact, I believe he thrives on it."

While walking toward the restaurant entrance, Genevieve kept looking back at the jeep with narrowed eyes. Teddy just laughed and grabbed her hand. "Come on, Gen. I'm sure those two are at least a drink or two ahead of us. You're certainly welcome to give him a piece of your mind if tha makes ye feel betta."

As they entered, they spotted the Santoros sitting in a booth towards the back of the dimly lit Mexican restaurant. Stopping at the bar first, Genevieve and Teddy ordered drinks—a Margarita for Genevieve, and a Guinness Stout for Teddy, then zig-zagged their way toward Sol and Cindy. When the Walkers appeared, Sol rose quickly. Teddy patted him on the shoulder, "Sorry we're a bit late."

Sol assured, "We just got here a few minutes ago ourselves, barely had time to take a sip." Walking over to Genevieve, Sol declared, "Lookin good there, Gen!" Then Sol pulled her close into a tight hug. As Teddy greeted Cindy, Sol kept a lingering hold on Genevieve, and she began to feel repulsed by the feelings he was emitting, the type she only wanted to experience coming from her husband. Not only was she feeling his erotic desire, but his confident expectations. Forcing herself away from the embrace, she gave him a frown. Being unaware of her ability, Sol looked puzzled. "Everything okay, Gen?"

Knowing men will be men, it wasn't that Genevieve was naive to a person's fantasies. What was so disturbing was that Teddy's *married* partner was feeling them for her, and the arrogant confidence and self-assuredness that he could indeed have her. With every fiber of her being, Genevieve wanted to slap Sol's face and run to the car, but she knew she had to play dumb. After all, it *was* an invasion of his feelings, even if she had no choice but to experience them.

Changing her expression, Genevieve reached for her stomach. "Oh, I'll be okay. I just felt some nausea a moment ago. It seems to be fading now." Genevieve turned to Cindy and gave her a warm embrace, then quickly moved next to Teddy and sat down.

The dinner would have been quite enjoyable had Genevieve not wondered what Sol was thinking every time she caught his lingering gaze focused upon her.

Visiting with Cindy always brought laughter as she had such a humorous way of talking about office gossip, or any other aspect of her life. She was beautiful, yet seemingly unaware, always looking at Sol, as if she needed his approval. As the evening continued, Genevieve wondered, *Does Sol realize all he has with Cindy?*

After dinner, the two women went to the restroom. Upon returning, both sensed a change in their husband's moods. Genevieve figured Teddy must have talked to Sol about his aggressiveness with their client, and it didn't go over very well.

Trying to act nonchalant, Sol deflected, "Anyone up for dessert?"

Everyone chose to pass, stating the dinner had been way too filling. After paying the bill, Genevieve and Cindy walked out in front of the men as they finished their "business" talk.

Before leaving, Genevieve was afraid Sol would want to give her another hug, so she gave Cindy a quick good-bye squeeze, and hurried into the car.

On the drive home, Genevieve and Teddy were quiet for the first few minutes, but Teddy knew something was off when he coaxed, "Ye seemed a bit troubled tonight. I guess the dinner wasn't enough to get your mind off Jorgia affta all?"

Genevieve was hesitant to tell Teddy, as he already was at odds with Sol, but whether it was good judgment or not, she let him know.

"Tha son of a bitch! As soon as ah drop ye off, I'm heeded te see tha wazzock! I'll knock tha dorty mind doon te the ground, smash him like a midgee."

Genevieve squeezed her eyes tight as she thought, *Oh no. He's talking full-on Gordie. Yep, terrible judgment, Genevieve.*

"Teddy, calm down! I won't have you going over there and getting in a fight with him over something he's not even aware I know. Besides, I don't *want* him to know, either. No matter what, it was an invasion of his privacy. Confronting him would jeopardize everything you two have built."

Teddy kept the scowl on his face as he stared ahead. "Ah saw the way he looked at ye and it fashed me aplenty!"

A smirk began to appear on Genevieve's face as she reminded him, "You know I don't understand what 'fash' means, right? Babe, calm your Geordie dialect down and let's talk about this. I know Sol isn't in your good graces right now but let this go. I realize I shouldn't have said anything. I know you two came to an agreement tonight on tactics at work, and we both know how important your partnership has become. I just think I'll keep a little distance from him for the time being. If professional and personal don't mix right now, then that's how it will have to be.

As Teddy drove without responding, Genevieve quietly coaxed, "Honey, look at me." Teddy turned, and when he saw Genevieve's crossed eyes, his face relaxed. Leaning over and speaking softly, Genevieve murmured, "I don't think it's *me* that needs a little distracting when we get home tonight."

Teddy's dimpled grin appeared. "Love, for better or worse, ye keep me in a constant state of distraction, and I don't see tha ever changin."

CHAPTER 22

LUCY LUCY

THERE HAD BEEN no message from Jorgia, so when the phone rang at around nine-thirty in the morning, Genevieve anxiously answered it. "Hello?"

It wasn't Jorgia, but Brenda, one of the nurses that cared for Lucy, also the same nurse who had mentioned Genevieve to Jorgia. Brenda had a soft spot for Lucy and knew all the details to the petite widow's heart-wrenching condition. She often would stand by the door as Genevieve held Lucy's hand, afterward inquiring if Lucy's Soul had anything new to tell Genevieve.

"Hi, Genevieve, it's Brenda."

Genevieve could hear a solemn tone to her voice and asked, "Brenda, is everything okay?"

"I just wanted to let you know that Lucy's vitals are showing signs that she's finally letting go. I thought you might want to come by soon, if you wanted to say good-bye."

Genevieve slowly closed her eyes. She knew this day was coming but hoped Lucy would be alive when she could finally tell her that they found her attacker and had put him in jail. Genevieve knew it was vital to Lucy—it had to be why she had held on so long.

"Thank you, Brenda. I'll leave right now."

As Genevieve grabbed her purse and headed for the door, the phone rang again. Rushing to answer it, she impatiently boomed, "Hello?"

This time it *was* Jorgia. "Genevieve, did I catch you at a bad time?"

"Oh, Jorgia, hi. I just now got a call from Brenda at St. Ann's. They think Lucy won't make it through the day. I was getting ready to see her one last time when you called." There was silence on the other end. "Jorgia, are you there? Are you okay?"

Genevieve could hear Jorgia holding her emotions in as she cleared her throat and murmured. "Do you think I could come by and see Lucy also?"

Genevieve smiled, "Of course. I think it would be really nice for you to meet her."

Jorgia continued. "So that you know, I waited until Victor had gone to work today to look for a hidden box. I figured if there were anything he was hiding it would be in that sacred shed of his out back. I'll tell you, Genevieve, I try to stay clear of that thing, as it has pretty much everything in it that I *don't* want in the house." Genevieve nodded, as Teddy used their garage in a similar manner.

With a deep sigh, Jorgia continued speaking, barely above a whisper, "Well I found it, Genevieve. God, I wish I hadn't. I wish you had been all wrong about this. But when I opened the box…" Genevieve heard Jorgia inhale sharply before continuing, "I can't believe what I found inside."

By the inflection of Jorgia's voice, Genevieve knew. She knew it would be over soon. But did Lucy already know what the outcome would be, and was now ready to move on? "Thank you for your courage, Jorgia. I can't imagine how hard this must be for you. If it's okay, however, could you bring the box with you, and I think I'll have Detective Chao meet us at the hospital as well."

Jorgia's voice was hushed yet resolute, "Yes, I think that would be a good idea."

After making sure Brunner could meet her and Jorgia at St. Ann's, Genevieve took off cruising down the streets, marveling at how every traffic light seemed to be in her favor. In record time, she was at her destination and was surprised when a parking spot opened up right in front of the nursing center—something that had never happened before. But then she realized, *There's a reason this happened today. Lucy must not have much time left!*

As Genevieve rushed to Lucy's room, Brenda was standing near the bed. The two smiled at each other. Taking Brenda's hand, Genevieve whispered, "You've been an angel to her, you know."

Brenda's chin quivered slightly. "With Lucy, it was more than my job. I just felt she needed to know she mattered. I hope she felt that when I was around. It saddened me that, besides you and Brunner, no one else ever came to see her. However, I believe *you* were the real angel, Genevieve. You were able to do much more than I ever could." Squeezing Genevieve's hand, Brenda then moved a chair next to Lucy's bed and said softly, "I'll give you a little space now."

Genevieve took a deep breath and let it out slowly. Sitting in the chair, she took Lucy's hand. Soon Genevieve began making a quiet humming sound as a feeling of bliss greeted her senses. Then joy settled in. *You're happy!* Genevieve thought.

Gratification and thankfulness responded.

Was this what you had been waiting for Lucy? A positive reaction was expected, so when conflicting feelings came back it puzzled Genevieve. *I don't understand. At first, everything felt positive, but now I feel a sense of foreboding. Is there more I don't know?*

With a short pause, anguish and dissatisfaction began to insinuate its way in, making Genevieve squirm in her seat.

Why are you feeling this way, Lucy?

An emotional void held Genevieve in a state of limbo. Then a thought occurred to her, *Not Lucy.*

Frowning, Genevieve hesitated, *So, this emotion is not yours then?*

A reassuring feeling rolled through Genevieve like a rumbling bowling ball.

As Genevieve thought upon each person that Lucy might be referring to, only silence answered back. It wasn't until Genevieve began reflecting on her own frustration, that a rushing response of enthusiasm made her sit rigidly upright.

Am I to understand that this anguish and dissatisfaction is mine, Lucy?

Lucy's Soul rallied both understanding and confident assurance in response.

Lucy, I'm seriously quite satisfied. Nothing will make me happier than to see justice for what happened to you.

Genevieve then felt two strong emotions rise from the pit of her stomach. They were feelings she had worked hard over the years to suppress. Yet, now, she could feel them pushing their way past the stable barriers she had built up, taunting her once again: unworthiness and utter loneliness.

Feeling as if she was a young child all over again, her thoughts questioned, *I don't understand! Why are you doing this to me, Lucy? Why are you making me feel this way? I thought you cared about me; that we had become friends?*

Genevieve closed her eyes before tears had a chance to fall. She hadn't noticed that Jorgia, Brenda, and Brunner were standing silently at the door as she began to cry.

Within a few moments, a sublime love had begun to sooth Genevieve and calm her. She allowed the euphoric tidal wave to drown the corrosive feelings that had started spreading inside her. Genevieve continued to hold tight to them, like a life raft, until Lucy's cherished adoration for her was all Genevieve could feel.

Then, Genevieve began to notice the Soul becoming distant, dispersing Its love outwardly. Its time was almost over. Lucy had finally found her release.

You can be with Vincent now. I love you, Lucy. Laying her head on the bed with eyes still closed, Genevieve smiled as she thought of the words again, *I love Lucy.*

A final emotion resonated with Genevieve as Lucy took her last breath… forgiveness.

CHAPTER 23

PEACE

HEARING THE HEART monitor being turned off, Genevieve looked up. Brenda stared at her from across the bed. "She told you something new today, didn't she?"

Staring back at her, Genevieve quietly inquired, "How did you know that?"

Brenda shrugged. "No mystery. I just heard you mumble, 'I don't understand.' That meant she must have been trying to tell you something. Did you get the answer before she was gone?"

Genevieve took a deep breath and looked at Lucy. "No. It made no sense to me. She was sending me negative emotions that were totally unlike her. The odd thing is, she said the feelings belonged to *me*, but they don't! I refuse to allow those types of emotions to possess me anymore—I haven't in a very long time."

As Genevieve moved in her seat, she saw Brunner and Jorgia standing at the door. Smiling at them and nodding, she added, "At least I was able to let her know she was loved, but I sensed she always knew. I could feel her affection and appreciation moving out toward all of you at the end."

Brenda took the back of her hand and wiped a tear from her cheek. With barely a whisper, she mouthed, "Thank you for letting me know."

Genevieve nodded. A few moments later, when Brenda began the task of removing everything that had been keeping Lucy alive, Genevieve and the other two quietly left the room.

As soon as Genevieve cleared the doorway, Jorgia gave her a gentle hug. "I'm glad I got to see her. I sensed you had become quite close to Lucy."

Genevieve looked back at Lucy, just as Brenda pulled a sheet over her head. "I had never spent that much time with someone in her condition. The more I visited her, the more I sensed who she had been by what the Soul revealed about her. That's why I don't understand why anyone would ever want to hurt her."

As they began to walk down the hall, Brunner put his hand on Genevieve's shoulder. "It's always amazing to watch you, Gen." Genevieve gave Brunner a fleeting smile and reached up to pat his hand but said nothing. Brunner hesitantly continued. "Say, I know it's been an emotional day for you already, so here's the thing, I met with Jorgia here, while you were with Lucy. She told me what she found. Gen, it's not going to be easy to see. I'm not sure you're up for it."

Genevieve gave Jorgia a puzzled frown. Jorgia looked back with concern and admitted, "I know. I too wasn't expecting to see much more than some old faded papers. But I actually got ill when I saw what was inside. You don't have to look, Genevieve, honestly. You'd be better off not putting yourself through any more misery."

But Genevieve couldn't help but wonder, *Was this somehow related to the feelings Lucy projected toward the end? Was it her way of preparing me?* Anguish and foreboding were now definitely bubbling beneath the surface, *Courage girl, don't bale out now!* Genevieve told herself.

"I know you could take it from here, Brunner. But it's something I have to see through."

With a nod from both detective Chao and Jorgia, they walked out to Jorgia's car. Upon opening the trunk, there sat a beat-up old rusty green toolbox. Brunner lifted it out and closed the trunk. "You can open it when you're ready," he cautioned.

Genevieve stood still, bracing, and acknowledging the fact that she wouldn't be able to "unsee" whatever was about to be revealed. Breathing in shallow breaths, she lifted the lid as a putrid smell quickly grabbed her attention. Brunner reached in his pocket and pulled out some latex gloves. "Here, you need to wear these."

Frowning even harder now, Genevieve put the gloves on and quickly lifted a pile of photos and newspaper clippings to see what could be causing the odor below. At first, she didn't recognize what she was looking at. Then her face became ashen with realization. Teeth, stained dark, lay at the bottom left corner. In the upper right, something small rested, shriveled. Genevieve would not have recognized it, if it weren't for a small pearl earring still attached to the dark prune-like remnants that had once been Lucy's delicate earlobe. Sickened by the revolting souvenirs, Genevieve gagged, "Why?"

Brunner cautiously urged, "Let's look at everything, Gen."

The first picture Genevieve picked up was after Lucy's beating. It was a polaroid of her mangled head and body with the word "Vindicated" scribbled over it. Genevieve shook her head as she began to cry. Wiping the tears clear, she picked up another polaroid. This one was of Victor, maybe at nine or ten, taken of himself with a vivid red handprint on his cheek. Another, with his shirt lifted, exposing several dark bruises on his chest and stomach.

There was one more. And when Genevieve saw it, she gasped. Victor must have been about fifteen or so. With his back to a full-length mirror, Victor took a naked picture of himself. In the reflection, it revealed his beaten and bruised back with what looked like several whip marks along his buttocks. Turning to Jorgia she asked, "You never knew?"

Jorgia shook her head. "I noticed some scars on his back, but he said they were from his boxing days."

Looking at the photos, Genevieve questioned. "Did his father do this to him?"

Brunner answered, "We don't know at this point. But we *do* know, without a doubt, it was Victor who attacked Lucy now. After he's arrested for murder, maybe he'll shed more light on the unanswered questions, including his hatred for his stepmother.

Genevieve lifted another picture bent and faded of his father in army fatigues, posing with several other soldiers. The last one was of his father holding Victor as an infant with Victor's mother sitting by his side. There were a few newspaper clippings in the box as well. One was a wedding picture and announcement between Victor's father and Lucy. Assuming it was Victor, horns and a devil's tail had been drawn on Lucy. The other two clippings were of Victor's mother and father's obituaries.

Jorgia took the wedding announcement from Genevieve and stared at the photo. "You've never seen Victor, but when I saw these pictures of his father,

I thought it could have been a clone of my husband when he was a little younger. Victor never talked about his father. It was a taboo subject from the day we met, so I never realized until I saw these yesterday, how remarkably similar the two of them looked."

Upon saying that, Genevieve studied the picture of Vincent and Lucy. Imagining herself in Lucy's shoes on that tragic night, Genevieve closed her eyes as she verbally surmised Lucy's state of mind...

"She was finally alone. The sun had gone down, and all the visitors had left. I imagine Lucy was sitting in her dimly lit living room, still wearing her black dress and pearl jewelry, staring at a picture of Vincent." Opening her eyes, Genevieve looked at Detective Chao, "You know, the one they passed out at the funeral that day as a remembrance. Brunner, you said that when they found her, Lucy had one clutched in her hand, right?" Brunner solemnly nodded.

Genevieve then turned and looked blankly ahead as she continued. "Lucy hears the doorbell. Thinking it might be someone still coming by to pay their respects, she opens the door without thinking. There, standing before her is her beloved Vincent. But wait, how could that be? Before Lucy has time to pull herself out of the wishful illusion, Victor pushes her back and closes the door."

Looking over at Jorgia, Genevieve confirmed, "I always knew the person responsible was full of rage. Yet, Lucy's Soul refused to lead me toward him. That's why I never got the answers I needed. Now I know why. A Soul only reveals the truth *if* Its host demands justice. Lucy didn't. In her mind, the last thing Lucy saw was her handsome husband standing before her. That was where time stopped for her. If it weren't for Mario, we might never have solved this crime for Lucy. It was Mario who gave Lucy justice, and hopefully something *she* had been waiting a long time for, peace."

"But what about Mario?" Jorgia muttered. "Who will give him peace."

Genevieve had no answer but, as she gave Jorgia a sympathetic look she thought, *I hope it will be Victor.*

CHAPTER 24

SUPERHEROES

Genevieve and Jorgia met Detective Chao at the station, staying until they knew Victor had been arrested and was on his way to the precinct. At that point, Brunner insisted both women leave. Victor was still holding onto a lot of anger, and Brunner felt it was better not to fuel the fire when Victor learned of the circumstances surrounding his arrest.

Jorgia, not wanting to go home alone, called her sister, Faith who lived in Flagstaff. Once she explained what was happening, Faith said she could be in Scottsdale later that evening. Until then, Jorgia chose to spend time with Mario. Genevieve offered to keep her company, but Jorgia insisted Genevieve go home and take a breather from the very trying day.

A breather sounded really good. Genevieve needed an escape to the safe haven of her family in the worst way. And, so, like Jorgia, not wanting to go to an empty house, Genevieve decided she'd go to her aunt and uncle's estate, also knowing Broc was there working in the stable. "I could use a Haddie fix," Genevieve mumbled as she got in her car. "I hope the ole girl is up for a little ride."

Once she was there, Genevieve called Teddy to join the family after work. She wanted to surround herself with everything and everyone she loved. She even called and coaxed Ella to leave campus and make the short trip since her daughter didn't have any classes until eleven the following morning.

Later that evening, as dinner was ending out on the patio, Uncle Steven quieted everyone down and asked Genevieve for the details that finally resulted in an arrest. Genevieve was taken by surprise. She would never expose her family to the startling discovery that clinched the case. They had all come to know and care about Lucy during the past year. It was hard enough to let them know she had passed away earlier that day.

As Genevieve felt everyone's eyes on her, showing pride in her ability to solve a difficult crime, she knew she had to say something. So, Genevieve explained the story of how she came to know Mario. The dots that connected him to Lucy and the clues Mario's Soul brought to Genevieve's awareness. Shaking her head, Genevieve concluded, "The only thing I don't know yet is why. Hopefully, Victor will reveal *that* to Detective Chao."

Everyone began clapping. Watching Genevieve squirm slightly in her chair, Teddy, grabbed her hand and held it under the table, tight in his own. He knew how uncomfortable she felt when she was being shown praise for what she did, even if it *was* only family. Leaning over, Teddy whispered, "It's ye we love. This is just another good excuse to show it." As Genevieve turned, Teddy was inches away. All she could see was his expressive blue eyes, reflecting everything he had just said.

Smiling back, Genevieve confessed, "I know. But we all have special abilities. Mine is just…unusual, so people think it's better somehow. Still, I really needed it today—love, I mean, not praise. It was a hard day. By the way, were you able to keep your cool with Sol today?"

Teddy looked around to make sure no one listening. "I told him I saw the way he was lookin at ye and tha he needed to keep his eyes on his own wife, where they belonged. To be honest, the guy looked a bit surprised. I'm not sure he even realized wha he was doin last night. Anyway, he apologized. I decided to leave it at tha."

Genevieve then noticed that Ella and Broc were headed toward the stable. With a grin, she uttered, "Broc's so proud of himself. Uncle Steven promoted him from cleaning the stalls and filling buckets with water, to teaching him how to clean a horse's hooves. He even went with his grandfather today to see a farrier hot shoe one of the mares headed for the east coast. I think this has been exceptionally good for him, honey—great idea of yours."

In the distance, Genevieve and Teddy watched as Broc bowed and put out his arm out in welcoming gesture after opening the stable's large outer door for Ella. With a wink, Genevieve added, "Looks like he's going to show-off to his sister a little tonight."

Just then, Aunt Melinda came up behind Teddy and Genevieve and wrapped her arms around their shoulders. "I love it so when we can get together. I only get to see Broc these days, which I *love*, of course! He's getting to be a good horseman!"

Teddy chimed in, "Aye, and tha reminds me. I think a thank-you dinner is way past due for helpin Broc to get his priorities straightened oot. How aboot an evening at our house next week? I discovered a new recipe for ribs. Ye and tha ole cowboy of yours can be my guinea pigs, Geoffrey too. Sound good, Gen?"

Genevieve's mood was rising steadily. "Nothing would make me happier than a little normalcy for a while."

Aunt Melinda sat down in an empty chair on the other side of Genevieve. "Have you talked to your sister lately?"

Genevieve shrugged, "No, not in a few weeks. When I last talked to her, Ryan was happily settling in as a professor at the community college. Selene and Sara were driving her crazy, nothing new there!"

Aunt Melinda smiled and raised her eyes, "Those two *do* give her a run for her money! Your uncle and I flew over to San Diego last week for Selene's ninth birthday. She's such a beautiful tomboy! Quite a few of her school friends were there, and I noticed how the boys hovered around her, but she seemed oblivious. I hope it stays that way for a while longer. Sara was her bubbling, rambunctious self. Six is a good age; much more engaging intellectually, but still ready to shower Grandma and Grandpa with kisses."

Genevieve had a smile on her face the entire time her aunt was talking. "Yes, six was a great age. I just wish I had a photographic memory. Every year is precious, and over time, you tend to forget the little things."

Aunt Melinda teased, "What, one superpower isn't enough?" Genevieve closed her eyes and stuck her tongue out at her aunt. Melinda took her niece's hand as Genevieve opened her eyes again. "I know you're self-conscious about your ability. But make no mistake, it *is* a superpower and like it or not, you *are* a superhero to me, honey."

Genevieve lifted Melinda's hand and kissed it. "I think the best type of superhero is someone who remains humble, never seeing themselves in that way, and I happened to be looking at that someone, right now."

Taken aback by the compliment, Aunt Melinda tipped her head and smiled. "You have such a way about you, Gen. I love you deeply. But that doesn't make me a superhero. That makes me human. Darling, not that I'm an expert on superheroes but I do know this, great superheroes are humble, true, but they acknowledge their power—embrace it. Don't shy away from accolades that come your way or deflect them as you did with me just now. It is who you are, and God gave you your unique ability for a reason. It's time you love that about yourself."

Genevieve lifted her eyes as a tear dropped from each of them. Glancing at Teddy, his head was bobbing as he said, "Damn, your aunt says the most profound things. I wish I could have said it so eloquently. I've got to agree, Gen, Melinda absolutely has superpowers too!"

CHAPTER 25

DAMAGED

WHEN THE WALKERS got home, the house was dark, save for a blinking red light from the message recorder. As Genevieve pushed the button, she hoped it was Brunner, and it was. "Hey Gen, give me a call when you get this."

Broc kissed his mom, "Hope he can tell you the reason why now. I'm heading up...night, Dad."

After Broc had closed his bedroom door, Genevieve and Teddy sat on the living room couch, and Genevieve called the detective. As soon as Brunner picked up the phone and started to say, "Hello..."

Genevieve rushed in, "Did he talk?"

"Geez Gen! And to think, I almost waited until tomorrow to give you a call."

"I'm glad you didn't. I would have been up all night wondering. Thanks for not waiting. So, how did it go?"

Brunner paused. "It was surprising and disturbing. For tonight, just know we have the answers we needed. Get a good night's sleep. Tomorrow, meet me at the station, and I'll show you the footage of the interrogation. Jazmine, and I are just finishing a late dinner right now."

Squeezing her eyes tight, Genevieve groaned, "I'm so sorry, Brunner. Of course, it's been an awfully long day for you *and* your wife. Please tell Jazmine I'm sorry for interrupting."

Genevieve could hear soft music playing in the background, and Brunner became utterly distracted by something that sounded like moaning. Realizing it wasn't dinner she had interrupted, Genevieve quickly wished Brunner a goodnight and hung up the phone.

"So, Brunner didn't feel like revealin anythin tonight then?" Teddy inquired.

Genevieve gave a sly, Cheshire cat grin, "No, just the bare minimum."

"Where're my glasses!" Brunner grumbled as he fumbled around his desk.

Genevieve, who was sitting in the chair next to him, stood up, walked over and lifted Brunner's glasses from the top of his head. "Still a little tired today, are we?" She asked with a smirk on her face.

Brunner gave her a curious frown. "Slept just fine, thank you." Adjusting his glasses on his face, he picked up a file. "Let's go to the conference room where we won't be interrupted."

As they walked down the hall, Brunner peered at Genevieve over his wired spectacles. "You seem amused by something. Anything you'd like to share?"

Genevieve glanced down and scrunched up her chin. "No, nothing comes to mind. Can't I feel good sometimes without the third degree?"

With a moment to consider her question, Brunner nodded, "Sure, no more prying. It's a good look on you, no matter the reason. Just wish I saw it more often."

Genevieve stopped in her tracks and stared blankly at Brunner as he entered the small meeting room. "Am I always that morose?"

Brunner walked back and took Genevieve's arm, pulling her into the room. "I just meant I don't get to see the 'Happy Genevieve' that often; a hazard of the job, that's all."

Genevieve nodded, "Yea, you're right. There's nothing about a crime that tickles the funny bone. But, deep down, I *am* always happy when a case is solved."

Turning on the overhead T.V. in the upper corner of the room, the detective deduced, "Well then, I'll have to remember that you're smiling on the inside while you watch this tape then. Are you ready?"

The smile dwindled as Genevieve sat down. Detective Chao turned on the monitor, and, as the image flickered into focus, Genevieve took a quick breath as she saw the stunning resemblance Victor had of his father. The man was sitting quietly, surveying the small room when Brunner entered and sat down across from him.

Wasting no time, the detective questioned, "Do you know why you have been arrested?"

Victor slowly lifted his cuffed hands from his lap and placed them carefully on the table. Staring at them for a few moments, then making a fist with his right hand, Victor replied, "For doing the one thing I swore I'd never do."

As Victor continued to stare at his fist in silence, Brunner coaxed, "And that would be?"

Looking up at the detective, Victor reluctantly admitted, "Doing what my mother told me to do."

Not expecting that reply, Brunner sat back in his chair and looked at Victor with a furrowed brow. "Mother? Your mother has been dead for years."

Dropping his head and staring at his lap, Victor let out a snicker. "I know. I genuinely rejoiced the day she died, thinking I'd be free of her once and for all. But even in death, the woman haunts me in my dreams as I hear her final words to me, over and over, 'You failed me, Son.' "

Brunner continued to frown as he shook his head in confusion. "Hold on. Let's back up. I need to ask you some questions. Did you know the person you attacked?"

Victor nodded, "Yes. Her name is, *was*, Lucille Granger."

"Lucille Granger, your stepmother." Brunner clarified.

Victor blinked slowly and said, "Officially, I suppose that would be correct."

"And with premeditation, you went to Ms. Granger's home to do her harm?"

Again, with a snicker, "Premeditation. That's an interesting word. Yes, I would say I meditated on harming her ever since I was a young boy."

Genevieve got chills listening to Victor. Reflecting on the pictures she had seen of his abuse, an eerie dark twist was becoming more apparent.

Detective Chao continued his methodical interrogation. "Can you walk me through the night of August 20, 1994?"

Victor looked at Detective Chao, and for the first time, Genevieve noticed a hint of vulnerability escape his stoic façade. "Do you just want details, or can I also explain why?"

Brunner retorted, "I'm not a lawyer. The why will have no bearing on how I proceed. You told the arresting officer you didn't want counsel. Is that still true?"

Victor nodded.

"Well then, if it is important to you to explain *why*, then, by all means, go ahead. But the only thing that matters to me is *how*. Just understand that."

Victor tipped his head upwards and stared at the ceiling. "When I was sitting in the police car, waiting to be driven over here, I heard two of the officers talking about the box. So, I assume you found it."

As Victor continued his focus upward, Brunner's eyes narrowed, "Yes. A disturbing assortment of keepsakes were brought to my attention."

Victor brought his head back down and looked at the detective. "Disturbing…yes." There was another pause as Victor's eyes glazed over and he blankly looked ahead in contemplation. "Another interesting word, 'keepsake.' For the sake of what, do we keep certain things? I chose to keep just a *few* pictures of my mother's handiwork. But in the end, I don't know why. You keep things for the sake of remembering. That box and everything in it has been seared into my memory and, no matter how I try, nothing lets me forget."

Genevieve's eyes closed for a moment as she thought, *It WAS his mother.*

Adjusting his posture to sit rigidly upright in his chair, Victor began his long disquisition.

"When Dad left, I was eight-years-old. As Mom and I watched him drive away, she told me emphatically it was my fault he left, that he couldn't handle being around a child; that I made too much noise. Funny though, I heard what they screamed about at night, after I went to bed, and it was never about me. Still, what did I know? Even when she'd look at me with contempt, I felt sorry for her, blaming myself for her misery.

"For a couple of years after that, she held the belief that he'd come back to her. I remember him calling a few times in that first year. Each time, I think he must have asked to see me because Mother would yell into the phone that he'd never see his son again if he didn't come back home where he belonged.

"Her frustration grew to the point I never knew what would be waiting for me when I got home from school. If it were a bad day, she'd take her aggravation out on me—even called me Vincent once while smacking me in the face." Victor closed his eyes and became silent, flinching as he undoubtedly was reliving that moment in time.

After a short while, Victor's eyes reopened, ready to press on. "Then one day, Mother saw Father's wedding picture in the newspaper, and her agenda changed—her anger changed too. Lucille was now the reason we'd never have him back. Thinking I was not the cause of her fury anymore, I hoped she'd leave me alone. But then, Mother started pleading with me to kill Lucille, saying the woman had purposely seduced my father to keep him away. When I told her I wouldn't, she found new ways to punish me, all the while, telling me I should blame Lucille for the pain I was receiving."

Victor nodded as he looked at his cuffed hands, "I should have hated my mother, but she was all I had. Father never came to rescue me. If he hadn't married 'that woman,' he might have taken me away...away from *her*.

"So, I came to believe Lucille was as wicked as my mother said she was. With every cut and bruise inflicted on me, I put the blame squarely on the woman who took my father away. Still, I refused to give in to my mother's demand for revenge

"Then, when I was sixteen, I'd had enough. I remember the day because it was my birthday. When I got home from school, I *thought* she'd have a cake and the Beatle's newest album waiting for me. She promised she'd get it for me. But as I walked through the door, I knew she'd had more than a drink or two. She snidely remarked that my father had called and wanted to wish me a happy birthday. It was the first time my father had reached out in years, at least as far as I knew. When I asked if I could call him back, she walked over to the fireplace and grabbed the poker. She muttered something about how ungrateful I was and then began to raise it. I knew what would come next. But this time I yanked it away from her and punched her with my fist, hard in her stomach. It felt good. She never touched me again, ever. From that day on, the only thing she abused was her liver, until eventually, that self-affliction became her undoing."

Looking around the room, Victor shook his head. "I thought I had moved past the anger and hatred. Boxing in college gave me a way to focus the dark energy until I finally didn't feel it anymore. For a time, things seemed normal. I married my dream girl, carved out a good living, and had a son. And I *swore* the day Mario was born that I'd be the best dad in the world to him."

Victor's chin began to quiver, and he wiped a tear quickly as it fell. Detective Chao offered, "Do you want to take a break?"

Victor shook his head. "No. I don't know if I'll have the courage if I stop now." Taking a deep breath, Victor moved on. "The day I saw my father's obituary, I realized how final everything was. I went out to the shed, wanting to see the few pictures I had of him. I hadn't touched that old toolbox since we had moved there. I thought I'd have a hard time finding it, so it seemed odd that the old thing was sitting on a corner shelf, by itself. I was sure I'd buried it deep, under other tool supplies when we moved in, twelve years earlier. But, it had been a long time, and things get moved around, so I didn't think any more about it. As I opened the box and started looking at the pictures, I began to have those old feelings of self-loathing and abandonment again."

Genevieve listened to the grown man as he walked in the shoes of his childhood, knowing the hardest thing to do was relive an abuse you'd fought so hard to forget. Harm comes in many forms. Victor's mother had left deep scars, inside and out. But like Genevieve, Victor had desperately wanted to believe his mother loved him; a lie they both knew better now. Still, the hurt they endured was their badge of survival—also a keepsake of their misery.

Victor continued. "After days of brooding, I decided it was time to meet this woman that had haunted my thoughts for years." Leaning forward, toward the detective, Victor quickly added, "*But not to harm her!*"

Leaning back in his chair, Victor paused and let out a sigh. "It was time to honor my father and pay my respects to his widow. I called the funeral parlor listed in the obituary. I said I was from the florist and had instructions to deliver flowers to Vincent Soblin's widow, but I had somehow lost her address. They didn't ask any other questions, just rattled off the address to me. The whole time I was driving out to Arcadia, I remember practicing what I'd say when I finally met Lucille.

"Then, as I made the turn down the street my father had lived on for so many years, I became disoriented. There, in the driveway of their home, sat my son's car. I froze, idling in the middle of the street, dumbfounded. Mario knew who Lucille was. He had gone behind my back. He had betrayed me!

"I don't even remember driving back home. I found a way to get Jorgia out of the house, and then just sat in the living room, alone, waiting for Mario to walk through the door."

CHAPTER 26

A MONSTER MADE

GENEVIEVE'S HEART BEGAN to race. "God, so he *did* hurt Mario?"

Brunner paused the recording. "I know this hasn't been easy for you, Gen. Victor wasn't thinking clearly that night. Here was his cherished son, and, in his confusion, Victor saw another loved one abandoning him for *Lucy*. He explains it all. Would you like to take a break, have some lunch first? It's almost noon."

Genevieve shook her head. "I don't have an appetite right now. Let's finish this if it's okay with you."

Brunner raised his eyebrows and tilted his head, "You got it." And the tape resumed.

"I felt like I was going to go crazy by the time Mario came through the front door. I stood up and asked him where he'd been. Mario lied, of course, said he'd been at a friend's house. When I told him where I saw his car earlier, he gave me that 'deer in the headlights' look.

"I realized at that moment, it was Mario who had moved the toolbox, and had found out who my father was. And, that he'd witnessed all the pictures inside it. So, I confronted him. He said he found it over a year ago, while looking for a small screwdriver to fix his old Game Boy. Mario said when he saw the pictures of me, he thought my *father* was the one who had beat me, so his instinct was to find him and hurt him as he had hurt me. Foolish, loveable kid. Mario thought *that* was why I never spoke of the man.

"When Mario found where his grandfather and Lucille lived, he drove there, prepared to avenge me. But my father was already bedridden. Mario said chemotherapy had ravished his body. After my father dispelled the notion

115

that he ever laid a hand on me, he wanted to know all about Mario, me and Jorgia. Mario kept telling me how nice my father was to him.

"At that point, I told Mario to stop. I didn't want to hear about my father anymore. It was too late. I had lost the chance long ago to know him. As I looked at Mario that night, I realized *he* got to receive the love of my father. The love I should have had, if it weren't for Lucille.

"Mario told me he had been helping Lucille take his grandfather to doctor and lab visits. Then, when he could, he'd stay with Vincent for an hour or two so *Lucy*..." Victor glanced at Brunner to clarify, "Mario kept referring to her as *Lucy*. So, *Lucy* could get a break outside the house."

Genevieve flashed a slight grin. She was always Lucy to Genevieve.

"When I told Mario, she had been the reason my father left, Mario looked puzzled. They had told him they met at an AA meeting, becoming friends first, as both were dealing, unsuccessfully, with complicated divorces."

There was a long pause before Victor spoke again. Brunner waited patiently for him to continue.

"I've thought about what Mario said that night, many times." Victor tried to hold his emotions in, but as he stared down at his shackled hands, his forehead became furrowed, and a slight tremble showed on his lower lip. "I should have been proud of my son's behavior. He's such a good, kind young man. But instead, I yelled at him. Told him he no right to go behind my back; that he didn't have the whole story.

"That's when Mario told me he figured out it was his grandmother who must have hurt me. He said his grandfather almost got ill when Mario described the pictures he had found in the toolbox. My father told Mario he knew how volatile my mother could be. Then my boy explained how my dad had tried to get custody of me as soon as he left, but my mother knew enough to make him look entirely unfit. In the divorce, she was granted full custody and didn't even request child support because she didn't want my father to have access to me, ever. So, after several failed attempts to change things in the courts, he eventually gave up, met Lucy, and she helped him to move on. She saved him.

"I remember Mario saying the words 'helped him to move on' and realized if my father had never met Lucille, he might have tried again and again to save *me*. So, I forbid Mario from ever going back to that woman's house. She had ruined my life."

Victor stopped and looked again at the ceiling. "Mario got mad at that point and said he planned to go to his grandfather's funeral. He said he had promised Lucille...*Lucy*, he would stay with her for the reception afterward and that I couldn't stop him. I grabbed his shoulders and told him, 'Over my dead body!' That's when he gave me a disgusted look, pulled away, and stormed out of the house.

"I assume he was on his way to Lucille's house because the accident was just a few blocks from where she lived. He had lost control, spinning around a corner and hit a light pole."

Victor finally broke down and began to cry. Brunner excused himself and left for a minute, coming back with a box of Kleenex and a glass of water. By then Victor had composed himself, finally ready to talk about the 'how,' which Detective Chao had been waiting patiently to hear.

"The next day was surreal. Jorgia was a mess. We thought Mario would die. Still, all I could think of was that I had to go to the graveyard and be there when they buried my father. I *had* to see this woman. I made an excuse to leave the hospital and drove to the cemetery, waiting in my car until the funeral procession arrived. I parked far enough away, not to be noticed, but close enough that I could see Lucille. I was rather surprised at how attractive she was, for her age anyway."

Genevieve remembered seeing the wedding picture of Vincent and Lucille, as well as a stunning studio picture Brunner had shown her when Lucy was in her thirties. But it was only the disfigured aftermath that Genevieve had ever known, something she'd gotten used to seeing over the past year. Yet, sight was only one sense, and often deceiving. Genevieve believed without a doubt, that emotion was another way to navigate life, another sense. And she got to *feel* the real beauty that was Lucy.

Victor continued, "There were just a handful of people there. I remember thinking there would have been so many more attending if my father had only been a part of my family, instead of hers.

"When I got back to the hospital, Mario's condition had become unstable, and he was having a hard time breathing. The doctor had just finished a procedure to relieve fluid that had been building in his chest. By the evening, his condition hadn't changed much, and I kept seeing Lucille in my mind. This conniving woman had taken my father and now would take my son from me as well.

"I don't even know what I told Jorgia. I really don't remember much of anything until I pulled up to Lucille's house and she opened the door."

Victor looked back down as he made a fist with his right hand again. "I can't give you the blow by blow description. I just don't remember. It didn't feel like me. I could hear my mother screaming, 'You need to kill that woman' over and over in my head. By the time I stopped, my heart was pounding so hard I thought I'd explode.

"Then, I saw it—my Polaroid camera on her fireplace hearth. I don't know if Mario had been using it or why it was there. I had always kept it in the toolbox. It was like my mother was inside me. I picked it up, walked over to Lucille, thinking she was dead, and, after I took a picture of her, I wrote 'Vindicated' on it. Something my mother felt she needed, vindication. But, honestly, that night I can't tell you where she left off, and I began."

Victor swallowed hard. "I think my mother would be quite pleased with me. I finally did as I was told."

Genevieve felt an icy chill roll down her spine.

"Then, it was like my mother was gone and I realized what I had done. Lucille didn't even look human."

Brunner stopped the tape and looked at Genevieve's sallow face. "There's really not much more. I think you've heard all that matters."

Genevieve turned and gave Brunner a blank expression. "Finish it."

The detective shook his head.

Slowly blinking Genevieve whispered, "Please."

With a deep sigh, Brunner hit the play button.

"I remember I felt like I had to clean up for some reason. I cleaned the blood from the floor and the walls and wiped fingerprints as best I could. I didn't know what to do with the..." Victor glanced up at the detective, "things you found in the box. So, I wrapped them in one of the clean-up towels, took the camera and left. I kept thinking I'd missed something—surely I'd be caught."

Victor stared at Brunner for a long moment before continuing. "I guess that woman, Genevieve was real after all, huh?"

Detective Chao nodded.

With his lips turned downward, his head bobbing up and down, Victor remarked, "You probably expect that I'll use all this as a defense or claim insanity. I won't. I realize I'll never know freedom again. But I was never actually free, anyway. We all have choices, and I won't defend mine. Monsters need to be locked up. I just wanted you to see how *this one* was made."

HAPPY FACE

Broc held his hands to his ears as his parents howled downstairs. Studying was impossible with all the noise. Stomping downstairs, he could see his mother wiping tears from her eyes. "Can you *please* tell me what's so funny!"

Genevieve snorted, "Broc, you have to come watch this. George has gotten himself in trouble again!"

Broc couldn't help smiling as his parents continued to watch an episode of Seinfeld. Walking over and sitting on the arm of the couch he watched a flustered George on an animated rant. Then Broc glanced at his mom who was mouthing George's words.

As his parents cuddled and laughed together, Broc's eyes narrowed with suspicion. "Wait a minute." Walking over to the entertainment console, he saw that the VCR machine was running. "No wonder! How many times have you watched this episode?"

Genevieve smirked and looked at Teddy, "I don't know, maybe three or four times." Teddy raised his eyebrows and nodded in agreement.

Broc shook his head and started to go up the stairs, but half-way up he heard his parents burst into laughter again and hollered, "Hey kids, can you keep it down already?" Broc had a big grin as he closed his bedroom door. *It's so good to see her laughing again!*

It was the best medicine Genevieve could have imagined. After telling Brunner she would be taking a little time off, which he was in total agreement, she had spent the past month bingeing on laughter, watching one sitcom after another.

When the show was over, Genevieve grabbed the empty ice-cream dishes from the coffee table and headed for the kitchen. "I think I'll start to get fat if we keep eating desserts every night!"

Teddy watched Genevieve walk away, her knit sweater and jeans hugging tightly to the slender curves of her body. *Not a chance*, he thought. "It's not the ice cream ye need to watch. It's Aunt Melinda's turkey stuffin tha can put an easy ten pounds on ye."

Genevieve returned from the kitchen and had a big grin on her face. "That's so true! And that reminds me, I'm supposed to make my cheddar-broccoli casserole and bring a dessert."

Finding her spot next to Teddy again, Genevieve laid her head on his shoulder. They sat quietly for a minute when Genevieve whispered, "I don't know what I'd do without you, taping all these shows for me. It always seems that you have to lift me out of some dark hole."

Teddy kissed the top of Genevieve's head. "The thing is, ye wouldn't *have* to do wha ye do. I don't think most people would. It's hard, and it takes a special type of person to brave the unknown. I like to think wha ye do is akin to a policeman or firefighter. Ye nivvor run away from wha scares ye but have the strength to endure it, helping others, no matta wha the cost might be to ye. I'll pull ye oot of any hole, any time, just like I know ye would for me."

Genevieve lifted Teddy's hand and kissed it. "In a heartbeat."

Teddy glanced at the clock. "Ye want to catch a little of the 'Tonight Show'? I think Jay's supposed to have Rodney Dangerfield on it."

Genevieve smirked. "Ah, now that man's funny, even if he *does* pick on his wife way too much! Let's tape it too."

Thanksgiving was the one day of the year that Aunt Melinda showed just how talented she was in the kitchen. Occasionally, during the year, she'd boot young Gidda, their cook and housekeeper, from the kitchen, and whip up a fanciful creation. Yet, without fail, Thanksgiving was Aunt Melinda's day to remind everyone and herself, that, although she wore many hats, a chef's toque was one of her favorites.

When the Walkers arrived at the estate, Tess, Ryan, and their girls were already there and hurried to greet them. After an hour of what the kids considered boring chatter, Geoffrey agreed to take Broc, Selene, and Sara out to the stable. Ella chose to stay behind and enjoy time with her parents and grandparents, which, although she would never admit, missed them a lot.

Late in the afternoon Tess rang the large cowbell that was strategically positioned on the back patio. It was loud enough to get everyone running from the stable, except Geoffrey, who used a cane to maneuver around these days.

As Aunt Melinda carried the main course to the table and Genevieve poured wine into the last piece of crystal stemware, everyone stood around the table and let their sight and smell feast on what their taste-buds could still only imagine.

After everyone was in place, Uncle Steven began with a prayer. It started out thoughtful and reverent. But, being Uncle Steven, he couldn't help but end it with, "And Lord, while you're blessing this heavenly meal, could you also bless these?" Taking a small bottle of antacid pills from his pocket, he stared at them briefly, then added, "Oh, and maybe make them multiply. I know the crowd will need them." With a big grin, Uncle Steven looked around, pleased with his biblical reference until he spotted his wife. Then, realizing how it may have sounded, he quickly added, "You know, too much of a *reeaally gooood* thing, Lord!"

The men and children tried to stifle a laugh, while Tess, Genevieve, and Ella glanced at Melinda with a smile on their face.

Uncle Steven watched his wife to evaluate just how much trouble he had caused for himself. After giving him "the look" she grinned and said, "A-men."

After the meal was over, the men offered to do the clean-up—a pleasant surprise. Aunt Melinda figured it was because Uncle Steven was still treading lightly, making sure he was in her good graces. But after forty-two years of marriage, what he didn't seem to realize, was that she enjoyed his oddball levity. It was part of the loveable package she signed on for, many years ago, and why people were always at ease with him. Still, the women all agreed, a little busy work would do wonders for all that indigestion.

While the women retreated to the living room, the kids took a late afternoon swim. Uncle Steven kept Teddy, Ryan, and Geoffrey reeling in laughter with his more, *colorful* humor as they cleaned and watched football on the kitchen television.

Early that evening, Gidda arrived back from spending the day with family. At that point, everyone felt they had room for dessert, so Gidda and Ella served pie and coffee.

Aunt Melinda however, had gone upstairs just before Gidda arrived, and still was absent as the final pie crumbs were being consumed. Beginning to get concerned, Genevieve headed up the stairs just as her aunt was heading down. "Is everything okay? Genevieve quizzed. "We should've waited on dessert until you were back. I'm sorry. We just thought you'd be coming right back down."

Although Aunt Melinda tried to act nonchalant, Genevieve sensed something was upsetting her. "You know, honey, I wasn't going to have anything anyway, so I'm glad you didn't wait."

As the two walked down the stairs side by side, Aunt Melinda took Genevieve's hand and held it tight. When Genevieve looked over, she could see that her aunt was fighting tears. Within moments Genevieve began to feel a plethora of emerging emotions: remorse, sadness, powerlessness, and worry. Genevieve stopped and faced her aunt. "Something is wrong. Is there anything I can do to help?"

Aunt Melinda blinked slowly and tipped her head to the side. "No, dear. I wish you could. I just got some bad news, that's all. One of the children I sponsored in Kenya had an accident, and they don't think she'll live."

Understanding the emotions better at that point, Genevieve responded, "I'm so sorry. I know you are a charitable sponsor to several children on top of everything else you do. But I didn't realize you had been sponsoring one in Kenya."

Letting go of Genevieve's hand as they moved down the stairs again, Aunt Melinda took a deep sigh. "I didn't talk about her much. She didn't write letters to me like the others. From everything I knew, she had a difficult, sad life. And now this has happened."

Genevieve shook her head as they got to the foyer. "Let me know if she pulls through, okay? No matter what, her life would have been worse without *you*, remember that."

CHAPTER 28

TWISTS AND TURNS

BRIINNGG!

Teddy jumped. "Aww, come on. It's Black Friday already. Why isn't everyone oot shoppin instead of wakin me up at..." Teddy glanced at the clock, "7:15!"

Genevieve barely moved. She too had been looking forward to sleeping in after a late night with her aunt and uncle.

Lifting the phone from the cradle before it had a chance to ring again, Teddy mumbled, "Hello?" Genevieve pried her eyes open when she heard Teddy say, "Hold on, she's right here."

With eyes closed, Teddy passed the phone to Genevieve. "Hello?"

"Genevieve it's Jorgia. He's awake! Mario's awake!"

Genevieve's eyes flew open. "Oh, my God! When?"

Teddy lifted his head and looked over at Genevieve, alarmed. Patting his shoulder, she mouthed, "Don't worry, nothing's wrong." Dropping his head back down on the pillow, Teddy closed his eyes again.

"Hold on a minute, Jorgia," Genevieve whispered. Getting up and taking the cordless phone to the bathroom, she continued, "Sorry, Jorgia. What were you saying?"

"During the night! The nurse said when she went to check on Mario, his eyes were open. But as you know, that's not unusual. Then, as she was adjusting his blanket, he asked where he was. The poor thing said she almost had a heart attack! Then she called me right away. I've been slowly filling Mario in on a lot of things, a years-worth, including his father. Surprisingly, he took it better than I expected he would, especially when I told him about Lucy.

"But here's why I couldn't wait to call you. Mario told me, he and Lucy had visited together from time to time, that she was always happy. The crazy thing, Genevieve, was when I began to talk about you, he said he already knew you! That he and Lucy thought of you as a friend!"

Genevieve was speechless. She had never known anyone that had come out of an extended vegetative state after communing with their Soul. But she always remembered Dillion, the young man poisoned accidentally by cocaine as he innocently drank a green beer on St. Patrick's Day. It was back then when his Soul confirmed Genevieve's suspicion that Dillon was aware of her thoughts. It felt surreal now, to know they could retain Genevieve's emotional communication once they were awake.

"God, that is amazing!" Genevieve marveled.

Jorgia interrupted before Genevieve had a chance to continue. "I can't tell you how happy I am, or how stunning your ability truly is, Genevieve! Anyway, Mario asked if he could see you. Can you come by today for a visit?"

Genevieve felt a flutter in her stomach. It was like having a pen-pal you never expected to meet, and they suddenly show up out of nowhere. "I can't wait! I'll be there as soon as I can."

Still feeling sluggish from the day before, Genevieve set the coffee on brew while getting ready. After leaving a note for Teddy, explaining the situation, Genevieve grabbed a banana, and a hot cup of coffee then hurried out the door.

When she got to Mario's room, Jorgia and Jorgia's sister, Faith were there. Genevieve's heart skipped a beat when Mario turned and smiled at her. "Oh my God, Mario, it's so nice to meet you."

Mario, sitting upright in bed, put his arm out. "I think we're way past the meeting stage. How about a hug instead?"

Genevieve could feel her eyes getting misty. "I'd love that." As she walked over to Mario's bed, she glanced at Jorgia, who was wiping a tear from her eye. Wrapping her arms around the young man, Genevieve felt overwhelmed by his love, not just for her, but for life itself.

There was one more question that still needed answering in Genevieve's mind. Something she could finally ask the human host. "Mario, since you could understand my thoughts and feelings, did you also know what your Soul was conveying to me?"

Mario looked puzzled. "I felt everything. I understood *everything*." He frowned, looking for a way to explain it. "I never realized that feelings were a language, and by far, much more revealing than words could *ever* be. I don't have the perfect clarity now that I had, but I still can remember how amazed I felt when the communication was going on. It was then that I understood feelings were the language of our Souls.

"I also recall how much communication was being transmitted to you through those emotions. It seemed so simple and clear to me at the time, but I sensed how difficult it was for you to understand the subtle nuances within the feeling, and then convert it into words, yet you did!" Mario became silent, and his expressive hazel eyes stared at Genevieve in reverence. "Do you know of anyone else that can do what you are able to do?"

Genevieve felt a tear drop, and she let out a laugh. Finally, there was someone who truly understood what she went through, first-hand! "I've heard rumors, but I can't say if there is any truth to them."

Looking over at Jorgia and her sister, Faith, Genevieve smiled and asked, "I know I'm taking up very special catch-up time, but do you mind if I ask Mario one more question?"

Jorgia let out a laugh. "You, my dear, are more than welcome. As long as Mario feels up to it."

Mario interjected, "Feeling better than I have a right to be—ask away."

Genevieve took a seat on the edge of the bed. "What was Lucy like when you used to visit her and your grandfather?"

Mario's expression changed slightly. Looking down, Genevieve sensed he was searching for happier times to reflect on. Within a few moments, a broad smile appeared, "She was wonderfully eccentric!"

Genevieve's eyes grew wide as she glanced at Jorgia. Bringing her focus back to Mario, she pleaded, "Explain, *please*."

"Well, I guess you never saw their home then?" Mario exclaimed.

Genevieve shook her head.

Mario laughed. "Lucy loved color. She told me she used to live in Tacoma, Washington, and had flowers year-round. But once she moved to Arizona, nothing she planted stayed alive very long. So, she crocheted flowers, hundreds of them, and put them in flower beds around the yard. Each year she'd replace them, so they never lost their bright color."

Genevieve revealed a warm smile, then winked at Mario. "Always with the *rosy* attitude. I got that sense from her."

Mario's eye's narrowed. "Okay, but did you know she was a belly dancer?"

Genevieve shrieked, "What!"

Mario nodded in 'gotcha' satisfaction. "She sure was. I had noticed a large picture of her in a costume when Lucy was a young woman and asked her what she was doing. She said when she was young, her parents took her to Turkey for their friend's wedding. A belly dancer performed at the reception and, from that moment on, Lucy said she was hooked. She even took out her old finger cymbals and danced around the room for me that day."

Genevieve shook her head. "Well, you surprised me with that one...did *not* see that coming!"

Mario smiled and nodded. Then after a moment, a frown appeared. "I wish I'd talked to my dad after I met my grandfather and Lucy. But, since I didn't know why he seemed to hate my grandfather so much, I was afraid to approach him. Who knew it was actually Lucy he hated. My grandfather once told me that it was Lucy who didn't want to give up on the court order and continued to urge my grandfather to try again for partial custody of my dad. She always wanted to know my father, to have Victor as part of their family. Something I suppose you didn't know either, right?"

Genevieve took a deep breath and let it out. "No, I didn't. But again, I'm not surprised. I'm just glad you got to know them. I'm sure they felt blessed to have you in their lives. Thank you, Mario, for sharing your memories of Lucy with me. I'm seeing her in a new way now. A dancer! What a kick!"

As Genevieve slipped off the bed, Jorgia came over and hugged her. "Mario should be coming home in a few days. I'd love it if you and your family came for dinner once he gets settled in."

"Nothing would make me happier, Jorgia. I know my husband, Teddy, and son, Broc would like to meet Mario. They've heard so much about him."

After saying goodbye to Faith and Mario, Genevieve headed down the corridor, beaming. The hallway was almost empty, so she began awkwardly twisting her hips while tapping her fingers above her head. Within a few moments, however, a sharp pain froze Genevieve in her tracks. Taking a deep, slow breath, and gently straightening up, the spasm in her side subsided. Glancing upward Genevieve murmured, "Pretend you didn't see that, Lucy."

With a humble respect for a dance that was clearly more difficult than she imagined, Genevieve guardedly continued walking when she began to hear a woman crying at the far end of the corridor. It sounded familiar somehow. Going past the exit door, Genevieve continued down the hallway until there was no mistaking who was standing alone, crying with such a mournful wail it made Genevieve shutter.

CHAPTER 29

BLINDSIDED

"AUNT MELINDA!" FORGETTING the pain in her side, Genevieve hurried toward her aunt. When Aunt Melinda saw her niece, just steps away, her expression changed from morose sadness to dread.

"Aunt Melinda, what's happened?" Is Uncle Steven okay? Why are you here?" Pulling her aunt into a tight embrace, Genevieve quickly felt the woman's despair, but confusion and panic were swirling around as well.

Breaking Genevieve's hold on her, Aunt Melinda stepped back and wiped at the black streaks of mascara that stained her cheeks. "I don't understand, Genevieve, why are you here?"

Unsure why her aunt seemed unhappy to see her, a frown crossed Genevieve's face as she responded, "I got a call this morning that Mario, the boy that had been in a coma, had awakened last night. I was visiting him in his room down the corridor. When I was leaving, I heard crying that sounded familiar, and that's when I saw you. So, tell me, what's happened, please!" Aunt Melinda stared at Genevieve in silence. With tears swelling, Genevieve concluded, "It's Uncle Steven, isn't it?"

As Genevieve looked into the adjacent room, she saw a body covered by a sheet. "Oh my God, Uncle!"

Genevieve turned and started to go into the room when Aunt Melinda grabbed her arm. "Don't! It's not Steven."

Genevieve looked down at her arm and the firm grip holding her from going forward. Lifting her eyes, Genevieve tilted her head and studied the outline of the sheet in the dark hospital room. Finally, she turned to her aunt, who's trembling lips mouthed, "I'm so sorry."

Shaking her head, Genevieve began to tremble. "Sorry about what?"

Melinda released her hand from Genevieve's arm and gave her a pleading look. "Go home, Gen, please."

Genevieve turned back to the room again. Her heart was pounding, and her thoughts were racing. Slowly she made her way to the bed. Looking back, Melinda stared at her and shook her head. Reaching down, Genevieve lifted the sheet. In the darkness of the room, she only could distinguish that it was a woman. Reaching over for the overhead light, Genevieve heard her aunt, still standing near the doorway, pleading for her to stop.

As the iridescent light flickered on, Genevieve instantly felt faint and nauseous. The woman's face was weathered and seemed much older than she should have been. "Mother." Genevieve whispered.

Touching the face of the slightly warm corpse, Genevieve felt only her own confused emotions. The Soul was gone. Her mother was gone…again.

"No!" Genevieve uttered while trying to make some sense out of the surreal moment. "This can't be happening. No one dies a second time!" As she pulled the sheet back further, Genevieve could see how emaciated her mother was. Lifting her mother's arm, she noticed the bruised and abused veins from what looked like years of addiction.

Aunt Melinda came up next to Genevieve and gently wrapped her arm around her niece's waist. Genevieve, still in shock, never took her eyes off her mother. "You told me she died, that she had committed suicide long ago."

Turning to her aunt with fire in her eyes, she challenged, "Did you know she was alive all this time?"

Just then, Uncle Steven walked in. "Genevieve," he hesitated. "You're here. How did you know?"

Still looking at her aunt, Genevieve's lip began to quiver as she watched tears rolling down her aunt's face. As she turned to look at her uncle's contrite expression, Genevieve began to let out a guttural moan, realizing the two she loved, cherished, and *always* trusted without question, had been lying to her all along.

"Honey," Aunt Melinda finally blurted. "Please, give me a chance to explain."

Releasing her aunt's arm from around her waist, Genevieve took one last look at the woman on the bed, that once upon a time, she had called, Mom.

"I suppose you had your reasons. But you knew how I blamed myself all these years. That maybe she would have loved me if there had been more time. If nothing else, had I been here, just a little earlier, I could have felt the love of her Soul. Love that we could have shared if only for a short time."

With that, Genevieve ran out of the room, shaking off her uncle's attempt to hold her hand, and ran until she was safely alone in her car. Then she sobbed.

CHAPTER 30

SECRETS

As GENEVIEVE LAID her head on the steering wheel and the tears began to subside, only questions remained. She knew she had to talk to her aunt and uncle, but the betrayal was unforgivable. That she knew for sure.

Just as she was about to start the car, Genevieve stopped as she began recalling the interaction she had with Lucy just before she died. At the time, nothing made sense. The feelings the Soul assaulted her with were those Genevieve had as a child, unworthiness and debilitating loneliness. But why did the Soul choose to remind her of them? Was Lucy's Soul trying to forewarn her of what was going to happen? Genevieve had been so terrified of the emotions themselves as they came forth that day, that she never thought to relook at them more objectively.

When Genevieve finally understood her ability, in her mid-twenties, she was able to reflect on the feelings she experienced at an earlier age and, for the most part, was able to decipher which had been her feelings and which were others. But of these raw emotions of uselessness and loneliness, Genevieve had been sure they were genuinely her own, until now. *Maybe they had never been my emotions after all, but my mothers. Or, perhaps, having felt them from her for so long they became a part of me as well.* As she closed her eyes and pondered the possibility, she remembered the final emotion coming from within Lucy… forgiveness. *Who was that meant for Lucy? Me? My mother? My aunt and uncle?*

A loud knock on the window made Genevieve jump. Standing outside the car were her aunt and uncle. Genevieve rolled down the window. "Genevieve," Aunt Melinda pleaded, "Can we *please* sit somewhere and talk."

Genevieve's heart sank, looking at the two of them. Her life was shattered again by people who were supposed to care for her. But, if they honestly had, there would have been no secret as crucial as this. Genevieve had the right to know the truth, whatever it was.

Nodding, Genevieve opened the door. Uncle Steven gave her a quick pat on the back, and Aunt Melinda tried to hold a smile, but it soon disappeared when Melinda saw the same look of heartbreak and betrayal Genevieve had as a child, when Genevieve thought her mother was happier dead then coming home to her children.

There were many places scattered around the vast hospital grounds that were set up with benches, or patio tables and chairs. Walking by two such areas, both already occupied, they kept walking, as this was not a conversation anyone wanted to be shared. Genevieve knew a place along the perimeter of the hospital grounds that was seldom used and led the way there. In actuality, it was one of the nicest spots on the property, with several benches near a fountain and two large trees for shade.

Genevieve motioned for her aunt and uncle to sit, but she, herself, remained standing near the fountain. Uncle Steven was trying to look relaxed as he stretched out his arm behind his wife. Yet his right leg was bouncing fiercely, and his eyes wandered in anticipation of a conversation he must have hoped would never happen.

As Genevieve stood looking at the only real parents she ever knew, she could feel tears start to fill her eyes again.

Aunt Melinda had been trying to think of how to start, when she finally began with, "There were things I never wanted you to know about your mother, but, now, if I'm ever to make you understand why I did what I did, I'll have to tell you everything. Please don't blame Uncle Steven for any of this. It was my decision to handle things the way I did."

Brushing a tear away, Genevieve moved to the adjacent bench and whispered, "I'm listening."

Clearing her throat, Aunt Melinda moved her downcast eyes back and forth before considering her next sentence. "Do you remember much of your father's funeral?"

Genevieve had kept that time vivid in her mind since it was the last time she saw her mother alive. "Yes, I remember it very well."

"You were such a brave little girl, so protective of your mother and sister. I saw the way you looked at your mother, staying close by her side, trying to relieve her pain. Knowing what I do now, it must have been excruciating to experience that kind of agony."

Genevieve instantly became eleven-years-old again, remembering her mother's anguish. "I would have done anything for her. I knew she needed me."

Aunt Melinda slowly nodded. "I know. You were so precious, and, to this day, I remember your hopeful look when you watched your mother leave for the mental hospital, thinking she'd be back soon."

Genevieve looked sharply at her aunt. "What do you mean, thinking? You and my mother both told me that she just needed a little time away. Another lie, then?"

Sighing, Aunt Melinda continued. "Your mother and I talked almost the entire night before the funeral. She told me things that I couldn't wrap my head around."

Aunt Melinda stared at Genevieve, still wishing she could have gone to the grave keeping her sister's conversation a secret from her niece. "Honey, your mother was mentally ill. Her sole existence was to love and be loved by your father. Liv told me that night that she never wanted to have any children. That Zeffran, your father, loved kids, so, she thought if she had some, he'd love her more, and become the family man she wanted him to be, and finally leave the military.

"Liv said she tried to love you and Tess, but every time she looked at you girls when he was gone, she felt trapped, and wanted to escape. When your father died, Liv said she just couldn't pretend to be the loving mother you girls needed her to be and said she was going to give you both up."

Genevieve kept shaking her head in disbelief. "You're lying. She would never do that!" Genevieve watched a tear roll down her aunt's face as her uncle reached over and took Melinda's hand in his but remained silent.

Aunt Melinda continued, "I told her she was only grieving, that it would get better and not to make any rash decisions. I said maybe it was time for some professional help, where she could get away and reflect on what was vitally important in her life, which was you girls.

"At that point, I thought I had gotten through to her. She agreed to a hospital stay, and I said I'd take care of you and Tess for as long as she needed me. But as she was getting ready to leave that day for the hospital, there was something in her demeanor that felt final. She went on at length about what you two girls would need, and to be sure to pack up as much as possible. Then she wanted *me* to have several things she had kept from our childhood. A favorite book our mother read to us called 'A Country Girl.' I think that was the main reason she wanted to move to the country when you were small. She loved that story. She also gave me several photos she kept of the two of us as young children. When I asked why she was giving me those things, she laughed, and just said she wanted them in a safe place.

"As the car drove out of sight, I hoped as you did, that she would see life differently soon. But then days later the call came."

CHAPTER 31

BETWEEN A ROCK
AND A HARD PLACE

GENEVIEVE REACTED, "YOU mean the call that she committed suicide, I presume?"

"Yes. After I broke the news to you, I flew back the next day. First, I went to the police station, and they showed me a cryptic suicide note, that just read, 'I can't go on.' It was in your mother's handwriting. Then they showed me an empty bottle of Actomol, which was an anti-depressant they had prescribed for her at the hospital, yet no one knew how she was able to acquire a bottle of the pills. Her clothes, even her underwear was left on the beach, along with her hospital I.D. and a half bottle of cheap vodka, lying half-buried in the sand. A witness swore he saw a naked woman with the same height and hair color as your mother enter the surf but didn't think there was anything to report since the beach was pretty secluded, and occasionally people shed their clothes there."

Genevieve's facial expression softened. "So, you truly thought she had died."

Aunt Melinda nodded. "Then I went to the hospital and found out she had the right to leave, since she admitted herself voluntarily. The doctor told her she wasn't ready, only having been there less than two days. He, too, had no answer as to how she got the pills as they were carefully guarded at all times, and there were no missing medications when they took inventory after hearing about Liv."

Genevieve got up and walked over to the fountain, watching as the water bubbled up and over the opening at the top, then plummeted to the bottom. Without turning, she asked, "So when did you realize she was still alive?"

Now the part had come that Aunt Melinda was dreading. "I decided to make one more trip to your house since I was there anyway, and see if there was anything else I could bring back that might comfort both of you. When I got there, the door was open, yet I knew I had locked it when we left. Guardedly I pushed it open just as your mother emerged from her bedroom. We both screamed, not expecting to see the other. At first, I was so relieved I ran and hugged her as tight as I could, but the feeling wasn't mutual. She pulled away and angrily asked what I was doing there. I stood looking at her, bewildered for a few moments, then realized what was going on.

"I remembered asking her how she could do that to us, to you! She said she had dreamed of faking her death many times before, but never had the courage to follow through. But once Zeffran was gone, and she was away from her girls, knowing they'd be safe and loved, she saw her escape and took it."

Genevieve spun around and demanded, "So why didn't she come back, then? You should have made her!"

Aunt Melinda lowered her head. Uncle Steven showed distinct disapproval for the way Genevieve was addressing her aunt. Patting his hand to let him know she was okay, Aunt Melinda answered the question.

"I *told* Liv she had to come back with me or face the police. She ran to the kitchen and took a knife and held it to her wrist, saying she couldn't do either. I didn't know if she would actually harm herself, but I backed off. I asked if we could just sit and talk before I left. Your mom kept her distance but agreed. Liv explained after she was discharged, she went to the back of the hospital and rummaged through the trash until she found an empty bottle of the drug they had prescribed for her. Then she went to the liquor store and bought the vodka and staged the scene. She said she couldn't let you go through more pain because of her and knew I would be the kind of mother you children deserved. She felt you'd move on much better if you thought she was dead."

Genevieve's face was wet but made no attempt to dry it. "Don't you see that she *did* love me? If she hadn't, she wouldn't have cared if I was in pain. She wouldn't have cared about our wellbeing. She wouldn't have staged a suicide. She just would have left. I could have confirmed that if you had told me all this last night. *She* was the reason you were upset, right? It wasn't a child in Kenya was it?"

Aunt Melinda nodded, but became defiant. "You weren't there to see the desperate look in her eyes or watch the knife pressing against her wrist. You didn't have to make the hard decision that might cause her to actually kill herself! The only thing I could get her to do was to take back a picture she had given me. I wrote my private office phone number on the back and pleaded with her to call me, anytime; that I would be there whenever she needed me.

"But I never heard from her again. I never knew what happened to her until Wednesday. I was cleaning up some things in my office, and the phone rang. I only had given that private number to a handful of people, and rarely heard it ring. When I picked it up, it was a hospital in downtown L.A. They said they had found a woman, unresponsive, near an underpass. She had a few meager belongings with her, but otherwise, they only found a faded photograph with a number on the back. After I confirmed it was Liv, I arranged for her to be flown here to the Mayo Clinic. When she arrived, I was waiting. After the E.R. staff examined her, a doctor told me she only had a day or two, at most, to live. Her lungs were riddled with cancer, and she had liver failure due to contracting Hepatitis-B, which they assumed was from her obvious drug use. The doctor said there was no evidence she was being treated for either of the life-threatening illnesses. Yesterday, I had her moved here. I had just gotten off the phone with the hospital when you met me on the stairs. When I got here this morning, I held her hand and read from the book she loved until her heart stopped. She never regained consciousness."

Genevieve let out a moan. "I didn't need her to be conscious. I just needed to know she was capable of love; that there was love for *me*, somewhere, deep inside her. I know there was, but now it's too late. You stood right next to me last night and could have given me what you *knew* I always wanted from her, yet you robbed me...because you were afraid.

As hurt as Genevieve felt, she couldn't utter the words she thought, *Maybe you aren't a superhero after all.*

CHAPTER 32

WHAT TO DO

UNCLE STEVEN STOOD up, "Alright, that's enough."

Genevieve's chin was trembling. "I love you both, but I just can't get past this. I've seen over and over again how secrets poison the lives around them. I always felt so blessed that our family was one of those rare exceptions. Funny thing is how well you both kept it hidden from me. But then, no matter what emotion I felt from you, I would never have suspected this kind of deceit in the first place. I know your perspective is different than mine, and you feel justified, *but she was my mother!*"

Aunt Melinda looked at Genevieve with pleading eyes. "But I'm your mother too."

Genevieve began crying and turned and ran for her car. Starting it up, she left before she could be stopped again, driving in a haze until she arrived home.

Sitting in the driveway, Genevieve thought of how the day had begun. She was so happy to see Mario, basking in the joy of his recovery while looking forward to the holiday weekend and spending some rare time with Ella while her daughter was home. *Why today? If Mario had stayed unconscious just until tomorrow, I never would have known. Life, as I knew it, would be unchanged... ignorance would surely be bliss.*

Every movement felt like a struggle. As Genevieve made her way slowly into the house, Teddy was waiting for her. "I just got a call from your uncle."

Genevieve walked up to him, and, as he wrapped his arms around her, she began crying uncontrollably. Broc and Ella ran down the stairs when they heard their mother sobbing. Both had a concerned frown on their face, and Ella mouthed, "What happened?" to her father. Teddy just shook his head and motioned for the two to go back upstairs. Broc slowly headed back, but Ella lingered. Again, Teddy motioned for her to leave. With a distressed, hurt look, she turned and went back upstairs.

After a few minutes, Genevieve looked up at her husband, "You know then?"

Teddy moved Genevieve's wet, matted hair out of her face. "Steven filled me in on the main points. He said he had to give your aunt a sedative. She's inconsolable, feelin like she just lost a sister and a daughter today."

Another tear ran down Genevieve's face. "It didn't have to be this way. It wasn't just losing my mother all over again, but the betrayal of two mothers *and* a father hurts in ways I can't even explain."

Taking Genevieve's hand, Teddy led her to the living room couch. He knew talking about Genevieve's mother, Liv, was a tricky subject to maneuver through, and, luckily, for him anyway, the woman rarely came up in their conversations at all. So, as he studied Genevieve's face, he knew he had to tread lightly in his attempt to try and mend fences and cut through the hurt that was blinding her.

"Love, I won't pretend to know wha you're thinkin. I know ye blame your aunt and uncle for keepin ye from knowin your mum was alive, but don't ye think it was your mum, affta all, who made the decision to nivvor see ye again when she could have come back at any time?

Genevieve closed her eyes, trying to slow the spinning that was clouding her thoughts. "I don't absolve my mother from her unbelievable selfishness, but I was just a little girl when she left, and I didn't understand what mental illness was. I didn't comprehend the magnitude of her depression, yet I lived with it, day in and day out as if it were my own. So, in retrospect, I understand how debilitating it really was for her.

"My aunt, however, knew better back then. She knew my mother was sick. She said she had no choice but to let my mother flee after she found her alive in our house. But she had to know my mother would never find peace in running away. It was just easier to be rid of her."

Teddy squinted and rubbed his eyes. "If I recall, didn't ye say, it had been your aunt tha talked your mum into goin to the hospital in the first place?"

Genevieve nodded. "Yes."

"So, it looks to me like she *did* care aboot her sister and wanted her to get betta," Teddy reasoned.

Genevieve interjected, "On the day of my father's funeral, my mother told me she was going to a hospital because she always felt sad and didn't want to live without my dad. I remember running into my room, crying. My aunt came in and, it was way back then she told me that, even as a child, my mother felt incapable of handling life on her own. As years past, my aunt watched my mother get worse and worse. Aunt Melinda's gesture to get my mom help after the funeral was too little, too late."

Teddy grumbled, "It must be nice to nivvor make mistakes."

Turning to her husband and looking horribly forsaken, Genevieve got up and hurried up the stairs, closing their bedroom door and locking it. Teddy knew he'd let his frustration spill out, making a big mess even bigger. As he sat, defeated, Ella slowly maneuvered down the stairs and toward him.

"I know it was a private conversation, Dad, but I was really worried, so I listened anyway."

Teddy lifted the side of his mouth and nodded, not surprised.

With her father having nothing to say, Ella continued, "So, Liv was alive all this time?"

Teddy looked up at the bedroom door and spoke softly, "Aye, she died today. Mum had gone to the hospital because Mario came out of his coma, and she was anxious to see him. As she was aboot to leave, she heard your grandmother cryin doon the hall. Tha's when she saw her mother and found oot aboot Liv faking her suicide and choosin to abandon your mum and everyone who loved her."

At that point, Broc was coming down the stairs, so Teddy decided to fill both of them in on all the details.

Broc shook his head. "I don't understand why she's so mad at our grandparents. They didn't abandon her. They did everything for her and Aunt Tess. This makes no sense!"

Ella emphasized, "You weren't in her shoes, Broc. You don't know what it must have been like to have a mother like that. I can only imagine how much

I'd crave mom's love if she couldn't give it to me. I don't imagine you'd ever stop wanting to feel that maternal love of your mother if you had the chance. Mom could have had that opportunity, Broc, just before Liv died. It could have finally given her some sort of peace."

When Ella looked up, she saw her mother standing at the rail at the top of the stairs. No one realized she had been listening. As Genevieve made her way down the stairs, the family became silent, waiting for her to say something.

As she sat down on the loveseat, adjacent to the couch, Genevieve smiled at her family. "I know how conflicting and probably irrational this all seems. But you're right, Ella, there is something that can't be explained about the need for a parent's love. Your father and I love you both so much, and you'll *never* know the feeling of it being denied to you.

"Every time, as a Soul is about to leave the body, all the host's filters, life-long traumas, and heartaches simply disappear. All that is left is the sweetest and purest love you could ever imagine. I've learned over time, that the feeling coming through was not just meant for my benefit, but so I could convey the person's genuine love for those they hurt along the way. I often imagined what it would have been like to feel that from my own mother. That's why it hurts so much. Your grandmother *knew* I longed for that because I'd talked to her about it before.

"Fear can be a great motivator, but more often, it can paralyze a person from helping someone in need. Right now, I can't reconcile what my aunt and uncle did. Maybe in time, things will change, but they can't be a part of my life right now."

Everyone had a shocked look on their face, and Broc pleaded, "But I don't want to stop seeing them. I have my job there, and Grandpa needs me!"

Genevieve shook her head, "This is only about me and *my* relationship with them. I would never take that away from any of you.

"I've decided that I'm going to try and find who had been a part of my mother's life during those missing years. If I can, maybe at least I can understand more about the woman through people who knew her in a different life."

Teddy cautioned, "Gen, wha is the point? This can only give ye more heartache. Ye know the condition she was in when she died."

Genevieve reached over and touched Teddy's leg. "I do. But my mother thought she'd find a better life somewhere else, away from all of us. Nothing cuts deeper than that heartache.

"Whatever happened after she left, had nothing to do with me. When I looked at her today, I knew who she was, yet she was a shadow of the past; a complete stranger who lived a life I never knew. Maybe, this journey is what I need to absolve myself as well as my aunt for the guilt we both share of failing to save someone who was screaming to be saved."

A DAUGHTER'S CONCERN

ELLA SHOOK HER head, "I can't imagine where you would even start."

Genevieve replied, "My aunt said there had been a few belongings the police found with her. I assume my aunt has whatever they are. I can start there, but I'll need one of you to get them."

Teddy implored, "Gen, don't leave things this way with your aunt and uncle."

Genevieve had held a calm demeanor, but as she looked at Teddy, the emotions began to surface again and, as her eyes became misty, she shook her head and whispered, "I…"

Broc, not wanting to see his mother break down again, said, "I'll get them if someone can drive me over to the estate." Ella felt it was more important to spend time with her mother, so Teddy agreed to take the uncomfortable trip with Broc.

As he and Broc were heading for the door, Teddy looked at his wife with frowned concern. "We have a lot to talk aboot when I get back."

Ella looked at her mother. Never before had she seen her parents at odds, on anything. Genevieve looked so lost, confused, and alone when she forced a quick nod in reply.

When Teddy and Broc left, Ella got up from the couch and squeezed into the small loveseat with her mother, putting her arms tight around her. She let her mother cry some more and couldn't help but join her.

Ella had never given her actual grandmother much thought in the past. Liv was one of those relatives that no one brought up in conversation, so it never occurred to her the depth of despair her mother had lived with and was having to relive now.

Lifting herself from the tight embrace, Ella wiped her eyes and said, "And I thought we'd be half finished with our Christmas shopping by now!"

They both let out a cathartic laugh. Genevieve sighed as she stared at her daughter, "If only I could change the way this day turned out..."

Ella cut her off, "Mom, don't blame yourself for what happened today, or the way you feel. It doesn't matter if Dad, Broc, Grandpa, or Grandma think you are acting irrationally. They could never understand what it was like for you, none of us could. But one thing is for certain. Without any doubt, we *all* love you, and we want you to finally have peace where your mother is concerned."

After a moment, Ella continued, "I imagine it must have been a horrible secret in which Grandma and Grandpa ultimately felt trapped. Once a certain path is taken, it can feel impossible to find a new one. But like you always say, there is a reason for everything; there are no mistakes in the universe. So, what were the odds you'd be at the hospital today, on that floor, at that specific time? I refuse to believe it was to punish you or my grandparents. You were simply meant to know the truth, Mom. Now you have to learn why. There must be something more you are destined to discover, and I believe you'll find it. You seem to have an exceptional guardian angel that continually helps guide you, so, follow her lead. I'll talk to Grandma before I go back to school and do my best to try and make her understand."

Genevieve shook her head in amazement. "You're much too young to be so wise, Ariella."

Ella shrugged. "No, I've just spent a lifetime listening to one that is." Genevieve smiled but became distracted about something. Trying to keep the lighter momentum moving along, Ella jumped out of the chair and blurted, "We only have a few hours left until dinner so, hurry and get your coat on. The mall is calling us!"

Genevieve just sat looking at her daughter with a puzzled expression on her face. "Say, how do you know my guardian angel is female, anyway?"

Ella rolled her eyes. "Because, before I was born, I talked to her."

Genevieve relaxed and smiled, "Oh, reeeally."

Ella smiled back. "Yes. And when I told her I had chosen *you* to be my mother, she laughed and said, 'Are you sure? Have you read the fine print before signing on?' "

Genevieve's eyes widened, and jumping from the chair, chased Ella through the house until she caught her. With both panting and out of breath, Genevieve admitted, "That's about what I'd expect my angel to say! Nevertheless, I'm certainly glad you signed on the dotted line, even *with* the dire warning."

Ella walked over and grabbed their coats. "She didn't have me worried. Anyone who did what you did, just to have me, was already perfect in *my* mind."

CHAPTER 34

LEFTOVERS

WHEN TEDDY AND Broc got back, there was a note on the kitchen counter, in Ella's scribbled handwriting, "Went shopping."

Broc looked at it and said, "Looks like we're on our own for dinner, pizza?"

Teddy placed the box of Liv's belongings near the door and turned to chastise his son, "Eee! Don't be dafty, lad. There's a refrigerator full of turkey, stuffin, cranberries, and desserts. Best to enjoy wha's left of Thanksgivin now, who knows wha next Thanksgivin will be like."

Broc started pulling left-overs out of the refrigerator and putting them on the counter. "Do you really think Mom will punish Grandma and Grandpa that long?"

Teddy shook his head. "It isn't tha she *wants* to punish them. But right now, she's blinded by bein hurt by them. I think, if your mum lets this go on, *she'll* be the one feelin punished the most. She loves them too much, and not havin them to talk to will kill her. I hope she realizes tha, and soon."

Broc looked over at the box. "Why didn't you look inside, Dad?"

After Teddy set the temperature on the oven, he turned to Broc, "When your grandma handed it to me, she said it would be best if only your mum saw wha was inside it."

Frowning, Broc stated, "Why make it sound so mysterious? I thought it was just some old clothes and stuff?"

Teddy shrugged. "Aye, me too, but I didn't question her. It was hard enough to ask for it in the first place. Aunt Tess was in the room, and at first, I wasn't sure if she knew. But your grandma said since Tess and the family were still visiting, she felt it best to let her know wha was happenin, saying, 'It was just a matta of time before she'd find oot anyway.' Thing is, Aunt Tess doesn't remember her mum, being only three years old when Liv disappeared. So, your aunt hovered near your grandmother, afraid, maybe, of wha I had come to say. When I told your grandma tha your mum wanted Liv's belongings, and why, she said she had hoped they could have gone through them together and almost started cryin. She said she'd do anythin for Gen, and if your mum needed company, she'd gladly go with her to L.A." Broc just stared at his dad with a disheartened expression but said nothing.

When Teddy and Broc arrived at the estate, earlier that afternoon, Broc had gotten cold feet about asking for the box, and instead, headed straight to the stable, hoping things would be "as usual" there. Now, as Teddy observed his son, he had a strong feeling "as usual" wasn't the case there either and questioned, "So, Grandpa didn't have much to say when ye met him oot at the stable?"

Broc walked over to the table and sat down. "I could tell he was upset, cause he didn't joke around, and was really quiet when he was working. I told him I was sorry Mom was so upset about everything."

Teddy nodded. "Did he say anythin back?"

Looking at his dad and slightly nodding, Broc responded, "He said he was always afraid Liv would appear one day. Grandpa said that he and Grandma had even thought about telling Mom last night, after dinner, but Mom was in such a good place, Grandma didn't want to see her hurt after all she'd been through lately."

Teddy turned and put the casserole dishes in the oven. "And figurin, at tha point, your mum would nivvor know, as Liv was on death's door, I too would have seen no good in openin old wounds. But, for whatever reason, the secret wasn't supposed to die with Liv. The circumstance today made tha crystal clear."

"Spooky clear," Broc shot back.

As the two nodded at each other, they heard the girls coming through the door. When Genevieve and Ella entered the kitchen, only Ella was carrying a bag.

Testing his wife's mood, Teddy lightheartedly questioned, "Wha? Only *one* bag?

Ella forced a yawn, "I don't think either of us were up to the challenge today. It took over a half-hour, standing in line, just to buy this one thing."

Genevieve went and sat at the table next to Broc. "Ella is being kind. I thought shopping would be a good distraction, but nothing appealed to me today. I kept wondering how things were going for the two of you."

Teddy pointed to the box. "I was told it was for your eyes only."

Genevieve frowned, "So you don't know what's inside?"

Teddy shook his head, "Your aunt wants ye to be the one to open it."

Genevieve stared at Teddy and shook her head with a puzzled look.

Teddy felt he should mention the news about Tess. "By the way, your sister knows."

Genevieve looked relieved. "That's good. Best that it didn't come from me. Was she okay?"

Shrugging Teddy said, "She's concerned. But mostly aboot how it's affectin the relationship between ye and your aunt and uncle. She was keepin a close watch on Melinda and said she would call ye tonight."

Glancing at the box, Genevieve lamented, "I suppose my sister feels like I'm the villain."

Although Teddy got that vibe from Tess, there was no point in speculating. Tess would be calling soon anyway. Trying to divert the conversation, he asked, "Have ye two had dinner yet?"

Ella took a deep breath, "No, but even if we had, I'd partake of whatever it is I'm smelling!"

Teddy looked at Genevieve who drew a slow smile and affirmed, "Nothing better than Thanksgiving Day leftovers. I'll set the table."

Dinner was quiet, but even Genevieve seemed to have a decent appetite.

Off the hook for clean-up, Broc and Ella headed to their rooms for the night. Genevieve knew Teddy wanted time to talk to her alone.

Just as Genevieve was about to break the awkward silence, the phone rang. Teddy nodded, "It's your sister."

With a hesitant glance toward her husband, Genevieve put down the dishes she was carrying and answered the phone. "Hello?"

Genevieve took the phone into the living room. As Teddy cleared the dishes, he kept his ears alert in case things went south with Tess, but barely a word was heard coming from the other room.

Once the dishwasher was full and the rest sat, soaking in hot water, Teddy walked into the living room. Genevieve was off the phone. She had been crying, but now was sitting on the couch, staring at the darkness outside the window. When she noticed Teddy standing near her, she motioned for him to sit next to her.

Taking her hand and squeezing it, Teddy murmured, "Looks like it didn't go very well."

Genevieve sighed, "Why is it, I can empathize with the motives of almost anyone else, but not my aunt? What *is* it about my mother? Why do I care so much?

Teddy wondered, "Were those the questions Tess asked ye?

Genevieve looked up at Teddy with watery eyes. "Those, and many others, not one of which I had a reasonable answer that she would understand."

Turning back to look out the window again, Genevieve continued, "When you came in, I was thinking about something Ella had said in jest earlier today. She joked that before she was born, she told my guardian angel that she chose *me* to be her mother. What if we *do* choose our parents. Would I have known the person Liv was? And if so, there had to have been something that would have drawn me to that predestined relationship."

Genevieve paused as if she expected, or at least hoped, the answer would instantly reveal itself. When it didn't, she finally shook her head and concluded, "I guess, if that's the case, it will always be a mystery to me, *now*."

Teddy knew Genevieve was referring to Melinda when she said, 'now.' With his wife's myopic view of her aunt's motives, arguing for reason would only cause more distance between Genevieve and everyone, including Teddy. It didn't matter whether he shared the same questions as Tess. For the first time that he could remember, Teddy felt an uncomfortable distance from Genevieve. There was no way to comfort her this time. She had to find peace, if there was to be any, on her own.

With nothing else he could do, Teddy suggested, "Maybe it's time to see wha's in the box?"

Genevieve looked at him and nodded.

Teddy got up and brought a box the police use to hold evidence in and placed it at her feet. "I'm goin to honor your aunt's wishes and leave ye alone."

When Teddy had closed the bedroom door upstairs, Genevieve walked over and put a cassette in the cassette player so she wouldn't feel so isolated.

As the music quietly began to play, Genevieve sat back down, took a deep breath and lifted the lid.

CHAPTER 35

THE BOX

THE STENCH COMING from inside was almost more than Genevieve could stand. Several worn and torn sweaters filled the majority of the box. As Genevieve lifted each sweater with her thumb and index finger, she gave it a cursory glance and dropped it to the floor. Next, she removed a filthy water bottle, a pair of worn-out socks, and underwear that had not seen a washing machine since maybe—ever.

Genevieve couldn't believe the squalor her mother must have lived in as she removed a few scattered plastic bowls, a baggie which held one metal fork, a metal spoon, and one plastic knife. Finally, only three items remained: a small pan, a dirty hairbrush, and a knit scarf that looked homemade with the initials D.B. on one end. That was everything.

So why was it so important I see this alone? Genevieve mumbled.

Staring at the sweaters, she decided to take a closer look at each one of them again. The first one was an awful mustard yellow color, the fabric, definitely wool. Moths had feasted on the organic material at one point as Genevieve noticed over a dozen holes. Originally, it must have had decorative buttons down each arm. But now, they were all but gone, save for one near the wrist on the right sleeve, and two up near the shoulder of the other. *How did she ever come into possession of this?* Genevieve thought.

Dropping it again, she picked up the next sweater which she realized was actually a sweatshirt. The color was navy blue with grey flowers, or maybe they had been white once upon a time. As Genevieve held the limp garment up, she knew the size was at least three times larger than it needed to be, and, other than being very dirty the shirt seemed to be in decent shape. Genevieve pondered, *Maybe she used this as her outer layer at night or on cold days.*

That got her speculating, *Were these the clothes she was wearing when the police found her? If so,* (Genevieve rechecked the box)*, where are her pants and shoes? Why aren't they in the box? She certainly would have been wearing those things too.*

As Genevieve dropped the shirt and began reaching for the last sweater, she noticed that, as the sweatshirt fell, instead of landing in a limp, crumpled mess on the floor, a noticeable bulge was sticking out, keeping part of the fabric rigid and taut.

Frowning, Genevieve picked it up again and felt the center front. There was something hard on the inside. Quickly turning the fabric over she observed a large, cloth pouch that had been sewn in by hand. The thread used was so perfectly matched, Genevieve didn't notice the tiny stitch marks on the outside of the garment. The pouch was closed with three small snaps. Nervously, Genevieve pulled them apart and took the contents out.

Pictures. There must be ten or more. Genevieve fanned them out like a hand of cards. Then, placing them on the coffee table, she picked up the first one. *Dad.* In the black and white studio picture, she whispered, "You were so young here." Turning the picture over, in faded handwriting, Genevieve read, "Zeffran Clarke, graduating class of 1950.' What a handsome young man you were, Dad."

The next two were of Liv and Zeffran. One, also in black and white, had them both in their early twenties—a cheek to cheek close-up, smiling broadly at the camera. The following one was a studio picture of Genevieve's dad in his Marine uniform, and her mother in a beautifully tailored white dress and navy jacket, standing solemnly next to him. *I know all too well how you felt to be a soldier's wife, Mom. I felt your sadness every day he was gone.*

When she got to the next picture, Genevieve knew why Aunt Melinda wanted her to be alone. Liv was nude, bent in a provocative pose. On the back, in her mom's handwriting, 'Don't forget what's waiting for you at home, xoxo Liv.' *She must have given this to Dad once when he was headed overseas,* Genevieve surmised. Turning to look at the picture again, Genevieve knew wives and girlfriends did this sort of thing, and it came as little surprise that her mother would also.

Closing her eyes, Genevieve listened to Luther Vandross sing his soulful hit, "Endless Love" on the cassette player. The lyrics brought surprising empathy for Liv, knowing the desperation that was behind the suggestive imagery. *Keeping her man hungry for more was the only ammunition she felt she had against Dad's formidable mistress, the military.*

Suddenly Genevieve's eyes began to tear up as she looked at the next photo. It was an old colored polaroid. The entire Clarke family was sitting on the couch. Even Genevieve's cat, Tutu, which she hadn't thought of in ages, was, with her face to the camera, sitting gracefully on Genevieve's lap. Tess was maybe two years old, sitting on her daddy's lap and holding her cherished, stuffed bunny. Everyone had a big smile on their face.

Brushing a tear away, Genevieve went to the next picture. *Who's this?* The image was of Liv and a man, kissing and wrapped in a tight embrace. Liv didn't seem much older than when she disappeared in 1968, but nothing about her resembled the mother Genevieve remembered. As if straight out of Haight Ashbury, Liv's clothes rang "Hippie" from the garish striped bell-bottoms to the fringed vest, and a headband, wrapped tightly around her forehead. *I guess it would have made sense for her to join the anti-war movement and all the peace/ love of that Woodstock time period. Was that the beginning of her drug use? Free love?* When Genevieve turned the picture over, all it said was, '*Darren.*'

As Genevieve lifted the next one, it looked to be around the same time. It was a group picture of eight people, Liv being one of them as well as Darren, sitting next to her. All were dressed in similar garb. A joint was held in Liv's right hand while holding up a peace sign with other. One guy in the picture was holding some type of liquor that looked like whiskey. Everyone was either sitting on or around a beaten-up old couch, laughing. A big poster of Jimi Hendrix was on the wall behind them." Genevieve began feeling a tinge of anger. *While I was mourning her, she looked like she was having the time of her life.*

Then Genevieve's heart sank. The next photo was again of the same man, Darren. But this time he was standing alone, holding an infant in his arms. Genevieve just stared at the picture with a lump in her throat. *She started a new family.*

The last few pictures were only of a boy. They were all taken when the boy was young, the last one being maybe five or six years old. The first two were in black and white and had nothing written on the back. But the last one was in color and had the initials, *'DM'* on the backside.

Recalling a conversation, Genevieve had with her mother before Tess was born, the two were mulling over names, and Genevieve remembered her mother saying, "If you had been a boy, your father and I would have named you David Michael. That's what we've decided to name this baby if it's a boy. But what do you think of Teresa if it's a girl? We could call her Tess."

Did she finally have a son?

Twenty-seven years had passed since her mother left. So much more than the relatively short time Genevieve had known her. The pictures told a little of the story, but not enough. If Liv had finally found someone that made her happy enough to bear a child, since now Genevieve knew her mother never wanted children, then why? Why did she end up a homeless, forgotten drug addict?

With only more questions than answers, Genevieve decided it best, for the time being, to put the pictures back where she had found them. Gathering them up, she slid the stack back into the pouch when a cold object touched her finger. With her fingertip, Genevieve felt the slender rim of a small object and realized it was a ring. Lifting it out however was impossible, as Liv had *sewn* it into the pouch.

Quickly removing the pictures again, Genevieve opened the pouch as wide as she could. The ring appeared old, the stone was dark, but that was all she could discern without more light. Hurrying to the utility drawer, Genevieve grabbed a small flashlight and scissors. As she pointed the light into the pouch, Genevieve stopped breathing. It was a blue diamond ring, somewhere between one-half, and three-quarter carat, tied up inside, like a prisoner.

Aunt Melinda had made it a point, long ago, to teach both girls about the grading of diamonds; what to look for, as well as understand the secure investment of rare gems. Although it had fascinated Genevieve to learn how different one diamond could be from another, personally, there was never a desire to collect jewelry she knew she'd never wear. Genevieve had always been more of a relationship investor. But now, some of those she had invested heavily in, were, at best, unstable.

Cutting the thread so she could take a closer look, Genevieve took an educated guess that it was a rare, "fancy" diamond. With its radiant cut, the natural color saturation was deep, dark, and even. The crown was high, while the flat, table facet was small. Aunt Melinda used to wear a very similar one on special occasions and wore hers while their family portrait was being made, when Genevieve was thirteen.

After considering the intricate details of the antique gold setting and smooth, claw edges, Genevieve slowly closed her eyes. It *is* Aunt Melinda's ring. *Another lie. She said she never saw my mother again after that day at our house. But if that were true, then how did my mother get possession of this ring when Aunt Melinda was wearing the same one two years after that?*

Had the two been in contact all along?

CHAPTER 36

A CONFUSED
SENSE OF SELF

GENEVIEVE FELT NUMB. She was past tears, past anger. The day had utterly devoured her. There were too many questions to contemplate. Lies seemed to be growing, and all Genevieve wanted to do was go upstairs and be held by Teddy.

Putting everything back in the pouch, then in the box, Genevieve set the cardboard container in the kitchen corner and went upstairs.

As she opened the door, the room glowed softly with only the small lamp on Teddy's nightstand to illuminate it. Propped up, he had fallen asleep with his reading glasses still on, a land proposal laying on his bare chest. With a resigned shrug, Genevieve removed the papers and glasses. As she began to leave for the bathroom, Teddy reached for her hand, "I've been waitin for ye."

Genevieve turned and looked at him. His penetrating blue eyes implored answers to the mystery box, but Genevieve didn't want to talk. She wanted to *feel* the kind of love her mother had craved.

Without either of them saying another word, Genevieve stood next to the bed and took her clothes off. Her facial expression was far from playful, almost desperate in nature. Coming to lay next to him, she whispered, "I'm sorry for everything I put you through today." A faint smile appeared on Teddy's face. Reaching over and untying the string on Teddy's pajama pants, Genevieve breathed, "I need you."

Genevieve's lovemaking was out of character, more forceful than usual, and Teddy wondered what spurred her to try something they had never done before. Nevertheless, he happily obliged, keeping words to a minimum since they only got him in trouble anyway.

When they were through, Genevieve pulled herself tight next to her lover, her arm wrapped snuggly over his mid-section, holding on as if she was afraid he might escape. Twenty minutes went by, and Teddy knew Genevieve was still awake as he felt the flutter of her eyelashes as they brushed against his chest each time she blinked.

Taking a chance that she might want to talk, Teddy murmured, "Whaever ye discovered doon there, it will nivvor change wha we have, love. I may not *understand* ye sometimes…"

Without moving, Genevieve interrupted with barely a whisper, "What makes you stay with me, Teddy?"

Teddy lifted Genevieve's arm so they could face each other. He frowned when she seemed serious. "Where's this all comin from, Gen.?"

Genevieve's eyes glazed over. "My mother did everything she could to make a man love her. She was beautiful, desirable, and did everything she thought would make them happy, yet she died alone and in pain. I *know* I am more than a handful at times. So, why was I blessed with someone like you?"

Teddy diverted from the question, and his eyes narrowed, "Wait, back up, *them*?"

Genevieve closed her eyes. "I found pictures. It looks like she had another family, once.

Teddy was silent for a minute, contemplating the possibility, then shrugged, "Maybe she thought there'd be a different outcome the next time. But, Gen, there was somethin tha caused your mum to have her obsessive behavior with your fatha. I'm sure it wouldn't just disappear. She needed help. She *needed* to stay put in tha hospital. Obsession isn't love—it kills love. Ye aren't *anythin* like your mum!"

Genevieve laid her arm, relaxed now, on Teddy's chest again. Within moments she began her habit of tapping her fingers on his skin. It was after one in the morning, but Genevieve's fingers were an indication her mind hadn't turned off. Since the pictures sounded intriguing anyway, Teddy inquired, "So, did the photos reveal anythin else?"

Ironic choice of words, Genevieve thought. She told him about all the pictures she found in the cloth pouch, except the nude of her mother. After a short pause she added, "I also caught my aunt in another lie."

Teddy squeezed his eyes tight. He had hoped the pictures would, if anything, absolve Melinda of her subjective misdeeds. Hesitantly he asked, "Somethin ye saw in the pictures?"

"No. She told me she had no contact with my mother through all these years. But when I was putting the photos away tonight, I found, sewn in the corner of the pouch, the blue diamond ring Aunt Melinda cherished. The one she was wearing when our family portrait was done, two *years* after my mother had left!"

Teddy's frown reappeared, "Ye really need talk to your aunt. There probably is a reasonable explanation. Besides, why would she give the ring to your mum anyway?"

"I don't know," Genevieve grumbled. "It's very valuable. Maybe it was to pay her off to stay away. All I know is I'm afraid if I see my aunt again, I may say something I'll regret. I just need time and distance to sort things out."

Teddy didn't believe Melinda would be so calculating. He had known the Teels for twenty years now, and their altruistic behavior had no pretense. They used their money and status to do more for others than anyone he had ever known. As much as Teddy wanted to talk to Melinda directly, Genevieve would see it as another intrusion and mistrust. There was enough of that going around already.

Turning to lay face to face, nothing else needed discussing. Bringing Genevieve close, Teddy put his arm around her waist, and within minutes, both finally drifted off to sleep.

Hearing some muffled commotion downstairs, Genevieve woke to see that Teddy was up. Looking at the clock, she saw it was almost ten in the morning. As Genevieve laid in bed, she knew the kids would want to know what she found in the box. She just hoped they wouldn't question the mysterious reason Melinda wanted only Genevieve to look at its contents. There were two things she wouldn't show them—obviously, the provocative picture of her mother, and also the ring. No matter what Aunt Melinda's intentions were, they had nothing to do with Broc and Ella. Their relationship with their grandparents was beautiful and genuine. Genevieve wasn't about to take that away from *any* of them.

Sitting on the edge of the bed, Genevieve realized she wasn't sure she even wanted to know about her mother's other life, anymore. Would there be anything to gain by looking for Darren and his son?

There were only two days left to spend as a family before Ella was back to college. Deciding to pretend the previous day never happened, Genevieve got ready and came down to meet the family in the kitchen as her old cheerful self. With great relief, everyone played along, ignoring the elephant sitting in the corner of the room.

After breakfast had finished, Genevieve looked at Teddy and winked. "I'm sure there must be a football game on soon, so, Ella and I will join the masses and head for the mall once again."

Extremely surprised by the suggestion, Ella jumped from her seat and wrapped her arms around her mom. "Thank God, Mom! I'll gladly take insanely long lines over watching grown men plow *insanely* into each other for hours on end."

Teddy and Broc turned toward each other, smiled broadly and nodded.

CHAPTER 37

NIGHTMARES

FOUR MONTHS LATER.

"Why aren't you listening to me?"

Genevieve squirmed in her sleep. In her dream, she had been trying in vain to hide from Lucy. But no matter which room she ran to, Lucy was already there, her disfigured face showing hurt and sadness for Genevieve's refusal to let her come close. "You can't hide from me, Genevieve, I'll stay until you listen to me."

Genevieve had never felt fear for Lucy while she was alive, but she did now. She knew why Lucy was there, haunting her. She wanted to touch Genevieve; to make her feel the pain and loneliness once again. Scurrying from one dark corner to another the feeling of unworthiness was closing in, no matter how hard Genevieve tried to outrun it.

As Genevieve cowered in the darkness of a frightening, dilapidated old wood cottage, she watched helplessly as Lucy moved in. However, with every step closer, Lucy was transforming. By the time she was within reach of Genevieve, Lucy had become the beautiful, shapely belly dancer of her past. When her hand touched Genevieve, the only feeling pulsating through her was forgiveness.

Tears escaped Genevieve's sleeping eyes as the dream continued. "I don't know how to do that, Lucy. Everything that has happened to me seems unforgivable."

Lucy looked puzzled. "Genevieve, pay attention!" As Lucy reached to touch Genevieve again, the nuance of redemption was felt, making Genevieve tremble. Then Lucy whispered, "You can't possibly forgive them before you forgive yourself."

Genevieve bristled and wiped away an angry tear, "It wasn't *me* that did anything wrong!"

As Lucy lifted her hand away and began to fade, she echoed, "It's only true if you believe it, Genevieve."

Gasping, Genevieve's eyes flew open. It was pitch dark in the bedroom. She could feel her heart racing; her body was clammy and cold. *It was just another dream, Genevieve. It's wasn't real!*

Rolling to her side Genevieve knew, although she couldn't see it, the box with Liv's belongings was lurking in the corner, next to her nightstand. She had moved it several times over the past months, not ready to store it away out of sight just yet. Closing her eyes Genevieve pondered, *Is seeing the box regularly bringing on these dreams, or is it the dreams that keep me from letting the container and everything inside it, go?*

Genevieve had had three dreams so far since she discovered the truth about her mother. The first was of Liv, chasing Genevieve through a labyrinth made of thick, tall rosebushes which had no blooms, and were laden with sharp thorns. Every time Liv got close to Genevieve, the bush nearest to Genevieve would reach out and prick her. Although no blood resulted, the merciless jabs repeatedly made her wince. Eventually, picking up the pace, Genevieve ran until she couldn't see her mother anymore. Yet, she couldn't escape her mother's voice calling from within the maze, "Don't leave me this way, Genevieve. You'll be sorry if you do!"

In the second dream, Genevieve went to the estate to ask for Aunt Melinda's forgiveness. When Aunt Melinda opened the door, she looked right through Genevieve as if she wasn't there. As Genevieve pleaded with her aunt to let her back into her life, Melinda said nothing—heard nothing. With a puzzled look on her face, Melinda finally took one last look around, then, slowly closed the door. As Genevieve pounded on the door, screaming for her aunt, the dream abruptly ended.

Fumbling in the dark for her dream journal that was now always kept nearby, Genevieve took it and quietly went downstairs to write down what she could remember of her latest dream. Each one seemed symbolic in nature: abandoning her mom in a sort of limbo. Losing her aunt's love and feeling as if she didn't exist to her, and now the dream of Lucy. *What does all this mean? Running, hiding, being invisible? I sometimes wish I could do all these things; escape from everything that haunts me. If I go to California what will I find? Will doing it save my sanity somehow? Is redemption still possible? It's too late to show my mother the compassion she sorely needed, and my aunt, she's probably disowned me by now.*

As Genevieve thumbed through the worn book, she began re-reading dreams that she had forgotten. There was one she had journaled over a year prior, in which she was standing at a gravesite. It was a windy day, and the large brimmed hat Genevieve was wearing blew off her head and got caught in the forceful breeze, bouncing and rolling toward a young man standing a fair distance away from her. He grabbed the hat and held it out for her. Smiling, Genevieve walked over to him. The gentleman never uttered a word, but as he handed her the hat with a nod, she saw something familiar in his features, the certain way he smiled—the way his eyes looked at her.

The dream ended with the mystery man walking over and kneeling at the same grave Genevieve had been visiting.

Closing her eyes, Genevieve tried to recall the features of the man more clearly. But too much time had passed now. All that was left were notes that, at the time, she had felt held the most meaning.

Rubbing her tired eyes, Genevieve closed the book and chuckled to herself. *I have a feeling these dreams are going to continue, aren't they, Lucy? You'll make sure of that. I never realized how pushy you could be.* Then, closing her eyes, Genevieve added, *or how much you must care.*

The next morning after Teddy was at work and Broc had gone to school, Genevieve decided to relook at the items and pictures in the box, acknowledging she had nothing else to do anyway. Brunner was on a special assignment in Las Vegas, so Genevieve had plenty of time to herself. No words had been spoken between Genevieve and her aunt or uncle. Still, through the Broc and Teddy grapevine, the three had a gist of each other's goings-on. As time had passed, reconciliation seemed less likely. But it didn't change the fact that the gaping hole in Genevieve's life was agonizing.

The only way to escape the purgatory Genevieve was in was to begin the search. The first step was reexamining everything in the box again. Then, hopefully, Genevieve would find clues she had missed, before starting on a journey that seemed to be beckoning her.

After filling a large cup of hot coffee, Genevieve took it and went upstairs. Putting the steamy cup next to her journal, she picked up the box from the corner and placed it on the bed, hesitantly staring at it for a minute before opening the lid.

The smell hadn't dissipated much. Genevieve's first thought was, *Who was this stranger I once called Mom?* Trying to stay focused, Genevieve took the pictures out of the sweatshirt and spread them out over the bed. The "hippy" pictures had been taken so long ago there was no way to know precisely when or where they had been taken. But when Genevieve took another long look at the picture of Darren holding an infant in his arms, she studied the surroundings better. The photo had been taken on the sidewalk in front of a small, modest house with a chain-link fence. The window had Christmas lights around it and a holiday wreath decorated the door. Putting on her amateur detective hat, Genevieve deduced, "So, assuming the child's name is David Michael, it looks like he was born during the Christmas holiday, within a few years after Mother disappeared."

There was a small sign next to the door. Genevieve strained to make out the words but couldn't. Knowing Teddy's reading glasses worked like a magnifying glass, she grabbed his spare pair and glared at the picture again. The sign was either an address or a name. The first symbol looked like an 8 or possibly the letter B. The next was either an I or the number 1, and the third was an S or a 5. Genevieve shook her head in mild frustration as she thought, *You've got to be kidding me!* With Darren's head blocking the rest of the sign, it resulted in either BIS or 815.

While Genevieve peered down at the mishmash of clothes, her eye caught a glimpse of the scarf buried towards the bottom. Pulling it out, she remembered it had letters on it. *D B.* Picking up the photo again, Genevieve speculated, *If the sign were letters, then maybe Darren's last name starts with Bis? Still, even if I've got this much correct, it's very little to go on. Where do I start?*

Genevieve laid the picture down and lifted the picture of the child—the one that was in color. *Hazel eyes. Exactly like Mom's.*

Supposing her mother headed to California, where? Darren and his son could be anywhere in the large state or could have even moved to another by now. But Liv was found in L.A. As Genevieve glared at the box, she saw the cover stamped with "Los Angeles Police Department, Central District." The evidence sticker said it was "Case 15699." The officer listed was "Sean Kirpatrick." As for the location, it had "Rueter Street Underpass" scribbled with a black marker.

I guess I'll see if Officer Kirpatrick is in today.

Dialing information, Genevieve asked the operator for the phone number of the Los Angeles Police Department, Central District. Then she took a deep breath and waited.

CHAPTER 38

A GUT FEELING

As the phone rang, Genevieve's heart was pounding.

"Hello, Central District. How may I direct your call?"

"Hello. Do you have an officer by the name Sean Kirpatrick working at the precinct?"

No other response followed except, "I'll transfer you now."

One, two, three, four. At the fifth buzz, Genevieve began to hang up when she heard, "Kirpatrick here."

"Hello, officer. My name is Genevieve Walker. A few months ago, you found my mother by an underpass. She had hazel eyes and brown hair. She was a drug addict."

As Genevieve uttered the words aloud, emotions swelled in her throat, and she had to pause a moment before continuing. "I had thought she died when I was a young girl, but when you called my aunt, I found out she had been alive all this time. Unfortunately, she died shortly after you found her, and now I'm trying to find out what I can about the people who may have been close to her. I thought a good place to start would be with you."

The officer cleared his throat. "Was this the homeless woman over near Rueter?"

Genevieve smiled. "Yes! So, you remember. I have the box of belongings you sent with her, but is there anything else you might remember? Was she with anyone? Do you think I might find more information about her if I go to the area in which you found her?"

The officer quickly replied. "No, please don't! Unfortunately, in the area I patrol, Rueter is where some of the most mentally ill, desperate drug addicts can be found. Dealers snake through there, in and out, all day looking for vulnerable prey. If someone can't pay for a fix, the dealer will find a "job" that can be done for payment instead. Crime often leads back to that damn underpass. It's patrolled several times a day *just* to try and keep things under control. We've done a number of sweeps in the past to clear that area. But every time, within days, they're migrating back. So, again, I wouldn't recommend nosing around in that area."

There was a slight pause, then the office continued. "Normally I wouldn't remember your mother from anyone else I pick up from that godawful place. Over-doses and serious health conditions come standard in that territory."

"But there was something that seemed to draw me to her that day. My partner and I had just broken up a fight, and before leaving, I decided to take a quick walk around. I discovered your mother on the edge of the scattered encampment. At first, I thought I was looking at a discarded mound of trash until I saw movement under some black plastic sheeting. When I lifted it, I could see her mumbling incoherently. She was shivering and had a high fever. She was wrapped in a soiled blanket, and her pants and shoes were gone. It may seem hard to believe, but most likely, someone stole those things from her at some point. The only thing she had on was some underwear and a sweatshirt. There was a trash bag with a few other items lying next to her.

"The reason I remember her so clearly is because when the paramedics arrived and put her on a gurney, she grabbed my hand, pulled me close, and whispered, "I love you Zeffran. I knew you'd find me."

Genevieve could feel the hair on her neck rise. "That was my father's name."

The officer paused, then said, "Ah… Well, Zeffran is my *legal* first name. I just go by my middle name, Sean." Letting out a chuckle the officer added. "It was just one of those bizarre things that have kept her on my mind, you know. Anyway, to answer your other question, no one seemed to be with her, at least no one came forward at the time to help, and no one seemed to know her name."

Genevieve whispered, "Liv, her name was Liv."

"Yes," The officer responded. "When I called the number on the back of an old picture, I luckily got a hold of her sister, and she told me. Nice lady, your aunt then?"

Genevieve could only utter a quiet, "Uh-huh."

Having the feeling that Genevieve didn't want to elaborate any further, the officer concluded, "Well, that's about all I can tell you, Ms. Walker. But if you want to start someplace around here, there's a place that a lot of the drug addicts and homeless go to get off the street and get a decent meal. I'm sure your mother would have gone there occasionally if she lived in the area for any length of time. It's worth a shot anyway. It's called the Bethlehem Refuge over on the corner of Sylvester and Blane. If you decide to go, ask for Legor. He's run the place for years and knows most the regulars, an amazing man! Maybe he can help you."

For the first time since the conversation began, Genevieve had hope that Legor or someone at the refuge might give her something new to go on.

"Can I help you with anything else then, Ms. Walker?"

"No, thank you very much for speaking with me, and thank you so much for being kind to my mother and helping her in her final hours."

Genevieve slowly put the phone down and stared at the picture of her mother, cheek to cheek with her father. *I guess no one ever truly replaced my father after all.*

Sitting for close to a half an hour lost in her thoughts, Genevieve jumped when the phone rang. "Hello?"

"Hey, love." Teddy sounded a little off.

"Hey back. Is there something wrong?"

There was a long pause, then Teddy asked, "Did ye see the news today?"

"No, I was talking this morning with the police officer who found my mother. He gave me a lead on where to start my search. Why, what was on the news?"

"Well, don't panic, but whaever Brunner was doin in Las Vegas got him shot."

"Oh, God, did they say what his condition is?"

"Before I called ye, I called the station. Brunner had just come oot of surgery. A bullet hit him in the leg, fracturing part of his right femur. They say he's in stable condition."

"Did the news go into detail as to what happened?"

"Naw, naw really. He and a bystander were hit. All they would say was it was a police sting tha went bad."

Genevieve looked at the clock. "If I leave now, I can be in Vegas by dinner time."

"Hold on, Gen. The detective is goin to be *fine*. He'll probably be back here in a couple of days."

Genevieve sounded uneasy. "I can't explain it, but when he left last week, I sensed something. I felt an urgency to go with him for some reason. My gut said go, but I knew the case didn't need my services, so I ignored the feeling. But now it's back Teddy, that urgency. Maybe he'll have a turn for the worse. Maybe I'm supposed to be there when…"

Teddy knew where she was headed. "Come on, Gen. He's doin fine. Look, if ye insist on makin the trip, I'm goin too. Once ye see for yourself, we can make a night of it, maybe even see a show. I'll pack up here and be home within the hour."

Returning everything to the box, Genevieve hastily placed it back in the corner and pulled out a suitcase.

Hoping they would be back the next day, she packed just enough for herself and Teddy for one night. By the time Teddy got home, Genevieve had called the school, talked to Broc and made arrangements with the Jergen's family for Broc to stay with them for the night. Hoping she remembered everything, Genevieve quickly packed a bag for Broc as well, which they dropped off on their way out of town.

CHAPTER 39

SOMETHING IS MISSING

ARRIVING INTO THE town that never sleeps, Teddy weaved in and out of the late afternoon commuter traffic, staying clear of the strip, toward Centennial Hills Hospital, north of the downtown's Fremont area, where the shooting had occurred.

The sun was still beating down by late afternoon, but at 80 degrees, it was comfortable enough. When they arrived at the hospital, Genevieve could see in the distance, high-rise casinos and large cranes that were assisting in building, or in some cases replacing, the older "Rat Pack" type casinos.

She had been reading about the Vegas goings-on lately, in Ella's favorite magazine, G.E.N., the acronym for Great Entertainment News. Although aware of the abbreviation now, when Ella was little, Teddy told her the magazine was all about her mother, Gen. Genevieve was so amused when she saw Ella's face light up, that she and Teddy let Ella believe it was real until at about six years old, Ella eventually figure it out on her own.

Now Ariella had her own subscription, and the order went to her parent's address. Then when Ella came home, she'd binge on all the happenings in the entertainment world. But in the meantime, as the periodicals piled up on the Walker's kitchen counter, Genevieve's inquiring mind would occasionally have a look inside.

As the car entered the parking structure, obscuring Genevieve's view, thoughts of the new and improved, family-friendly Vegas, popped like a balloon from her mind. By the time the two had reached the hospital lobby, Genevieve's gut feeling was back, telling her she was right where she was meant to be.

Now that Brunner was deemed stable, the woman at the reception desk said he had been moved to a private room. When Genevieve and Teddy entered his room on the second floor, Jazmine was already there, sitting by her husband who seemed to be sleeping. Surprised to see the Walkers, she got up and greeted each with a gentle embrace.

Whispering, Genevieve asked, "Is he really going to be okay?"

Jazmine smiled and began to say, "He's going to be…" when Brunner opened one eye and peered over at his new visitors, interrupting his wife in mid-sentence.

"Ah, so you thought if you hurry, you might get a good secret or two from my Soul before I croak, huh? Sorry darlin, I just got nicked. Didn't quite get out of the way in time."

Seeing how taken aback Genevieve was by the detective's callous remark, Brunner blinked slowly and snickered, "Geez! I was just teasing! Come here. I know you want to hug me."

Genevieve's expression changed slightly as she turned to Teddy with a wry smile, "The man is so full of himself!"

Walking over to the bed, Genevieve bent down and hugged Brunner. Noticing his hand resting at his side, Genevieve touched it while Teddy moved next to her, and gave Brunner a solid nod, saying, "I'm glad ye are okay, Brunner."

Genevieve quickly noticed that Brunner was presenting a happy face, but inside she felt a profusion of contrary emotions. Anger, confusion, and anxiety were expected. But she could feel a strong sense of sadness. *Why sad?*

After a little idle chit-chat, Brunner's dinner tray arrived. With the initial relief that the detective's death was not imminent, Genevieve and Teddy headed to the cafeteria to eat as well, promising to bring Jazmine a sandwich upon their return.

The two sat down at an empty table with the Special-of-the-day: Chicken enchiladas, rice, and rather watery refried beans. Genevieve's mind was elsewhere, picking at her meal while staring at it with a distracted frown on her face.

Teddy didn't seem to notice, however. After quickly devouring one of the two enchiladas on his plate and most the rice and beans, he glanced up and said reassuringly, "I told ye he was fine, Gen."

Genevieve shook her head. "There's something I'm missing. I felt a lot of sadness coming from him, and that gut feeling I've been having isn't going away."

"Maybe he's just sad the bust or sting or whaever, didn't go as planned."

"No, it felt more personal, like a heartache."

Teddy looked at Genevieve and tipped his head to the side. "Everythin okay with the Chao's marriage as far as ye know?"

"Yes, I'm as sure as I can be. No, I don't think it's about Brunner necessarily. Maybe when we get back, I can find out more."

With Teddy's plate now clean, he was eyeing Genevieve's almost untouched dish of lukewarm food. Genevieve watched him stare at her enchiladas as if they might grow legs and take off if he were to look away. Pushing the plate slowly across the table, she saw a dimpled smile appear on his face. With narrowed eyes, Genevieve concluded, "You never ate lunch today, did you?"

Teddy shook his head. "I thought I'd grab somethin when I got home. But when ye were standin at the door with the suitcases, I forgot all aboot it in the rush to leave. Ye go ahead, Gen. I might look for some dessert after I finish this off. I'll get somethin for Jazmine too, on my way back."

Genevieve got up, walked behind Teddy, and wrapped her arms around him, whispering, "You're awfully cute with all that enchilada sauce around your mouth." Then smiling, she kissed him on his head, handed him a napkin, and headed back to Brunner's room.

While Teddy wiped his mouth, he began studying the desserts in the display case, not far from his table. *Cheesecake—aye! My favorite, no mess dessert.*

CHAPTER 40

CAN'T STOP HER NOW

WHEN GENEVIEVE ARRIVED back at Brunner's room, a fellow detective Genevieve had never seen before was talking to him. Jazmine was sitting at the end of the bed, listening quietly to their conversation. Genevieve stayed outside the room for a few minutes until the man had left. Then, peeking inside, she asked, "Is it okay if I enter?"

Brunner signaled her in with a wave of his hand. Both Brunner and Jazmine had somber faces, but then the detective forced a smile. "How was dinner? Did you get the same mushy enchiladas they gave me?"

Genevieve looked at Jazmine, who flashed a quick, brief smile.

Bringing her focus back to Brunner, Genevieve coaxed, "Is everything okay? I don't mean to pry, but if I can help, please let me know."

Brunner dropped the smile and looked at Genevieve. "How much do you know about what went on today?"

Genevieve looked down and to the right as she tried to recall everything Teddy had told her. "I didn't know anything until Teddy called around noon-time. He said he caught your name on the news. That you and someone else had been hit by gunfire in a sting operation, that's all."

Brunner nodded. "Yea, that's the typical news blurb. Everything is being looked at under a microscope right now, so I can't tell you the whole story. What I *can* say, is that I was assisting in this operation because an infor-mant of mine had given me information that led me here. There was to be an important meeting at nine this morning. It was going to be at an obscure diner with just my informant, and a 'person of interest.'

"Two local detectives, myself, and my informant were parked in a sedan two blocks away. Just before nine, I opened the door to let him out when a car drove by, spraying bullets everywhere. I dove back into the car but got hit in the leg. Someone *had* to have tipped them off. They knew exactly where we were parked."

Genevieve listened intently but was still confused. "So…this feeling of sadness you have, it's because the shooter got away? I understand the frustration and anger, but…" Genevieve shook her head slowly.

Brunner stared at Genevieve for several moments, then said. "The other person hit was a young girl, well young woman, just twenty-two years old, simply walking to work. She was at the wrong place, wrong time. She's here, in I.C.U., but they don't expect her to live much longer. She was hit twice, in the chest and abdomen. The detective that just left, came by to let me know her condition."

Genevieve hadn't thought about the *other* person and wondered, *Is she the reason I'm here?* "Brunner, do you know who she is? Is she alone?"

Brunner slowly shook his head. "You know how I am with names, Gen. But I do remember him calling her Daisy something". Giving his wife a smile, he continued, "I only remember *that,* because it's Jaz's favorite flower. Do you remember any of the other details, Jaz?"

Jazmine frowned. "I'm sorry, no, not really, other than the officer said the woman had an I.D. badge that showed she worked at the Nugget Casino."

Brunner winced as he repositioned himself in bed, his leg heavily bandaged. Turning back to look at Genevieve he shrugged, "I really don't know anything else. Everything happened so fast, and it was so damn chaotic. Before I knew it, the paramedics were getting me ready for transport. As they wheeled me to the ambulance, I could hear another one heading off, sirens blaring. It wasn't until then I realized someone else had been hit. I never got a glimpse of the woman, before, during, *or* after."

Genevieve hesitated, "It may seem odd, but I think I'm supposed to see her."

Brunner snorted, "Don't make me laugh! It hurts my poor aching leg. Ms. Walker, you have to know I'm way beyond seeing anything you do as odd—not after all these years. Your *'odd'* my friend, is what I depend on."

Jazmine nodded in agreement.

Knowing it might even do some good, Brunner encouraged Genevieve, "If you think you're supposed to see the woman, then you probably should."

Genevieve smiled at both Brunner and Jazmine then turned toward the door. But there, leaning against the wall, with a Styrofoam "to-go" container in his hand, was Teddy.

Walking over, Genevieve mouthed, "Thank you" to her husband, took the container and handed it to Jazmine. Then grabbing Teddy's arm, Genevieve instructed, "We have one more stop to make."

While opening the door for his wife, Teddy turned to Jazmine. "There's some cheesecake in there too. Ye may want to start with tha. It's by far the best part."

Before the door closed, Brunner called out, "Hey, thanks for coming! Don't be a stranger now, *and don't get into any trouble!*"

Genevieve popped her head back in and winked. "Who, me? I'll be seeing you both later, and again, Mr. Chao, I'm over the moon that you're going to be okay."

Walking up to the elevator, Genevieve quizzed Teddy, "So, do you know where we're headed?"

Teddy quickly replied, "I do, I came in just when Brunner told ye aboot the lass gettin shot. I.C.U., it's two floors up."

Reaching to push the elevator "up" button, Genevieve began to feel nervous. "I've never done this before, Teddy. I mean, I've always been asked by the police or a loved one to reach the Soul before it departs. What if I'm supposed to know something and a relative tells me I can't see her?"

As the elevator door opened, they stepped in. It was just the two of them, alone, for the short ride up. "If ye are supposed to do this, everythin will fall into place. Ye know tha betta than anyone."

Genevieve was hesitant. "I guess. But this time it feels different, more crucial. Maybe she knows more about the crime than anyone knew? Who is she, really?" Genevieve took a deep sigh.

When the doors opened, Genevieve realized they needed to check in at the nurse's desk first. Since they were total strangers to Daisy and her family, if anyone was with her, how would she explain why she was there? Thinking fast, Genevieve needed to improvise. Stopping Teddy just outside the elevator door, she said in a hushed tone, "I'm going to have to pretend I'm here on police business if I have a chance of seeing Daisy. Stay here. If I get the okay to see her, I'll wave you in. Hopefully, they won't notice you following me!"

"But Gen, she's u n c o n s c i o u s. Wha are ye goin to say to the nurse, 'I need to speak with the victim's Soul?' "

Genevieve shook her head. "Ye of little faith. My assumption is that there is at least someone she loves with her right now. I'll tell the nurse I just came to check on the family and let them know the police department is doing all they can to find the shooter. If the nurse is still skeptical, I know Brunner will back me up."

Teddy watched his wife straighten up and confidently walk to the nurse's station, immediately addressing a nurse sitting at a computer. Being too far away to hear the conversation, he watched Genevieve reach into her purse and pull out a business card as if it was just another day at work. Teddy couldn't help but grin at his wife's tenacity.

After a few moments, the nurse picked up the phone and called someone. Genevieve looked at Teddy with raised eyebrows while strummed her fingers on the counter in front of her. After the nurse hung up the phone, she pointed to a room just past the elevators. With a nod, Genevieve headed toward Daisy's room, rolling her eyes at Teddy as she passed, signaling him to follow.

Peering at the nurse, Teddy noticed she had quickly resumed starring at her computer, so, trying to be as stealthy as he could, he shadowed, or, more like hovered, behind Genevieve as she strutted down the hall. Still keeping a watch over his shoulder to make sure the nurse wasn't glancing their way, Teddy didn't realize Genevieve had stopped abruptly outside Daisy's room and stepped on her heel.

"Ouch!" Genevieve winced. Then, with panicked eyes, she quickly turned and put her index finger to her lips so Teddy wouldn't say anything. Cupping her hand over Teddy's ear, Genevieve whispered, "There *is* a man sitting next to her, holding her hand. It's probably her husband or boyfriend."

Teddy nodded affirmative.

The two moved closer to the door.

Genevieve watched the young man, trying to figure out how to approach him. Within a minute, however, Genevieve and Teddy turned to each other, speechless.

Finally, Teddy murmured, "This goes *way* beyond any gut feelin!"

CHAPTER 41

UNCANNY

GENEVIEVE WATCHED THE young man as if she was watching herself. With his eyes closed and hand holding tightly to Daisy's, his facial expressions changed from smiling to shaking his head in confusion. Soon, a stifled laugh escaped followed by deep sharp breaths that Genevieve knew was the ecstasy felt when love coming from the Soul is so overpowering, one can hardly breathe.

Looking at Teddy in utter amazement, Genevieve slowly entered the room. It was dark, with only the light of the monitors, and the outside hall for illumination. The beeping sound of Daisy's heartbeat was slowing down.

The man put his head on the bed, and Genevieve heard him whisper, "I know, but how is this happening?" There was a long pause, and he began to laugh and cry at the same time.

Daisy's heartbeat got slower.

He opened his eyes slightly but didn't notice Genevieve, just the dying woman in front of him. The mysterious man brought Daisy's hand to his lips as he stared at her. Tears began to flow down his cheeks as he choked out, "I wish I had understood all this earlier—known those emotions were yours and not mine. Then I *never* would have let you leave."

As Daisy's heart was about to stop, the young man closed his eyes again. Within a few moments, his head tilted up, and Genevieve knew the Soul was departing. She watched him mouth, "I love you too."

The monitor fell silent. Genevieve wiped a tear away while thinking, *This was his first time.*

With a flashing memory, Genevieve relived her first 'Soul' encounter with the little girl, Chrissy. Remembering her own guilt, sadness, and confusion, but also the redemption in understanding there was finally a purpose behind feeling other people's emotions. Beyond it all, however, nothing compared to the rapture felt by the unspeakable love of the Soul.

As the young man brought his head back down and wiped his wet face, Genevieve realized he had just discovered everything it had taken her years to know. He now understood the confused feelings were someone else's emotions, not his own, something Genevieve hadn't learned until holding her infant, Ella. At the same time, he also found the purpose behind it, saving him years of turmoil, not understanding the *why* behind it all.

There was one distinct difference in this first Soul encounter. Chrissy had survived, this woman had not. A heavy thought crossed Genevieve's mind, *Was her death a self-sacrifice to show this man his ability, like Chrissy's spirit was willing to do for me?*

Just then, two nurses came in, turning the lights on. It was protocol to physically check the body and pronounce the time of death.

That was when the young man noticed Genevieve and Teddy standing near the door. Genevieve's heart began to race, expecting him to feel, at the very least, violated to see complete strangers intruding on such a personal, heart-wrenching moment.

Instead, after staring at her for several moments through bloodshot, blurry eyes, the man slowly got up and walked closer, until he was just a foot away from Genevieve's face.

"You're Genevieve," he quietly uttered."

Genevieve frowned in confusion. *How could he...* Then, she studied his face. *Mom's hazel eyes.*

With everything in the room now clearly visible, Genevieve looked at the hospital board on the adjacent wall that gave current details of each I.C.U. patient. At the top it read, Name: Daisy Bishop.

Genevieve's eyes widened, and she took a sharp breath as she thought, *Bishop. It was letters, not numbers, BIS...BISHOP!* With a shiver running down her spine, Genevieve whispered, "Are you, David Bishop?

The man seemed baffled by the question, since it was Genevieve, after all, that somehow had found *him*. With a trembling lip, he nodded. "Mom told me about you once, not long before she left my father and me, when I was young. After she was gone, I found an old picture of you that she had left behind. It had 'Genevieve' written on the back. I guess you were about seven or eight? I would study it as a kid, wondering where you lived, always hoping to meet you one day." David paused and stared at Genevieve's misty eyes. "But now, seeing you and those emerald green eyes—I just knew it had to be you."

He put his arms out, welcoming Genevieve in an embrace. As they pulled tight to one another, both began to cry. Genevieve felt an overwhelming flood of emotions coming from David, many mirroring her own.

The nurses had finished turning off the heart monitor as well as the I.V. pump that had been administering several strong pain medications to Daisy. Quietly leaving, one told David he could stay as long as he needed.

Teddy, still standing by the door, shook his head in confused awe at the chain of events that had just occurred. Still not sure how Genevieve knew the young man's name, he was confident both he *and* David would be enlightened very soon.

Deciding to give the two siblings time to acclimate to their new circumstance, Teddy motioned to Genevieve he'd be back soon and headed to Brunner's room. Once there, he explained how the detective's investigating journey, and the subsequent shooting that morning, had all been an integral part in an elaborate, other-worldly orchestration. Not only had it brought two lost siblings together, but also the discovery that they both had the same exact empathic ability!

When David and Genevieve released their hold on each other, Genevieve said, "So Daisy is your wife then."

David looked over at the still body. "Yes, well, our divorce was final just a month ago."

Even though Genevieve felt more emotions than even she could discern coming from David, she could only imagine what was swirling around in his head. The shocking death of his wife, a half-sister that shows up out of the blue, and then the revelation he just discovered about himself. Genevieve was unsure what to do or say next, as David seemed lost in thought while he continued to stare at his wife.

"David?"

David blinked out of his trance and looked at Genevieve. "Sorry, I'm just feeling very disoriented right now. It all seems so unreal."

Genevieve took David's hand. "If you'd like some more time alone with Daisy, I can wait outside."

David shook his head. "No. I can't really explain it to you, but I'm positive she's okay and that after everything we'd gone through, she truly loved me. It was something I didn't believe when she left last year. I just had the strangest experience a little while ago. I…" David shook his head and looked back at Daisy.

"Her Soul talked to you," Genevieve whispered.

David's eyes quickly shifted to Genevieve. "How would you know about that?" As David's brow furrowed, he asked, "Now that I think about it, how did you even find me, *here—and now?*"

CHAPTER 42

A COSMIC WORMHOLE

GENEVIEVE REACHED FOR David's hand. "Close your eyes."

David kept his frown but decided to oblige for the moment.

"Now, what do you feel that seems different," Genevieve quizzed.

With his eyes closed, David's frown slowly relaxed as he stood close to Genevieve, fingers interlocked. Soon he showed a hint of a smile, moments later it broadened."

Genevieve grinned. "Do you feel a giddy, joyfulness? A feeling that seems odd and out of place right now?"

With his eyes closed, his smile faded as he murmured, "Yes."

"What else do you feel?"

David stood silent, concentrating on Genevieve's question. Shrugging, he replied, "I feel lots of things."

Genevieve clarified, "What feeling seems strange, even dominating others you've been having?"

David took a deep cleansing breath, letting it out impatiently while tipping his head from side to side. Genevieve closed her eyes too, concentrating on the emotion she wanted David to recognize.

David's face made all kinds of contortions, trying to siphon out what seemed foreign from his own feelings. Then his eyes opened as he peered at Genevieve. "It's a feeling of protection, almost obsessive protection."

Genevieve smiled and opened her eyes. "Good."

David blinked. "Good? That's it? So, you have been doing this for a while I'm guessing. How did *you* find out about it? Are there others out there that can do this—thing?"

Letting go of David's hand, Genevieve turned to see that Teddy had just arrived. Nodding to her husband, Genevieve looked back to David, and confirmed, "I have a lot to talk to you about, more than you can imagine really. And there's so much I want to learn about you. But I know it's getting late. Do you have a place to stay?"

David shook his head. "As soon as I got the call, I drove straight here from Riverside."

Genevieve questioned, "Riverside, California?"

David nodded.

Genevieve's heart skipped a beat, knowing she would have been headed in the right direction. However, due to powers far beyond her understanding, a sort of wormhole had opened that saved her months if not years in finding her brother."

"David, this is my husband, Teddy." The two men gave each other a quick nod and cordial handshake.

"Teddy and I don't live here either. As wild as this sounds, I happen to work with the other person who was shot in the gunfire today. My husband and I rushed here after hearing what happened from our home in Scottsdale."

David's eyes widened. "No! That's quite a coincidence, wouldn't you say?"

Genevieve didn't believe in coincidences, but she needed to take baby steps with her brother, or she might risk scaring him away.

"Yes, quite an amazing turn of events," she responded. "You know, David, you probably have some calls to make, and you'll need to make arrangements for Daisy in the morning, so let's all find a place to stay for the night, okay?"

With a sudden look of exhaustion, David turned to Daisy. Her skin tone had begun to look ashen. He walked over and held her hand. "There's silence now. But I could *feel* the peace she felt, yet I'm still not understanding why. No one had the right to take her young life away like that. Why was she okay with it all?" David let go of his wife's hand and crossed his arms to his chest, trying his best to keep the anger and despair from overflowing.

Genevieve grabbed Teddy's hand and held tight as they looked at each other. Knowing and *understanding*, that a loved one has gone home in total peace, doesn't make the heartache any less for the ones left behind. Just entertaining such thoughts of Teddy tormented Genevieve, and she could feel similar feelings resonating within her husband as their gaze continued.

After a few moments, Genevieve turned to her brother, "David, you were right, I have been doing this for quite some time. But even now, I can't always know why a person had to die the way they did. The Soul has Its reasons, and I've learned to make peace with it because I have no say in the matter anyway."

Letting go of Teddy's hand, Genevieve walked over to David. "When I first realized I could communicate with the Soul, it was because of a precious child; one I knew and loved. She had been in a horrible accident. By that time, I had already discovered I could feel other people's emotions, which I'll tell you about later." Genevieve gave Teddy a faint smile

"Our friends, Chrissy's parents, knew about my ability and pleaded with me to relay the emotions their critical, unconscious daughter was feeling. I was petrified, but I did it anyway. I thought I was doing it for their sake, but what I learned that day, was that the entire accident had happened by design."

David shook his head, "I don't know what you mean by that."

Genevieve gathered a deep breath. "Nothing is worse than knowing you can feel someone's emotions but finding no purpose behind it. There were many times, especially when I first discovered my ability, that I would wear gloves. I was afraid of the dark and disturbing feelings that might be encountered when touching someone, even casually.

"Then, being asked to tune-in to feelings I was positive, in my mind, would be darker than any I'd ever encountered, almost paralyzed me. But Chrissy's Soul trusted I would come, that my love for her would win out. It was in that communication I found a calling, a reason for my ability. You see, David, the only way to communicate with the Soul is to touch a person who has fallen far from consciousness. Chrissy's Soul had been willing to sacrifice the life It inhabited, without any regret, just so I could understand what I was always meant to do, to communicate with the Soul."

David raised his eyes to the ceiling for several moments. Then his eyes became watery and he looked straight at Genevieve. "Are you trying to say that Daisy died, *sacrificed* herself to do the same for me?"

Knowing David's tenuous acceptance of his ability, Genevieve tried her best to tread carefully. "I'm not saying that. In my case, Chrissy eventually recovered. But that day, as she lay teetering between life and death, the Soul made Its' intentions clear. It did what was needed, no matter the consequence. I still don't understand it fully, even today, my worthiness, the Soul's unwavering faith in me and Its' *determination* to show me what I was able to do."

Genevieve shook her head as she implored David, "Whether or not that was the case with Daisy, you will probably never know. Nevertheless, the gift was given; an understanding you never knew before.

"It must have been torture not knowing why you'd feel such strange feelings from time to time. I know it was for me. However, before I learned the truth, I had no way of discerning the difference. There was no one to tell me that it *wasn't* normal. Daisy's Soul has now *told* you by the only way it communicates, through emotion! Maybe, just maybe, I was meant to be here too. Think about it. Who better to help you understand all that happened today than someone who's gone through it already? Do you still think it's a coincidence that that person was me?"

David squeezed his eyes closed and rubbed his forehead. "All I know is that I lost the love of my life today. I found a sister that I never thought I'd meet, and I've discovered something I guess God gave me, that I'm supposed to be happy about."

As his eyes opened, David wondered if Genevieve would be disappointed in his last remark. However, he only saw empathy on her face. Putting his hand on her shoulder, David said wearily, "If I can just get some sleep tonight, I'm sure things will make more sense in the morning."

Teddy stepped forward, "Aye, it's aboot midnight. Let's go doon and get the cars."

David grinned and raised his eyebrows, "Ah, a Scotsman! Love that Gaelic accent."

Genevieve smiled, "Me too, but it's a *Geordie* accent, and he's from Northern England.

Teddy just gave a sleepy grin and nodded.

CHAPTER 43

COMMISERATING

FINDING A HAMPTON Inn just a few blocks away, Teddy paid for two rooms for the night. However, he had an important meeting the following afternoon, so Teddy had no choice but to leave in the early morning if he was going to make it back in time.

Genevieve, however, had barely scratched the surface with her brother and needed time to get answers that only he could provide. Although Teddy offered to come back and get her, Genevieve reasoned it was better to rent a car for the ride home, whenever that would be.

After a quick breakfast, Teddy said his good-byes and headed back to Arizona. As Genevieve and David sat together afterward, Genevieve looked for similarities between David and herself which seemed only to be that his hair was dark brown and wavy like her own. He sported a popular cut that Mel Gibson wore; curly and longer along the top and back, shorter on the sides. His eyes were just like their mother's, but that was where all resemblances ended. David stood tall, taller than even Teddy, who was 6 feet 2 inches. Her brother was on the thin side, but well built, with an engaging smile and he wore a dental retainer.

Noticing that Genevieve was observing his mouth, David remarked, "I had terribly crooked front teeth. Dad never had the money to pay for braces, so, now that I've got a decent job, I'm taking care of that!"

Genevieve wanted to follow the "Dad" trail. It was an excellent lead-in to learning about David's life as a child. However, keeping the conversation on the lighter side seemed to be the way he preferred it, for now, so Genevieve continued to oblige for the time being.

"Oh, I hope I wasn't staring! I was just noticing what a nice smile you had. What type of work do you do, anyway?"

Taking a sip of coffee and placing it back on the table, he stated, "I'm a molecular scientist, well, with a good step in the door anyway. I received my bachelor's degree last spring, and I'm now working towards my masters. Last year I got an entry-level position at Raydon Labs. It's a fascinating line of work I have to say. Ever since I was a kid, I would watch shows like Ninja Turtles, Spiderman, even Star Trek, but I was more interested about how something inside changed a person, the science behind the story, ya know?"

Genevieve looked star-struck at her brother, always wondering if there might be a scientific reason behind her "gift." Now, maybe, she might get the answer, especially if David were curious enough to explore his newfound ability. *Could it be a genetic thing?* She wondered.

David continued to talk about his passion for cell genetics and mutations when he stopped abruptly, and his demeanor became sullen.

"But like anything, there needs to be a balance in your life. I kept feeling like I was failing, that I wasn't giving my all. *I thought* it was about my work and studies. But no matter how much time I spent on them the feeling kept coming back, especially at night, and I felt tremendous anxiety."

David looked down at his coffee cup as his finger moved slowly around the rim. "Now I know they weren't *my* feelings, but Daisy's. Yesterday I learned those were the feelings *she* had for *me*, that no matter what she did, it was never enough. She finally gave up on us and moved here for a fresh start." Looking painfully at Genevieve, David asked, "How could I not know that?"

Genevieve felt it was time to tell him about her early life; the confusing emotions she felt when around her mother, and how she finally discerned the differences, holding newborn baby Ella for the first time.

"You see, David, it took an extraordinary event to realize I was different from other people. We all are very similar otherwise with feelings we all have in common. How could you have known? Just like me, it took an unmistakable event to show you differently!"

David's lips turned down as he shook his head, eyes still transfixed on his finger as it continued its umpteenth rotation around the coffee cup. "So, what about our mother? I mean, she must have been an empath as well, don't you think?" Finally prying his eyes away, David looked at Genevieve who just shrugged and shook her head.

Having no answer to that mystery, David decided to ask Genevieve about another one that had haunted him for years. "I always supposed that Mother went back to you and your sister after she left my father and me. Was that what happened?"

Genevieve took David's hand away from the coffee cup and held it tight in her own. She could feel her tears welling up as the emotions she was receiving from her brother were all too familiar.

Tipping her head to the side, Genevieve gave him a gentle smile, "Aw, David—no, she never came back to us."

David's chin slightly trembled as he nodded to Genevieve. She could feel a sad sort of relief settle within him.

Genevieve spent the next hour talking about her father's death and mother's supposed suicide, leaving her crushed and guilt-ridden. Then, she went on to explain how her aunt and uncle took her and little sister, Tess home with them, "...becoming the kind of family I had never known. I always believed our mother to be dead..." Genevieve held her gaze on her brother, "...until about five months ago."

David frowned. "She came to see you?"

Genevieve's eyes didn't move but became glazed and distant as she remembered the shock of seeing her mother's almost unrecognizable face as she pulled the sheet back in the hospital. "No, not really."

"What does that mean, not really?"

Genevieve shook off the memory and studied David's face, hoping he was up for another punch to the gut. "She came back, yes, but only because my aunt, her sister, brought her back—so Aunt Melinda could be near, as Mom died."

David sat silently, eyes darting from left to right as it sunk in. "She's dead?"

Genevieve, still holding his hand, felt her brother's utter disbelief. She explained the day she found her mother in the hospital—the confusion, lies, betrayal, and the missed opportunity to feel her mother's underlying love for her, just once before she died.

David blinked. "How could they do that to you?"

Genevieve gave a slight shrug, "You don't know how many times I've asked myself that question. I haven't talked to my aunt since I found out. She was the one that I loved and trusted in everything. I don't know how to reconcile our relationship now. That's why…"

David waited silently for several moments before finally raising his eyebrows, *"And?"*

"The only way I'll ever make peace with my aunt and my uncle's part in allowing the deception, is to understand my mother and what happened to her. She was found dying by a police officer as he made his rounds at a homeless encampment in central L.A. She was a drug addict, dying from years of abuse and other diseases that were never treated."

David nodded. "I can't say I'm surprised. When I was young, my parents had some wild parties. I was always sent next door where an older couple looked after me. One night, when I was about six, I heard screaming coming from my house during one of those parties. People began scrambling as an ambulance arrived. I didn't find out until the next morning that Mother had overdosed."

Genevieve shook her head in empathy as David continued. "She lived of course, but things changed after that. Dad started going to meetings and stopped using altogether. He tried to get Mother help, but she refused. She started spending more time away from home, until one day she just never came back. Dad seemed to know something because when I wanted to look for her, he said it was no use, that she chose to leave."

Genevieve was staring at her hands, now folded in her lap as she lamented, "Now I don't know which was harder, growing up believing Mother killed herself, or like you, living with a drug addict and the belief she abandoned you to reunite with her first family. Either way, we both lost her long ago."

Both sat silently for a short while when David challenged, "What if Mother never had that extraordinary moment as we did? What if the only way she dealt with the chaotic emotions was to run away from loved ones, even herself, through drugs?"

Genevieve began to feel sick inside. "You know David, as long as I knew her, she was depressed and was *always* taking some sort of anti-depressant.

What if the medications masked her ability to feel natural, unaltered emotions? What if feelings had become some type of nebulous purgatory, and she was never clear-headed enough to see through the drug-induced fog. *What if* she never experiencing the incredible feeling of an infant in her arms because the drugs suppressed or altered them?"

Genevieve gave David a startled stare, "You're the scientist, what do you think?"

CHAPTER 44

ESCAPE

AUNT MELINDA HAD been packing for days. Loneliness had tipped the scales, and the only way to escape the void Genevieve had left in her life was to leave for a while. The plan was to go for a week-long visit with Tess, Ryan, and the girls, then continue to Maui for at least a month and stay at the condo she and Steven owned. Steven would meet Melinda whenever work allowed.

She was feeling even more detached from Genevieve's life than ever. Teddy had called during the day to tell Melinda what had happened in Vegas. Disclosing how Genevieve had miraculously found Liv's son, and, that he too, had the same ability as Genevieve. "Can ye believe tha Melinda? Wha are the odds?"

Two large suitcases laid open on the king-size bed. The Teel's bedroom was beautiful, open, and airy with a walk-in closet to die for. As Melinda stood in the middle, surrounded by her vast wardrobe, she made a slow circle, looking for several books she wanted to pack and reread.

Stopping, she spotted them on an upper shelf where she put particular books she didn't want lost in the living room library. "I knew they had to be here," Melinda mumbled to herself. Taking a stepping stool from the closet corner and placing it just so, she took two steps up and found a treasure of past memories. There were old love letters Steven gave to her when they first dated, framed pictures of Liv and herself as young children, mementos of her life *before* Genevieve and Tess.

After pulling the books from the shelf and gently dropping them to the floor, Melinda grabbed one of the framed pictures of her and her sister, then descended from stool.

Leaving the closet and taking the picture, Melinda walked over and sat in her elegant reading chair which rested next to a large window overlooking the pool. As she surveyed the expressions on their young faces, a memory suddenly flashed through her mind from the day the portrait was taken. Melinda was about eight years old, sitting in a child-size chair, hair curled tight, wearing a crisp, short-sleeved cotton dress. She had her hands crossed neatly in her lap and displayed an awkward, forced smile. Liv, almost six years old, stood by her sister's side, hand on Melinda's shoulder with an identical dress, hairdo *and* smile. Melinda remembered Liv's resistance to having her hand placed the way the photographer insisted, telling him it made her feel mad.

As Melinda stared at the picture, she remembered she had been invited to a friend's birthday party that day, but their mom demanded that Melinda have her portrait done instead, since it had been scheduled for weeks. *I remember being so mad as I sat there. Was it possible Liv wasn't being obstinate but, instead, felt angry because she felt what I was feeling?*

Melinda held the framed picture in her hands and closed her eyes. *Liv was always so unsure of herself, always looking to me to handle things because Mother wouldn't indulge her moods, but what if her moods were beyond her understanding?*

Feeling a tear slide down her cheek, Melinda grappled with the possibility, knowing that Liv not only had one child that could feel other's emotions, but *two* now!

Taking a deep breath, Melinda made herself acknowledged the simple fact, that Liv was gone, and speculating on possibilities and probabilities would only cause more sadness and regret.

Putting the picture on the side table next to her chair, Melinda got up and went to the closet to retrieve the books from the floor. When she came back out, Steven was standing in the bedroom doorway.

"Oh my God, you scared me. I didn't expect you home until later."

Steven smiled, walked over to Melinda and pulled her close, causing her to drop the books she was holding. "We're going to need another couple of suitcases, my beauty."

Melinda only responded with a wrinkled brow.

Steven chuckled, then kissed Melinda's forehead, moving to her pixie nose, then held a long kiss on his wife's ruby red lips. "I'd never have you leave me the way you're feeling right now. Our marriage and the vows we took are sacred to me. I know things will change. I truly believe Gen will come around and see things differently. But, until then, I'll follow you around the globe, wherever you want to go. I'll just take the business with me. I have a good back-up system here, and everyone at work is more than glad to help. So, like I was saying, we'll need some more suitcases."

Melinda took a deep breath. "You've had more than your share of the 'worse' part when it comes to our vows, I'm afraid, but, honey, nothing would make me happier than spending time away with you."

Steven looked puzzled. "I beg to differ with that skewed assessment, Mrs. Teel! The only 'worst' part would be not seeing you every day. That would be brutal, *torture* honestly. The closer it got to your leaving, I realized nothing mattered, nothing but you."

Melinda knew Steven hated to see her cry, so she buried her head in his chest.

Shaking his head, Steven lifted Melinda's face with one hand and wiped her eyes with the other. "Damn, I knew I should have thrown a joke in at the end of that mushy dialogue. Well, never too late, I always say. Did I ever tell you the Foggy Bottom joke?"

Melinda broke into laughter, "I'm not sure, b u t t…"

Steven raised his eyebrows, then nodded and winked.

CHAPTER 45

SIBLING EXCHANGE

SCIENTIST OR NOT, David had no answer for Genevieve, and they both knew it, at least for now. Yet, it opened the door for David to show his knowledge in the field, as he explained the great strides scientists were making in gene mapping. As David's discourse continued, chromosomes, genes, DNA, and double helixes muddled Genevieve's mind, just like the chemistry class she had failed *twice* in high school!

When the waitress came by to ask if anyone wanted more coffee, David realized he'd been talking for over a half-hour and apologized for monopolizing the conversation for so long.

"One last question, Genevieve, and then it's your turn to ask me anything you want. I never understood how you knew who I was when you came to the hospital room last night. If you only learned about Mother a few weeks ago, and never were able to talk to her, how could you have known about me?"

Genevieve told him about the pictures she had found, hidden in one of her mother's shirt. "She had several pictures of a man named Darren. Your dad, correct?"

David nodded. "He died six years ago when I was a junior in high school, a boating accident. I went to live with my Aunt Diane, his sister, until I was eighteen. We never had much money when I was growing up, but Dad had taken out a rather substantial insurance policy. Surprising, due to his less-than substantial income. I was the sole beneficiary. That's how I was able to go to college."

Genevieve smiled and nodded. "I'm glad you had him. At least we both had people in our lives that loved us when she couldn't." Genevieve felt a sudden heaviness in her chest, remembering all the love her aunt and uncle had showered on her and Tess when they came to live with them.

Looking at David's chameleon hazel eyes that appeared greener now, next to the blue tee-shirt he was wearing, Genevieve continued. "Then I saw pictures of you. A couple of them were you as an infant, but two were taken when you were older. When I saw your eyes, I knew. I took an educated guess on your name since Mom had wanted to name Tess and me David Michael if we'd been born a boy."

The only other thing Genevieve divulged of what she found in the hidden pouch was the picture that had the partially hidden sign by the front door of a house he lived in as a baby. "When I saw Daisy's last name on the hospital board, everything came together."

David had a stunned expression, "I still don't think I could have put all that together as you did. That's quite remarkable."

Genevieve let out a small chuckle and shook her head. "I learned long ago, it has little to do with me, and to trust my gut feelings, intuition, signals, and dreams—things most people dismiss or ignore. And, if you let me hone your ability, you'll be able to understand the nuances within every feeling you encounter which will also heighten other senses."

David shrugged. "I don't see myself using this the way you do unless it can somehow tie into what I'm doing now, and that doesn't seem likely."

Genevieve raised an eyebrow. "Oh, there *is* a reason. If not, Daisy's Soul would not have engaged with you. Our sister, Tess doesn't possess the ability, neither do my children or my Aunt Melinda. Maybe it was designed to happen through heredity, or perhaps it was simply an incredible coincidence, not that I believe in coincidences. Either way, the gift will become vital to you, sooner or later."

Looking at the clock on the wall, David murmured, "Well, you'll have to convince me of that later. Right now, I've got to call work and let them know I'll be back tomorrow. Daisy's parents have arranged for her to be buried in her hometown, Des Moines, Iowa. They've made it clear I am not welcome and to stay clear of the funeral. My father-in-law was one of those, 'You'll never be good enough for my daughter' types. He believes her death would never have happened if I'd been the loving husband I was supposed to be, and he's absolutely right."

Genevieve wondered if anything she might say would change his point of view. She felt however, she had to try and show him a different perspective. "We all have choices, David. Daisy could have made the choice to stay with you while you worked hard to make a better life for both of you. I remember when my husband, Teddy was going through the same thing, buried in work and studies. It was very hard for a while, and like Daisy, I doubted that I was enough; worried that he'd lost interest, but I chose our love. I chose to believe it would get better. She had that choice too. She also decided to move here. Again, it was *her* choice, not yours.

"I guess what I'm trying to say is we sometimes see things as arbitrary choices. Yet think of all the pieces that *had* to come together, so that we'd meet at this particular momentous time in your life, and mine. How far ahead did the universe have to orchestrate the different components that seemed unrelated for it to happen?"

David sat for a few moments thinking, "Are you saying we don't have a real choice? That everything is already predestined, and we're just playing a part in something that's already been written?"

"Not at all! I'm saying how incredible the unseen powers are, that can take each choice a person makes and connect it to a choice another person makes and another, and another, like a bridge that ultimately takes *each* person where they were meant to go, whether they are aware of the dots or not."

"What do you mean, meant? So, Daisy was *meant* to die yesterday?"

Genevieve looked confidently into David's eyes as she replied, "With all the Souls that have blessed me with their knowledge, I've learned one thing that is absolute. Each person has a purpose here, a sort of Soulful contract to fulfill. Our *Soul's* purpose may be for the sake of someone else and not our own. The contract may be multifaceted or of simple intent. Our choices *are*, and always will *be*, ours to make, but it's our Soul who knows the end game. It's our Soul and the guidance of the unseen that help each of us toward that goal."

Taking a deep, slow breath, Genevieve concluded, "So, was Daisy meant to die yesterday? Daisy was *meant* to help you yesterday. A loved one, who's Soul knew you were ready for a truth you were meant to know. Beyond that, her Soul was at peace, ready to go home. If there were more to accomplish, the circumstance would have been different."

David's eyes had become misty. "She loved me that much?"

Genevieve smiled. "That feeling you felt just before she died? *That's* how much!"

CHAPTER 46

ALWAYS AWARE

IT WAS ALMOST mid-morning before the two left the hotel restaurant. Check-out time was 11:00 a.m. Stopping at the front desk, Genevieve asked if they could have a late check-out, just another hour would do. The front desk clerk said it would be fine, so David and Genevieve went to their respective rooms to finishing packing.

As Genevieve looked around, most her clothes were already neatly packed, just a few toiletries to gather. Thinking she'd just take a moment to close her eyes, since she got very little sleep the night before, Genevieve laid down and without realizing it, fell asleep.

An ear-piercing shrill cut through the silence. Tess was crying. At two-years-old, she had tripped and hit her head on the side of a doorway, leaving a red line indentation, straight down the side of her little face. Running over, ten-year-old Genevieve gathered her sister and held her until the toddler began to calm down."

"You always knew, Genevieve."

Startled, Genevieve turned and saw her mother, beautiful, young and *alive*, standing behind her. Confused, Genevieve only frowned, as Tess, oblivious to anyone but Genevieve, quietly rested her head on her big sister's shoulder while Genevieve stroked her sister's short curly hair.

With a smile, Liv continued, "You were always such a smart girl, so much more than I at your age. You weren't afraid to embrace emotion, even if it was hard. Like now, as you hold your crying sister. Before you picked her up, you instinctively knew you'd feel pain. You didn't understand the correlation yet, but you didn't shy away from it either. You were there for her. It mattered more that she be comforted than knowing you'd feel an odd discomfort by doing it, just as you did with me. How hard it must have been for you."

Young Genevieve put her sister down, and Tess scampered off, plopping down on the floor next to her favorite stuffed rabbit to begin watching Captain Kangaroo as the grinning mustached man jingled his keys to the opening theme song.

Turning back toward her mother, ready to deny such an absurdity, Genevieve watched as Liv reached out to touch Genevieve's shoulder. As her mother's hand grew closer, Genevieve could feel her muscles constrict in preparation for the dismal feeling she knew would come.

"You see," Liv entreated. "I never had even an inkling, you did! Like I said, you were so smart." When Genevieve finally felt the touch of her mother's hand, only pride and respect filtered through, like the sun warming her chilled body.

Coming around and sitting next to her daughter on the couch, Liv took Genevieve's hand and continued. "Forgive me for not being smart enough to understand, Gen, but even more, forgive yourself for knowing. Deep down, it's been a guilt you've carried your whole life about me. You could never have saved me, only yourself."

Liv's demeanor became pensive as she hesitantly continued. "Only the strong find their way, by endurance. It's *those* that will be needed. Don't lose your connection with your brother, Genevieve. You'll rely on each other in ways you can't imagine." Kissing young Genevieve on the forehead, Liv's smile returned, "And I *do* love you, Gen."

Genevieve felt her throat close up, barely able to utter the words she needed to say. "Aunt Mel..."

Liv didn't wait. She seemed to know what Genevieve was trying to say. "She wasn't lying to you, Gen. I knew at your father's funeral what I planned to do, so I told Melinda I had never wanted to have children. I saw the shocking hurt on her face. I knew she'd hate me but shower the two of you with all the love you deserved. I *knew* she was going to be a great mom to you and Tess. Don't blame her for the things *I* did wrong."

Liv studied Genevieve, as if hesitant about confiding a big secret to a small child. Then after several moments, she began to whisper, "Gen, something's happening, and you will..."

Genevieve's eyes burst open as she heard a loud pounding at the door. With watery tears blurring her vision she looked around, disoriented. She was

back in the hotel room. Squeezing her eyes tight, Genevieve felt the tears rolling down her cheeks. Blotting them with her sheet, she focused on the alarm
clock by the bed: *12:20 p.m.! Ah, I need to write this down!* Getting up, she
hurried over and answered the door. It was David. "I know it's late. Come in.
I have to do something before we leave."

With his large backpack in tow, he gave Genevieve an amused grin,
walked in, and closed the door. "Is everything okay?"

Genevieve ran to the desk and grabbed a notepad and pen and began
scribbling without allowing any time for a response. Giving her an odd frown,
David dropped his pack and sat at the end of the bed, watching his sister as if
she was in a possessed trance.

After a couple of minutes, she stopped and closed her eyes. David watched
silently with intrigue. Slowly opening her eyes again, Genevieve fingered
through her notes and nodded. Finally, turning her head to David, she smiled
with slightly trembling lips. "It was one of those powerful dreams."

David raised an eyebrow, as he questioned, "You mean part of that instinct
thing you were mentioning at breakfast?"

Genevieve nodded, still reeling from the emotional exchange with her
mother, "Sort of. Come on, let's head to the lobby to check out and I'll try to
explain." After throwing the remaining toiletries in her overnight bag, the two
headed down the hallway to the elevator.

"I have dream journals at home, and they're jammed packed with dreams
I've had since I was first married. I started one soon after I had a bizarre
dream of people in floating beds chanting my name, and a young girl talking
about how things would become clear after my daughter was born. I didn't
even know at the time of the dream that I was pregnant. It was after Ella was
born, like I had mentioned earlier, that I understood part of my ability. Since
then, I've followed leads and connected dots, often referring to the dreams I've
noted in my journals. Some made no sense to me until years later."

As the elevator doors opened, five people were already standing inside
taking the downward journey as well. Genevieve and David halted their conversation until the check-out process was complete, then moved to a bench
outside the hotel to continue.

David began, "So you had one of those notable dreams then, just a short while ago?"

Genevieve nodded and told David how the dream took her back in time. How Liv showed Genevieve how much more aware Genevieve had been of her ability as a child, than Genevieve had ever realized.

Continuing, Genevieve told David that their mother had, indeed, the same ability but was scared and shied away from it. Yet she was proud her two children had the courage to maneuver through it. Genevieve left out the part about her aunt, not sure if it was just her own wishful thinking that had insinuated itself into the dream. She also left out whatever Liv was about to say when it was cut short by David's knock on the door.

With an awkward silence, Genevieve began to squirm uncomfortably on the bench, then added, "There was a part that had an ominous tone to it. Mom said only the strong, like us, endure, or survive, in her case. And she said it's those, *the strong*, that will be needed."

Genevieve and David looked at each other with a puzzled frown. "Finally, Mom said that you and I would need each other in ways we can't imagine and not to lose our connection with each other."

David looked away and shook his head slowly. Being a scientist, he was having a hard time believing what Genevieve was saying, and yet, he couldn't account for the phenomenon he experienced with Daisy. There was no scientific test that could confirm or deny what he and his sister were able to do.

Seeing the doubtful expression in her brother's face, Genevieve stopped talking and took a deep breath, deciding to take a minute and admire the Vegas skyline. However, the sun's blinding reflection bouncing off a high-rise tower next door caused Genevieve to abandon her perusal and quickly return her focus on David.

"I know what you must be thinking right now. How fast can I get away from this very peculiar woman and this "Twilight Zone" I've entered? Does that about sum it up?"

David grinned. "Well, that's a bit harsh. I agree these two days have been surreal and I'm not sure what I'm supposed to believe or what will be *needed* of me. I am, however, glad—no, more than glad, that we've finally met, and

I don't need a dream to convince me to stay in touch. We don't live *that* far away, we've got phones, and hopefully, you have a computer with internet and an email address? I don't at home, but I *do* at work, which is where I am most the time anyway."

Genevieve nodded. "Yes, Teddy always has to have the latest, *hot* fad out there! I have a computer, Netscape, and just got an AOL address a few weeks ago. It's come in quite handy with Ella, who has access to the internet at college and Detective Chao who emails me from work, taunting me with his horrendous bad spelling." Leaning close to David, Genevieve smirked, "I know he does it on purpose just to get my blood pressure up."

David smirked "Yeah, I'm not the greatest speller either, but numbers…" David beamed with a confident smile.

Genevieve took David's hand. "I'd like to see how you're doing in a couple of days if that's okay. Once you get home, the enormity of all that has happened will hit you. Call or email me *any* time. Then, maybe I can come and visit, or you can come to Arizona and hang out with your big sister." Genevieve winked and nudged David.

"David, I think now that the door has been opened, you won't turn your back on what you *know* is on the other side. Scientists live for new discoveries, right? If other senses or abilities start to be apparent, follow where they lead. That's what I've done."

The two got up and held a long embrace. Genevieve grinned and quizzed, "Do you feel that?"

David kissed the top of his sister's head, "The feeling is quite mutual."

CHAPTER 47

WHY HER?

WHILE DRIVING HOME in her rented Saturn, Genevieve had hours to replay everything that had happened recently. She realized David had been the man in her dream at the cemetery. The grave in common, their mothers of course, one that Genevieve had yet to visit.

Mind jumping, Genevieve went from Brunner, who would be headed back home tomorrow, to Daisy and David. *What could he be thinking about with all that just happened, especially now that he's all alone?*

As she began jogging through the dream about her mother, Genevieve frowned with a tinge of regret. *If only I could have asked Mom about the diamond. Why did she have it? When did Aunt Melinda give it to her?*

By the time Genevieve was on the outskirts of Scottsdale, it was almost 6:00 p.m. yet the desert drive seemed faster than it ever had before. Finally, Genevieve let her mind drift to another dream, the one of Lucy in the dark shack. *'Forgive yourself.'* Genevieve felt a tear tickling her cheek and brushed it with her shoulder. *From the time I was a young child, I always blamed myself for Mom's sadness, even her death. Then, after I found out she was alive, it was easier to divert the anger to her, or my aunt, anyone that could take the blame away from me, where deep down, I always believed it belonged. Now I understand what you meant, Lucy, and Mother helped me realize I really couldn't have saved her. Only the* **strong** *endure. Her fate was always beyond anything I could have controlled.*

Hoping her mother was near, Genevieve spoke softly, "I forgive you, Mom. Do you *hear* me? And I'm ready to forgive myself now, too."

Genevieve took a deep breath, feeling free from the bondage she had inflicted upon herself, but it was short-lived. Within moments, deep regret and longing began to squeeze like a vise to her chest as she lamented, *Aunt*

Melinda. Why did I let my anger go so far, and for so long? God, I don't care that she knew Mom was alive, and I don't care about the diamond. Nothing matters anymore but asking for her forgiveness. Just please, don't slam the door in my face, even if I do deserve it.

Changing direction, Genevieve took the 303 West. Fifteen minutes later she was pulling up to the estate's large gates. *Home*, Genevieve thought.

It had only been a little over five months, but it seemed like a lifetime. As Genevieve pulled into the circular drive, she could hardly breathe. Walking up to the front door, Genevieve noticed it was uncharacteristically quiet. When perking her ears, even the stable was oddly silent in the distance. Nothing was moving, save for the quickening pace of Genevieve's heart as she lifted her hand.

Knock, Knock. Genevieve's breath halted as she put her ear to the door. Nothing.

KNOCK, KNOCK. *Gidda is always here, even if no one else is.* Putting her ear back to the door, Genevieve finally heard someone coming.

When the door opened, Gidda, the housekeeper stood, red-eyed. "MS. GENEVIEVE!" She wailed.

Genevieve's eyes opened wide as Gidda fell into her arms. "Gidda, what's wrong?"

"Mrs. Teel." She sobbed.

Panic set in, as Genevieve demanded, "What about Mrs. Teel? Gidda, what's going on?"

"Come in, come in." Gidda moaned. When the door closed, Gidda took Genevieve's arm, and they both sat together on the stairway. "Mr. and Mrs. Teel were leaving to visit your sister today, then after that, Mrs. Teel toll me they would stay in Hawaii for a while."

Genevieve looked stunned. As she held tight to Gidda's trembling hand, she replied, "I had no idea. Had their trip been planned for a while?"

Gidda shook her head. "Oh, Ms. Genevieve, she missed you so much. She decided days ago that she had to get away for a while. Mr. Teel refused to let her go alone."

Guilt and shame—the vise was squeezing tighter. "Was there a car accident? Is she dead? **What** happened to my Aunt, Gidda?"

Gidda had a strained look as she held her gaze on Genevieve. "Your uncle toll me that their jet was only in the air for about fifteen minutos. Mrs. Teel got up to get a libro, um, book, from her small duffle bag that was on the bench across from her. Then, turbulence—bad shaking, came out of nowhere and threw her to the ceiling. When she came down, she hit the side of the table, hard, with her cabeza! Mr. Teel hadn't taken his seatbelt off yet." Gidda looked up and made the sign of the cross, before turning back to Genevieve. "He said he had been working and forgot." Then Gidda added, "He also said the stewardess hit the ceiling too, but was okay, just some bruises.

"Oh, Ms. Genevieve, Mr. Teel was crying when he called. I never heard him sound so…, and now I haven't heard *nothing* for horas!" Gidda began to cry again.

Genevieve put her hands over her face. *Why now? Why her? I don't understand.* After a minute, Genevieve wiped her wet face, gathered her composure, and with a deep sigh, uttered, "Gidda, I'm going to the hospital now. I promise I'll give you a call as soon as I know anything, okay?"

Gidda nodded. Genevieve squeezed her tight and quickly left. *She can't die, not now!* On autopilot, Genevieve headed for the hospital.

Walking down the halls of yet a different hospital, the despair of possibly losing her aunt made Genevieve feel faint. Stopping and clinging to a nearby doorway, she felt herself shutter. Her hands and face were cold and clammy. Everything became fuzzy and out of focus. Silence ensued, except for the deafening rushing sound in her ears.

Feeling unsteady, Genevieve closed her eyes and took several deep breaths. Forcing herself, she continued to breathe slowly and methodically. Within a minute the dizziness began to subside. Vision and voices began to appear again. One voice was distinct and particular—Teddy's.

With squinted eyes, Genevieve saw Teddy and Broc talking down the hallway. As if shot with adrenaline, Genevieve ran. She flew past them both, coming to a screeching halt just inside her aunt's room. Uncle Steven was sitting attentively at his wife's side. When he saw his niece he slowly smiled, closed his eyes and nodded as if saying, "Thank you, God."

Melinda's head was wrapped in bandages, her eyes closed. As Genevieve quietly moved closer, her aunt opened her eyes and looked at Genevieve. A moment later, a slight grin appeared, and Melinda reached for Genevieve.

"Oh *God*," was the only thing Genevieve was able to utter before she grabbed her aunt's hand and began to cry.

Teddy and Broc quietly stepped in. Teddy moved a chair over so his wife could sit down. Genevieve glanced back with a tearful grin and nodded.

Turning back at her aunt, Genevieve allowed Melinda's physical pain to envelop her, hoping that in doing so, she might funnel it away from her aunt, and put it squarely where it belonged, with Genevieve.

In surveying all the damage to Melinda, Genevieve realized, for the first time, how small, precious, and fragile she was. Melinda's neck was in a brace, her eyes were dark and swollen by the force of impact which Genevieve could now discern had been her forehead. Her left wrist was wrapped as well.

Melinda brought Genevieve attention back by squeezing her niece's hand. When Genevieve's eyes met Melinda's, Melinda blinked slowly with a content look on her face. Genevieve closed her eyes. Besides the physical distress her aunt was experiencing, she also felt a strong emotion Genevieve was praying for—hopefulness.

Opening her eyes as tears continued, Genevieve whispered, "I'm *so* sorry for all I've put you through. *Lord*, you never deserved such harsh words from me or my judgmental attitude. If I could just go back in time…"

Melinda's pale lips smiled and, as she closed her eyes, a tear escaped and skipped down her cheek. Genevieve gently raised her aunt's hand and kissed it, noticing the imitation blue diamond on her ring finger. When Melinda opened her eyes again, Genevieve quickly returned her gaze to her aunt.

Smiling, Genevieve tipped her head and murmured, "You get some rest. I'll be right here." Then, leaning closer, and with her voice beginning to crack, Genevieve added, "I will *never* hurt you again, *ever!*"

Aunt Melinda gave a slight nod, tightening her grip on Genevieve's hand, then relaxed it, as she slowly closed her eyes.

CHAPTER 48

HEALING WOUNDS

GENEVIEVE GOT UP, and the other three followed her out. Leaving Melinda to rest, they went to the nearby waiting room. As soon as they were inside the doorway, Genevieve wrapped her arms tight, around her uncle, and held on as if making up for the months she had sorely missed. After a full minute, Uncle Steven began to laugh but was in no hurry to break the embrace. Finally, Teddy inquired, "Ye think I could get a little of tha action, lass?" Genevieve turned and smiled at Teddy and Broc, pulling them into a group hug.

Finding a quiet corner in the large waiting room, the four sat huddled together. With a furrowed brow, Genevieve implored her uncle, "How serious is it?"

Uncle Steven rubbed the back of his neck. "Well, she sprained her wrist and fractured her frontal bone. She has a concussion that they are watching closely. The doc's got her on some meds for pain, but he won't fully sedate her, saying they need her alert enough to assure there won't be any complications with the hit to her head."

Genevieve stressed, "But she'll be okay, right?"

Steven nodded. "I think so. And now, being that you're here, I know it will make a big difference."

Genevieve just looked at her uncle for a moment with a pained expression of guilt and regret. "You heard about what happened in Las Vegas?" Genevieve asked softly.

Steven nodded again. "Yes, Teddy told Melinda all about it earlier today."

"Oh, Uncle, that trip opened my eyes to so many things. It clarified my understanding of my mother, myself, and Aunt Melinda. I was on my way home earlier, but something inside became overpowering and urgent.

I couldn't wait any longer to ask both of you for forgiveness, so I made a detour and went straight to the estate, not knowing…"

Teddy interjected, "So ye didn't *see* the note I left ye on the kitchen counter then?"

Genevieve shook her head. "Gidda told me what had happened. *Oh,* I've got to call her. She's out of mind with worry!"

Uncle Steven stood up, "You sit. I should have called her myself by now. She'll be happy things aren't as bad as I thought when we last spoke." Genevieve took a deep breath, reached out, and held her uncle's hand for a moment before he left to make the call.

When Steven left, Genevieve turned to Broc, who was sitting next to her. She smiled and touched his hand, "Are you okay?"

Broc made a quirky nod, "I'm just glad we can be a family again. I never understood how you could have let this go on so long, Mom."

Teddy cautioned, "Don't judge your mum for things we can't understand, son."

Genevieve quickly appealed, "It's okay Teddy. I know how upset he's been, along with you and the whole family. All this time, I misunderstood the intentions of my mother as well as my aunt, and in doing so, I unfairly put all that I love in a state of purgatory—*hell* maybe a better term."

Broc looked pleased by her confession and smiled with a slight nod. Teddy raised his eyebrows, "I guess there was a lot I missed affta I left earlier today. Ye want to talk aboot it?"

"I do, but right now I have to go home and get something. You want me to bring back some Mc Donald's burgers and fries?"

Broc's eyes got wide. "Better hurry, Mom, I'm starving!"

When Genevieve returned, an hour and a half later, everyone was back in Aunt Melinda's private room, along with the addition of Ella, Geoffrey, and finally, Tori, a good friend of Aunt Melinda's. Genevieve realized, as much as she wanted to have a heart-to-heart talk with her Aunt, it would have to wait.

Melinda was resting in the bed, slightly inclined, her dinner tray off to one side. Genevieve smiled when she noticed most of the food had been eaten—an excellent sign.

Laden with four large bags of food, Genevieve remarked, "Wow, I guess I should have brought a little more!"

Broc hurried over and helped relieve his mom of her heavy load. Ella quickly followed and put her arm around her mother. "I'm so happy to see you, Mom. Wish the circumstance was different, but it would have been so much worse if she didn't have you here right now."

Genevieve nodded and could feel stormy emotions begin to rise but took a deep breath and quickly blew it out. "I have a lot of making up to do. I don't think I could ever have recovered if she had…"

Ella blurted, "But she's going to be fine, just *fine*, Mom."

Genevieve focused on Ella's reassuring smile, "Okay."

Giving her mom another encouraging hug, she added, "Aunt Tess just called a few minutes before you arrived. She booked a flight and should be here later tonight."

As Ella watched the mass exodus heading to the waiting room to grab their share of the burger dinner, she entreated, "Man, that smells good. I haven't had anything to eat since breakfast. Mom, if it's okay…"

Genevieve frowned. "Ariella! What's the matter with you? You're already so thin you disappear when you turn sideways. Go. Hurry, before the men take it all!" Ella rolled her eyes, then dashed down the hallway.

All that was left in the room besides her aunt, was Tori Miles. Tori had become a close friend of Aunt Melinda's ever since her aunt began the foundation for abused women, in which Tori was an integral part. Genevieve didn't know Tori's entire backstory, other than she had been a nightclub singer when she was young, and Aunt Melinda had been a big fan. Then one night, Tori was raped while leaving the nightclub. She never sang again.

When it happened, Genevieve remembered the way her aunt became almost obsessed with Tori's circumstance, visiting Tori at her home and having her over for dinners, followed by private talks in which young Genevieve was never invited to join.

Around that time, Aunt Melinda founded "Healing Wings." She had asked Genevieve to help her with the name, thinking "Wounded Wings" might be a good name, but Genevieve had questioned, "Aren't you trying to heal them, Aunt Melinda?" Genevieve could still remember how important she felt when her aunt acknowledged, "That's exactly what I want to do, Gen!"

Tori, now teaching civics in high school, was aware of the situation between Genevieve and her Aunt and made the transparent excuse of having to grade papers before morning. "But I'll be back tomorrow, after school's out.

Giving Melinda a quick kiss on the cheek, Tori rounded the bed and hugged Genevieve whispering, "She's been watching the door for you. I think she still can't believe you're back."

Genevieve knew the feeling and whispered back, "Thank you for being such a good friend, Tori."

Smiling, Tori nodded, then loudly bemoaned, "Well, those papers aren't going to grade themselves, so I'm off."

When Genevieve turned to her aunt, Melinda spoke to her for the first time, "Come here."

Genevieve had been fine, until she heard the voice of her aunt, and remembered the dream in which she was invisible in her eyes. Hurrying over, Genevieve draped herself gently over her aunt's chest and began crying softly.

Melinda smiled, eyes filling with tears. As she stroked Genevieve's long dark hair, she asked, "What's changed, Gen?"

Lifting her head, Genevieve looked at her aunt. Even with her eyes dark and swollen, no one looked more beautiful. Putting her head back on Melinda's chest, Genevieve whispered, *"Everything."*

CHAPTER 49

NEW BEGINNINGS

GENEVIEVE ONLY WANTED her mother back—*this* mother. The one that even now, held no bitterness or blame that Genevieve could discern, only joy. An emotion so potent it had begun to dissolve the self-loathing Genevieve had long-been harboring.

Still stroking her niece's hair, Melinda waited until Genevieve was ready to explain. Looking up at her aunt, Genevieve quavered, "Is it too late to call you Mom?"

Aunt Melinda took a sharp breath, and her eyes became a watery blur. "No, honey. I don't think it would *ever* be too late."

Genevieve smiled and moved her hand to Melinda's face. With barely a sound, her trembling lips mouthed, *"Mom."*

Melinda's swollen wet eyes were imploring Genevieve to explain the extreme turn of events.

Clearing her throat, Genevieve continued. "It feels *so* right; so *good* to call you that. In the past, I would catch myself about to call you Mom, but then, I'd see her face and stop myself. I could never unlock the mysterious hold Liv had on me through all these years. I couldn't fully break free. Beyond her deception, a larger truth was revealed, one I was destined to understand and now do. It didn't end with her death, and somehow, deep down I knew that. There was still more to the story she and I shared.

"However, it didn't change the fact that many years ago, she willingly gave up the right to be called Mother. A title which is really so, so much more."

With her voice beginning to crack, Melinda sounded cautious, "Then I can finally call you my…"

"Yes," Genevieve choked, closing her eyes and kissing her *mother's* cheek. *God yes!* She thought to herself.

After a few moments, Genevieve slid from the bed and sat down in the chair next to it. "I had a dream this morning."

Melinda spoke quietly. "I hear you've had many over the last few months."

Genevieve raised her eyebrows in surprise.

Producing an impish grin, Melinda added, "Your husband has been a blessing for me. He always knew to tell me what was happening with you, otherwise, I would nag him. Maybe he divulged more than he should?"

"No, he was my lifeline to you as well. A blessing, yes. A very patient one."

"So, what of this dream?" Melinda coaxed.

"I was very young. Tess was just a toddler. Liv was there too, at our house in the country. She showed me things that I never realized about myself."

With an impassioned look, Genevieve leaned closer to Melinda. "Liv showed me something I never knew about her either. Mom, your sister had the gift too! But, in the dream, she showed me the differences between her and myself.

"Like me, she didn't understand it yet when she was a child, but she very much feared it. She let the fear of emotions destroy her, telling me I was the strong one. Then she told me, *'only* the strong survive.' "

Melinda listened with rapt attention. "And I hear her son has the same ability as well."

Genevieve nodded. "Yes. *He* was the one that tied everything together. He *was* the rest of the story."

Melinda squeezed Genevieve's hand, "I was amazed you found him, David, is it?"

Genevieve smiled slightly and nodded.

Melinda struggled to nod back, despite the stiff brace around her neck. "After I heard about that discovery today, I recalled a time when Liv and I were children that made me wonder. However, because Tess never had the ability, the memory held no significance, then. Yet now, I can remember time after time that Liv recoiled from people, always unsure, confused, and sad.

Genevieve shook her head. "It's okay. *Everything* is okay now." Then Genevieve reached in her jacket pocket and pulled something out, placing it in her mother's hand.

Melinda looked at the blue diamond ring and paused, as a single tear began trickling down her cheek. "Where did you find it?"

Watching Melinda's bewildered reaction, Genevieve smiled with anticipation. "I found it in Liv's tattered clothes, along with all the pictures."

Melinda's blackened eyes blinked quickly at Genevieve, in stunned amazement. "It was with the *pictures?*"

"Uh-huh, I almost missed it. She had it sewn to the bottom of the pouch."

Melinda turned and stared at the ring. "Did I ever tell you that your uncle, um, should I say, father now?"

Genevieve grinned and nodded.

Melinda looked tearful, "Did I ever tell you that your *father* gave this to me the day before we got married?"

Genevieve looked intrigued and shook her head.

"I was having terrible doubts and insecurities about getting married, and Steven knew it. After the wedding rehearsal was over that evening, we all got into our cars to go to dinner. My mind was a million miles away, and I didn't notice at first, that Steven had waited until everyone else had disappeared down the street.

"It was then, sitting in the darkness, with only the distant moon for light, I could see the deep and desperate love that man had for me. As we sat in the car, he pulled this ring out and placed it on my right ring finger. He said, and I quote: 'The stone's rare beauty symbolizes eternity, and, although eternity doesn't sound nearly long enough to love you, this might have to do.' "

Genevieve brushed a tear away and laughed. "That sounds way too serious for that man. But I always see *and* feel the rare love he has for you."

Melinda smiled and gazed at the beautiful symbol in the palm of her hand. "I missed this ring so. I thought it was long gone; spent on drugs, lost or stolen. But Liv had watched over it, *kept it close* with all the things that meant the most to her."

Genevieve gently removed the imitation diamond off Melinda's finger and replaced it with the real one, as she said, "I never knew the difference until I found this one."

Staring at the brilliant diamond as her hand rested in Genevieve's, Melinda recollected, "Liv and I were arguing in her house, the day I discovered she was still alive. I knew she didn't have any money, and I only had forty dollars in my purse to give her. Then I glanced down and saw my ring. She always admired it. I took it off and told her to take it. She refused, but I walked over, put it in her hand and closed her fingers tightly around it, telling her to use it. It would help her survive."

Genevieve again felt the sting of her wrong assumption. Cocking her head back and looking at the ceiling, her chin began to tremble. "So, you had a fake one made when you got back home."

Melinda murmured, "Yes."

Bringing her head back down, Genevieve mumbled sheepishly, "And you never saw your sister again until just before she died, just as you had told me."

Melinda looked puzzled by the question. "I actually tried to find her *once*, about five years after she disappeared, but all leads came up empty. She did an excellent job of staying invisible.

"I was so proud of you girls. If nothing else, I wanted to let her know how amazing you both were. In the end, however, I came to the sad conclusion that she always knew where she could have found us if she had wanted."

Genevieve shrugged, "She'd moved on, started a new life, a new family. As it turned out, she disappeared from that one also."

With downturned lips, Melinda looked at her daughter and slowly nodded.

Genevieve quickly changed her expression, sat up straight and beamed, "Enough of that. No more wasting time on the past and no more secrets! That chapter is now over, once and for all, as well as the burdens that haunted us both for too long."

Melinda took a deep cleansing sigh, "Looks like a new chapter has started, and we've turned the page."

Genevieve eyes widened, "Ah, very clever, *Mother*."

CHAPTER 50

CAVEMAN

FALL-1999, FOUR YEARS later

She had been watching it for almost ten minutes. As Genevieve finished putting on her make-up for an early morning meeting with Brunner, she kept a watch on a harmless daddy longleg, working a web in the bathtub/shower next to her vanity. What usually took Genevieve five minutes to splash a bit of color on her face, now had been fifteen. She had become entranced by the painstakingly intricate workings of the arachnid, trying to build a distorted web ladder to escape the slippery jail, in which it was trapped.

Feeling a sudden tinge of empathy for the creature's plight, Genevieve decided to help it out—literally, by capturing it and releasing it outside. Getting up, she went to the bathroom's attached walk-in closet to see if she could find a container that would suffice, when Teddy walked in to the bathroom, turned on the shower, and washed the fragile crawler down the drain.

Standing naked and groggy while waiting for the water to get hot, Teddy blinked a sleepy dimpled smile at Genevieve as she emerged from the closet, empty button jar in hand. Giving her husband a shocked look, she rushed past of him and peered into the tub.

Resting his chin on the back of her shoulder, Teddy whispered, "Wha's the matta?"

Genevieve watched the raining hot water as it pelted the side of the tub, then turned to look at her bewildered husband. With a thwarted shrug, Genevieve dropped the jar onto the rug and wrapped her arms around him. "It was just a little spider I was trying to set free. Something you probably would have done if you'd seen it."

Teddy frowned, "Naw, I saw it. It had to go. Spiders are our enemy!"

Genevieve smacked Teddy's bare butt yet couldn't help grin under her furrowed brow. "I thought you'd be more compassionate."

Teddy raised his eyebrows, and his blue eyes came to life, "Ah, I'd be more than happy to demonstrate just how compassionate I can be."

Genevieve's eyes widened as Teddy grabbed her waist and began pulling her toward the shower. "Stop!" She screamed. "*Compassion*, not passion! Besides, there's no time! I have a meeting in less than an hour."

With a mischievous look, he implored, "There's always time. Come—passion—ye—me—shower," Teddy grunted as he ran his hands over Genevieve.

Letting out a loud laugh, Genevieve pulled away from Teddy's clutches. "Okay, caveman, maybe we can rendezvous later. That's *if* your little enemy doesn't climb back out of the drain and bite you in your British arse!"

Teddy's eyes peered into the steam of the shower. "Naw, all looks clear, so I'm advancin!" With that, he stepped into the shower and winked at Genevieve before closing the glass door behind him.

Grinning, Genevieve shook her head and picked up the jar. Gathering the buttons she had dumped on the closet floor, she filled the jar back up, and after placing it on the shelf, headed for the stairs.

Halfway down, Genevieve heard a voice and realized someone was leaving a message on the phone recorder. By the time she reached the machine, just the red blinking light was flashing. Pushing the "Play" button, Genevieve knew right away it was Teddy's partner, Sol.

"Hey, Ted. Say, can we meet a little later this afternoon? First, I need to meet with someone. I think you know who. It's important, call me."

Sounds mysterious, Genevieve thought.

It had been four years since she last saw Cindy and Sol. Genevieve always felt guilty about her abrupt disassociation with the Santoro's after the *revealing* dinner party. Guilty, only because poor Cindy had to be left in the dark as to why Genevieve was a no-show from that day on.

It also seemed of late, that Teddy had a frustrated tone whenever speaking of Sol. When Genevieve asked if things were okay at work, he'd just give a curt, "Sure, it's fine" or "Just goin through some growin pains." but it was obvious that's where he wanted to leave it, as then, the subject would quickly change.

Looking at the clock, Genevieve gasped. *Late again.* Scribbling a note to Teddy, to "Call Sol," Genevieve grabbed her purse and flew out the door.

As she drove to the station, she began to ruminate over the fragile existence of the long-legged, insect. In a matter of moments, because of Genevieve's mere impulse, it would have been roaming free in the yard. One of a plethora of future possibilities. However, circumstances and choices made by another seemed to seal its fate. Still, what of the spider choice that took it to the place where it ultimately died?

Genevieve began getting lost in her thoughts of cases in which people had seemingly lost their lives due to a choice made by another. *Yet, what about the victim's decision that led them to that fateful moment? Each morning we wake up with the assumption that our day will end when we go to bed. Still, where are our choices taking us each day, as they rendezvous with the choices made by others?* Although life at times, had its serendipitous moments, it was never about luck, but the perfect melding of decisions made, from all those involved.

Frowning, Genevieve wondered why she was even contemplating something that many Souls had already made her aware of. Good choices, bad choices, right or wrong, they all proceed from a thought. Each one, even the most impulsive or insignificant, can change a life: that of their own, or someone else's. The Soul will never interfere with that free choice, but, *the Soul only*, decides if It's ready to move on. Whether it be to end some type of suffering or Its purpose for coming has been fulfilled, *no one, not me, or anyone else's choice or circumstance will ever trump that of the Soul's. Its decision is the final one,* she reminded herself.

When Genevieve entered into the station's parking lot, the space where Brunner always parked his treasured white corvette was empty. Reaching into her purse, she pulled out her new Nokia cell phone that she got from Teddy for her birthday, and dialed Brunner.

After just one ring Brunner answered, "I tried calling you, but you'd already left. No one answered, and I don't have your new cell number yet, sorry."

Teddy must have still been in the shower, Genevieve figured. "That's okay, so, what's up?"

"Had a robbery three days ago, a pawn shop. The owner was shot, yet nothing was taken. The guy didn't have any security cameras, and we couldn't find any witnesses. His wife had an alibi.

"Anyway, the victim was still unconscious last night, so I called you in to see if you could find out something we could work with. However, this morning, he came out of his coma and told us it was his *ex*-wife. We're following up on that now. Sorry for the false alarm."

Genevieve closed her eyes and wrinkled her nose, "It's alright. Glad you didn't need me, but it's been a few weeks with nothing to do. Maybe I'll be out of a job soon."

Brunner snorted, "From your lips to God's ears. I'll call you later. I'm sure it won't be too long before you're needed again."

When Genevieve got back home, she heard Teddy and went to his office. He was sitting on the stool by his drafting desk, talking on the phone with Ella, who was soon to be working on the latest acquisition of Teddy and Sol's. With her degree in Architectural landscape, Teddy wanted to see how Ella would use her knowledge and incorporate it into the land project that was now in the beginning stages of urban development.

Taking a seat on the office couch, Genevieve watched Teddy's body language and facial expressions with amusement as Ella most assuredly was talking about her latest boyfriend.

Ariella was drawn to men in uniform and had already dated a marine cadet, a med student, and now a baseball player on a full scholarship at Fresno State, who she had met at a party earlier that year. The young man was athletically built, self-assured, and, as Teddy observed, much too openly affectionate with his daughter. However, Ella seemed hooked, gushing, whenever she talked about her new love or his talent at playing ball.

Ella had her father's striking blue eyes, and although her dimples weren't *as* deep as his, a smile from the slim beauty had always produced plenty of interest. *With* that interest, Teddy felt obliged to examine each specimen under his fatherly microscope.

After a few minutes, Teddy ended his conversation with, "Well, now tha you're back, come by later and show me the designs you've done for Market Street."

Teddy placed the receiver down and gave Genevieve a blank stare. "She's so in love," Teddy said as if reading it on the side of a bus.

Genevieve grinned, "I think he may be the *one*, Teddy. She's made the trip to Fresno twice now, and he's come here several times as well. That's a lot of traveling in a very short time for a fleeting romance."

Teddy stretched his neck from side to side, trying to crack it. "Maybe, but we'll see. She said he told her there's new Triple-A team comin to Sacramento, and he's pretty sure they're interested in signin him. Sounds like he's quite full of himself, not the kind of fella Ella needs."

Genevieve shook her head, "His *name* is Finn, you know, and he seems to be *just* what she needs. I've never seen her happier."

Getting up, and walking behind Teddy, Genevieve began kissing the back of his neck. "Don't you remember the powerful feeling of *our* new love?" Teddy closed his eyes. "The constant craving to be held in each other's arms?" She breathed in his ear, "The **ache** to be together?"

Teddy turned and pulled Genevieve toward him, "Aye, I do."

As Teddy brought his lips to hers, she once again felt the power his love had on her. After a few minutes, Genevieve caught her breath enough to whisper, "Sometimes, it all comes down to a feeling, *caveman*."

CHAPTER 51

SMALL WORLD

AFTER THEIR ROMANTIC tryst was over, and Genevieve was getting up to leave, it dawned on Teddy, "Wha happened to your meetin?"

Genevieve lifted the side of her mouth, "Wasn't needed," She said with a hint of disappointment. "Say, did you call Sol? Are you meeting with him later?"

"Aye. I may call Ella back and have her meet us at the office later. I think Sol will be quite impressed with our little girl's talent."

Genevieve nodded. "I'm sure our *little girl* will do just that." She said matter-of-factly.

As she turned toward the door, Teddy reached for her hand. "I almost forgot. Broc called and asked if I could pick him up affta practice, but since ye happen to be home...?"

Broc rarely needed a ride home from school now, since his grandfather, sold him (for a fraction of what it was worth) his vintage, pine green,1953 Chevy pickup, when Broc started his senior year. However, currently it was sitting in the Walker's garage, waiting for a vintage carbonator to get moving again.

Genevieve nodded. "Sure, what time?"

"He said aboot four-thirty." Teddy responded,

After lunch, Genevieve made a call to her mother. Melinda finally met David last year, when Genevieve went to visit him for his birthday and Melinda came along. It was a bittersweet introduction as Melinda could see her sister, Liv, in David's eyes and mannerisms. For David, it was a reminder of all the relatives he never knew due to his mother's secrecy. Despite this, within hours of their meeting, a cohesiveness began building as a family, which had only gotten stronger over the past year when David also met Steven, Tess, Ella, and Broc at Christmas time.

"Have you spoken to your brother lately?" Melinda inquired.

"I spoke to him about a week ago. It's funny. I wasn't sure exactly what he might do with his ability. I had a feeling though, that he'd want to explore its relevancy from a different angle. He's still looking for that scientific link. He knows everything is essentially energy, and he thinks there must be a way to measure the intensity of that energy when the Soul communicates with us. He's looking for someone else in his field that he can collaborate with but says he has to be careful, since science and spirituality mix about as well as oil and water.

"He said he'd found another instance where someone, like us made the news, this time in Spain. Of course, it's not the mainstream news, in fact, I don't know how he finds these stories, but he's constantly looking. Obsessed, really. He thinks there may be more empaths than we might imagine."

Melinda acknowledged, "He is a very intense person and seems to have tunnel vision. I'm just afraid he'll make the same mistake again, and lose his new girlfriend, Janet. I know you and I both have tried to stress balance with him, and I know he tries, but…"

Genevieve sighed. "I know. But at least Janet has a busy life also, traveling all over the U.S. as a Pharmaceutical Sales Rep. Unfortunately, his deceased wife, Daisy, had no life outside of him. For now, anyway, he's happy again, fulfilled, and in love. Live in the moment, right, Mom?"

Genevieve knew Melinda was smiling when she concurred. "It's all we have."

By the time Genevieve was done on the phone it was a little after 4:00 p.m. Before leaving for the office earlier, Teddy said he'd be home by dinner time and would probably bring Ella with him. *Feels like a pizza night to me*, Genevieve thought smiling, as she pulled out of the driveway to get Broc.

On her drive to the high school, she remembered when Broc was around four, and no matter how Genevieve tried, he refused to eat anything that didn't resemble a pizza. He literally would starve himself if it weren't round with cheese on it. So, for a little over a year, Genevieve became a world-class maker of round dinners, using anything that could be flattened and baked. Biscuits, omelets, pancakes, baked yams, even Portobello mushrooms fooled the little guy. Sprinkle some cheese, add a few vegetables, sliced meat or poultry, and *voila*—a Broc pizza!

As she approached Dillard Street, she slowed to make the turn. *I love taking this scenic route.* But, glancing at her watch, Genevieve changed her mind and hit the gas, as Broc was probably already waiting. So, she continued down Butchart Boulevard, toward the intersection. "Good, the left turn signal just changed to green." She whispered.

Out of nowhere, a black BMW raced ahead of Genevieve, pulling in front of her so close it would have hit her front bumper had she not slammed on the brakes as the driver forced his way over. With her heart racing, Genevieve closed her eyes for a moment, body tensed, praying no one would hit her from the back due to her sudden stop.

Then she heard it. The sickening sound of screeching tires and metal on metal.

Genevieve's eyes flew open. The BMW that demanded its way ahead of her, was now sliding, on its side, in the opposite lane. A car coming from the other direction had run the red light, and T-boned the BMW as it made its hasty left turn.

A stunned Genevieve, paralyzed in her seat, slowly turned her head to the left. There, facing her in the middle of the opposing lanes, twenty feet from where the BMW was now resting, was the other car.

Genevieve took a shocked breath. The older Cadillac's entire front section was crushed and smoldering. The driver had gone through the windshield; his head a dripping mass of mangled flesh and blood. Feeling faint, Genevieve started to turn away when she caught a glimpse of what looked like a woman on the passenger side. With the windshield a mosaic of fragmented, opaque red shards, there was no way to ascertain her condition.

Knowing time may be short, Genevieve took a courageous breath and held it a few moments, before turning off the car motor and opening her door. The center-divide was made of cement, about three feet high. Climbing over the barrier, Genevieve forced herself to look at the driver. The glass was wrapped around his neck like a jagged frame. A stream of blood that had been running off the mangled hood had the acrid smell of iron and motor oil, assaulting Genevieve's senses. The blank stare in his one open eye let Genevieve know that he was gone. With traffic now stopped in all directions, several people were approaching the scene.

Quickly moving to the passenger side door, she noticed the window had been blown entirely out by the impact and, as Genevieve reached for the car door, she thought her eyes were deceiving her.

Cindy? Cindy Santoro?

With dread steamrolling through her veins, Genevieve pulled open the door and looked again at the driver. His hair, that wasn't matted with blood had a brownish color to it, and it was straight, unlike Sol's black wavy hair. The driver was also wearing a flannel shirt, something Genevieve was positive Sol would *never* be caught wearing dead *or* alive. And then there was the car. Sol only drove his bright red jeep. *Who is this man with Cindy?*

Luckily, Cindy had been wearing a seatbelt, but her legs were pinned under the dashboard. With only a few cuts to her face, Cindy was beginning to come around, moaning.

Hearing sirens in the distance, Genevieve spoke loudly, "Cindy!"

Sluggishly, Cindy opened her eyes and stared blankly at Genevieve.

"Cindy, it's Genevieve Walker. You've been in a car accident."

In a dazed state, Cindy strained to lift her head, and briefly surveyed the horror that had befallen her car companion. Gasping, she turned her head toward Genevieve. "I've got to get out of here!" As Cindy struggled to move, she arched her back in alarm, screaming in pain, "My legs!"

Genevieve could see that trying to move Cindy might make matters worse, as she detected a small pool of blood on the exposed mat underneath Cindy's trapped legs. Genevieve didn't know what condition the driver of the BMW was in, but if Cindy didn't get help soon, she might bleed to death.

"Cindy, the ambulance is almost here. Can you feel your legs? Does anything else hurt?"

Becoming still, Cindy closed her eyes as her tears mingled with blood from the cuts on her face, "Everything hurts."

Feeling panic begin to take over, Genevieve started to step away from the car so she could flag down the ambulance coming down the street, but Cindy grabbed her arm. "Don't leave me, Gen!"

Looking around frantically, Genevieve spotted several people standing nearby. "Please, call the firefighters and ambulance over, this woman is critical!"

A young woman began waiving and screaming, "Over here!"

Genevieve took Cindy's hand, moving in close. "You're going to be fine, Cindy. There are people here to take care of you now."

Cindy opened her wet eyes, "Tell Sol, I'm so sorry."

Genevieve flashed a look of confusion as the emotions pouring out of Cindy were too chaotic, and Genevieve didn't have the luxury of time to understand them. With a reassuring reply, Genevieve uttered, "Don't you worry about anything right now. You can talk to Sol later."

As the first responders began the extrication process, Genevieve stepped back and looked over at the snarled BMW. Firefighters had just pulled the driver out of the car and laid him on the pavement. No one was working on the young man who looked to be only in his teens.

He didn't make it. Watching a firefighter drape a yellow covering over the body, Genevieve could only stare. *If he'd just been patient; chosen differently, he wouldn't be lying there—but would I?*

When the paramedics got Cindy on the stretcher, Genevieve veered from thoughts of what might have been to what was real. Cindy was urgently calling her. "Genevieve, I'm scared. I can't feel my left leg, come with me, please!"

Genevieve looked and saw that traffic on the other side was moving again and that her car was the only one left abandoned in the turn lane. Looking at the paramedic she asked, "Can I move my car and come with you?"

The woman shook her head, "We don't have that kind of time."

As they started to wheel Cindy to the ambulance, Genevieve held her hand. "I'm going to be following right behind you, Cindy. I need to call Sol too."

When the doors closed, Genevieve ran and climbed over the center-divider and back into her car. When the light changed to green, Genevieve glanced over at the wreckage and saw what can happen when one choice rendezvous with another. *I'm sure they both thought they were going to be sleeping in their beds tonight,* Genevieve thought with a nauseating feeling in the pit of her stomach.

CHAPTER 52

OUTSIDER

THE MOMENT GENEVIEVE got to the E.R., she called Teddy who was still at the office with Sol and Ella.

The conversation was quick and urgent, "Cindy's been in a car accident. She's hurt pretty bad. Two others didn't make it. Tell Sol, and hurry!"

After hanging up the phone, Genevieve stood just inside the E.R. room so Cindy could see she was nearby. The attending doctor had just walked in as well and was reading Cindy's chart. After observing the I.V. drip pumping blood, he made a quick adjustment. His demeanor was thoughtful as he tried his best to calm Cindy's fears. When he asked her if she was allergic or had ever had any adverse reaction to morphine, Cindy shook her head, and it was promptly ordered.

By the end of the full visual examination, the doctor had decided to keep the cervical collar on Cindy's neck, and told the attending nurse, "She needs a neck and chest X-ray, and I want an MRI of her left leg.

As a patient transporter got ready to wheel Cindy to X-ray, the doctor walked over to Genevieve. "Are you family?"

Genevieve shook her head. She couldn't even say she was a good friend at this point. It had been years since she and Cindy had spent any significant time together. "Our husbands have a business together. I just happened to be there when the accident occurred. Her husband is on the way. Please, can you tell me about her injuries?"

Looking at Cindy who was in a conscious but dazed state, he confirmed, "As best I can tell, she sustained two, maybe three fractured ribs. The X-ray will show more. I'm more concerned about the deep cut on her left thigh. She may have some nerve damage. We'll know more once we get all the test results back."

As they were wheeling her out of the room, Genevieve took Cindy's hand. "Sol is on his way, Cindy. We'll all be here when you get back."

Genevieve couldn't tell if it was the morphine or possibly a concussion, but Cindy started shaking her head from side to side and rambling incoherently, "He wouldn't...I just wanted out." Then her eyes burst open wide, "Sheena! Oh, God, where is Sheena, you have to find her!"

The feelings coming from Cindy were drenched in remorse. To calm her, Genevieve nodded, "Yes, I'll find her."

Once Cindy was out of sight, Genevieve began walking to the waiting room when her cell phone rang. *Oh no, Broc!*

"Mom, where are you? I've been waiting over an hour." Broc questioned.

After Genevieve explained the situation, Broc said he'd call his grandfather to pick him up. "I'll see you later at home. I hope Mrs. Santoro will be okay."

Genevieve's questions were propagating in a flurry, as she arrived in the waiting room. *Who was it that died? Who's Sheena? Was that the mystery man's wife? Why were they flying through the red light?*

After ten minutes of torturous waiting, Sol, Teddy, Ella, and the Santoro's son, Leo came through the door. Seeing Genevieve, Sol hurried forward, "How is she?"

Genevieve relayed everything she knew, including the fact it had been the car Cindy was riding in that caused the accident. "The driver ran a red light at high speed, hitting the person that was *just* ahead of me, as he was making a left turn, killing him. I don't know if you knew who Cindy was with, but he didn't make it either."

Genevieve could see the wheels turning in Sol's mind and added, "When Cindy was being wheeled to X-ray, she asked me to find someone named, Sheena. Do you know who that is? Is it the man's wife?"

Everyone but Sol shrugged or shook their heads. Sol murmured, "Yea, I know who she is. She's Greg's daughter."

At that point, Teddy and Leo appeared to have realized who had been in the car with Cindy. Teddy knowingly remarked to Sol, "I had a feelin I knew who it was. She was with Greg. Greg's dead."

Sol looked at Teddy solemnly and nodded.

Genevieve stared at her husband. For the first time, she realized all that he had been holding back from telling her. She had made it clear, years prior, that it was better to keep her distance from Teddy's partner for everyone's sake. Ever-after, Teddy never disclosed his conversations with Sol, or what was happening in the Santoro's personal life, dutifully keeping the two worlds from touching.

Now it was crystal clear, all that had been sacrificed by Genevieve's cycloptic view of things. *Where was I when Teddy needed to vent **his** frustration? Where was I when I should have been cheering him on at award dinners? How could I not see that I had become an outsider in so much of his life?*

Teddy looked at Genevieve. Seeing her bewildered expression, he said, "Let's take a little break."

Ella echoed, "I'll come too."

As they walked outside the large double doors of the E.R., Genevieve lamented. "I feel like half my life is spent in hospitals."

Teddy put his arm around Genevieve's shoulders and kissed her head. "As long as you're just a visitor. Sounds like it was a close call for ye."

Genevieve recalled just *how* close it had been and shuddered. "It was very close."

At the far end of the parking lot, Teddy spotted "Jose's Meals on Wheels" food truck. "Let's grab a taco, and I'll fill ye in on wha I know."

While the three sat on a grassy knoll by the food truck, the smell of onions and fried tortillas wafting in the warm breeze acted as an invisible invitation for others nearby. Within minutes, the line for Mexican cuisine had grown fifteen people deep.

Throughout the time it took the Walkers to eat their spicy snack, Teddy explained that Cindy had started an affair several months prior with a mutual friend of the Santoro's, a man named Greg. The discovery had blindsided Sol, and, in his haste, he kicked Cindy out of their home. "She's been stayin at Greg's ever since. I didn't know he had a daughter though. Sol has nivvor mentioned her."

Genevieve was having a hard time with the story. "Cindy was always so devoted to Sol. I don't understand *her* being the adulterer."

"Sol plays God's gift to women, ye know tha Gen. Cindy told Sol she believed he had been goin oot on her for a long time. He hadn't though, not until she hurt him like tha. He's been seein someone lately. I haven't met her. It seems casual though. I think he's just tryin to fill the void. I see him starin at Cindy's picture on his desk all the time."

Ella looked dispirited, "How sad. Do you think they have a chance to get back together, now?"

Before Teddy's response, Genevieve got a flash of something Cindy said, '… I just wanted out.' Genevieve wondered, *Was she talking about her marriage, the car, or the affair she was having?*

Teddy shrugged at Ella. "I hope they can at least open up honestly to each other now."

Genevieve knew just how important those words were, as she took Teddy's hand. "Not just the Santoro's. I'm sorry we haven't been able to be open with each other either."

Then, glancing at Ella who was giving her mother a puzzled frown, Genevieve continued, choosing her words carefully. "I know I've had my differences with Sol. He can be hard to deal with at times, but I'm sorry you didn't feel you could talk to me about him, or the upheaval it was causing at work. I know you've been struggling lately, and you didn't feel you could turn to me. It was my fault for making you feel that way. I had no idea how much things had changed."

Teddy shrugged at his wife, "There wasn't anythin ye could do. When he told me aboot her affair, I wasn't tha surprised. Sol's wanderin eye is cheeky, yet I've come to realize, impotent. Obviously, though, Cindy didn't see it tha way. When Sol kicked her oot of their house, she went straight to the office and packed up all her personal stuff and left a note sayin she quit. We've had a temp workin there ever since."

Genevieve was dumbfounded, shaking her head. "*Teddy,* you could have told me. You *should* have told me, she stressed, softly.

Ella's eyes narrowed as they darted back and forth from her father to her mother. It was apparent something was missing. Something had happened that they were tiptoeing around. Putting two and two together, Ella came to the logical conclusion that Sol had caused trouble for her parents. Knowing her mom's ability and what she might have felt coming from Sol at one time or another in addition to the way they made him sound…

Ella cringed, *Eww!*

CHAPTER 53

WANT AND NEED
FOR CHANGE

WHEN THE THREE got back, Cindy had finished the tests and was back in the E.R. room. Leo was sitting next to her. The two were alone in the room, talking quietly as Cindy continued to wipe at her eyes. Looking around, Genevieve noticed Sol was nowhere to be seen.

"Can we come in?" Genevieve asked.

Cindy looked up, flashed a miniscule smile, and nodded. By the time the Walkers had squeezed into the small available space, Cindy's head was downcast. "It's my fault," she cried. Wincing in pain as she tried to move, "Greg had picked me up from my temp job. As we were driving, I told him it wasn't working with us, that I was leaving. When I told him Sol wanted me back, Greg got so angry, he swung and hit my right shoulder. I was shocked. He had never been violent before. It scared me. I asked him to pull over so I could get out, but he became withdrawn and began to drive faster. The more I pleaded with him, the faster he drove."

Genevieve shivered at the thought, murmuring, "It must have been absolutely terrifying, Cindy. So, Greg didn't know you were seeing Sol again?"

Cindy blinked slowly and smiled slightly, "I wasn't seeing Sol. But he had been leaving notes on my car. Yesterday, he sent flowers to where I'm currently working, saying how sorry he was and how much he wanted me back. Sol swore he had never gone out on me. It was all I needed to hear. I was going to leave Greg anyway. His controlling nature was smothering me, something I never witnessed until I began living with him."

There was a short pause, then Cindy's face melted into despair, "But, I should never have done it the way I did. I didn't realize how desperate he could be, but I should have known better! If I'd just waited until later this evening and let him down easy, he'd still be alive. He didn't deserve to die like that."

Leo held his mother's hand as she started to cry again, but reminded her, "Mom, to me, it looked like Greg didn't care what happened. He was on a mission of destruction with his recklessness, probably hoping you'd both meet the same gruesome fate. No matter the timing, his instability would have been aimed to hurt you for leaving him. You know that now. There was just no excuse for what he did, plain and simple. He also took the life of a teenager, did you know that?"

Cindy's chin quivered. "Your father told me."

Teddy interjected, "Speakin of Sol, did he leave?"

Cindy nodded. He said he'd go by Greg's house and break the news to Greg's daughter, Sheena."

Lifting her head upward, Cindy began moaning, "The poor girl's mother died of cancer when Sheena was only five. She's only had her father all these years, and no matter what else, the two of them were very close. There was never a time he didn't have a smile when he talked about his daughter. I just don't understand why he would do this, to *her!*"

"I take it she's not a little girl then?" Teddy inquired.

"She's around nineteen or twenty. I don't see much of her. She's taking a full load at the community college and hangs out with her friends—even more, lately."

When the dinner tray arrived a few minutes later, so did Sol. Genevieve could see a humble, contrite change to his demeanor. Taking Leo's place by Cindy, Sol never took his eyes off his wife, and, knowing the two had a lot to discuss, everyone excused themselves for the evening.

On the way out, Sol ran up to Teddy, "Say, Ted, I need to talk to you later. Can you come back by after you've had some dinner?"

"Aye, sure, but can't it wait until tomorrow? Ye should spend some time with Cindy."

Sol shook his head, "No, it won't take long, just a few things I need to discuss. Say, I'm parked over by the main entrance. I'll meet you there at eight-o'clock, is that okay?"

Teddy shrugged, "If ye insist."

Sol patted Teddy on the shoulder. "Thanks, partner. See you then." As he started to head back to Cindy's room, Sol turned back, "And thanks for all *you* did today, Genevieve. It was amazing you were there to help Cindy like you did. It was good to see you again. Oh, and Ella, come back to the office tomorrow afternoon so we can continue where we left off today. I'm really impressed with what I've seen so far. I think you'll be a great addition to our company one day soon!"

As Sol headed back down the hall, Teddy, Genevieve, and Ella watched his swagger before Teddy concluded, "Well, there's no denyin, one man's loss today, was another man's gain. I just hope Sol realizes it was *his* behavior tha started everythin in the first place."

When Sol got to Cindy's room, he turned back smiling and gave the Walkers a quick wave before entering.

While the three made their way to the parking lot, the conversation was minimal until Ella asked, "Do you think someone can really change their underlying behavior, who they are?"

Genevieve proposed, "I think it can be done, yes. But only if the person chooses the change for themselves, and not to satisfy others. However, that's not the real test for Sol. I believe he *wants* to make the change in his flirtatious behavior, but he seems to be totally unaware when he's doing it. If you aren't conscious of what you're doing, how then can you change it?"

Teddy cracked a smile, "I can always smack him upside the heed when I see him doin it."

Genevieve raised her eyebrows and followed his lead, "I can flick his ear with my finger when *I* see him doing it."

Ella gave her parents a concerned look, "Why don't you just zap him with a taser, geez!"

Teddy and Genevieve gave their daughter a surprised look. "Boy," Genevieve blurted, "That's even a better idea, Ariella! In fact, I just received one from Brunner the other day. Looking at Teddy, "Since you see him all the time honey, I'll give it to you."

Teddy beamed, "Perfect!" And the two gave each other a high-five.

Frowning, Ella shook her head. "You're just kidding, right?"

When Teddy and Genevieve gave her a "What do you mean?" look, Ella crossed her arms and sneered with stark disapproval.

Within moments Genevieve grabbed Teddy's arm, and they both began laughing, "You're so fun to tease!" Genevieve chirped.

Looking annoyed, Ella closed her eyes and turned away. *When will I learn? Like those two would ever **tase** anyone!*

CHAPTER 54

A DEADLY SECRET

JUST BEFORE EIGHT o'clock, Teddy was on his way back to the hospital. Reflecting on the day, he was puzzled why Sol felt the urgency to meet. *Must be important.*

The parking lot had plenty of open space now, so Teddy found a spot reasonably close to Sol's jeep. Sol was standing near it, smoking a cigarette. *Bad sign,* Teddy thought. The habit always laid dormant unless stress became overwhelming for him.

As Teddy walked closer, Sol dropped the cigarette and snuffed it with his shoe. "Hey, Ted. Hope you got some dinner."

Teddy nodded, "Aye, Gen called in a pizza tha arrived just affta we got home."

With a nervous smile, Sol murmured, "Good, good."

A frown began to appear on Teddy's face when Sol didn't continue talking. "So, I see you're smokin. Wha's goin on?"

Sol raised his eyes, "I've got myself in a mess, Ted."

The first thing that came to Teddy's mind was the railyard project. "Did ye get in another argument with the buildin inspector again? I told ye to let *me* handle it. Ye always rub tha guy the wrong way!"

Sol reassured him, "No, no, it has nothing to do with work."

Teddy sighed with relief. "Okay, so?"

Sol took his pack of cigarettes out again and was about to grab one when Teddy swiped the pack away. "It can't be all tha bad. Now you've got a chance to have your wife back, tha's good, aye?"

Sol's head bobbled between nodding yes and shaking no. "Yes, of course. Cindy's all I want. But I've got myself entangled with someone else now, and I don't think I can just break it off."

Teddy crossed his arms and questioned, "I thought ye said it was just a casual thing?"

Sol put his head down. "I know. That's what I told you. That's what I told myself as well." Looking back up Sol stressed, "First, Teddy, you have to understand how angry I was when Cindy left me for someone like Greg. About two weeks after she left, I decided I was going to confront him and have it out. I went to his house, and when the door opened it was his daughter, Sheena. I knew Greg had a daughter but didn't realize how old she was, and beautiful."

Teddy's eyes widened with alarm. "Ah, Sol ye didn't?"

Sol hesitated and cleared his throat. "I asked if I could speak to the man of the house, and Sheena said that it was her father, but he wasn't back from work yet. I should have left, I know, but we started talking and she actually seemed attracted to me. Still, I said I'd come back another time, when I knew he'd be there alone, and then I left.

"About a week later, I was getting coffee at a donut shop near the community college. You know, the one a few blocks from work." With narrowed eyes, Teddy stayed silent and nodded. "Well, as I was leaving, Sheena was walking in. She recognized me right away. She said she needed a good jolt of coffee before her next boring class or she'd surely fall asleep. I don't know, Ted, we started talking again and she asked if I was married. I told her I was separated and probably headed for divorce. Then she asked to meet me again. I wasn't thinking anything through Ted, I know that. But I was so lonely, and she was so…"

Teddy shrugged, resigned, "Ye always get yourself into trouble. So, wha? Ye reasoned tha Cindy would marry Greg, you'd marry Sheena and your ex-wife would then become your mother-in-law?

Sol thought about it for a moment and began to laugh at the insanity of it all. Teddy looked down and shook his head but couldn't help but let out a quiet chuckle.

After a long moment, Sol confessed, "Man, I really screwed up. But I didn't think Cindy and I were ever going to get back together, no matter what I wanted. I knew that Sheena and I couldn't last, but I really *do* care for her. What do you think I should do, Ted?"

Before Teddy could answer, Sol's attention was caught by something happening behind Teddy, and his expression morphed into sheer panic. "NO! Don't!"

Teddy turned in the direction Sol was looking, and there, about fifty feet away, a woman was pointing a gun in their direction. Her hand was shaking, and it looked like she was crying. "YOU SON-OF-A-BITCH!" she screamed.

Teddy stepped forward, "Hey lass, don't..."

BAM.

Teddy felt a sting. Looking down, a dark circle, right below the A on his University of Arizona T-shirt was turning bright red and quickly growing larger. Looking over at Sol's petrified expression, Teddy staggered backward, fell against the side of the jeep and slid slowly to the ground.

The woman screamed, "GOD, now see what you made me do! I hate you!"

Running toward Sol, she unleashed her furor, BAM-BAM-BAM.

The force from the barrage of bullets threw Sol off his feet, landing him flat, face toward the night's sky.

As he laid twitching, she stood over him and said, "I went to see her, and there you were—kissing her! God, Cindy is your wife? Were you hoping to hurt her by screwing me? Or, was it some sick revenge on my dad for stealing your wife from you? Oh, Lord, what a fool I've been!"

With only moments left, Sol gurgled, "Sheena, please."

Screaming with sheer anger and despair, Sheena dropped to her knees and dissolved into sobs as Sol took his last few gasps of air.

Teddy felt cold. Laying frozen after falling on his side, he watched as the young woman next to him began to lift the gun again. With every fiber of his being, Teddy tried to move, to take the gun away, but he was coughing up blood that was filling his throat and mouth, each breath getting harder to take.

"Why did you have to be so deceitful?" Sheena bellowed. "You knew how much I loved you, that you were my first." Slumping and putting the gun in her lap, Sheena stared at Sol's lifeless body, then continued, "Cindy never mentioned her husband's name. She had no idea, did she? Now I see why you didn't want to meet my dad. And you had me believing it was all about our age difference."

Lifting her face to the sky, Sheena let out a loud, mournful cry. Then after a few moments of silence, she brought her focus back to Sol. Her demeanor had become stoic as her voice softened to a mumble, "Everyone I love is gone."

Wiping her wet face with her free hand, Sheena concluded, "Cindy was bad for my dad—and *you* were bad for me."

Noticing several security guards closing in, Sheena lifted the gun and put it under her chin. Teddy pulled every ounce of strength he had left and reached outward, knocking the gun from her hand.

The three officers swarmed in as Teddy's world began to fade. His fear was gone.

As Sheena looked back toward Teddy before being taken away, she mouthed, "I'm sorry."

Teddy felt a tear escape before slowly closing his eyes.

CHAPTER 55

TIME TO MOVE ON

THE SMELL OF the fresh salty air burned at Teddy's lungs as he rode his Kelly-green bike up a steep grassy hill. The sky above was moving from east to west in a cyclical rotation of colors. Like an artist, creating a watercolor master-piece, using the sky as the canvas, drops of green appeared from nowhere, seamlessly blending into the purest blue, to create a brilliant turquoise, then fading to a muted yellow. Soon, invisible brushstrokes of red swept broadly across the mellow yellow, producing an "Awe-inspiring" burnt orange before gradually fading to a calming rose.

Billowy clouds frolicked leisurely above him, and, to Teddy's amusement, he only had to imagine one taking a particular form, and it quickly complied, making him laugh.

Yet everything seemed as it should be for the twelve-year-old, as he and his best friend went exploring the lands and cliffs near Bamburgh, England.

As the hill got steeper, Teddy's friend, Deeker started to fall behind. "Wait up, Ted!"

Looking at his buddy, Teddy laughed and pressed the peddles harder. The path upward was obscured and overgrown, but Teddy knew the way blind-folded. When he finally got to the top, Teddy dropped his bike and beheld a view that existed beyond human sight. To the far reaches, the ocean stretched out before him. The water was colorless, moving like waves of bending glass, while every creature and plant below, navigated their habitat in technicolor brilliance.

Suddenly, a forceful wind rushed up the steep wall of the bluff, just thirty feet away from him. Teddy watched as it shot above him like a glittering stream rising in the air, then sliding down an invisible slope, where it gathered speed, sprinting through the long grass toward him. Stretching out his arms, Teddy felt its refreshing energy flow through him. Then, quickly turning, he watched the sparkling current as it swiftly rolled over a large rock nearby, then gleefully continued down the hill, where it disappeared.

With a huge dimpled grin, Teddy began to turn back toward the ocean, when he noticed the mesmerizing activity, inside the large flat rock. Stepping closer, Teddy stood perfectly still and watched the almost undetectable movement within it. As if looking through a high-powered microscope, Teddy could clearly see each molecule. He likened it to a billion marbles crammed into a cookie jar, all jostling for position. Then he imagined them wailing, "Move over, you're crushing me."

Whether it was the shimmering light energy of the wind or the dense energy within the stone, Teddy could only shake his head and marvel at the energy of all life—observed from this new perspective.

Finally, Deeker reached the look-out. Teddy nodded at his friend, who stood panting, then laid his bike next to Teddy's. With his husky structure, Deek, as Teddy called him, was several inches shorter than lanky Teddy. He had inquisitive green eyes, a sprinkle of freckles along his nose, and short curly dark hair that glistened with sweat, while his cheeks flushed a rosy red from the laborious climb.

Teddy motioned Deek to have a seat, and the two proceeded to get comfortable on the large boulder. "You're really playin the part well, my ol friend," Teddy complimented.

Deek took a deep breath, "It's been a while since ah felt like me ol self. Thought it waad be easier if ye saw me, as me."

Teddy held a long moment looking his friend over. With a satisfied nod, Teddy turned and looked outward. Deek grinned and followed suit.

Staring at the galaxy of colors beneath the sea, the two remained silent for a time. Finally, Deek spoke. "Ah wish wi could hev foond this place together, Ted."

With a nod, Teddy gently scolded, "We were *supposed* to, ye know. If only ye had waited for me to finish my chores."

Deek didn't say a word but got up and walked to the edge of the cliff. "Sure is bonny up heor."

"It's my favorite place in the world." Teddy quietly replied.

"Ah knaa. Ye took yer wifie heor when ye two had barely met. Ye had kept this place a secret until then. When tha happened, Ah knew she wez the one."

Teddy nodded again. "Aye, it was my secret place. I always felt closer to ye up here. It was where I could talk to ye; figure things oot. But when I met Gen, I felt ready to share it. I hoped you'd approve."

Deek sat back down and nudged Teddy, "Aye, Ah did."

Teddy sat peacefully, watching a florescent Blue Whale, more than a mile out, feasting on a cloud of flashy hot pink Krill.

"Wha ye thinkin Ted?"

Teddy scrunched his nose. "Just thinkin how I've missed bein near the sea."

Deek nodded, "Ah suppose movin te a desert *was* a big change."

"Aye," Teddy murmured, "But Gen loved it there, and I loved her, so…"

Another few quiet moments passed when Deek suddenly jumped up, "Say, Ted, would ye like te see yer fatha? Maybe yer older brother James? Sol isn't far frem heor either and many others who are waitin. Are ye ready te move on?" Deek questioned.

Teddy looked at Deek, contemplating his suggestion, "I think I'd like to stay here a while longer. Will ye stay with me?"

Deek grinned and sat back down, close to Teddy, and put his arm around Teddy's shoulder, "As long as ye want, Ted."

Looking back out at sea, Teddy admitted. "I sure missed ye all these years."

Deek murmured, "Ah knaa, Ted. Ah wish Ah could have convinced ye tha it was nivvor yer fault. Ah tried through the years te let ye know; te give ye peace, but ye nivvor heard me."

Teddy chuckled. "I don't think many know *how* to listen, my friend—I guess I nivvor really tried. I always left the spiritual end of things for Gen. She understood it much betta."

Then Teddy's tone changed, "But, no matta! I was the one who showed ye tha old well. I should have known where to look for ye."

"Ted!" Deeker boomed, "Ah hit me heed on the way doon. Ah wez gone in a minute. Time would not hev matta'd. Me choice led me there, not yers. Just like it wez yer choice to step in front of tha bullet."

Teddy raised his eyebrows and shook his head. "Aye, I didn't expect tha to happen."

"HA!" Deek exclaimed. "And Ah didn't expect the rocks te crumble when Ah leaned over the well, either. Ah just wished ye wouldn't hev waisted so much time mournin fer me. Ah always was quite fine, felt betta than ever affta it happened. Tha's wha comin home always feels like."

"So, Theodore Ian Walker, are ye ready te move on then?"

Teddy looked at Deek, then up at the sky that was beginning to turn a light rose. Nodding, Teddy acknowledged, "I understand more than ever now, wha led me here, to *this* bluff. I could always grasp the enormity of *everythin* betta here."

Looking earnestly at his buddy, Teddy stood up and decided, "Movin on sounds like a wonderful new journey. Thank ye Deek for letting me talk things oot with ye. I told ye I always felt closer to ye up here."

CHAPTER 56

EXPLANATIONS

SITTING QUIETLY, GENEVIEVE stared at the blank wall. It had become a movie screen of memories playing out before her. Closing her tired, red eyes, Genevieve imagined smelling Teddy's musk cologne that always drew her like a cat to catnip; feeling his warm breath as he caressed her neck—aching to hear his comforting accent tell her "Everythin will be just fine, love."

Genevieve's tears had subsided for now. On a dime, her world had shattered.

Feeling the soft touch of her sister's hand, Genevieve opened her eyes and saw Tess gently intertwine her fingers among her own. Squeezing them tight, Genevieve sighed, "Thank you for being with me."

Tess made a slight frown, "Gen, where else would I be? I know you have the family to surround you, but before anyone else here, it was just you and me. You've always watched over me. It's my turn to watch over *you* now."

Holding a sandwich out in front of her, Tess urged, "Please, Gen, you need to eat something."

Genevieve just stared at it, "Maybe later. I was thinking about the time we all met Teddy in Bamburgh. Do you remember that trip?"

Tess gave a little chuckle. "How could I ever forget? It was like 'Where's Waldo' trying to figure out where you were hiding out with Teddy each day!"

Genevieve smiled. "I wasn't hiding. It was just that I had this annoying sister who wanted to steal my new boyfriend away from me."

Tess rolled her eyes, "As if I could. I was nine! I did have quite a crush on him though. That bellman outfit really made his blue eyes sparkle."

Genevieve could feel her lower lip tremble. "Yes, it sure did."

Seeing that the memory was about to bring on a new wave of tears, Tess brought Genevieve back to the present by asking, "So, where is everyone?"

Genevieve looked around, just realizing the room was empty. "I'm not sure. Mom and Ella were here a little bit ago."

Just then, the surgeon walked into the surgical waiting room and, as if he were the Pied Piper, Steven, Melinda, Ella, Broc, Geoffrey, and Ryan followed closely behind.

Quickly standing, Genevieve searched Dr. Breaman's face for a sign as he walked in her direction. She thought she read confidence and possibly a hint of relief. If she could only hold his hand, then there'd be no possible pretense or misunderstanding, for nothing could be more honest and revealing than what the doctor's feelings could tell her. Still, Genevieve resisted the impulse and waited for his words.

"Mrs. Walker?" he guessed. Melinda moved to the other side of Genevieve and put her arm around her waist.

Genevieve nodded, "Yes. Did my husband survive surgery?"

The doctor's lips formed a narrow line and his eyes were weary but intently focused on Genevieve as he nodded, "Yes, he made it through surgery, but he is still critical. Honestly, if he hadn't been just outside these hospital walls, I don't think he would have had a chance. The bullet did a lot of damage to his left lung. I was able to repair the superior lobe but had to do a lobectomy on the inferior. There was also damage to his costal cartilage and splintering of his sixth rib which caused a diaphragmatic rupture. I was able to spot it quickly, so no herniation occurred. However, he lost a lot of blood and coded once during surgery."

Genevieve felt like collapsing, but Tess and Melinda held her close. Observing the color quickly fading from Genevieve's face, the doctor urged, "Mrs. Walker, it's been a long night, you should sit down."

Annoyed at her own frailty, Genevieve agreed and sat back down. The doctor approached and put his hand on her shoulder, "Will you be okay?"

With a nod, Genevieve realized the doctor's clinical, forthright approach had taken her by surprise. His candor of the situation, no matter how blunt, had been understood. Before his hand lifted, however, Genevieve felt all she really needed to know. His feelings, although exhausted and drained, revealed self-confidence and positive expectations. It was unclear if the doctor was playing it safe, or it was his nature to be less then hopeful when addressing a patient's family. But his feelings were positive, and that was good enough for now.

"Can I be with him?" Genevieve pleaded.

The doctor shook his head. "He's in recovery, but as soon as we get him to a room, I'll let you know. It shouldn't be too long. Do you have any more questions for me?"

Genevieve shook her head, "No, and thank you doesn't seem nearly enough. I can't tell you how grateful I am for all you've done for my husband."

Dr. Breaman smiled and nodded. "I'll keep a close eye on him. In the meantime, now would be a good time to get something to eat."

Tess once again held the sandwich in front of her sister. "Okay, okay." Genevieve murmured.

As the doctor turned and headed toward the door, Steven stopped him and quietly asked if he'd explain things in 'simple cowboy terms.' The other men closed in for a better explanation as well.

When the doctor was finished, Steven rubbed his hands briskly together and looked firmly into the doctor's eyes. "Okay, so a bullet hit the bottom part of Ted's left lung. It was damaged so bad you had to remove that part. The bullet also hit a rib that caused a piece to it to put a hole in the thin muscle that separates his top half from his bottom half. However, you repaired it before his guts could, what did you call it, 'herniate' or seep into his upper half, which would have been very bad. So, do I have that correct then?

The doctor couldn't help but smile. "Close enough."

Choking on her fourth bite, Genevieve looked at Melinda who in turn shrugged. "In simple terms, the man *has* to be thorough in his understanding of things."

As the doctor was leaving, Brunner walked in. Spotting Genevieve, he walked over. "How's Ted?"

Making a hard swallow of her fifth bite, Genevieve quietly reported, "He's in recovery right now. There was a lot of damage, Brunner. The surgeon said he's still critical. But there was a moment when he touched my shoulder, and I was able to feel his emotions. That's when I was able to breathe again. The doctor has hope. I'm going to trust in his feelings—I have to."

Brunner smiled, "Ted's strong Gen—and *s t u b b o r n*. He's not going to let a little bullet take him down."

Genevieve laughed as a tear fell. "You've got that right. What was I thinking?"

Everyone agreed; some smiling and nodding in concurrence while others broke the tension with a healthy laugh.

After a moment, Steven asked Brunner, "Did you find out what happened? Who shot Sol and Ted?"

Brunner's demeanor turned solemn. "I read the woman's confession in the police report. I don't know what Mr. Santoro was thinking, but he had been playing with dynamite."

Melinda interjected, "So this was about Sol then?"

Brunner nodded. "For whatever reason, Mr. Santoro started an affair with the young daughter of his wife's boyfriend."

Genevieve quickly shook her head back in forth in confusion. "Wait. Are you saying Sol was seeing Greg's daughter?"

Brunner raised his eyebrows and nodded. "It's really convoluted, I know. Her name is Sheena Gossman, and in her eyes anyway, she and Mr. Santoro, or Sol, were in love, and it had become very serious. After the accident that killed her father yesterday, Sheena went to the hospital to see her father's girlfriend, Cindy. When she arrived at Cindy's room, Sheena's boyfriend, Sol was there, kissing Cindy.

"It wasn't until that moment that Ms. Gossman put two and two together. In the report, Sheena said she ran home, blinded with anger, and got a gun from her father's safe. Then she came back, planning to sit and wait for Sol to leave the hospital. But, when Sheena arrived, she spotted him standing by his jeep, smoking a cigarette. When she got out of the car, she noticed him talking with another man, which was Ted, of course. Sheena said it didn't matter, that she had a clear shot at Sol. However, just as she was pressing the trigger, Ted stepped in front of Sol. She said she never meant to hurt anyone but the man that ruined her life."

Melinda whispered, "Oh my God."

Genevieve stared blankly at Brunner as she recalled, "I remember Teddy saying Sol was seeing someone. But Teddy said he thought it was casual, that Sol was only trying to fill the empty space Cindy had left."

With a sharp focus back on Brunner, Genevieve fumed, "Why would Sol *do* such a thing?"

Brunner replied, "I guess we'll never know for sure. In the report, Ms. Gossman believed Sol had used her to hurt either his wife, Cindy or her dad, Greg, or maybe both. One of the security officers said Sheena was about to pull the trigger on herself, when Teddy leaned forward and knocked the gun from her hand just before he fell unconscious. I thought that was heroism at its best, and you should know, Gen."

Genevieve blinked a tear away as she smiled and nodded.

Brunner nodded back and concluded, "In the end, I don't think Sol imagined a scenario that would ever have him getting back together with his wife. Then, all of a sudden, well, like I said—dynamite."

Ella inquired, "Has anyone talked to Cindy yet?"

Brunner vacillated, "I'm not sure. A police officer should have advised her, but they may still be trying to sort everything out."

Genevieve put the sandwich down. "I'll go and see her. Ella, come with me. If Leo isn't with her, I'll need you to find him. He needs to know what has happened to his father as well. Everyone else, *please* get me as soon as..."

Broc grabbed his mom and hugged her. "We will."

CHAPTER 57

YOU'LL NEVER
KNOW WHY

WHEN GENEVIEVE AND Ella found Cindy's room, it was dark. Cindy appeared to be sleeping as Leo sat in the shadowy room next to her. Seeing the two, Leo got up and came to the door. Genevieve instantly knew Leo had heard the news, his eyes were as red as her own.

Reaching out, Genevieve pulled him close. "I'm so sorry, Leo."

After Ella took Leo's hand and dittoed her mother sentiment, Genevieve looked at Cindy and asked, "Does she know?"

Leo looked at the floor, then at his mother. "Yes. I was sitting with her when an officer entered the room, about an hour ago. We thought he was here to take Mom's account of the traffic accident. However instead, he told us there had been a shooting and Dad had been killed. Mom refused to believe it. When the officer told her *who* did the shooting, she became hysterical, and they needed to sedate her.

Then, turning to Genevieve, "After she was out, he informed me that Mr. Walker had been shot too but he didn't know his condition. Is he alive?"

Genevieve's face remained somber, "Yes, he's out of surgery but critical. I haven't been able to see him yet."

Leo shook his head, "I don't understand any of this. Why would Greg's daughter go on a shooting spree, presumably aimed at my father? When I asked the officer if he knew why, all he said was that it was a love triangle, gone bad, but Dad wasn't even seeing my mom. Why would Greg's daughter blame him for anything?"

Genevieve and Ella looked at each other. Leo saw the expressions on their faces and asked, "You know why, don't you?"

Genevieve wished Leo and Cindy already knew the heartbreaking news, as she thought, *How will Leo remember his father, after learning Sol was far from an innocent bystander? What about Cindy, who believed Sol when he said he never was unfaithful to her. Will she recover when she hears of his ultimate betrayal?*

With a slow nod, Genevieve explained what Brunner had told her, but reminded Leo that he would never hear his father's side of the story—and there was *always* another side to every story.

Leo shook his head, "No, there is no explanation that absolves my father from this. He is, or was, a manipulator. I was never ignorant of that fact. Hell, that's what his job was all about, and he was mighty proud of that. Did he deserve what he got? No. But his calculating scheme, whatever the reason, was never going to end well."

Out of the corner of her eye, Ella saw Cindy wiping a tear away. Nudging her mother, they all turned and saw that Cindy was awake and had been listening.

"Mom," Leo murmured, walking toward her.

Cindy was subdued, holding her emotions in check. "I'm okay, Leo."

Genevieve and Ella moved to the bed. Cindy put her arm out, and Genevieve took her hand. Within moments deep despair ripped through Genevieve's chest. Anger and betrayal danced sadistically around Cindy's own guilt and powerlessness. Cindy's calm exterior scared Genevieve, knowing what was harbored beneath.

Pretending she was unaware, Genevieve hesitantly asked, "Cindy, did you hear everything I told Leo?"

Cindy blinked slowly; her face almost devoid of emotion. "I heard enough."

Genevieve looked at Ella bewildered, unsure what she could say that could soften the titanic blow to Cindy's world.

Deciding that her own story was all she could offer, Genevieve began, "It wasn't that long ago, that lies, and betrayal almost destroyed me. I let the hurt, perpetrated by those I had loved, poison my outlook on just about everything good in my life. Don't let that happen to you. It will rot you from the inside out. These two days have been tragic; the accident, Sol's lies, even Sheena's revenge and rampage which spilled over into our lives as well when she shot Teddy."

At that moment, horror covered Cindy's face, "Teddy was killed too?"

Genevieve felt Cindy's anger racing in circles, trapped, not knowing what direction to take. Quickly, Genevieve continued, "Cindy, Teddy is alive. He's in bad shape, but I have to trust he'll make it. What I want *you* to know is that I have learned the hard way, that I can never control what someone else does. We can never truly know the mindset of others at any moment, or the choices they will make. Our only control is in how we let what happens define us."

Genevieve tightened her grip on Cindy. "*Cry*, Cindy. Grieve your loss. Scream in anger, and shout how it hurts just as loud as you want. You have every right to feel all those emotions. Just don't let them consume you. They each have their purpose, as all feelings do. Yet if you start internalizing them, holding them back, you'll become a real victim. It's not what was done to you that holds you as one, but what you do to yourself that does.

"Trust me, Cindy. I know all too well, how the feeling of betrayal can make you doubt everything about yourself. It's a fate much more tragic than the actual transgression, which, in time, will only hold the power you've given it. You are no victim Cindy! Not Greg's, Sheena's, or Sol's. Let your family and friends, let *me* help you get through this, *please,* Cindy."

Cindy began to cry. Leo bent over and kissed his mother. Before Genevieve released her hold on Cindy's hand, she could feel the potency of anger waning ever so slightly. It would take time, but with a lot of love and continued reinforcement, Genevieve hoped Cindy would find her way again.

Ella took her mom's hand as they took a step back. Cindy's, uncorked emotions were flowing freely now. After a minute, trying her best to smile, Cindy choked out the words, "Go, be with that wonderful man of yours."

Genevieve smiled back. "We'll see you a little later."

As Ella and Genevieve approached the elevator, Broc lunged out when the doors opened. "MOM! The nurse just came by and said Dad's been moved to a room in I.C.U. We can see him now!"

The elevator felt like it was in slow motion as they climbed two floors. When the doors opened, the rest of the family stood nearby at the nurse's station.

"Good, you found them, Geoffrey exclaimed to Broc. The grandfatherly figure then turned his walker and began scooting forward, "He's in room 4221."

Genevieve's heart was pounding wildly as they all, in turn, passed Geoffrey by. As much as she treasured the communion with the Soul, she wasn't ready to hear Teddy's. *Please, not now!*

When the entourage arrived, Teddy's eyes were closed. He was on a ventilator to assure his lungs were getting adequate oxygen. An I.V. pole behind his bed had several bags attached, running through an infusion pump located to his right. The heart monitor to his left sounded heavenly with the familiar, quiet but steady, "beep." There was a chest tube drainage system hanging off the lower end of the bed, siphoning excess fluid from Teddy's pleural cavity that surrounded his lungs. All familiar equipment Genevieve had grown to know during the times spent in hospital rooms with those close to death.

Everyone quietly surrounded the bed. Genevieve reached under the blanket to locate Teddy's hand. It felt deliciously warm in hers. As she closed her eyes, Genevieve held her breath and waited. Never was she so petrified of the unknown as she was now. Not even the fierce trepidation she felt before holding little Chrissy's hand, years ago, could match the angst Genevieve felt as she now entered into this unpredictable realm.

Slowly an infusion of emotions began emerging. Confusion and some irritation were noticeable, but the feelings were nebulous and murky. Genevieve took a deep breath. *All normal. The pain medication is doing what it was supposed to.*

Smiling, Genevieve opened her eyes. It's him I feel!"

Everyone knew what that meant. Death was for another day. The Soul had nothing to convey. Ella let out a gasp and nodded while Steven put his arm around Broc and squeezed hard.

Within minutes a nurse stepped in. "I'm sorry but only two people at a time can stay in the room."

Genevieve looked at the nurse, imploringly, "Can you at least let my son and daughter stay with me for a little while?"

The nurse nodded. "Okay. I'd let you all stay, but there's just so little room in here."

It was now lunchtime, so the rest of the relieved family headed to the cafeteria.

As Genevieve settled in a chair next to the bed, she noticed Ella quietly crying as she sat at the foot of her father's bed. "Ella?"

Ella brushed at her face. "He's my *dad!* He's the strong one—my protector. I never imagined he could look like this, so helpless, so weak."

Genevieve tilted her head and stared at her husband as she felt her own emotions mirroring that of her daughters. Still, knowing what Teddy would surely say, she looked tenderly but resolutely at Ella. "Everythin will be just fine, love."

CHAPTER 58

A HARD MOVE FORWARD

AN HOUR HAD passed, and Teddy hadn't moved. Ella and Broc were talking quietly in the back of the room, while Genevieve sat next to the bed, resting her head on the bed's edge and monitored Teddy's emotions as she held a firm grip on his hand.

Confusion…disorientation…struggle…PANIC!

Genevieve shot to attention. Teddy's eyes were wide open and moving around. Letting go of Genevieve's hand, he began reaching for the ventilator tube going down his throat.

Genevieve stood up quickly so he could see her while the other two hurried to the other side of the bed. "It's okay, honey."

Once Teddy saw Genevieve, he let go of the tubing. Turning to his left, his children smiled, and Broc assured, "We're here, Dad."

With a slight nod, Teddy turned back to Genevieve. As she gently stroked his arm, a sudden spike of negative emotions arose within him. Although his eyes never veered away from his wife's, Teddy's face began contorting in heart-wrenching misery.

He remembers. Genevieve acknowledged as she took his hand and squeezed it, hard.

Inwardly, his shock, anger, and bewilderment translated outwardly to despair. Teddy's eyes became watery as he struggled to mouth the word, "Sol?"

With a trembling lip, Genevieve slowly shook her head. "He didn't make it."

Teddy closed his eyes tight and shook his head.

Kissing a tear that was beginning to fall, Genevieve held her face close to his and whispered, "You did all you could have done. You were *so* brave and heroic."

The sides of Teddy's mouth turned downward as more tears fell.

Like Cindy, Teddy was reeling from similar emotions. Both were not only dealing with their significant physical pain but also coming to grips with Sol's destructive secrets and sudden, devastating death.

Becoming agitated, Teddy began pulling on the ventilator tube again. Broc tried to keep his dad's hand away, as Genevieve pushed the call button to advise the nurse. "Let me see if I can reach Dr. Breaman." The nurse quickly responded.

Genevieve, Ella, and Broc tried their best to calm Teddy, and, within minutes, the doctor had made his way to the room.

Moving to the end of the bed, Dr. Breaman introduced himself to Teddy who was slightly inclined. Then, to Genevieve's surprise, the doctor explained the surgery and Teddy's condition with simplicity and the kind of encouragement Genevieve had only *felt* coming from the doctor earlier.

"Mr. Walker, that ventilator is only temporary, to help you breathe. Hopefully, I can have it removed by this evening and just an oxygen tube will suffice."

With a nod, Teddy laid his head flat on the pillow in compliance.

With a quick check of the monitors, the doctor, looking pleased, said he'd be back later, and departed.

When Genevieve turned back to Teddy, he just stared back at her. The spark of mischief and lightness was missing. Although not surprising, Genevieve could feel his emotions sinking into an abyss and it worried her.

The following ten days were a blur. Several times police came by to gather facts or take a statement from Teddy. Visitors stopped by, along with the rotating cycle of doctors, technicians, and nurses that did their duty, day and night.

No matter how exhausted Genevieve became, she refused to leave Teddy's side. Therefore, along with him, Genevieve was awakened every time an alarm went off at 2:00 a.m. alerting the staff of an empty I.V. bag, or, when the night nurse popped in to check on Teddy's vitals every two hours. But, without a doubt, it was when the two were sleeping at their best, that a lab technician would come to draw blood at the sadistic hour of 5:00 a.m. which *sucked* the most.

Cindy had come by earlier in the week and, after a brief visit, Genevieve excused herself, so Cindy and Teddy could commiserate privately about the man, even they came to realize, was unknowable. Two of the security guards came by as well and shook Teddy's hand, commending him for his selfless act when disarming Sheena.

Finally, the day had come. Teddy got the word he was going to be released tomorrow. The physical healing was going smoothly. The emotional healing, however, seemed far from repaired.

When the nurse left the room late in the evening after her final check before lights out, Genevieve sighed with relief, *one more night,* she thought. As she began to get up and move to the reclining chair that had been her bed the last ten days, Teddy held her arm and softly uttered, "I love ye, Gen."

Genevieve felt tears instantly rise in her eyes, as this was the first time since the shooting that he had uttered the words she longed to hear. Sitting back down, she began to feel some of the old familiar feelings she had missed. However, with his love and longing for her, Genevieve also felt anxiety, confinement, and a type of yearning for something that *wasn't* her. A frown quickly appeared on Genevieve's face as the emotions seemed contrary to each other.

Teddy carefully turned to his side. He studied Genevieve's face, not sure how to tell her. "Gen, from the moment I woke affta surgery, I've had this desperate urge to run away."

Still frowning, Genevieve questioned, "From the hospital?"

Slowly closing his eyes and shaking his head, he whispered, "Naw."

Genevieve's body started to shake, "From me? Teddy, I'm so sorry for all the things I've put you through. I *know* our life hasn't been easy…"

Shaking his head, Teddy grabbed Genevieve's hand, pulled it to his lips and kissed it. "I'd nivvor run from *ye,* love."

There was a moment of hesitation, then Teddy confessed, "But I've got to start over, move away from here. I need to be near the sea again. It's somethin I've wanted to do for years. If only I had, maybe this nivvor would have happened. I just need to know you'll come with me wherever tha may be."

Genevieve felt a teardrop as she closed her eyes and felt Teddy communicate his need for change, his love for her, his *need* for her, in a way words never could. As her misty eyes opened and met his, she whispered, "If *only* you could feel how much I need you. When I heard that you had been shot, my world stopped. I couldn't breathe, I couldn't think. I know it sounds cliché, but *you* are my home, Teddy. *Nothing* matters beyond that."

Teddy looked for signs of doubt, "But ye just reunited with Melinda and Steven not tha long ago. And wha aboot your job with Brunner?"

Genevieve smiled and repeated, "Nothing."

The darkness Genevieve had been feeling from Teddy the last ten days became a few shades lighter. Before midnight, the two had agreed the move would be somewhere along the California coast, but only after Broc graduated from high school. And, there were high hopes that Ella would accept a fast-track position as Teddy's new associate and move as well.

Genevieve felt electrified by Teddy's change in mood. That night, as the two discussed coastal areas to check out, Teddy kept imagining a familiar voice saying, "Ye still hev more movin on te do, Ted."

Teddy hadn't thought of his childhood friend, Deek, in a while, but that night he felt ready to open up the part of himself no one had ever had access to before, not even his wife. For Deek had been Teddy's best friend since they met in first grade. They thought alike, acted alike, *were* alike—inseparable.

When a scouting party found Deek's lifeless body at the bottom of a deep well, three days after he disappeared, Teddy began having nightmares, believing that his friend had been calling out for his help as he laid dying. That was when *Teddy* became the victim. Letting someone else's actions define him. Teddy used the feeling of guilt to victimize himself.

"If only I had skipped my chores tha day and takin off with Deek when he came by affta school. We would have taken a different path, to the bluff instead, which was where I had planned to go explorin tha day."

Softly Genevieve replied, "If only. I guess we've both tormented ourselves plenty with those two words over the years. What a wonderful friendship you two had. I can imagine all the fun you and Deek reveled in by the animated way you talk about your adventures. Do you have any pictures?"

Teddy nodded. "Aye, a couple. I've kept them in a box I brought from England when I moved here. I have nivvor looked at them though."

With a warm smile, Genevieve encouraged, "Maybe you're ready to now. Honey, if you've learned anything from my experiences with the Soul, then you know, it never blames, never regrets, and *never* stops loving you. As it was with my mother, there were ways, I'm sure, Deek's Soul tried to relay that to you. You just needed to be open to it.

When the words stopped, Teddy stared into Genevieve's compassionate eyes, and finally allowed himself to cry. Not for Deek, as he somehow knew Deek was fine, but for the relief in telling his story and finally giving himself a pardon from *his* self-imposed prison.

As Genevieve, stroked his dark, wavy hair, Teddy relaxed and closed his eyes. He couldn't be sure whether it was just his imagination, but he chose to believe his friend was smiling when he heard a faint whisper, "Glad ye *finally* listened! Ah knew she wez the one fer ye."

Teddy had moved on.

CHAPTER 59

BIRTHDAY SURPRISE

JUNE 2010

When Sol died, he left a fifth of his well-endowed estate to Teddy, with the remainder going to Cindy and Leo. Sol's generosity helped enormously in their move to California. The Walkers finally settled in the quaint seaside town of Cambria, and Teddy re-established his business with Ella as his junior partner. The area had many of the things Teddy loved when growing up in Bamburgh. Besides the refreshing damp, salt air, there were a few excellent bluffs to take in the vast coastline, and even a castle nearby—Hearst Castle. An enormous estate that had belonged to newspaper tycoon, William Randolph Hearst.

Genevieve sometimes missed her part-time job with Brunner. However, she had accepted his offer to stay on the payroll when she left, and flew to Scottsdale on occasion to help the detective out if he needed her.

She also began some of the work her brother David, had started, years prior, researching articles of people who had the same empathic abilities they did. The more Genevieve looked, the more she discovered. David was now reaching out to those he had found, hoping to put some type of cohesiveness together. If nothing else, at least there might be a support group who could relate to each other and give feedback on their experiences.

A year after they moved, Ella said, "I do" to Finn Weebly in an intimate ceremony on the beach. Finn's plans to become a professional baseball player didn't pan out. However, he did land an assistant coaching position at the community college in San Luis Obispo. Then, using his minor in web design, Finn had created, and now maintained, the revamped Walker and Weebly Inc.'s website, as well as several other lucrative accounts. Life for the Weebly's only picked up speed as their family grew to five. They now had three sons, Richard, now age seven, Steven, age five, and Zeffran, who just turned four.

After graduating high-school, Broc enrolled at the community college in San Luis Obispo with no real direction until he happened upon a speaking engagement that changed his life. The speaker's emphasis was on endangered marine life and, from that moment on, Broc had a laser focus for his goal. On his way to becoming a Marine Biologist, he also met the love he'd been waiting for, Adira.

But life has its seasons. Springtime was in full bloom for some, while others were feeling chilled by the harshness of winter. With the entire family surrounding him, Geoffrey passed away in 2001 after a brief, but deadly, bout of pneumonia. Genevieve caused everyone to smile through their tears when Geoffrey's Soul relayed a whimsical happiness. As he departed, she felt the deep love he had for his adopted family, and freedom that went beyond anything Genevieve could find equivalent words to describe.

Steven and Melinda were taking life easier these days. After *fully* retiring from real estate in 2002, Steven's sole focus had been on his horses. Then, the following year he had a bad fall when the horse he was riding got spooked by a branch that cracked and fell from a nearby tree. After recovering from a dislocated shoulder and broken femur, Steven decided it was time to sell off his six prized stallions. Now, after downsizing, only three mares remained in the once-bustling stable.

Traveling for the two seniors was for leisure purposes now. It consisted mostly of bouncing between visits to Genevieve in California, Tess who now lived in Florida and spending time at their condo in Maui.

Early afternoon, Friday

Sitting in oversized lounge chairs on their large front balcony, that overlooked the ocean a few blocks away, Teddy and Genevieve were each finishing off a glass of Long Island Iced Tea, Teddy's newest discovery. "Best drink ever!" Teddy beamed while holding the glass out in front of him.

"Well, *old* man," Genevieve teased, "Happy Birthday!"

Holding her almost-empty glass out, the two toasted Teddy's 56th birthday.

With one last gulp, Genevieve put her glass down and moved over to Teddy's chair. Burrowing in next to him, she pulled Teddy's arm around her to shelter her bare shoulders from the brisk sea breeze. "Glad you decided to take your birthday off, finally. I've been telling you to do that for years. It only took a momentous occasion to make that happen."

Teddy closed his eyes and felt the sun warm his eyelids. "Aye, a great occasion tomorrow. My boy is finally gettin married."

Genevieve grinned, "Finally? He's 28. That's a perfect age, I think. He waited until the right one came along. I love Adira. The stories she tells of living in Israel ten years ago are so harrowing! I can't imagine seeing your best friend killed by a suicide bomber!"

Teddy opened his eyes slightly and winced.

Genevieve paused for a moment. "She's so strong and energizes everyone around her. She could've been so bitter over all that has happened in her past, but instead, she's kind and loving. Speaking of *loving*, the heat between Broc and Adira is palpable. It reminds me of us."

Teddy gave Genevieve a side glance. As his fingers stroked her upper arm, he whispered, "I'm beginin to feel some of tha heat now!"

Genevieve blinked seductively and smiled. "Are you sure it's not the stiff alcohol warming you up?"

Teddy raised his eyebrows and shook his head slowly, "Naw, this heat is quite specific."

With a laugh, Genevieve looked at the mischief in Teddy's eyes. Pulling herself up, and over, she straddled Teddy's lap in her summer dress. The peppered grey on Teddy's temples, and deepening wrinkles where his dimples were gradually carving their mark in his cheek, added a whole new sexy she adored. "Well, it *is* your birthday, and there's plenty of time before the rehearsal dinner tonight, so…"

Bending down, Genevieve began teasing Teddy by brushing her lips slightly along his. As his pulse quickened, Teddy removed the clasp holding Genevieve's long hair and, as it fell over her shoulders, he grabbed the back of her head, pulling her in, kissing her hard.

Moments later, with inhibitions numbed somewhat by the alcohol, Teddy began slipping Genevieve's strap down from her shoulder, then he started to unzip her dress from behind. Genevieve didn't want the momentum to stop, yet, with the exposure to the chilling breeze *and* other people, Genevieve forced herself to pull back. "Probably best we avoid getting arrested and end up spending your birthday in jail. Let's go inside. You can make another Long Island if you like, and I'll be any appetizer you want me to be."

Teddy only nodded but was thinking, *Can this day get any betta?*

Once inside, Teddy headed to the kitchen, Genevieve to the bedroom, when the doorbell rang. Going to the door, Teddy's anticipation for an afternoon delight, quickly deflated when he saw Steven and Melinda standing outside. Genevieve peered into the living room with a slight frown, quietly asking, "Who is it?"

Teddy mouthed, "Your folks are here."

Genevieve's eyes widened as she whispered, "I didn't expect them until tonight."

"Hello! Anyone home?" Steven shouted.

Running and standing next to Teddy, Genevieve could only shrug and give Teddy a quick kiss on the cheek before opening the door and smiling, "Hey, you're here! What a nice surprise!"

Melinda felt an odd vibe and scrunched her forehead, "Did we interrupt something?"

Looking at each other with a feigned, puzzled expression, Teddy sputtered, "I was just gettin ready to make a cocktail, would ye be interested?"

Nodding, Melinda entered with a long garment bag and gave Teddy and Genevieve each an air kiss as she brushed near their cheek.

A bit winded, Steven turned toward the road and waived off the limousine service driver, then rumbled through the door, pulling two suitcases behind him and huffing, "I'll say, and can you make it a stiff one, son?"

Teddy looked at Genevieve, "I've got somethin tha should do the trick."

After taking their luggage and garment bag to the spare bedroom, Teddy headed back to the kitchen. Melinda gave Genevieve a proper hug before having a seat on the couch, "I know we're a bit early, but the pilot had a scheduling mix up. I figured if you weren't home, we'd just relax at the beach for a while."

Steven sat in Teddy's leather chair opposite them and quickly spotted a coffee table book that he grabbed and placed in his lap. It was a large book with beautiful pictures and descriptions of the different points of interest in California. "Now, this is what I've been talking about, Melinda!" As he turned one page after another, "Look, Catalina, Solvang, Yosemite National Park, the Monterey Aquarium, where Broc works. Hell, I haven't even seen that Hearst Castle yet. We've been clear around the world yet haven't seen what's in our own back yard."

Melinda nodded. It will take some planning, but you know that's what I do best. Still, first things first. We have a wedding to go to!" Looking at Genevieve, "So, everything is going as planned?"

Genevieve smiled. "Yes. It's really been Ella and Adira's show."

"Any word from Adira's parents?" Melinda asked, hopefully.

Genevieve shook her head, "Nothing has changed. We didn't think it would. They sent Adira to live with her aunt and uncle for a reason when they went underground nine years ago. What they've done has made them a target, and Adira knows they'd never risk putting her in danger by coming here."

Melinda nodded. "Well, hope she's prepared to be a part of *this* crazy family!"

"I'm sure she's not," Steven said matter-of-factly, then winked as he proceeded to empty the nearby candy dish into his jacket pocket.

"STEVEN!" Melinda scolded.

"For my diabetes, honey, when my sugar gets low."

Genevieve just shook her head, while Melinda's eyes narrowed, "You don't have diabetes."

Steven unwrapped a piece and put it in his mouth, "Things change, best be prepared."

CHAPTER 60

MISGUIDED DREAMS

"Soul Seekers! That's ridiculous." Genevieve exclaimed to David over the phone.

"Well, that's what we've been called," David grumbled.

"We don't seek the Soul, we translate it—relay a message. Wouldn't it be more accurate if we were called Soul Messengers?"

There were a few seconds of dead silence on the other end of the phone, then David responded thoughtfully, "Maybe it's more accurate, but it has a lousy ring to it. In a way, we *do* seek the Soul. Otherwise, we wouldn't reach out for it at all. We do *seek* the message it has to tell us."

This time Genevieve was silent on the other end. "It just sounds like we're some kind of super-hero brigade, THE SOUL SEEKERS!" Genevieve mocked.

"It'll grow on you," David said. "It's time we call our group something. I just verified another one, Haruki from Sapporo, a city on the island of Hokkaido, Japan. He now makes eighty-four."

"And here I thought I was the only one, years ago." Genevieve sighed. "Doesn't it seem strange that so many of us have this particular ability?"

"It does, and fascinating in the way each of us discovered it," David agreed. "Maybe someday I'll write a book."

Genevieve smiled, "You'd need to categorize it as fiction. That's still what most people believe."

"That's why I said, *someday,* when people finally believe we're legitimate."

"And you expect that will actually happen in our lifetime?" Genevieve questioned. "I've been doing this for almost 25 years. If something is going to change, hopefully it will be someday *soon*. I'd love to see your book in the non-fiction section and flying off the shelves!"

David snickered, "Well, life is all about change. Think positive. So, are you ready for that long-awaited trip to England?"

Genevieve looked at the bags by the door, "Can't wait," she beamed. "We leave tonight. Just wish it could have been longer, but I want to be back here when Mom and Dad show up in ten days after their extensive California sightseeing tour. Teddy may stay longer though. I'm hoping he does. It's been such a long time since he's been back home."

Genevieve could hear her call-waiting beeping. "David, I'll call you later. I have another call coming in."

After switching over, Genevieve answered, "Hello?"

Tess was on the other end, "Gen, have you heard from Mom and Dad?"

Genevieve wrinkled her brow, "No, not since they started the road trip, three days ago. I was going to call them today, before we left for the airport to see how things were going, why?"

There was tension in Tess' voice, "I've been calling Mom's cell, and leaving messages since yesterday morning. You know Dad hardly ever answers his, but I even tried his earlier, and *no one* is calling me back!"

"Okay," Genevieve said in a reassuring, calm voice, "When I talked Dad a week ago, the gentleman they hired to drive them in their Lincoln Town Car for the two weeks was there going over the final details. I talked to him for a bit. He had an impressive resume and seemed very capable. I know Dad thought *he* could do all the driving on his own, but Mom and I put our foot down on that one. Did you call home? Has Gidda heard from them?"

"Yes," Tess answered. "She heard from Mom the first night and thought she would have checked in again, but nothing."

Now Genevieve was beginning to feel her heart beating faster. She pulled Melinda and Steven's driving itinerary out in front of her, "Okay, so after they left Scottsdale Sunday morning, three days ago, they were supposed to make it to Long Beach, which was about a six-hour drive and stay the night on the Queen Mary."

Tess confirmed, "Yes, they did. I called, and the front desk clerk confirmed it. She said they left early the following day. She remembered because

Dad made her laugh by saying they had to leave because he wasn't going to have '*those lurking ghost sailors*' drooling over his gorgeous wife any longer."

With a slight grin, Genevieve answered, "Good. Everything sounds normal so far. Then they were headed to Solvang Monday, which was a few hours north. They planned to stay there one night then head to Yosemite. They were supposed to stay at the Bakker House, did you call there?"

Tess hurried the conversation along, "Yes. I actually *started* with the Majesty hotel in Yosemite, as that's where I expected them to be last night. But when I called yesterday, late afternoon, I was told they had not shown up. I called again around 10 p.m., and they still had not checked in. So, I started working backwards to confirm each reservation, thinking maybe they had stayed longer at one of the earlier stops. God, I should have called you earlier, Gen. I just didn't want to cause a panic, knowing how Dad has a tendency to change Mom's best-laid plans. But now I'm really worried since no one has heard a word from them in days."

Genevieve closed her eyes, trying to focus. "I'll call Brunner and find out what to do. I'll call you back."

Hanging up the phone, Genevieve speed-dialed the detective. After Brunner got the rundown on the situation, he said he'd contact the cell phone company and, as long as at least one of them had their cell phones on they'd be able to track their location.

After calling Tess back and then calling Teddy to come home early, Genevieve sat and waited. *Was there a dream I had, warning me of this day?* Genevieve went to the bedroom and pulled her latest, of now three dream journals, out of the nightstand, the newest entry being only a week old. Thumbing through the pages, none of the often-abstract descriptions seem to fit. As she was about to close the book, there was one that caused Genevieve to stop breathing.

In an entry, almost eight months ago, she had written the following:

The sound of the ravine was burbling as it gently rolled over the rocks and tree roots while meandering its way to an unknown destination. The lush green of the trees spread out overhead, like a spectacular umbrella, shielding me from the hot summer sun. There was a peaceful quiet and, after what felt like a long life, I was completed somehow, that things were done. Not over but finish on Earth. I felt the deep love of my husband, close to me, and the extreme thankfulness to have seen my children grow up.

As I write this, I never grow tired of how we truly feel in the end. If this is how my last day ends, it's incredible to know this is how I will feel.

When Genevieve had written the entry, she couldn't discern when it would happen, or why she was there, often knowing that her dreams were symbolic. But as Genevieve stared at the words, silent tears began to drop upon them. *I was mistaken. This wasn't about me.*

As the phone rang, Genevieve jumped. Before she answered, she knew.

CHAPTER 61

PEELING MORE OF THE ONION

THE RECORDED ACCOUNT of Josh Rockman, hired driver for Steven and Melinda Teel:

"I had been out most the night with an acquaintance, a woman I met at Hogan's Club. When it closed, just after two in the morning, we went back to her apartment for a while. I took a cab back to the hotel around four in the morning, I think.

"When I heard pounding on my door, I looked at the clock, and it was almost 9:30 a.m. I jumped out of bed but tripped and hit a chair, getting a bloody lip on my way to the door. When I opened it, the Teels were standing there, looking rather irritated. I told them I could be ready in about 15 minutes. Mr. Teel stepped closer, and I guess he could still smell some alcohol on my breath. He pulled his wallet out, took a one-hundred-dollar bill from it, and threw it at me, saying I could find my own way home. I called out after them, but Mrs. Teel, just gave me this disappointed look and Mr. Teel waived me off as they headed for their car. That was the last time I saw them."

Three weeks later.

The estate hadn't been this active in years.

After a beautiful service, the cremated remains of Steven and Melinda were buried at Green Oasis cemetery, under a colossal granite headstone with TEEL boldly etched in the center. Melinda and Steven had specifically picked the shady area after Liv died. Her ashes were buried next to theirs under a small but tenderly written headstone that read, 'She was whisked away by angels, where her love awaited to welcome her home.' The first time Genevieve visited Liv's gravesite, she got misty-eyed, believing her father, Zeffran, *would have* been waiting to wrap her in the arms she had longed for until the day she died.

At the estate, valets had been hired, and the reception was fully catered, yet Gidda, wanting to feel useful, busied herself like a drill sergeant, making sure all the hired help were doing their jobs, and then some.

Although admiring Gidda's stamina, Genevieve sat on the living room couch with Teddy on one side, Tess on the other, feeling tired and drained after an afternoon of mingling amongst family, friends, and associates of her parents that were all still in shock over the circumstances.

Once the police had located Steven and Melinda in their car, partially submerged in a deep ravine off a tricky stretch of highway outside of Solvang, the question became, 'Where was their driver?' Genevieve knew his name was Josh Rockman, and that he had once been the hired driver for an investment firm her father did business with years ago. On one occasion, Steven said the two had exchanged business cards. Apparently, Steven enjoyed the banter and humor of Josh, unlike most drivers who respectively only spoke when spoken to. When Genevieve questioned why her dad hadn't used a car service, Steven replied, "No one will ever fill Geoffrey's shoes, but if I *have* to hire a driver, at least this guy has a personality that fits well with mine."

Aware Josh wasn't working for that firm anymore, Steven took a chance that he might be available, and called the cell number on the business card. What Steven assuredly didn't know, was that Josh had been let go for excessive drinking on the job.

After their confrontation with Josh, no one knew for sure, but somehow, Steven must have convinced Melinda he could do the driving. The coroner said the impact was catastrophic, yet both lived for a short time before succumbing to their injuries. When found, Melinda's head was resting on Steven's shoulder, his hand on her knee.

Now, as Genevieve's brother David and his girlfriend, Janet, perused the overabundance of Teel family pictures in the room, lining the bookshelves and baby grand piano, Genevieve's attention drifted to the large family portrait over the fireplace.

Always impeccably clothed, Melinda had chosen that day, to wear her royal blue knit dress that hugged her beautiful figure, exquisitely. As she sat to the left of her husband, Melinda's flawless ivory face and meticulously applied red lips now held an everlasting smile Genevieve lamented she would never see again.

Steven's cowboy mentality, though not what one might expect, happened to be the perfect contrast to his elegant wife. With laughing eyes and a crooked smile, he had always been a straight shooter in business. That, combined with his charm, levity, and odd-ball humor, gave him the ammunition to win just about anyone over.

Finally, Genevieve's focus fell on her thirteen-year-old self, standing slightly behind the person she'd one-day call Mother. Genevieve's hand was resting on Melinda's shoulder, while five-year-old Tess sat primly at Steven's feet. As Genevieve stared, the young Genevieve staring back seemed a stranger. *That Genevieve had no idea what she was capable of doing. That Genevieve knew nothing of all that was to follow.* Genevieve's chin began to quiver as she swallowed hard. *And that Genevieve knew so little of all she already had.*

Feeling Teddy brush her check, Genevieve realized tears were falling again. Leaning on his shoulder, she held his hand as he kissed her forehead. Broc and Adira were sitting on the loveseat next to them. Adira was seven months pregnant with their first child, a girl.

When Genevieve set her gaze on the two of them, she noticed Broc was watching her. Genevieve had received a call from him almost daily since his grandparent's death, making sure she was doing okay, yet never shying away when she wasn't. His vigilant concern for her was a bit surprising and touched Genevieve deeply.

Smiling at her son, Broc smiled back and mouthed, "I love you, Mom."

Genevieve nodded and managed a wink to let him know she was okay.

By late afternoon, other than family, only a handful of friends were still present. The hired helpers were finishing their clean-up, while the younger half of the clan, along with Teddy, had donned bathing suits to swim in the lukewarm swimming pool.

While Genevieve stood at the front door, waving good-bye to the Farrows, who lived at the neighboring estate, Melinda's good friend, Tori Miles quietly came up behind her and put an arm around Genevieve's waist. "I'm sure going to miss your mother."

Genevieve turned and hugged Tori. "Are you leaving?"

Tori took a quick look around and said, "It's been a long day. It's time for this old lady to get home."

After advising the valet to bring Tori's car around, Genevieve sat with her on the front bench. "I want you to know something." Genevieve said softly. "Because of my mother's wealth, she was always a bit cautious of people's intentions toward her. Yet there was something that drew her to you, and I know why."

Tori's eyes widened. "You do?"

Genevieve nodded. "Mom told me about your rape. I hope you are okay with her telling me. I know *you* were the catalyst for creating her foundation."

Tori relaxed slightly and nodded. "She was such a lifesaver for me back then."

Genevieve sighed, "I'm glad Mom was there when you needed her, Tori. But I think it was more, somehow. You touched her heart when you used to sing, and then later, you did it again with all you went through. I think she sensed from the beginning you were a person she could trust; someone she could be vulnerable around. You two were the true definition of kindred spirits."

Tori nodded, "More than you know, Genevieve. I understand all too well, what it feels like when trust is lost, just as you've experienced the loss in your own way. All that used to feel normal becomes suspect, and you have to be brave enough to *be* vulnerable again. Melinda had many reasons to be leery of other's intentions, but I never knew anyone with a more open heart."

With a slight pause, Tori added, "I'm not saying this figuratively when I say she *showed* me how to live again."

After Genevieve watched Tori's car disappear down the street, she walked back toward the kitchen and noticed more and more of the family had found their way into the pool. Walking up behind Gidda who was tidying up at the counter, Genevieve put her hands on the back of Gidda's shoulders and insisted, "It's time you go home and get some rest, Gidda." Then looking at the mountain of left-over food on the large dining table, Genevieve added, "And *please,* take some this food for your family!"

With little argument, Gidda turned and hugged Genevieve. "I'll put as much as I can in the two refrigerators before I leave. Then I'll be back mañana."

CHAPTER 62

DECISION MADE

TEDDY WOULD BE leaving for England tomorrow. Although he had been resistant to go without her, Genevieve insisted he spend time with *his* family, which had eagerly been anticipated before the accident occurred.

After Teddy's father, Richard, died of brain cancer, four years after Teddy and Genevieve's marriage, Teddy's visits to England slowly dwindled. His mother, Ann, only visited the U.S. once, besides their wedding, and that was when Teddy had been shot. It had now been almost ten years since his last visit home, although Teddy regularly Skyped with his sister, Amelie.

With Genevieve's promise that she would join him as soon as the immediate legalities of the estate was finalized, Teddy eventually agreed to go.

Genevieve watched as the revived group, back from their swim, had regained their appetite and pulled all the leftovers back out for another go-round. Teddy, however, quietly went back to the bedroom to start packing. Genevieve didn't follow. She was dreading their separation and knowing she wouldn't be able to keep her emotions in check, stayed put and forced a smile, doing her best to stay engaged with her chatty family.

By late evening, everyone had retired to their rooms, and Genevieve welcomed the peaceful quiet as she laid next to Teddy, putting her arm over his chest. "I'm glad you'll finally get to go home," Genevieve remarked.

Taking his fingers and brushing them along her outstretched arm, Teddy bemoaned, "It hasn't been my home for a very long time. But it will be good to see my sister and my mum, even though I know Mum won't know who I am."

Genevieve lifted herself on her elbow, looking down at her husband, "Maybe she will."

Teddy stared at the ceiling, "Amelie said she doesn't even recognize *her* anymore, and my sister sees Mum a couple of times a week. I think it's pretty doubtful she'll recognize *me*."

Laying back down, Genevieve began strumming her fingers on Teddy's chest. "Well, if that's the case, then just be the friendliest stranger she's ever met. Even if her memory doesn't come back, I'm sure it won't take long for her to adore you all over again."

Teddy rolled over, facing Genevieve. "I just wish ye were goin with me."

Genevieve could feel Teddy's yearning for her companionship, along with the conflicting feelings of leaving for a place that couldn't possibly live up to the idealistic memories he had of it.

His searching eyes were soulfully pleading, and it took all of Genevieve's strength not to ask him to stay until she was free to go with him. But she couldn't. They both knew the separation that might be a month, or even longer, was inevitable.

Bending down to kiss her, the rolling of emotions left Genevieve dazed. Pulling the covers back, Teddy scanned Genevieve's naked body. She watched him, suddenly feeling self-conscious as his eyes moved down, then up, until their eyes locked on each other. At that moment, their need to love and comfort each other became overwhelming.

When the early morning alarm breached their silence, Teddy readied himself and was on his way to the airport within the hour. As the taxi disappearing out of sight, Genevieve quietly closed the front door and headed back to the bedroom.

Genevieve had done her best through the years to keep up with Teddy, and his exercise regimen. Still, as time passed, she was accepting that her body was changing, and with it, so would Teddy's desire. But as Genevieve stood at her bedroom doorway and stared at the disheveled bed, she got goosebumps. *Certainly, not yet, hopefully, never!*

After getting showered and dressed, Genevieve headed to the kitchen where Gidda had just finished preparing a large breakfast. By mid-morning everyone in the family had said their good-byes, leaving just Tess, Ryan, and Genevieve to begin the business of handling the affairs of the estate.

The Teel's had left a generous sum to their grandchildren and great-grand-children. They donated half a million dollars to Healing Wings, Melinda's foundation, as well as smaller denominations to a few close friends and several other non-profit organizations. But it was the surprised and grateful faces of several long-term staff, that brought a tear to Genevieve. Steven and Melinda had willed ten-thousand dollars to each of them. Still, the bulk of the assets went to the Teel's two nieces, which Steven and Melinda unofficially referred to as 'Their beloved daughters: Genevieve Walker and Teresa Seelig.'

Now Genevieve would have the kind of money most people could only imagine. Not that she was naïve to the fact that she would inherit a lot of money one day. But that *day* always was far-off and unimportant in Genevieve's mind. While other family members, including Tess, were looking forward to spending their windfall, Genevieve had no idea how she would handle her inheritance. The enormity of it even scared her a little.

Glenda Bardoum, the Teel's longtime accountant, came by early in the after-noon. to go over the immediate bills that needed to be paid. An appraiser came by, a little later to begin assessing the main contents within the home for an estate sale planned in two weeks. However, it was Genevieve and her sister's job to go through all the personal belongings and decide what needed to be done with them.

While Tess stayed with the appraiser, Genevieve went to her parent's closet to start the personal assessment. After taking only a few steps inside, she found herself paralyzed. Suddenly, the loss was all around her. Several of her dad's worn cowboy boots sat forlornly in the corner. One of Melinda's favorite flowered dresses hung alone on a hook by the door. Walking over, Genevieve pressed the fabric against her face. She could still smell traces of her mother's perfume and dissolved into tears, pulling the dress with her as she fell to her knees in despair. Hiding away, alone in the closet, Genevieve held the soft dress tightly to her chest and sobbed with abandonment.

After a time, Genevieve began to compose herself. As she stood up, she saw Tess standing at the closet door. Walking over, Genevieve, with her smeared mas-cara and bloodshot eyes, grabbed her sister as Tess broke down and wept as well.

After separating, Genevieve took a deep breath and grinned at her sister. With a shaky sigh, she vowed, "I'll try this again in a few days."

CHAPTER 63

THE PROCESS BEGINS

WHEN DINNER WAS over, Tess, Ryan and Genevieve took a dip in the pool. Then Genevieve walked out to the stable to bring the last occupant a few carrots; a filly named Piper.

Back when Steven had decided to sell his horses, a good friend offered him a handsome sum of money for Steven's most prized racehorse, Wind Runner. The plan was to stud the impressive stallion while still in his prime years. Steven made a deal that he'd sell his Arabian thoroughbred, well below market value, on one condition—that the first sired filly would go to him.

Early last year, Steven got his filly. After that, he spent most days doting on her and watching her begin to develop the same ability of her fathers; to run like the wind.

After Genevieve had spent an hour of bonding, she was headed back to the house when her cell phone rang. With the distinctive ringtone, Genevieve knew who it was. "Teddy! How was the trip? Everything went smoothly?"

"Aye. Although I kept thinkin how nice it would have been to fly in a private jet, spoiled now, I know. Bein the commercial flight was non-stop, I was comfortable enough. Anyway, I just got to Amelie's house an hour ago, and I'm exhausted, but, before I take a nap, I wanted to check in with ye. Everythin okay?"

"Everything's fine. But that reminds me, I was supposed to get back to the broker today on the sale of Dad's jet, but I forgot. Maybe that was a good thing. I never thought *you* might want it. Should I stop the sale?

Teddy laughed, "Heavens no, woman. But ye know...I could use a wee bit of an upgrade to my tired fishin boat, tha is, if presents are bein handed oot!"

Blinking slowly with a grin, "Oh, I'm sure that can be arranged, and more, when I come to see you." Genevieve promised.

With a quick-witted response, Teddy teased, "Now I'm gettin *all kinds* of excited!"

Laughing, Genevieve tried to get back on topic. "I'm glad. But, until then, Mr. Excited, at least some progress has been made here. The estate sale is on track two weeks from now. Tomorrow, Tess and I will be closing some bank accounts, and check to see what's in Mom and Dad's safe deposit box as well."

After a hesitant silence, Genevieve spoke softly. "Teddy, I wanted to talk to you about Piper. I'd really like to keep her."

Without any consideration, Teddy replied, "I had a feelin ye would. The filly meant a lot to your fatha, and horses were always your special connection to him. I think he'd be happy aboot tha."

Genevieve felt a lump rising in her throat. "We did love those horses."

Hearing the gradual tiredness in Teddy's voice as the conversation progressed, Genevieve conceded, "I know you're tired. Get some rest, then call me after you've visited your mom."

Feeling exhausted herself, Genevieve left a quick message with the broker to call her about getting the jet on the market, then she collapsed, not waking until after nine the next morning.

When she finally made it to the kitchen around ten, Tess was sitting at the table staring out the window. Seeing Genevieve, Tess quickly wiped a tear away and flashed a quick smile. Genevieve frowned and asked, "Feeling another wave of sadness, or is it something else?"

Tess just looked at her sister but didn't answer. Genevieve could see her sister's lip trembling and stressed, "What's wrong?"

Tess took a deep breath. "I wanted to spare you from the chore of cleaning Mom and Dad's closet out. So, last night I started going through some things. I was removing Mom's long gowns and packing them in containers, when I saw an old cardboard box that had been hidden behind them. When I opened it, there were maybe forty or more writing tablets and letters in it. I thought it would be fun to see what Mom had written. I could see everything was in her handwriting."

Then Tess, stopped and looked back out the window. "But there was a reason she kept them hidden. What could best be described as journals, I spent most the night reading the one I found at the top of the pile. It seemed also, to be the last one she wrote—when she was in her early twenties. I think you should read it."

Turning to Genevieve, Tess added, "Gen, just know that it was written long before you and I were ever part of their lives."

Genevieve shook her head and stuttered, "Are, are you saying there's some dark secret you discovered? That's impossible. After everything that happened with Liv, Mom swore she'd never keep another secret from us."

Tess blinked slowly, "I know. This is different though."

Genevieve's pained eyes stayed focused on Tess as she whispered, "Where are they?"

CHAPTER 64

IN A SPLIT SECOND

AFTER TESS FORCED Genevieve to eat breakfast, they went upstairs to their parent's bedroom. The cardboard box was lying on the bed.

Tess walked over and picked up an envelope. "There were a few letters scattered on top of the journals. I glanced at the other two and they were love letters between Mom and Dad, very sweet. This one however had me very confused. It's letters between Tori and Mom. You should read it first." Then Tess picked up a large notebook. "After that, read this. I'll be downstairs with Ryan. We're going through all the cabinets in the library. Just holler if you need me or want to talk."

When the bedroom door closed, Genevieve walked over to the side of the bed and looked at the bulging envelope. It had yellowed over the years and had nothing written on the outside. Next to it was a thick notebook. The cover had black and white sketches of young women in flared skirts, tucked in blouses and short wavy hair hairstyles; very much the 50's era.

Picking up the envelope, Genevieve walked over to her mom's favorite chair by the window and sat down. Her heart was throbbing in her chest. Apprehension and curiosity blended evenly as her fingers ran along the envelope's edge, removing six folded pages of stationary. Unfolding the pages and taking a quick glance, she noticed most of the pages were in her mother's handwriting, but the last two were in Tori's.

Genevieve took a cleansing breath and began to read:

> Tori,
> I have a box at home that contains volumes of notebooks. I started writing them when I was a young girl. The first time Steven saw my box, when we were dating, he laughed hysterically. Not in a mean way, of course, he just didn't understand how cathartic it can be, or how clear you can feel about something until you write about it.

Last week, as you and I were talking about your rape and the things that happened to you when you were young, I saw such similarities between us. We both had rather unstable families. When you spoke of your brother's drowning and your mother's drinking problem, I kept having flashbacks to my own childhood. I could see more clearly then, how our childhood impacts so much of our lives going forward.

I have a notebook I wrote years ago. I would like to send it to you to read while you are in Michigan. It might help you...at least that would be my hope. Still, whether you decide to or not, I wanted to share with you a little of my childhood. I was going to give you the notebooks that chronicled them, so you could hopefully see the resemblance that I saw. However, after looking them over, I thought it best to give you the "Readers Digest" version, since my childhood meanderings made more sense to me than someone who would read them now.

So, here it is. The summary of my childhood. I hope you'll see what I meant. Then, if you do, I hope you'll accept my offer to read one of my journals.

Genevieve turned to the next page.

As I interpret my first journal which I wrote at the ripe old age of six, I still can feel the frightened, lost child rush through me, as I read through my many misspelled words. Why? Maybe it was because my father was murdered by a husband who caught Father in bed with his wife. Perhaps, it was because my mother chose to sweep the incident, and her emotions, under the rug, by becoming a stoic, cut-throat maverick in the business world, laying waste to any semblance of a happy, normal family.

Frowning, Genevieve rubbed her forehead. *I knew grandfather had been murdered but was led to believe it had been a random shooting. Now it makes more sense why no one ever spoke of him.*

Still, in spite of it all, two floundering souls living in Boston's Back Bay, Liv and I survived. We didn't thrive by any means, but we did survive. Even though we were only two years apart, at seven, I had the enormous responsibility to care for my little sister. Since Mother worked, I was tasked with something I felt ill-equipped to handle. Nevertheless, Liv clung to me for dear life—I clung to her for love.

279

During the next several years, Mother made a point, quite often, to prance the two of us around town in beautiful, detailed dresses, showing off her talent and growing success as a dressmaker. It didn't take long before I found myself looking forward to the attention of women and girls my age, telling me how pretty I looked.

But my insecurity about not being enough still dominated my life, and Mother hated that weakness. Even though Liv and I excelled in school, it only mildly pleased her. Appearances, and the perception of success had become her credo. She never wanted to feel helpless again in her life, nor did she want to see that frailty in her daughters.

By the time I was a junior in high school, Mother had her designs in several stores in, and around Boston. She had married the year before but divorced soon after. The actual cause, in my opinion, was that it was a power struggle. She wasn't going to let anyone take over being the pants in her family.

Pushing on with her agenda, Mother insisted that both Liv and I go to finishing school in New York. Insanely expensive, she expected results for her investment. However, Liv had become an emotional roller coaster by the time she was fourteen, rebellious and obstinate. She lasted six months before being released. Without me at home, my sister looked to others, mainly boys, with whom to latch on to.

I, on the other hand, started to feel more confident. I had learned poise at school and felt more self-assured. I perfected the application of make-up and how to fashion my hair. After graduation, Mother literally beamed with pride over me for the first time in my life.

As her business spread, Mother began using me as her primary model. More and more retailers were continually accepting her designs. Within the following two years, Mother had become a force within the design industry, and I had been noticed by the well-known, prestigious, Ford Modeling Agency. At twenty-one, I signed on with them, thrilled to be on my own and headed to New York.

She **was** a model! Genevieve thought.

Laying the letter down in her lap, Genevieve shook her head. *Why keep that a secret? I still remember the day I told her she looked like a model, when I was a little girl. Mother (Liv) was sitting right next to me when I said it. They both just laughed as if it was absurd, why?* she thought to herself as she turned the page.

At that same time, Liv surprised everyone and eloped with her high-school sweet-heart, Zeffran.

The next year, I began modeling for Sears and Roebuck and was picked by a well-known cosmetic company to model their trademark, ruby red lipstick on billboards around the country.

Then two very important things happened that would change my life. My Mother had a sudden stroke and died at the exact same time I was in Dallas, Texas, meeting my future husband, Steven, at a high-end fundraiser where I had been paid to model jewelry for a silent auction.

When the auction was over, Steven asked me to have a drink. We couldn't take our eyes off each other. He was handsome, yes, but it was more than that. He was naturally relaxed and comfortable with himself which was wildly different from the narcissistic businessmen I had been dating. And, Tori, oh how he made me laugh!

When I got to my hotel room that night, a message was left for me to call my Mother's assistant. That's when I found out. I left for Boston, first thing the following morning.

Two days later, Liv and I were sitting on Mother's front steps, simply overwhelmed. It wasn't just due to the planning of her funeral, but also, the fate of her business was now our naïve young hands. Then, totally unexpectedly, a car pulls up to the curb, and Steven stepped out!

I just remember running to him, crying. Even though I barely knew the man, I knew instinctively that he'd be the one to save me. I felt he already had. Crazy I know, but who travels half-way across the country to be with someone after one short date?

Genevieve nodded. *I always loved that story, Mom. In hindsight, maybe it was a kind of deja-vu for you when you saw my attraction to Teddy. You seemed to know how I felt from the moment I met him. Crazy? No, love does that,* Genevieve mused before continuing:

With permission from Liv and myself, Steven met with Mother's assistant, accountant, and lawyer the very next day. Long story short, since neither Liv nor I had any interest in carrying on her business, Steven worked for almost five months, until the right offer to buy the company name and inventory came along.

The night he told me of the generous proposal, Steven nervously pulled a ring from his jacket pocket. It was the diamond ring I had modeled the day we met, which, unbeknownst to me, he had bid for and won, at the silent auction. Steven told me that when he saw it on my finger that evening, he imagined he had placed it there.

Tearfully, I accepted both proposals.

At first, Genevieve smiled at the story she had heard several times before. Then, as she continued to stare at her mother's penmanship, a frown crossed her face. *Why did Mom have a letter she sent to Tori?*

The last two pages were from Tori. The first one had the yellowing of age, like all the other pages in the envelope, but the final one, Genevieve decerned, had to have been written much later, as it had no discoloration on what looked like basic, lined tablet paper; more of a note than a letter.

The first one read:

Dear Melinda,

I'm sending you a quick note to let you know I received the journal you sent me. I started reading it last night and couldn't stop crying. I had to stop but will do my best to continue later today. I was not prepared to read this and have to admit I'm a bit scared to continue reading your harrowing journey. But I know you and trust you sent it to me for a reason and have my best interest at heart.

I'm glad I went home to Michigan for a while. My parents are such a blessing. My mother has changed so much over the years. I think in some odd way she blames herself for what happened to me, but I told her to abandon such thoughts. She hasn't left my side since I arrived.

I should be back in Phoenix by next week. I'll call you so we can talk.
Tori

The ominous letter had Genevieve scared too. But just as Tori trusted Melinda, Genevieve trusted Tess.

Then Genevieve turned to the final page:

> Melinda,
>
> I know you wanted me to keep the letters and the journal. I've held them close to my heart for many years. But the more I think about it, this is your story and it belongs with you and all your other journals. I hope that one day soon you will believe, as I do, that your daughters are strong women and that they will only love you more for all you have endured.
>
> So, with love, I am returning to you all that is yours.
>
> You're my blessing,
> Tori

CHAPTER 65

UNDERESTIMATED

GENEVIEVE PUT THE envelope containing the letters back on the bed, then stared at the notebook. Hearing Tess and Ryan downstairs, she decided to get a drink of water. When Genevieve got to the library, all the cabinets below the shelves were open, with scattered items laying everywhere. Ryan had just placed some old vinyl records on a card table when he noticed Genevieve. "Hey, sis. How are you doing?" Tess turned around from what she was doing and looked at Genevieve with raised eyebrows.

Genevieve only said four words, "She was a model!"

Ryan nodded and Tess relaxed her posture and smiled. "She was! Isn't that a kick." Then Tess paused before continuing, "You haven't started the journal yet?"

Genevieve shook her head, "Are you sure I should read it?"

Tess looked over at Ryan, then slowly turned back to Genevieve, "Like Tori said, we're strong women. I just know *I'm* glad I read it. If you'd prefer, I can tell you what it said, but I'll never be able to translate it the way it should be told. I really think it would be better if you learned what happened, from Mom."

Genevieve nodded and began to turn toward the kitchen when Tess disclosed, "By the way, I talked to the broker a while ago and he thinks he has a buyer for Dad's jet."

Squeezing her eyes tight, Genevieve uttered, "I totally forgot about that. Thanks. Are you two sure you don't need me to help you?"

Tess looked around the room. "No, we got this. Your task is more important."

After a quick drink of water, Genevieve headed back upstairs. Picking up the journal she decided to get comfortable on the bed instead.

Quickly flipping through the book, Genevieve could see that some of the words had been smeared and were barely visible. Without focusing on the content yet, Genevieve knew her mother had poured her heart and Soul onto these pages. She also expected it to be compelling since it had the power to change Tori's life.

But, after Genevieve and Melinda had promised never to keep secrets again, Genevieve could only hope she was making the right decision to continue.

February 10, 1955

Steven keeps forgetting I have money of my own. Today I insisted on buying my own wedding gown, and it's gorgeous!

I got confirmation of the reception hall yesterday, and both Cheryl and Amy screamed when I asked them to be bridesmaids. With Liv as my matron of honor, that now makes six. Steven rolled his eyes when I told him I added two more bridesmaids since now he's got to come up with two more groomsmen. I had to promise that six was it.

Tomorrow I have a photoshoot downtown. Swimwear in the dead of winter, fun!

February 16, 1955

Taking the girls out tomorrow to try on bridesmaid dresses. I'm so excited!

That swimwear shoot last week was interesting. I had never modeled a two-piece bathing suit before. But I have to say, I looked pretty good. The photographer was gushing over the proofs and said the camera loved me. Well, as long as Steven does, that's all that matters.

We're going out tonight after my sweetheart gets back from Dallas later this afternoon. Now that we've both transplanted to Phoenix, he wanted to say good-bye to some of his friends there. I'm still a bit confused about why we moved here anyway, but Steven said real estate was ripe for the picking and he needed to be near the action. All I could do was smile, as I have no idea about such things.

February 28, 1955

Liv called today. She's been angry and frustrated ever since Zeffran left for his second deployment last week. I told her to come and stay with me until the wedding was over, but she refused. I wish I understood her better. She said she plans to get pregnant when he comes back in six months for a visit. I don't know. Maybe a baby would be good for her, someone to think about besides herself.

Last night, Steven and I met with the minister we want to officiate at our wedding. Since Steven and I aren't avid church goer's, the reverend wanted to know more about us. What a can of worms that could've been! We just gave him some highlights, and I think he could see what we meant to each other. I really like him. He's a character, with a sense of humor I know Steven appreciated. All is on track for our April 23rd wedding!!!!!

I have to say it's been a busy work month so far! I have a big fashion show in L.A. tomorrow, and then another photo-shoot on Thursday. I guess I'm the hot item to model swimwear now. The photographer from the last shoot, a friendly English fella, named Godfrey, requested me specifically. Although flattered, I'd rather be modeling coats.

Next page:

March 3, 1955

I

There was nothing else on the page. The "I" was smeared, and the paper warped as if water had spilled on it. Frowning, Genevieve turned the page

The next page still had blotchy ink spots. In other areas the handwriting was so faded Genevieve wasn't sure she'd be able to read it:

I've had the reputation of being the good girl, something of a rarity in my field of work. But then, I never had the need to climb the ladder as I watched other girls, doing what they had to, just to be noticed. I was spoiled, I guess. Always sought after to model clothes, jewelry, make-up. I can see now just how fortunate I had been.

I enjoyed the attention I got, yes, but now, as I sit here, I wonder what I might have been, had I not felt the need to please my mother and, instead, chose my own path. I don't blame her, though. In all things, even if we don't think so, we have choices.

Today, I chose to do something. Something that felt wrong from the beginning, yet I decided to do it anyway. Now I may never recover.
I still can't believe how naïve I was!

Genevieve squirmed, and began getting a queasy feeling as she read on:

After I met Steven, I knew I had saved myself for the right man. So often I've had dreams of our honeymoon night, what it would be like; how it would feel...
I've been just sitting here for an hour, not knowing how to write this, or whether I should.
When I got to the warehouse today for the photo-shoot, Godfrey grabbed a bathing suit from the rack and told me to put it on. When I saw it, I told him 'No!' I had never seen a two-piece suite so small and revealing. I asked who I was modeling it for and felt confused when he said it was for the same catalog as before.
Why didn't I go with my gut and refuse? God, why?

Genevieve knew where it was all going now. Dropping the notebook on the bed, she ran to the bathroom toilet, sure she was going to be sick. *How would Tess think I'd want to know this?*

Clinging to the rim of the toilet as the room spun around her, Genevieve forced her eyes closed. *I know there's a reason for all this. I know that!*

Genevieve fell back, against the wall, next to the toilet; her body felt numb, her thoughts chaotic and unfocused. She didn't want to read further and endure the details that Melinda had penned while reliving a violation against her, so many years ago.

I made the wrong decision. I understand why Mother didn't want me to know.

As she sat in silence, Genevieve heard something fall in the bedroom. Slowly walking back, she saw that the notebook had dropped to the floor. As she stared at it, Genevieve swore she heard Melinda whispering in her ear, "Pick it up, Gen. You can't stop now!"

Shaking her head, Genevieve lifted the book from the floor and took her place back on the bed. But this time she sensed something—her mother's presence, sitting beside her as Genevieve opened to the page she left off.

Bracing for what she knew was ahead, Genevieve took a deep breath.

I felt very self-conscious as I stepped from behind the changing curtain in the narrow strapless top, and a bottom that went below my bellybutton! Godfrey had a disarming smile, saying that several models had already posed in similar suits, but he knew I'd show them off best.

I tried to get into a rhythm as he snapped shot after shot, but it was obvious I was struggling. Finally, Godfrey called a time-out and had me sit on the couch while he reloaded the camera. When he was done, he came over and sat next to me.

Photographers often adjust hair or clothing, so when he brushed my hair back with his fingers while suggesting different poses, I wasn't alarmed. But then his hand quickly moved to the snaps on the back of my bathing suit top, and within a second, it dropped into my lap.

Straining, Genevieve could barely recognize the words that followed, which were smeared and faded:

God, my hand is trembling so

I started to get up, but he grabbed my arm, pulling me back down.
Then he
I can't. I can't write what he did to me. The vulgar things he said!
I just can't.
God, only you and I know how hard I tried to fight him, how I pleaded for him to stop. I see the bruising on my arms, my face...my thighs. It still feels like a nightmare I'm desperately hoping to wake from.

All I want to do is forget.

After he was done, he sat up casually and stared at me. The macabre glare made me afraid of what he might be planning next.

Then his demeanor changed like a light switch. Noticing my uncontrollable shaking, he grabbed a blanket and covered me up. Suddenly, he feigned an act of contrition, saying he was sorry, that he had never forced himself on anyone in his life—that he never needed to, but there was something about me, he said, that he couldn't deny. He had hoped when I saw him again today, I'd feel the attraction too and want him as much as he wanted me.

Feeling sick, I got up, and I told him I was going to the police, but he quietly said I shouldn't. He said he'd never admit anything, and it would just be my word against his. Then he added, "Besides, the police all know the wild sex that goes on behind the scenes anyway."

I gave him a disgusted look as I gathered my clothes and headed to the door. As he sat on the couch, he hollered for me to give him another chance to prove he was a better lover than my fiancé. All I had to do is relax this time, he said.

God, you've got to help me forget the repulsive smug look on his face!

When I noticed his precious camera on the table, I grabbed it and bashed it as hard as I could against the wall before slamming the door behind me.

I guess he's right though. Who would believe I was a virgin, or that I didn't ask for it, wearing something that revealing?

I can't help but think he's done this before. I can't be the only one.

Genevieve closed her eyes for a moment, relieved that the graphic details had been left out. There had been a reason she became ill even before she read what happened to her mother.

In the past, Brunner had called Genevieve in, on two separate occasions, while trying to solve a rape case. Each police report portrayed the brutal and graphic attack upon the victim's body. Yet, words could *never* come close to what Genevieve felt, as each victims Soul relayed the emotional impact as the assault was happening.

Taking a deep breath, Genevieve returned from where she left off.

Before I could begin writing today, I had to take a bath first to wash his filth off me. As I sat there scrubbing every inch he had touched, I imagined how easy it would be to slip under the water. To end forever, this nightmare that replays over and over in my mind.

Then I thought of Steven. He'd never know why. My pain would end, but his would just begin. I know he'd blame himself for my death somehow.

So, here I am.

As Genevieve turned the page, she wondered how her mother's journey took her from being suicidal, to a champion for all battered women.

CHAPTER 66

COMPLICATED

How do I tell Steven? He'll surely notice the bruises around my arm, my cheek— my mouth.

Will he still want me? I don't know if I can ever love him, now, as a wife should. Sex is nothing like I imagined.

I'm so afraid, God.

How can you lose so much in one single afternoon?

I've decided never to model again. Not because of that depraved beast, but because I have to know if there is more to me than my looks. God, I hope that to be true.

I know the right thing is to release Steven of his obligation. He thinks he's marrying someone pure and innocent.

But, Lord, I honestly don't think I can live without him. Heaven help me. Give me the strength, please, because I don't know how.

I can't see a future anymore.

I'm so tired.

It was if Genevieve was reading about a stranger. Without wanting to, she found she was tapping into the same feelings she had experienced with the other two rape victims: the anguish, self-loathing, doubt, and guilt were all, very much the same.

Closing her eyes, Genevieve knew there had been a happily-ever-after to Melinda and Steven's story. Now she wondered if Melinda ever told Steven, or did their marriage begin and end with a secret?

March 4, 1955

I couldn't see Steven last night. Every part of my body ached, and I wanted one more night to pretend nothing had changed between Steven and me.

Today, I covered my bruises as best I could, and met him for lunch at Dillinger's. We love that place. I had hoped the romantically dim lights would keep him from noticing my uneven skin tone, and the quiet atmosphere would be less distracting.

I've probably written this a dozen times before, and I'll say it once again, Steven's big brown eyes are, by far, the warmest, kindest, eyes I've ever seen. When he entered and saw me, already seated at our usual booth, those eyes of his were beaming with happiness.

I could feel myself shaking with panic. I began to have doubts. Maybe I won't say anything. Pretend it never happened.

After he kissed me, Steven took a seat across from me. He didn't notice the bruises. I felt my heart racing as he joked with the waiter who came by to get our drink order. I remember thinking I still had the choice to bury everything, maybe I should.

He started talking about how his morning went. I found it odd how he spoke as if the world hadn't totally changed. I was a completely different person now. Couldn't he see that? I watched as he laughed at a silly joke, and then took my hand as it rested on the table.

"I was raped." I heard myself say.

At first, he couldn't comprehend what he heard. His smile slowly faded as he asked, "What did you say?"

I wanted to go back a minute prior, when he was still smiling—when I was sure he still wanted me. I felt my chest crushing me.

Quietly, I said it again.

For a moment, I could tell he was trying to process what that meant. Then I saw the rage on his face, and it scared me. He asked me who it was. I knew he'd murder Godfrey if I told him, so I said I couldn't, for that very reason.

After the initial shock, he must have realized how shaken I had become. He got up and moved to my side of the booth and just held me in his strong arms. I didn't want to cry, but when he told me it was going to be alright and kissed the side of my head, I broke down.

I could tell he wanted to say more but had no words. As the crying subsided, I let his embrace linger, knowing it was to be the last. When I sat upright, I was going to tell him I was calling the wedding off and releasing him. But then, he saw the bruises that my tears had washed away, and I could see the horrified look in his eyes. Trying to stay calm, he asked again who it was.

When I shook my head, he said if I wouldn't tell him, at least I needed to go to the police and tell them.

He could see I was going to cry again, and pulled me close, saying he'd be with me the whole time.

I began thinking maybe I could get the miscreant for what he'd done. Perhaps the police would believe me. So, I agreed to go.

When we got to the police station, I told Steven he couldn't be with me when I talked to the detective. He didn't need to know the details, nor did I want him hearing the rapist's name.

As I suspected, even after telling the details and showing the detective my bruises, he said all he could do was give the accused a visit, but the bruises, sadly, weren't enough evidence to prosecute. So, unless he confessed...

When Steven and I got back to the car, I told him what the detective had said. The look on his face gave me the feeling he might try taking matters into his own hands. That's how Steven works. That's how he always gets things done.

So, before he did something rash, I took his incentive away. I told him I felt it would be best if we didn't marry.

For the second time, I watched him trying to process something he found unbelievable. After a moment he belted, "Absolutely not!"

I told him, I was no good for him, that if he didn't see it yet, soon, he would look at me differently.

Shaking his head, he said emphatically, "Impossible." Then swore his love was only stronger. Taking my hand, he said the only way he'd let me go was if I didn't love him anymore.

God, I was happy to hear him say those words.

Then I realized he didn't understand the type of love I wasn't sure of anymore. I told him I didn't know if I was capable of giving him the kind of intimate love a wife should. That just two days ago I dreamed of our wedding night. Now, I was afraid of it.

Shaking his head vigorously, Steven told me he'd wait for me.

As long as I needed, he said.

Genevieve noticed the faded ink and knew Melinda had cried tears of relief as the page ended.

CHAPTER 67

MORE TO THE STORY

THE NEXT FEW pages of entries were full of hope. Steven was going overboard to prove his love with daily flowers, romantic dinners, and frequent calls. Melinda had called her agent, Troy Desmeer, and told him she had chosen not to model anymore, using her marriage commitment as an excuse. It wasn't received well by him or the half-dozen businesses that had hired Melinda in the upcoming weeks. One, had even gone so far as to threaten a lawsuit. They didn't, but Melinda didn't care anyway.

Genevieve, understood now, why her mother had given the notebook to Tori. Learning that someone you least suspected had gone through a similar trauma and came out stronger was undeniably a gift of hope.

It was now late afternoon. Genevieve could feel her stomach growling as she had skipped right past lunch. With her eyes tired and having a hard time focusing, she decided since she was almost there anyway, she'd read through the "Wedding Day" entry, then head downstairs for dinner.

Her finger moved quickly as it scanned the following two pages. Suddenly though, as the slender digit moved to the top of the next page, it made an abrupt stop. Genevieve blinked several times to make sure she was reading it correctly. On April 21st, the first line read:

The doctor confirmed my suspicion. Heaven help me. I'm pregnant.

Genevieve's eyes remained frozen on the word "pregnant." A cacophony of thoughts blared in her head. Pulling her gaze from the book, Genevieve whispered, "That's impossible. She wasn't—she couldn't have been!"

She looked back to the date of the entry and murmured, "Two days before their wedding? NO! I saw the pictures. I know how happy they were"

Swallowing hard to keep her emotions from interfering, Genevieve resumed where she left off:

I don't know why, but when the doctor told me the news, I blurted out what had happened. I guess underneath it all I still hoped he'd see me as virtuous, even if I feel far from that now.

Dr. Monroe is such a nice man. I could see his concern as he told me there were options for me. He went behind his desk and wrote down numbers from his Rolodex. One option, he said, was of course to keep the baby. The second option, as he handed me the piece of paper, was a phone number of an excellent adoption agency in town.

Then he paused, hesitant to continue. Third, and the other number on the piece of paper, was a doctor of whom he was aware, that took care of unwanted pregnancies.

I remember looking up at him in shock.

Shaking his head, the doctor said he hoped I wouldn't choose that option. It was risky, and he stressed that he had no idea what the long-term physical and emotional effects might be.

I hadn't imagined the third option, and I told him so. He looked a bit relieved, in a dire sort of way, saying he had never suggested that option before. But then, he added, he never had to counsel a patient that had become pregnant from a rape before either.

I began to cry, feeling overwhelmed by yet, another cruel twist of fate forced upon me.

The doctor sat down at my side and said sadly, that he'd seen women in desperate situations, pregnant, and believing their lives were ruined. Knowing my wedding day was approaching, he implored me not to panic or act rashly. Taking the piece of paper back, he added his office phone number, and his home phone number, urging me to call him if I needed to talk to someone.

Before I left, Dr. Monroe asked if my fiancé knew about the rape. When I nodded, he said, "Tell him you're pregnant, Melinda. Trust this man. I think he's proven that nothing means more to him than you."

Melinda ended the entry there.

Staring blankly at the page, Genevieve knew Melinda had never raised a child, or even mentioned one. *Could she have actually had an abortion*? Genevieve could comprehend how devastating the circumstance would have been, but still felt sick inside, knowing how hard she fought for each of her own pregnancies. Then another twist of fate emerged in Genevieve's mind, *Miscarriage.* As she turned the page she wondered, *Could that have been what happened?*

> *April 22nd*
> *Our families have all arrived now.*
> *I wish so much to be happy. But my heart aches all the time. It aches for Steven, for me and this life growing within me.*
> *I don't recognize the person I see in the mirror. My face is pale, and I feel nauseous all the time. When I tried my wedding dress on last night, it was so tight! That's what I get for not picking a fabric that had any stretch to it.*
> *Steven will be here at any moment. I wish I could have given him more time to think about the bombshell I'm about to drop on him. He has every right to back out now, and I'm bracing for that very real possibility.*
> *I just wish we both had more time.*

Genevieve turned the page.

> *I better hurry but wanted to write this down while I can remember the details.*
> *When I told Steven, I expected one of two things to happen, or possibly both.*
> *1: That he'd say to me he couldn't handle the situation and cancel the wedding.*
> *2: Demand the rapist identity, something I've been expecting him to pursue.*
> *But, as we sat on the couch, and I told him I was pregnant, the shock and hurt in his eyes still took me by surprise, making me want to die. I put my head down after that. I couldn't look at him. His beautiful eyes had never made me feel so sad before. He didn't deserve any of this. When I was finished talking, I waited for him to tell me what I expected.*
> *My heart sank when he stood up.*
> *There was a long, excruciating pause. With my eyes closed, I could feel tears moving down my face. I knew Steven's eyes were on me, but I couldn't bear to watch him say good-bye.*
> *Instead, I heard him whisper how much he loved me. I began crying out loud. Steven came back and sat next to me, pulling me into his arms. When I was able to speak, I whispered the same to him.*

After that, Steven's tone seemed to change as he asserted how terribly wronged I had been. He didn't say it angrily, but there was a peculiar look that made me wonder. Did he somehow find out who the rapist was? Should I be worried?

For the moment, all I need to know is that Steven loves me and, considering every-thing, still wants me. I gave him every argument though and he never faltered. I even found myself getting angry, saying he wasn't thinking things through. The man just laughed and said there wasn't anything to think about.

Who IS this angel, who loves jokes, cowboy hats...and me?

GOD, I'm REALLY going to get married tomorrow!

Genevieve wiped a tear and smiled. Then, she remembered a comment her mother made in the hospital after her accident in the jet. It confused Genevieve at the time when Melinda said, "I was having terrible doubts and insecurities about getting married, and Steven knew it." Another tear fell as Genevieve whispered, *That's why he gave you the blue diamond. It was his way of telling you, no matter what the situation might be, he'd love you for eternity.*

With a shuttered sigh, Genevieve continued reading.

Steven asked me if I plan to keep the baby. I already knew before I left the doctor's office, my only choice was adoption. I explained that it wasn't the baby's fault: the circum-stance of its existence. The child deserved life, a happy life, but it couldn't be with me.

I expected to see relief on Steven's face, but instead, he asked if I was sure about let-ting the baby go.

This is why, Lord, I love him so much! I don't even know how I'll handle the next seven months, and he's ready to accept the responsibility of raising another man's child if that's what I wanted.

I told him I was afraid of what the child would look like—a resemblance that I might never get past.

Before he left to pick up his suit for tomorrow, Steven kissed me and said that whatever I chose, he would love and respect me for it. I think I've made the right decision, and, although I told Liv about the rape, she doesn't know about the pregnancy. I haven't told anyone but Steven. I plan to keep a low profile until after the baby is born. I think it's best that way.

Okay, it's getting late. I've got to hurry! My makeup is a mess, and the girls will be here within the hour to pick me up for a drink before the wedding rehearsal.

I think I'll have myself a stiff drink of 7-UP!

Genevieve let out a muted laugh. When she turned the page, there was only one more entry and it was dated, nine days after the wedding.

May 2,

I can't wait to see the professional portraits of our wedding. The whole day felt like a dream. He keeps telling me how lucky he is. I still don't think he has any idea how deeply in love I am with him.

The wedding night came faster then I realized. Suddenly we were alone in the airport hotel's suite before our flight to Hawaii the next morning. I thought I'd feel panicked. Steven made no suggestions or advances while we laid casually on the bed, for hours, reminiscing about the day.

But I had been dreaming of this moment for so long, and I knew to wait was a dangerous choice. My fear would only grow; Steven's love could falter...

I imagined Godfrey's smug smile. The rapist would still be in control.

Steven got up and said he'd sleep on the couch.

That was the last thing I wanted. I watched him take off his shirt. He had his back to me and didn't look toward me at all. I knew it was because he didn't want me to feel uneasy or pressured. Leaving his pants on, he went to grab a blanket and pillow from the closet.

Before he got back to the couch, I was there. My heart was racing when I heard myself whisper, "Undress me."

Steven put his head down and smiled, pausing for a moment. Then he looked up at me. Studying my face for a few seconds, he admitted nothing would make him happier but said, "I'll wait until you're sure it's the right time."

I felt anxious, but as he stood before me, I unbuckled his belt and finished undressing him. Then, lifting my eyes to meet his, I smiled and whispered, "It's the right time."

There was no panic or fear when I felt his warm, masculine body on mine. I knew then the anxious feeling had only been my longtime yearning for him, and this moment.

Every movement he made was slow and gentle.

It was what I had always dreamed it would be.

I've decided this will be my last entry. I started writing as a child because I had no one that understood me. I could scream and cry with my words and it soothed me somehow. But I have that someone now. I'm not afraid to be vulnerable with him. Steven knows me. And he's proven he's strong enough to handle just about anything I throw his way.

Now it's time for me to become the wife he deserves.

End of page.

Closing her eyes, Genevieve had only one thought…*Wow!*

Before going downstairs Genevieve slowly walked to the bathroom and splashed water on her face. After drying it with a towel she stared into the mirror. The reflection only hinted at the confounded state she was in, taxing her mind, *A model, a rape victim, a child? What happened to Godfrey? Did he ever go to jail? And what about the child? Did Mom give birth or did she have a miscarriage?*

CHAPTER 68

QUESTIONS

WHEN GENEVIEVE GOT to the bottom of the stairs, she could hear Gidda working in the kitchen and knew right away the talented cook was making her famous enchiladas for dinner. The spicy aroma was summoning Genevieve, not to mention her empty stomach.

As she began walking past the living room, Genevieve paused for a moment, turned, and went in. Walking over and stopping in front of the family portrait, she stared at Steven and Melinda, wishing with every fiber of her being that she could wrap her arms around them just one more time. With a trembling lip, Genevieve searched her mother's face. *How do you get over something like that? How did you hide everything so well that even I missed those intense feelings that must have erupted in you from time to time?*

Melinda, with her radiant smile, only stared back at Genevieve in poised silence.

With a sigh, Genevieve started to walk out of the room. Then she turned and looked at the couch. *Maybe I did feel them after all. I remember a day, long ago, when I caught Mom crying as she held Ella in her arms. I felt such longing and regret coming from her. Did Ella remind her of her own baby and what she'd lost? What happened to that baby?*

As Genevieve turned to leave, Tess was in the doorway with her head tipped to the side as she watched Genevieve deep in thought. Seeing Tess, Genevieve shook her head, trying to hold her emotions back. Yet when Tess walked over and hugged her, Genevieve let out mournful moan and whispered, "Why didn't she tell us?"

That evening Tess and Genevieve talked at length about the journal. With both reeling from all the questions left in their minds, they deciding to call Tori the next day, knowing she hopefully could fill in some of the blanks.

When Genevieve finally got to her bedroom, she decided to call Teddy, since it was mid-morning in England. It was outside their usual time to talk, but she just needed to hear his voice. The conversation was short, however, as Teddy was on the fifth hole of a golf course, and his party was waiting for him to finish so they could move onward. With a promise to call before he went to bed, Genevieve turned out the lights and quickly fell into a deep sleep.

Why can't I move? Genevieve began to twitch in her sleep. *Uh! I can't see anything. The phone is ringing, where is it?* Grappling in the dark, Genevieve reaches down to free herself from whatever she's stuck in. Realizing, in her dream, that her eyes are closed, she tries fiercely to open them.

The phone rings again.

With tremendous effort, Genevieve forces her eyes open to reveal a morbid sight. She can't move because she finds herself standing deep in bodies that are laying contorted, as if dropped from the sky and spread out as far as she can see. Hesitantly, Genevieve glances down and quickly retracts her hand when she sees that it had been touching the face of a young, dead man.

The phone keeps ringing.

Breathing short and shallow, panic sets in. *The phone, I've got to call somebody, where is the phone!*

Then, Genevieve feels her body start to lift. As she watches, the space where she once stood quickly disappears, as the bodies drop into it. Looking up, Genevieve begins flailing her arms and legs in a frenzied attempt to control the uncontrollable as she rises higher and higher. Finally, coming to a stop, midair, ten-stories high, she looks below. Her arms and legs become limp, and she becomes perfectly still. In a hideous mosaic design, the corpses below spell out a message: **Save the rest**.

Within a few moments Genevieve begins to descend. She closes her eyes, knowing there is nowhere to land except on the bodies below. Yet surprisingly, she feels her feet land on solid ground and slowly peeks out of one eye. The bodies are gone and standing in front of her is a young woman, who takes her hand. The young lady looks familiar, and Genevieve quickly recognizes her face from a dream long ago. Without a spoken word, a blurry message begins to formulate in Genevieve's mind. Frowning, Genevieve shakes her head at the young woman as she tries to make sense of it.

Suddenly, with frightful urgency, the young woman's eyes open wide as she pulls Genevieve closer, and the message becomes crystal clear: ***Genevieve, it's almost time! Are you ready?***

With a sudden jerk, Genevieve's eyes flew open, her heart pounding wildly as her cell phone rang on the nightstand. As she reached to grabbed it, the ringing stopped.

Closing her eyes, again, Genevieve regretted not bringing her dream journals with her to the estate. She knew she'd had a similar dream before, long ago. She still remembered the young woman. *Why did I see her again? What's almost here?*

The phone dinged; a message was recorded. Hitting "Play" Genevieve heard her brother's voice:

"Genevieve, I know it's early, but I've got to talk to you. Something strange seems to be going on and I could use your input. Love ya. And don't forget to call me!"

Tossing the phone on the bed, Genevieve squinted to see that the time was 6:55 a.m. *Oh David, everything is so urgent with you. Sorry brother, but my first call, after I truly wake up, will be to Tori.*

After getting ready and coming downstairs she walked into the kitchen. Gidda handed Genevieve a cup of coffee. "Thanks, Gidda. Are the other two up yet?"

Gidda joked, "Mr. Ryan just headed to the grocery store to get more boxes. I think you might not need the estate sale after all, looks like you're taking everything with you!"

Genevieve choked on her coffee, then nodded. "It does look that way."

Although the majority of items *were* being prepped and staged for the estate sale, both Genevieve and Tess continued to find more and more personal belongings they couldn't bear to let go, hence the additional boxes.

Just after eight-thirty, Genevieve put a load of clothes into the washing machine, while Tess was finishing breakfast. From the time she got up, Genevieve had been rehearsing what to say when she called Tori. As Tess sat next to her at the kitchen table, a few minutes later, Genevieve nervously made the call.

It rang five times and just as Genevieve thought she'd have to leave a message, Tori picked up, "Hello?"

"Tori!" Genevieve boomed, as her adrenaline, *and coffee* were making her overly anxious. Clearing her throat, Genevieve turned her volume down a notch. "Tori, hi, it's Genevieve."

"Hi Genevieve. How are you and Tess doing? I was thinking about you both yesterday and almost called. Could you use a hand?"

Genevieve looked at Tess and said, "Actually, Tess and I desperately need your help. But not in the way you think." There was a pause, then Genevieve confessed, "We found Mom's journal, the one she gave to you."

There was even a longer pause, then Tori questioned, "Then I'll ask again, how *are* you both doing?"

With such a loaded question, Genevieve could only echo what Tori had written in her letter to Melinda. "Like you had said in your letter Tori, we weren't prepared. Right now, Tess and I would really like to meet with you. We have so many questions."

Tori suggested they meet at a Starbucks near Tori's house in an hour.

When Genevieve and Tess arrived at the coffee house, Tori was sitting at a corner table and waved them over. Standing up, she gave each a hug and said, "Can I get you a cup of coffee?"

Genevieve shook her head. "Thanks, but we called ahead. The order should be at the counter."

Tori smiled, "Very good." Looking thoughtfully at the girls, Tori let out a sigh, "After your mom died, I wondered what she had done with the journals. I didn't want to say anything if she had gotten rid of them, since it was her wish that you girls never know what happened to her. I'll be glad to answer any questions that I have answers *to*, but first, go get your coffee while it's still hot."

When the three were settled, and the small talk was over, Genevieve wasted no more time. Giving Tess a glance she stated, "After Mom's accident, she swore there would be no more secrets. This wasn't just one she forgot about. No one forgets such a thing."

"Tori shook her head. "Melinda believed if you two knew what had happened to her, it would change how you saw her; that you'd forever see a victim and feel sorry for her. I told her it would be the opposite. I believed you would only love her more and be in awe of how she rose above such a heartache. Was I wrong? Has your love for her changed?"

Genevieve softly replied, "Yes."

Tess frowned at Genevieve, and Tori's eyes widened, her lips turned down when she saw Genevieve's chin begin to quiver.

Quickly putting her hand over Tori's, Genevieve almost immediately felt the older woman's positive expectations morphing rapidly into confusion.

"I mean, yes, my love *has* changed. I thought my love for her couldn't get deeper, but it did. The only regret I have is in not knowing earlier, when I could have talked with her about it. My heart ached for her as I read each entry, and all I wanted was to comfort her, you know?"

Tori's tense posture relaxed. "You two were her greatest comforts. However, that part of her life was such an important element as to who she became. I *am* sorry for the way you both found out about it, but I'm not sorry that you now know."

Tess pleaded, "We have so many questions that were left unanswered. Starting with, what happened to the baby?"

Tori gently pulled her hand from underneath Genevieve's and patting it before taking it away. "After Melinda and Steven were married, Steven bought the estate that they ended up living their whole lives in. Melinda spent her pregnancy there, hidden away until the baby was born—a little girl. She told me it was one of the hardest things she ever did, giving her baby away."

With a hesitant look towards Genevieve, Tori continued, "While we're on the subject, I thought you two should know. After she gave the baby away and had a few months to heal, Melinda had high hopes of getting pregnant and giving Steven a child. However, during the next year and a half, she suffered *three* miscarriages."

Genevieve took a sharp breath. Starring at Tori, she had no words, feeling sick as painful memories of her own miscarriages began flooding back.

Tess, gently put her arm on Genevieve's. Upon reflection Genevieve now understood. The heightened anger and sadness Melinda felt at the time of

Genevieve's first miscarriage seemed oddly closely to her own. But in the end, Genevieve assumed it was her mother's strong empathy and heartache for her. It was, yes, yet it *had* been more, much more. "I don't understand." Genevieve stressed, "Why was it a secret? Why couldn't she have told me that when *I* miscarried?"

With a concerned look on her face, Tori continued. "Because…Steven never knew."

Tess and Genevieve frowned at Tori in utter bewilderment.

"You see, Melinda told me this in confidence after I got married and had a miscarriage myself. The first time, she didn't even know she was pregnant until she went to the doctor. Melinda told me she never had regular periods, so she didn't suspect what had happened until the doctor advised her. Then, almost eight months after that, she had a feeling she was pregnant but wanted to wait before telling Steven, to make sure. She lost the baby days later. Four months afterward, Melinda's hopes were dashed again, with a third miscarriage. None of her pregnancies made it past eight weeks.

"Your mother told me at the time, she thought she was being punished for giving her daughter away. Her doctor said to give it time, but the emotional pain was so great that, after that, Melinda started using contraceptives. Back in those days, women mainly used a diaphragm. To keep Steven from getting worried or suspicious, she told him she wasn't ready to be a mother again, and he understood. She never could bring herself to tell him she'd never be able to give him a child.

Tori reached across the table and took Tess and Genevieve's hands. "Do you both understand now, the Godsend you both were in their lives?"

Tess cleared the emotions that were building in her throat, turned to her sister and smiled. Genevieve smiled tenderly back and nodded.

Tori affirmed. "In the back of her mind, Melinda knew her sister *could* come back and rip you two away from her. So, she told me she did her best to embrace each day as if it might be her last with you girls. Then, after a few years had come and gone, Melinda realized her fear had gone away. The Teels had been blessed with two amazing daughters. That's when she had the family portrait made."

CHAPTER 69

A HYPOTHETICAL GAME

GENEVIEVE SWALLOWED HARD, thinking about the agony she once thrust upon Melinda after finding out her mother, Liv, was alive. Turning to Tori, she lamented, "I wish I could go back. Change how I treated her, the things I said that hurt her so deeply. I knew so little then, and how much she had already gone through, and the loss..."

Tori gazed out the large window toward the parking lot. "So much of our understanding is learned through reflection," she replied. "You can't change what you didn't know."

Genevieve let Tori's words coalesce. Quietly, Genevieve repeated the words, "Didn't know." Looking at Tess, then at Tori she continued to the next question. "I have a few questions about the rapist, Godfrey."

Tori blinked, "Okay."

With a puzzled look, Genevieve asked, "So, if Mom never told Dad who the rapist was, do you think he ever found out? I can't imagine Dad just letting that heinous crime against his wife go, not knowing what the man might try again. Did you ever hear anything more about it? Didn't you wonder also?

Tori rubbed the back of her neck. "*Yes*, I did wonder if there was more to know. But when Melinda said Steven never knew, I didn't ever bring it up again. Still, I worried about what Godfrey might have been doing all those years, to other unsuspecting women.

"A couple of years later, after the foundation had been established, Melinda sent Steven to my house to deliver a document to sign. By that point, he and I had become friends, and Steven knew my circumstance and trusted my friendship with his wife.

305

"He didn't know, however, that *I* knew who her rapist was. It had been a nagging question for years, and Steven, like you said, wasn't one to sit idly by when so much was at stake.

"So, when Steven came over that day, I was sitting on the front porch with a beer in hand and asked if he wanted one. He said, 'Sure.' We talked about your latest family trip to Africa, and, after accepting a second beer, I decided to test the waters to see if he would divulge anything.

"I told him Melinda and I had just gone to see a rape victim, which was true. I said how thankful I was to know the person that had raped me was in prison. I added that every victim wishes the same, otherwise, there is always the fear he might strike again. I said how sad it was that Melinda's rapist had never been caught. Then I took a slow sip of beer, waiting to see if Steven would respond.

"There was a bit of hesitation, but then he said, 'She's safe. I'll never let anyone harm her, ever again.'

"I looked at him, and we stared at each other for a long moment.

"Then I said, "Hypothetically, since I know how you must have thought about what you wish you could have done to put that rapist away, *hypothetically*, then, what would you have possibly done?"

Steven raised his eyebrows and seemed happy to play the hypothetical game. Laughing, he took a sip of the beer and said, 'Well, hypothetically, I would have had to find another way to put him in prison since the police were of no help. I first would have contacted a friend I know in the police department to confirm my suspicion as to who it was. Then, I *might* have hired a private detective to shadow the rapist's every move, and hopefully catch him doing what surely wasn't a one-time offense against my wife.

"Within a month, this hypothetical P.I. would report back to me that, although the degenerate had been seen twice picking up prostitutes down on Nader street, it was something else that got his attention. He'd tell me that the miscreant had met the day before *our* meeting with several men at a warehouse on the outskirts of town. He'd hypothetically throw me a curveball and tell me that the rapist was also trafficking guns."

Tori looked at the unbelieving eyes of Genevieve and Tess. "I know girls, but that's what he said—guns."

Genevieve slowly shook her head, never imagining Tori knew as much as she did.

As Tori nodded, Genevieve could see the relief in the elderly woman's eyes, as she finally could tell the girls what she knew.

After a sip of coffee, Tori continued. "Steven said that the imaginary P.I. would then tell him the gun sale was to go down the following night. Your father then gave me this satisfied grin and said, 'Hypothetically, an anonymous tip would be given to the police. Then, I imagine, the private investigator and I would enjoy sitting in his beat-up old Studebaker across from the warehouse and watch as *all* the criminals were taken away.'

Tori paused a moment when she realized, "You know, Steven was so smart. It just dawned on me that he never, not once, slipped and mentioned Godfrey's name to me in his story." Looking down at the table, Tori added, "I remember saying to Steven he had quite an interesting and detailed "hypothetical" story, but I wondered if anything would change when the man got out of prison in a few short years.

"Your father's face turned serious when he responded. 'I would imagine the criminal was sentenced for a very long time. In my hypothetical imaginings, mind you, as the police searched his apartment after his arrest, they'd discover reels of film he hid in his closet. *Quite* a hypothetical surprise, and, it would prove Melinda wasn't his only victim.'

"Steven sat for a minute as I watched him finish his beer. Then he added, 'If there were anything to be thankful for, it would be that no film was discovered with Melinda on it. With *that* silver-lining she'd never be identified as one of his victims. She'd *never* have to relive her nightmare in front of a jury. And, maybe, more importantly, she'd *never* have to see the rapist's evil smile when he found out she had carried his child."

Tori, took a deep breath and concluded, "Before Steven left that day, he told me Melinda used to shake uncontrollably for a couple of months after the rape, but he'd hold her tight and tell her over and over that she would always be protected, he would make sure of it.

"One day when she was about four months pregnant, Steven said Melinda whispered in his ear, saying he was her guardian angel. She told him she knew that the man who raped her was no longer a threat to her or anyone else. Steven said he had tried to keep Melinda away from the local newspaper that had reported the crime and the perverted discovery in his apartment. Still, Steven knew then, that she had heard the news somewhere—and she knew he must have had a hand in it."

Tess sat quietly trying to grasp all that she just heard, while Genevieve shook her head. "I knew it!" she exclaimed. "I knew Dad would've had only one priority until he was *sure* his wife and other women were safe. I just couldn't see any scenario where he would stay complacent. It just wasn't in his DNA."

Tess nodded in agreement, then looked at Tori, "My sister and I always thought the foundation was started because of your circumstance, that's what Mom told us. But it went much deeper and far more personal to her than we ever imagined. Thank you so much for filling in the blanks.

Tori had a satisfied look on her face, then looked at her watch. "I know you two have been here for almost two hours, but there is one more thing I want you to know."

Genevieve looked up at Tori, hesitantly.

Tori let out a chuckle. "Nothing bad, I promise. Once, I had asked Melinda if she ever kept any mementos of her modeling days. She said she kept a few in a cedar chest in the attic. She said she had locked it away in a far corner so you children could never access it. Well, that was then, when you were too young to understand. This is now. I don't know where the key could be, but I bet it would be glorious to see what she kept from those days."

Genevieve had a furrowed brow, "I might know where the key is hidden."

Tess and Tori's eyes opened wide with surprise.

Genevieve hypothesized, "We know she kept her journals hidden in that box. It was part of her past she wasn't willing to let go. Why wouldn't she hide the key there also? With a side glance to Tess, Genevieve noted, "The attic was going to be our next project anyway, right Tess?"

Tess nodded but grumbled, "Project is putting it mildly. Every time I've headed up there, I've turned back around. We'll be lucky to find that chest in this century!"

Genevieve nudged her sister. "Look at it as digging for gold, and maybe things will move along quicker."

Tess looked skeptical, "Let's just hope it's what we think it is. Mom, as it turns out, held many tormenting secrets throughout her life. I just pray we've learned the last of them."

The girls looked at Tori to make sure she had no other shocking revelations to tell them. Tori, shrugged and shook her head, "If there is, I can't imagine what it could be."

Genevieve blew out a cleansing breath and whispered, "Good."

As the three got up from the table, Genevieve and Tess each wrapped their arms around Tori, and Genevieve promised, "We'll call you after we've opened the chest, even if we have to pry it open. I can't imagine what she decided to hold onto, but I know it would have been very meaningful to her, and, *hopefully*, like you said, glorious!"

CHAPTER 70

---- ❈ ----

ATTIC TREASURES

WHEN THEY GOT back home, Genevieve noticed David had called again while she had her phone on mute. It was another voicemail pleading for her to call. While Tess went to the kitchen to grab a bite to eat, Genevieve went to her bedroom and called her brother.

With barely a ring, he picked up. "Where have you been?" he demanded.

"Tess and I had an important meeting this morning. We just got back. What's so urgent?"

David sighed, which annoyed Genevieve as she knew a reprimand was coming. "I called you early this morning to see if you've been checking your emails. By the tone of your voice right now, I'm *sure* you haven't read them."

Genevieve began to frown with concern. "I checked two days ago, and there was nothing out of the ordinary. So, something has happened since then?"

"Let me ask you this," David responded, "Has anything odd happened in the last day or so?"

Genevieve almost laughed. Her days were riddled with odd. "Can you be more specific, please?"

David cleared his throat, "Almost every Soul Seeker has received a message lately. I know yours tend to come in dreams. Have you had an ominous one in the last day or so?"

Genevieve suddenly felt her heart beating faster. "As a matter-of-fact I did, last night."

David murmured something under his breath, but all Genevieve caught was, "Oh God."

"Oh God, what? You're scaring me now. What's going on?"

David answered with another question, "Did the dream include a massive amount of dead people?"

With a halted breath, Genevieve answered with a hesitant, "Yes." Genevieve could hear a panicked humming noise on the other end of the phone. "David?"

"Okay, *okay*, Gen. Well, you know how you get messages in dreams as do others in the group. Then there is me, along with quite a few, that see messages in articles or other literature, while still others are bluntly interrupted, no matter what time of day, with a specific voice, that only they recognize, relaying a cryptic message."

Genevieve affirmed, "Yes, we learned about that long ago."

"Yes, but we've never singularly received the same message. My guess is you received the same one: "It's almost time! Are you ready?""

Genevieve inhaled sharply. "Oh, God."

David took a deep breath. "Something is coming, Gen, and it's terrifying me—something very bad."

Genevieve shook her head, "What are we supposed to do?

David didn't say anything at first but finally uttered, "I have no idea. Did you're dream reveal anything else?"

Genevieve tried to remember the details. "I remember I couldn't open my eyes at first, not sure what that meant. Then I began floating over a multitude of dead bodies. When I was high enough, I saw a message spelled out in the bodies below that read, 'Save the rest.' It felt oddly familiar with a dream I had long ago. I don't have my journals with me, and I don't remember all the details, but the message came from the same person; the same Soul, I'm sure of that."

David spoke softly, "Then this ability we share has all been for grander purpose after all."

Genevieve felt queasy, "But what if we're *not* ready? What then?"

David had no answer. Before hanging up, he asked Genevieve to email the group about her dream so that everything could be documented and shared. By the time she put the phone down, she could feel her head swimming from revelations of the past, and now, the foreboding future. Doing as she was asked, Genevieve logged into her laptop and composed an email describing her dark and foreboding dream to all the Soul Seekers.

After she sent it, she closed the lid. Sitting for several minutes and staring blankly out her bedroom window, Genevieve finally acknowledging, there was nothing she could do about the future, so she forced her focus back to the past. *I'm hoping the key is where I think it is—where I would have hidden it. Whether I find it or not though, that cedar chest is opening this afternoon.*

By the time Genevieve got to the kitchen there was a sandwich and some chips left on a plate with a note from Tess: I'll be in the attic. Bring the key if you can find it.

After hastily downing her food, Genevieve went to her parent's bedroom. As she sat on the bed, she pulled all the pads and journals out of the box then grinned slightly when she saw a small, maroon, velveteen pouch at the bottom. Opening the drawstring, she turned it upside down and a small key fell into her hand. "This has to be it," she murmured.

Tightening her hand around it, the conversation with David began resurfacing. As she stared at her fist, she noticed her wedding ring. Genevieve was missing Teddy more than ever. With him, the sky could be falling, and it wouldn't matter. And, by all signs, it was pointed to just that. *But when?* She thought. *A few days, weeks, years? The sooner I get to England, the better. I can handle anything as long as I'm with him.*

As she slowly stood up Genevieve put the key in her jean pocket. *Let there be no more dark secrets in that chest of yours, Mom. I couldn't bear any more bad news today.*

When Genevieve entered the attic, Tess was going through a large cabinet near the doorway, filled with files and books of Steven's. Genevieve began to survey the heavily packed room. Tess pointed, "It's over there under a lot of boxes." Genevieve spotted the cedar chest and nodded. Tess let out a sigh, "Of what I've gone through so far, I have a feeling this room is going to be mostly worthless keepsakes and mementos. This cabinet has nothing but old contracts, real-estate literature, and some old pictures of horses."

Genevieve drew her eyes back to Tess. "Can I see those?"

Tess grabbed a half-dozen pictures and handed them to her sister. There were a few of Patience, Steven's first horse and mother to Haddie. Trident and

Dodger, two beautiful stallions that each won local races, but then Genevieve felt an ache in her chest. The last picture was of Haddie, her horse, as a new-born, nestling with her mother. "Ah, I loved you so, sweet girl. I want to keep this one."

Nodding, Tess assured, "I thought you would." Then, pointing to a large container near the air-conditioning vent in the center of the attic wall, she added, "I found Haddie's old saddle up here too. Dad kept it in such good condition. Do you think you could use it for Piper?"

Genevieve shook her head, "Haddie was a Fresian, a dressage horse. Piper will be a runner. Two different types of activities—two types of saddles. Besides, a saddle needs to be fitted correctly to the length and size of the horse, you know that Tess."

Tess raised her eyebrows and shook her head. "I never paid any attention to those types of details. Guess I learned something new today."

Walking over to the container, Genevieve could see how meticulously wrapped it was, being kept near the cooler air to keep the leather from getting too hot and dry. Genevieve knew that her dad had preserved the saddle for her, as he was not sentimental in any respect when it came to equipment. But he knew that anything to do with Haddie would always be close to Genevieve's heart. "I don't know where I'm going to put this, but I'm keeping this as well."

Tess grinned. "I had no doubt."

The cedar chest was in the corner, by the small attic window. Several dusty boxes were piled on top of it. Walking over, Genevieve pulled the key from her pocket. "I found a key. It *was* in the box."

Tess quickly walked over, "Great! Are you ready to see if fits?"

CHAPTER 71

DRESS UP

GENEVIEVE AND TESS moved the boxes that were sitting on top of the chest. Kneeling, Genevieve placed the key in the lock and turned until she heard a click. With nervous anticipation, Genevieve looked at her sister, then slowly opened it.

The first thing she noticed was the woodsy-sweet smell of cedar filling the air around her. When the lid had fully opened, a hinged wooden tray attached to it, expanded outward to reveal a lavish assortment of glistening, fine jewelry. Necklaces, bracelets, rings—even a tiara with small red rubies, lay draped and sparkling like a newly discovered pirate's treasure.

Tess knelt next to Genevieve as they beheld much more than a few items which Melinda downplayed when she spoke to Tori about it. The chest itself was packed full. As Genevieve imagined, there were gowns of many colors, neatly wrapped in clear garment bags. Lifting them out, one by one, Genevieve envisioning a very young Melinda posing in them as Genevieve handed each one to Tess. At the bottom, were several pairs of long elegant gloves, six beautiful handbags, and four pairs of Stiletto's: black, white, red, and royal blue.

After lifting the final pair of shoes, the girls smiled at each other.

Tess remarked, "This is what I had hoped we'd see." Genevieve sighed and nodded. Tess stood up and held a classy black gown up to her and strutted back and forth as if she was on a modeling runway. With a laugh, Genevieve relaxed and leaned against the chest, taking in a few deep, calming breaths of cedarwood. Noticing an intricately beaded cocktail purse next to her, Genevieve picked it up and ran her fingers along it, imagined the fair amount of questions the chest contents would have brought, had Tess not found the notebook first.

Genevieve and Tess spent the next half-hour, speculating as to why Melinda chose to save each particular item in the chest. Each made up a story as they placed a gown, shoes and accessories together. It was a fun exercise even though they knew they'd never know the answer to the question.

Ryan popped his head inside the door, "By the sound of things, you must be happy with whatever Mom hid in the chest."

Tess grabbed his arm and walked him over to the sprawled attire lying about. Gen and I have been playing dress up. Aren't they all gorgeous?"

Ryan raised his eyebrows. "She must have looked spectacular in these."

The girl's faces turned a bit solemn and as they nodded in unison.

Realizing he had just dampened the mood Ryan diverted the subject. "Tess, Sara called a little while ago. She said she'd really like to have her grandma's doughboy cookie jar. She said it always made her happy when she was little, and grandma would always have her favorite cookies in it. I've been looking around for it, but I can't find it anywhere."

Tess replied, "I think I put it on one of the pantry shelves along with some of the other kitchen items to display at the sale. I'll go down with you and make sure it's there." Looking at Genevieve, she smirked, "It's funny how our kids keep thinking of special things *they* want to keep as well. Say Gen, are you okay to put everything back in the trunk?"

Genevieve grinned. "Quite okay." After a few more minutes to admire the beautiful array around her, Genevieve started putting things back.

While placing the second set of shoes in the chest, one slipped from Genevieve's hand and fell, clamoring, with an odd sound, to the chest floor. Frowning, Genevieve looked at the attic floor, and then at the cedar chest floor. There were no legs to the chest, yet the floor of the chest had to be almost five inches higher than the attic floor. There was no hollow sound when Genevieve knocked on the bottom of the chest, but when pushing down on it, it moved slightly.

Glancing around the base, she noticed a small wire loop protruding out of the bottom edge on the right side, almost undetectable. Raising her head slowly to the ceiling and shaking it, Genevieve whispered, "I should have known there would be more."

Bracing for what was hidden below, Genevieve put her finger in the loop and pulled upward. The artificial floor was hinged on the left side from underneath, and, as Genevieve opened it wide, a four-inch deep compartment appeared below. However, only one, very large, manila envelope occupied the hidden space. Wrinkled and worn, it was stuffed full. Taking it out, Genevieve got up and walked to the old fall-front desk. Her mother had used the antique desk in her office for years before modernizing it with a sleek desk made with tempered glass and a metal frame.

Laying the envelope down, Genevieve sat at the desk, put her hands on her cheeks, and stared at it for several minutes. Finally, she turned on an old floor lamp that stood next to the desk and began unwinding the string closure.

With a quick peek inside, nothing seemed ominous. *It's full of pictures— tons of them.*

Pouring them out over the desk, Genevieve stared at them in awe, starstruck. Melinda was as glamorous as any model she had ever seen from that time period. With flawless features, each professional photo showed a different aspect of her mother's beguiling personality.

In one 8x10 black and white glossy, Melinda wore a full-length fur coat and cap. With sunglasses covering her eyes, she stood outdoors, leaning against a snowy patio deck rail and was blowing a kiss toward the cameraman.

In another, a profile headshot of Melinda's right side, she was posing, head tilted upward. She wore a small, dainty tea party hat with netting draped over her eyes, a burning cigarette with its long holder held up to her puckered colored lips. So stylish for the time, yet it seemed curious as Melinda had a hard time breathing whenever she came in contact with cigarette smoke.

Amongst the many professional shots, were torn catalog pages, as well as candid snapshots, all of Melinda in various poses and attire. But one, in particular, made Genevieve giggle with delight. It was a professional color photo of Melinda strutting down a runway. However, she wasn't sporting the pouty look, like so many models Genevieve had seen in the past. No, Melinda had a big toothy smile, framed by her dramatic red lips. She was wearing a sequined deep red, strapless gown, and red strappy high heels. The designer accessorized his model with a billowy long white silky sash around her neck.

Then, to top it off, Melinda wore a jeweled tiara intertwined with her updo curls and swirls.

Looking over at the cedar chest, Genevieve compared the headpiece made of rubies, with the one in the picture. *It's the same one!*

Feeling giddy, Genevieve intently studied the large 8x10 glossy. Suddenly she noticed that Steven was there, sitting in the front row along the runway. With a beaming grin, he watched his girlfriend walk by him, dazzling the crowd around her.

Letting out a muted laugh, Genevieve wiped a tear that had begun to roll down her cheek.

She was beginning to understand why Melinda hid the pictures. If her mother's modeling career was never discovered, which Melinda assumed would be the case, Genevieve and Tess would have concluded the beautiful garments in the chest had been worn by their mother in the past, then packed away for safekeeping. The pictures, however, would have been a blindsided mystery for sure.

As Genevieve continued to go through the photos, she noticed a small white envelope amongst them. There were a handful of black and white pictures inside. When Genevieve took them out, the euphoria she had been feeling, rapidly dwindled, knowing who the photos must have been of. Melinda had been keeping a watch over her daughter—for years.

She must have found out who adopted the baby.

The pictures were all taken from a distance, possibly from across the street. One was of a tiny tot being pushed in a stroller by a nicely dressed woman. Another was of the little girl, a few years older, sitting on the front steps of her house with another little girl. Each one was taken at the same place, presumably the girl's home. As the child grew, Genevieve could begin to see her resemblance to Melinda. The last one looked like the little girl may have been ten or so. She was standing by the steps of her house, in a school uniform, looking directly at the camera.

You never told anyone about these, not even Tori.

The pictures stopped after that. *Did something happen? Did the little girl see you taking her picture and frighten you away? Or, maybe Tess and I filled your days at that point and helped ease the pain of a loss that had clearly haunted you for years.*

Another question that would never be answered.

As Genevieve put the final pictures back in the envelope, she picked up one small candid black and white photo and held it in front of her. In it, Melinda was wearing the same sequined gown from the runway. Standing backstage, someone had snapped a picture of Steven tipping his love backward and giving her a passionate kiss.

With a trembling smile, Genevieve closed her eyes, brought the photo to her lips, and began to cry.

CHAPTER 72

READY OR NOT

THREE WEEKS LATER.

"Really, ye don't hav te help me, Gen. Go oot back and take Ted with ye. I'll come roond when I'm done washin the dishes," Amelie assured.

Genevieve looked at Teddy. who just shrugged and shook his head.

Anxious energy was bottled up in Genevieve. She was ready to get home and get her life back on track after flying straight from Arizona to London, ten days ago.

Once the estate sale was finished, the girls asked Tori to come over so she could see *everything* that was in the chest. Then Genevieve and Tess left the empty estate in the capable hands of the realtor. With excellent references, Gidda had already found new employment with only the groundskeeper left to manage—well, the grounds, until the property sold.

Piper was transferred to a stable facility near the Walker's home. Ella promised to visit the filly often until her parents got back. The plan being that when they returned Teddy and Genevieve would search for a new home that had more land to house Piper, yet, still be close to the ocean.

Then there were all the boxes, several pieces of furniture, and the Teel family portrait, which took some persuading to coax away from Tess. All had been shipped from the estate and were now sitting in Ella's garage.

Before the death of Melinda and Steven, Genevieve and Teddy had been talking about downsizing. Now instead, they were going to need a larger house *and* more acreage.

Adira was due any day, and Genevieve wanted to be home to greet her first granddaughter as soon as she arrived. Broc and Adira had finally decided on a name, Shani, after Adira's close friend that died in the Israel street bombing.

As Genevieve and Teddy sat huddled together on Amelie's back-porch swing, Teddy had his arm around Genevieve's shoulders as they sat quietly rocking back and forth. Genevieve had sorely missed his touch while he was away, the smell of him as well as his comforting dimpled smile.

She had decided not to tell her husband of the forewarned apocalyptic future. What would be the purpose? No one—not a single Soul Seeker had yet to be shown the what, when, where, why, or how it would happen.

Teddy and Genevieve's reunion, that first night in Bamburgh, was as intense as their good-bye was in Arizona. Only this time, Genevieve understood more than ever, how precious each moment together was.

Trying to keep her fears at bay, she murmured, "I wish your sister would come and live with us. She's got to be so lonely here."

One who never wandered far from Bamburgh, Amelie had raised two boys with her husband, Oliver, who died of a stroke, five years prior. She now lived alone in a quaint 3-bedroom stone cottage near Budle Bay, as both her grown children had moved across the border to Edinburgh Scotland.

Teddy turned and looked through the window behind them, watching Amelie move around the kitchen. "She's too much of a worrier, ye know. It would be harder for her to leave all she's ever known here. She has a few friends nearby, and the boys come around to visit a couple of times a year. Besides, she'd nivvor leave Mum. She frets over the old woman every day, even though Amelie is a stranger to her now."

Hearing Genevieve's wistful sigh, Teddy looked at her and whispered, "But I think I'm beginin to soften Amelie up for a visit to come see us, soon."

With a nod, Genevieve patted Teddy's knee, "Well, I'm going to finish packing up our things. Amelie is going to really miss you, Teddy. Those dishes in there can wait. Make your sister come sit out here with you, one last time before we leave."

Leaning over, Genevieve closed her eyes and brushed her lips along Teddy's and whispered, "One thing is for certain. I *never* want to know what it feels like to miss you, ever again."

With a prolonged kiss, Genevieve got up, went into the house, and began roaming from room to room, gathering Teddy's things that were still sprawled around. After packing everything she could find, she walked into the kitchen to see Teddy and Amelie having a lively conversation on the swing outside.

Genevieve had almost finished cleaning the rest of the dishes, when she heard Teddy yell, "Gen, come oot here!"

Looking out the window, Genevieve saw the panicked look in Teddy's eyes as he looked back at her. Running, Genevieve opened the back door to see Amelie in the midst of a violent seizure. "What happened?" Genevieve screamed.

"Nothin! She just started shakin, call 999!"

Genevieve shook her head, "What?"

Teddy pulled his cell phone out of his back pocket, "It's like 911." With shaking hands, Teddy dialed the numbers and pleaded for help.

By the time the phone call was over, Amelie's body had gone limp. Genevieve checked her sister-in-law's pulse and could see her chest moving. "She's alive. Did this happen before?"

With frowning concern, Teddy shook his head. "Naw while I've been here."

Within a couple of minutes, Amelie opened her eyes. When she saw Teddy, she smiled, but immediately went into another seizure, this one stronger than the first. By the time the ambulance arrived, she had become completely unresponsive.

As the sirens blared down the narrow street, Genevieve and Teddy jumped into Amelie's car and hurried behind.

When the Walkers stepped through the hospital doors, Genevieve was blasted with a feeling of Deja vue. As she took in her surroundings, she felt a pressure as strong as a G-force weighing her down."

While Teddy stood in line at the desk to sign in, Genevieve looked for a place to sit down. The emergency room was packed full, and the intake line was getting longer. It seemed very odd for such a rural area.

Near the corner of the room, Genevieve spotted just two seats still open and sat down. As she settled in, she noticed a woman a few seats down, wiping her eyes and mumbling quietly to herself. In another part of the room, a man was pacing up and down the floor while shaking his head. Heavy concern filled every face that Genevieve looked upon.

While Teddy made his way over to her, the woman directly across from Genevieve was on her phone when Genevieve overheard, "They sez they don't hev any more beds—none o the hospitals roond heor do. They're resortin te cots or whaever else they can use, just te accommodate everyone. Doesn't tha seem strange?"

Shaking her head, Genevieve could feel the fear and anxiety pulsating through the room as if it was one big nervous heart.

Just as Teddy sat down, Genevieve's phone rang. She knew the ringtone. When Genevieve looked at the display, it read: David. The urge to ignore was strong.

But then Genevieve took another look around the room. Dread began to pour over her, smothering her in the emotion. *Those dreams. The one long ago with people lying on beds, cots and mats, all rising into the dark clouds. And the one recently with bodies surrounding me. So many...Oh God! This can't be how it all begins, I'm not ready!*

Turning to Teddy, they stared at each other with anxious eyes. He was frightened only for his sister; Genevieve was frightened for all that was coming. But she knew Teddy would be her strength when things would feel hopeless.

As Genevieve reached down to answer the phone, she stayed focused on Teddy's eyes—for that strength started now.

"Hello, David?"

There was silence on the other end.

"David, are you there?" Genevieve spoke louder.

"They're dying, Gen. Five Soul Seekers have called me in the last few hours advising me that people they knew—people that seemed in good health have died suddenly within the last two days."

Genevieve couldn't look at Teddy anymore. Her heart sank as she thought about Amelie. "Do you know what's causing it?"

David responded, "No. The cause has been different each time. At least that's what it seems like so far. We have to talk with the Soul of someone close to death to see if It's ready to shed some light on what's happening. Where are you anyway, still in Bamburgh?"

Genevieve knew what she had to do—before Amelie died. "We're at a hospital in Northumberland. Teddy's sister, Amelie was just rushed here after having two violent seizures. She had been fine, now she's unconscious."

David was silent on the other end.

Genevieve whispered. "I know what I have to do."

I truly hope you enjoyed the story. If you have a moment, a review is always greatly appreciated.
For more insights on this book and information on the upcoming sequel, please visit:
www.SherylMFrazer.com
Be sure to sign up while you're there, for perks no one else will have access to!